'Good period bac
a skilful writer who keeps everything spinning
merrily.'

Publishers Weekly

Suddenly she realised as she faced his set, furious gaze where sharp words were taking them. Tears stung her eyes, for she feared she had lost him. He was standing aloof with his auburn head high and his lips held very tight. The admiration she was accustomed to seeing in his murky eyes was gone, as though it had never been. She made a blind, frustrated gesture. "Oh, go then and call him out. And when he has killed you and I am left to face the scandal I suppose you will be satisfied." A sob broke from her.

Also by Deborah Chester in Sphere Books:

A LOVE SO WILD

Summer's Rapture

DEBORAH CHESTER

SPHERE BOOKS LIMITED
30-32 Gray's Inn Road, London WC1X 8JL

First published in Great Britain by
Michael Joseph Ltd 1982 under the title of *French Slippers*

Published by Sphere Books Ltd 1983

TRADE
MARK

Printed and bound in Great Britain by
Collins, Glasgow

Equidem, Martha!

Chapter One

Above the tired streets of Calais, late afternoon storm clouds were massing, gray and swollen, with an occasional grumble of thunder offered as a warning to those individuals still venturing about out of doors. The wind began to pick up, galloping over the choppy waves in the harbor, then gusting into the town proper to rattle all the window panes and howl down and up chimneys. Wickedly, it darted into the private parlor of Madame Chérare's inn with a great, startling tumult of the chintz draperies, and lashed them so madly about that the teapot on a nearby table was upset and half the things with it.

"Oh, for heaven's sake!" Brought abruptly out of the deep abstraction which had held her prisoner since morning, Julia jumped from her chair to combat the wind, jerking the draperies from about her neck and panting as she strained to push the window closed. Then it was done and the catch fastened, just in time to avoid a venomous clap of thunder and the subsequent roaring downpour. Julia frowned at the rain lashing across the pane. "France has the most beastly weather imaginable," she said out loud to no one in particular and crossly twitched the draperies in place to shut out the sight.

She had intended to return to her overstuffed armchair and that complete absence of thought which had safely harbored her throughout the day, but a damp little sob, inexpertly muffled, came from the far corner of the room. Julia looked sharply in that direction, then bit back the words of rebuke which had almost risen to her compressed lips. There was no purpose to be served by scolding her aunt, save to make the poor woman more steeped in misery than she already was. Averting her face, Julia clenched her fists, willing the resentment in her heart back into submission. It was not right that she should feel so bitter about her aunt's tears just because her own would not come. She sat down again and suddenly buried her face in her hands, squeezing her eyes shut in a tense effort to force them to weep, but they remained dry, giving her pent-up grief and misery no relief.

A quiet knock sent her up from her chair as rapidly as the wind had done, and angrily she wrenched open the door. "Yes?" she said with freezing hauteur to the landlady, determined to repudiate any vulgar curiosity. Really! Had the woman not sensibility enough to realize they desired nothing but the strictest privacy?

But madame faced her impassively, looking stout and capable in her white apron. *"Pardon,"* she said, her unreadable black eyes narrowing ever so slightly as they looked past Julia and observed the shattered teapot in ruins on the polished floor. "Eh? There has been an accident. I will send the *bonne.*"

Yes, thought Julia rather wearily, and you will tack another handful of *sous* onto the bill as well. "Thank you," she said, not bothering to conceal the hostility in her voice. Next this dreadful woman would be wanting them to make another payment on their bill, or else ask whether they desired fish or capons for their dinner.

Madame Chérare gathered up her fresh apron between her strong, broad hands, and this time, for the merest instant, her expression wavered. "Mademoiselle,

I regret to ask, but I must know about monsieur your father and his *cadavre.* I have need of the room."

The threads of numbness which had swathed Julia for most of the day suddenly snapped. How could she be expected to think of arrangements *now* when her mind still told her he should be walking in with a jaunty whistle at any moment? She supposed it must be done, but she refused to be rushed into a display of her uncertainty and indecision. If she stood here and dithered, it would mean a loss of dignity before this woman, who most assuredly was prepared to pounce on the least opportunity, in her shrewd Norman way, to take advantage of a mere chit of a girl and an elderly woman, alone, without servants, and in a state of fresh bereavement. Her chin came up. "I shall have your instructions within the hour. Please come back then." She started to shut the door but Madame Chérare raised a hand.

"And the parlor?" she wanted to know, avarice overcoming the tone of respect in her voice. "You require it for tonight? That is—"

'Yes, I am well aware of the cost!" snapped Julia despite her efforts to keep control of her frazzled temper. "Of course we shall require it."

Unperturbed, the woman bowed. "I shall come back at the next hour."

As Julia shut the door and turned away in exasperation, she caught a glimpse of her reflection in the wall mirror with its too-ornate frame. She looked wan and tense, her eyes mere smudges of shadow and her lips drawn down into a thin line that was anything but pretty. The shock of seeing herself so out of curl helped dispel the last of the befuddled horror which had gripped her. With a small pang of guilt she realized her father would have had no patience with this frozen behavior. But it had merely been yesterday when he had returned from one of his outings with a grievous wound from a duel she had not had the faintest inkling was going to occur. Summoned, a French doctor had shaken his head, cupped him, and murmured condolences in poor English. This morning, Sir Geoffrey Swanton—baronet, confirmed rake, and incontinent gamester—had put out his hand to Julia and breathed his last. It had all been so sudden she had been stunned, unable at first to comprehend that her rackety parent was gone, leaving her, to all useful purposes, very much on her own devices in a hostile country.

And it was indeed hostile; there could be little doubt of that, even if there was not the cheap picture of the emperor's Corsican profile brooding over one wall. The very air was rife with ill will, although admittedly no one had uttered a word against her. She clenched her hands into fists of despair. If only they had never come to France! If only her father had exercised the sense to stay away from the sordid little salon where he had met his demise over the cards. If only he had been a prudent man to begin with and had never run himself so far aground on the spur of debt. If only—she stopped herself with a curt mental shake. Standing here like Mrs. Siddons in one of her famous throes of despair served them no better purpose than did her aunt's vapors in the corner. Decisions must be made; actions must be taken. Lady Elizabeth was not the one to perform either. Julia sighed. Where was she to begin? How could she possibly manage?

Necessity, however, dictated that she must do so without delay. Inwardly bracing herself, she began to walk slowly about the room. The first decision was easy; without question, they must return home to England at once. The prospect of vagabonding across war-ridden Europe on her father's jaunty notion of a grand tour had been exciting to contemplate at first, for he had possessed that glib ability to gloss over the sour point of their fleeing to escape his enormous debts. Sir

Geoffrey could have carried it off with a high hand, but Sir Geoffrey was dead and therefore no longer in charge of them. Julia was staggered by the new weight of responsibility for herself and her aunt, and she had little difficulty in realizing how much the practicality inherited from her French mother offset the romanticism and love of gaiety imparted by her father. The danger of being in France might have been thrilling before; now it was a dreadful specter which she was eager to flee. She gave a little nod. It was settled; they would go tomorrow.

And then what would become of them? That horrifying question loomed up immediately and refused to go away. She sent a quick, sidewise glance at her aunt. Dear Lady Elizabeth, who was not really her aunt at all, had no one of her own family branch to go to. And that left—

"Oh, Julia!" Lady Elizabeth wailed suddenly, seeing her standing by the window. "You are frowning so. I'm terribly sorry, truly I am, but I can't stop weeping. I know how much you detest watering-pots!"

"No, no!" At once tumbling down from her gloomy thoughts, Julia ran across the room to kneel and grip the plump little woman's hands. "Dearest Aunt, you mustn't think I am cross at *you*! Never!" Her clasp tightened lovingly on those pudgy, beringed fingers. "You see, I am trying to think of what we must do next, and the prospects are making me feel low." With a fierce frown she pushed herself to her feet and began pacing about the room. "But I *must* think of what to do. Papa is no longer here to tell us not to worry, and I simply haven't got his ability always to muddle through the worst situations."

Lady Elizabeth Pelling, a plain, rather dumpy woman with a predilection for too much rouge and bonbons, raised her crumpled features anxiously, her plump hands still gripping her scrap of a handkerchief.

"But you mustn't distress yourself, dear. We simply have to write to Gaylord, and he shall come to take charge."

Incredulous at the suggestion, Julia turned with a short laugh. "Gaylord? Good heavens, ma'am, I seriously doubt if he could find his way off England's shores."

"No, he has never been terribly clever," agreed Lady Elizabeth unhappily. "But I suppose he is *Sir* Gaylord now. Do you think that will give him a longer lease with his creditors?"

Impatient, Julia replied with a snap, "No, Aunt, I do not. He has inherited all of Papa's debts now. But I do not wish to discuss Gaylord!" She added before her aunt could speak, "Nor Papa. That may be callous of me, but indeed I dare not allow either of us to grieve any longer in this fruitless way." She saw her aunt frowning again in bewilderment and sought a blunt statement in hopes of making her point clear. "We have ourselves to worry about now. Don't you see, Aunt? Where are we to go? Any hope of Gaylord's assistance is out of the question, for he cannot manage his own ramshackle affairs. And as for Sophie—"

"Why, yes!" broke in Lady Elizabeth, brightening. "We shall go to her and all of us will retire together into the strictest mourning."

Julia looked up, holding back the first instinctive word of protest, then giving way to the force of her feelings. She shook her head. "No, Aunt. Do not think wrong of me, but I cannot face such a future. Sophie and I do not suit—never have—and for me to throw myself upon her charity would surely strain the small bond we have for each other."

Shock spread across Lady Elizabeth's features. "Julie! Such a thing to say! We need not be charity. Why, I could serve as her companion, for although I am not clever I can be agreeable company, and you could govern her child." She smiled coaxingly. "There are ever so many ways we could be of use to her, and I know she is not the sort of selfish creature who would be forever throwing our dependency in our faces."

"No," Julia agreed, but then frowned. "But I should feel it every moment. Sophie is"—for a moment she searched for words to describe her half-sister—"very well in her own way. But I am certain she would not want us."

"Not want us?" Lady Elizabeth's hands flew up in astonishment. "But, Julia dearest, have you not considered how lonely she must be with Lewing away?"

"Stuff. She is surrounded constantly by friends and admirers," said Julia with a toss of her head. "And if next you mean to say she would give me a push toward making a brilliant match, I wish you would not. I *know* the future awaiting me if I put on mourning and become a governess. I know it as plainly as if I see it." Defiance shook through her. "If I go under her roof or any other's, my seasons shall end. Well, I shan't finish out my days as a downtrodden spinster. I shan't!"

"Very well, my dear," said Lady Elizabeth mildly. "Oh, dear me, it *is* distressing to be obliged to discuss these measures, but I suppose we could continue to live at Swanton House in our old style, if that is what you prefer."

"Yes, it is. Only—" Julia paused and bit her lip with acute shame. They were in such a basket! Why could Aunt Beth not see the desperate straits they had been reduced to? It was quite impossible to open up Swanton House when they were as poor as churchmice. Besides, she shuddered to think of the horde of creditors which would descend upon them. Aunt Beth *must* be made to understand the problems besetting them from all sides. She put up her chin to conceal the despair trembling through her every limb and faced her aunt squarely. "I had a long talk with Papa before we fled—*left* England," she said in a rigid little voice, ashamed of what had to be confronted. "You did understand, didn't you, Aunt, that Papa's debts made it necessary for this sojourn on the Continent?"

"Oh, yes." Lady Elizabeth gave a jerky little nod, applying her handkerchief to the corner of her eye once again. "*Poor* Geoffrey. I fear he suffered the Swanton inability to practice economy."

"Yes," said Julia. "His debts are quite overwhelming and there is nothing to pay them with. Nothing. I went through his belongings yesterday and all the money we have is a few pounds and francs. That is *all*, Aunt Beth. And I seriously doubt that Swantoncourt brings in any revenue at all. Papa wrung every farthing out of it to waste upon the faro tables."

"Dearest, you really shouldn't speak ill of his poor memory," admonished Lady Elizabeth with a sigh. Abruptly her round face puckered. "Oh, dear! And I did think I had quite cried all I could."

"We must face facts, Aunt," said Julia with some severity to counteract her own strong urge to give way to despair. She could not afford to be womanish now; she must keep sharp wits about her. For a moment she moved away from her aunt, doubtful of ever making the woman understand, but then with a shrug she turned back. "Papa gambled everything but our present funds away. We cannot live in our old style again unless—" Something constricted in her throat and for a moment she could not go on. Unless what? Her wits churned for a solution to no avail.

"I suppose," said Lady Elizabeth thoughtfully, "that tomorrow we could go out and buy a few mourning clothes to suffice until we can engage a London dressmaker."

The iron band of panic in Julia's throat fell away. She shook her black ringlets in emphatic denial. "We cannot afford to waste our money on weeds, Aunt."

"Oh, yes, Julia." Lady Elizabeth's two chins came up with unexpected stubbornness. "Geoffrey may have permitted you a ramshackle upbringing—and since you aren't my dear sister's child I could scarcely protest without getting my nose snapped off in that *way* of his—but I cannot bear to be thought scrambling or improper in that regard. We must observe mourning. What would everyone say?"

"No one will know about it." The words popped out of their own accord, but at once Julia could see the solution. It would require intrepid behavior as well as a ruthless disregard of the proprieties; still, she had little choice but to go for it. Making her decision on the instant, she steeled herself to be firm in carrying it out, for from this moment on to waver in doubt would mean her downfall. "Listen, Aunt! No, please do. I must be very ruthless now, a true Swanton. And you must help me. We shall go back to London at once, where I will endeavor to bring an eligible suitor up to scratch at the first opportunity."

"Julia!" Lady Elizabeth's weak blue eyes fairly popped. "Oh, no, no, my love, you cannot seriously be thinking of anything so grossly improper. It would not do at all, not with poor Geoffrey still to be put in his grave and—"

"He will be buried here in Calais, and we shan't tell anyone in London what has happened—not even Sophie and Gaylord. We will tell people we are back because we could not bear to miss town during the season gaiety."

"But, gracious!" Lady Elizabeth's handkerchief dropped unheeded to the floor. "What an unchristian suggestion. My sweet, you surely do not mean to be leaving Geoffrey here in this heathen land? What if we should be obliged to use a priest for the ceremony?"

Julia made an impatient gesture, suddenly so weary she could not bear to stand another moment. Seating herself, she pushed back a straying strand of her raven hair and said in a flat, fatigued voice, "Papa had no morals. I do not think it would have troubled him at all. Aunt, we must!" she cried, making a last desperate effort. "I know I sound shockingly mercenary and—and *grasping*, but it is the only way I see. Once I am safely betrothed to—oh, someone, whoever—then I can pretend to receive a letter telling me Papa is dead. We can go into mourning officially with no harm done. You know *he* would have approved the plan. Please, Aunt Beth, help me! I promise you may always make your home with me." Tears burned at her eyes, but with fierce self-control she held them back and put one slender, well-shaped hand out in appeal. "It is horrible to contemplate, I know, but I shan't let any middle-class scruples defeat me. Oh, please, *please*, Aunt! Only think of how you shall hate moping about the house in black, unable to accept any invitations."

A knock on the door startled her for the second time that afternoon. She looked up, her heart fluttering rapidly, then sent a scared, desperate glance her aunt's way. It must be the landlady; they had no more time to waste coming to an agreement.

"Aunt!" she whispered so fiercely Lady Elizabeth jumped.

"Oh, dear lamb, I don't *know*." Lady Elizabeth put her hands to her cheeks in a helpless way. "It would be agonizing to have to bow out from everything, but the proprieties! If only it weren't so wickedly tempting . . . I suppose you must do as you see fit. It seems so dreadful but—"

"Thank you! Thank you!" Breathless with relief, Julia flew from her chair, then drew herself up in an effort to regain her composure. Carefully she opened the door and faced Madame Chérare's uplifted eyebrows, and began to give her orders in a clear, unhurried voice.

* * *

It was arranged. The funeral would be the following morning—a private affair since Julia had not the faintest conception of the names or directions of her father's French acquaintances here; nor, in view of the fact that he had met his demise while in their company, would she have sent for them had she been able to. The fact that her parent had engaged in sordid violence could only disgust her, and if he had survived it, she would have read him a terrifying scold. But of course there was nothing now to do except reaffirm her loathing for low gambling places and men who considered no one but themselves when they challenged one another to these tedious combats.

After spending the rest of the afternoon packing their trunks, for she and her aunt would go aboard a packet as soon as the grim little ceremony was over, they sat alone in the private parlor, silently picking over a repast of underdone turbot, cold ham, and a fresh sauce of mediocre quality. Outside, the storm continued to rage with undiminished energy, and drafts all but guttered the candles lighting the room. Julia sat at her place in glum spirits she could not quite conceal, and was thankful her aunt was too preoccupied to notice her case of blue-devils.

What harebrained course *had* she set for herself? Julie wondered, flinching as lightning clawed at their window. Being but twenty, she had already enjoyed two seasons and, to her gratification, had never lacked for beaux. But although she did not consider herself an excessive romantic, this cold-blooded course to snare a wealthy gentleman solely for his riches seemed an increasingly vile one to pursue. She had rejected all previous suits to her hand out of a capricious desire to enjoy being a belle of the *ton* as long as possible. Now she reviewed her past behavior with dissatisfaction. What a perfect goose she had been! She would not be in this tangle now if she had not previously refused to settle down to a matrimonial status.

Although the very thought of doing so depressed her, she began to think of whom she should throw her cap at. Heavy-footed and incompetent, the waiter served the second course, but she scarcely knew he was there. Should she go for a title? No. She would be a fool to encourage such high desires. She need concern herself more with the gentlemen's means rather than with their positions or faces. There was Wrexham, but he was so terribly young and callow. Sir Robert—but he was a fool who rarely had a feather to fly with; no, she must keep far away from any of those in her father's set. Mr. Tate perhaps, but she could not bear his poetry. Who then? She frowned with such intensity the waiter did not serve her a portion of the ham after all and she was obliged to help herself once he had departed.

And then, quite without warning, she remembered the name her father had spoken with his last breath. *Garde.* And he had said it as though solving a puzzle. Could that be his wish for her future? Her thoughts turned back to Lady Sefton's ball last year when on a dare she had consented to dance with the Earl of Garde. He was recognized as something of a nonpareil among the Corinthian set for his prowess at marksmanship and curricle racing. He was also a libertine and gamester addicted to the gaming hells in the notorious Soho quarter. He would never see thirty-five again. But he was wealthy and unattached, and the memory of his attentions paid to her during last year's dance still put her to the blush.

The new green peas upon her plate turned cold as, unheeding, she thought of that habit he had had, of running his eyes over her as though she were a morsel made delectable purely for his consumption. How wicked he was! But it was rather heady to contemplate the prospect of bringing him to the point of marriage.

And such a brilliant match it would be—could she contrive to pull it off? He was rich enough to see her secure the rest of her life. But more than that, he was no stripling coxcomb but a man, one who could throw any lady's pulse into confusion. Smiling, she gave herself a nod for courage. It was no easy task she was facing, for not only must she conceal her true circumstances, she must entrance one of the most determined bachelors in all England. Perhaps she had set her aims too high. But now that the challenge was before her, she could not back away to a lesser ambition. The end of the season would see her a countess, or she was not Julia Swanton!

But scarcely had she come to her resolution than the door flew open with a crash, causing her to jump and Lady Elizabeth to overset her glass. Words of rebuke flew to Julia's lips and promptly died there, unspoken, for it was not the waiter or the serving girl who stood in the doorway, but instead an aristocratic gentleman of medium height whose chiseled patrician features and modish caped driving-coat contrived to look elegant despite the water dripping from him in a small downpour of its own.

'Hah!" pronounced Madame Chérare, puffing from behind him. "Now do you believe? The parlor is engaged by two English ladies. You must eat downstairs, milord."

For answer he removed his sodden driving coat and low-crowned beaver and thrust them at her, revealing a superbly tailored coat of blue superfine, fawn pantaloons without wrinkle, and Hessian boots which were still glossy beneath their spattering of mud. His cravat gleamed in snowy, intricate folds beneath a chin taut with arrogance while his crisp chestnut hair, cut in the severe Bedford crop, attempted unsuccessfully to curl across his wide forehead. Beneath thin, dark brows a set of exceptionally keen gray eyes flickered over Lady

Elizabeth before settling upon Julia. One thin, haughty brow lifted, and a corner of his mouth quirked in a brief show of approval which set Julia at once on her mettle.

"You will please excuse us, sir," she began, but to her chagrin and doubled annoyance he merely bowed with a faint but charming smile.

"Not at all, mademoiselle. But please. You must not give up your so charming privacy on behalf of myself." He flicked a curt glance at Madame Chérare. "Lay another setting, *Tout de suite*."

Indignant at having been so ruthlessly misunderstood, Julia started to rise and give him a more final setdown, but removing the glove from his left hand, he waved her to regain her seat. Much to her vexation, she found herself obeying this lazy command before she realized what she was about. Why must the impudent coxcomb be foisting himself on them in this detestable way? she wondered, fuming as she took up her napkin again.

"I regret to say this, sir," she said in her proudest manner, hoping his conceit was not so great as to prevent him from realizing he was being snubbed. "But we have no desire to share your company."

"Yes, indeed," added Lady Elizabeth with a melancholy expression. "We are in mourning, and very dull it is too."

"Mourning?" He had a slow but precise way of speaking his very fluent English; this, coupled with his accent, only seemed to add to the air of elegance which hung about him. "But how sad. You must accept my condolences." With languid grace he advanced into the room, then half-turned and snapped his long fingers in dismissal of the landlady, who was still lingering. Her round face impassive, she departed without further delay. The stranger frowned ever so slightly. "How churlish the *canaille* have become."

But Julia's temper had soared at his thick-skinned persistence, and she was in no mood for desultory conversation. Cutting short her aunt's reply, she sent him a furious look. "You are quite past the pale of acceptable behavior, sir! Perhaps you believe your company is delightful, but we desire the strictest privacy. Need I be plainer?"

"Non." He was quite close to the table now, close enough for the frozen expression in his light gray eyes to be read; close enough, too, for her to see the tautness of the stern lines bracketing his mouth. It was enough to check her anger. She blinked at him a moment in uncertainty, and thus lost the advantage. This was no strutting tippy to be snubbed into place with a few haughty words; this was a gentleman of the first rank, one, moreover, whose breeding and natural hauteur gave him a formidable air of authority not easy to ignore. His expression had changed but little, yet with mounting unease she perceived her own peppery reception had aroused his annoyance. Cowed, she sat in silence and returned his stern gaze as squarely as she could while reassuring herself she need not feel obliged to back down from her position. He did not belong in their company; there was not the least reason to accept him.

"You need not be rude, mademoiselle," he continued in a voice unaltered from his previous tones, yet with the chill in his manner quite prevalent. "I comprehend that you do not want my presence. But since I refuse to dine in the common room you must accept me, I fear." Grasping a chair, he seated himself at the head of the table, and a minute later the waiter had arrived with a plate for him.

Resentful at having not only failed to rout this imperious stranger but at having been deftly snubbed herself as well, Julia bent smoldering violet eyes to her food in the strictest determination not to address herself to him again.

"Oh, yes, you poor man," said Lady Elizabeth, much to Julia's disgust. "The common dining room is never agreeable, is it? One is obliged to rub shoulders with the most out-at-elbows people imaginable. Would you like some of these peas? I am Lady Elizabeth Pelling, and this is Miss Swanton, the daughter of my brother-in-law by his second wife."

Thus betrayed, Julia sighed and raised her eyes in curt acknowledgement. "How do you so?"

The gentleman graciously inclined his head. "*Enchanté,* madame. Mademoiselle. I am the Marquis du Vallon. Ah, *merci,* but, no, I will decline the peas."

The fastidious curl of his etched nostrils seemed to indicate he found the majority of their repast less than satisfactory, but he made no further comment, instead addressing himself to his food in a well-bred silence which soon had Julia ashamed at herself for supposing he would vex them with unwanted conversation and questions.

It was difficult, too, not to avail herself of the opportunity to study him. After all, it was not every day that she dined, however unwillingly, with a marquis. She wondered if he was one of the new nobles of Napoleon's empire, but decided not. There was too much blood-lineage in the thin nose and high cheekbones for him to have come from bourgeois ancestry. Well, then, at least one member of the old order had survived the Terror, but she could not help but wonder if he had always dared to exhibit such *grand seigneur* airs.

She also noticed he had not removed the glove from his right hand and kept that member strictly in his lap except when obliged to cut his meat, as he was doing now.

"You stare, mademoiselle," he said, glancing up to catch her squarely.

Julia flamed scarlet with mortification. Nor did her aunt's look of mild reproach help. She bit her lip, so chagrined by her own reprehensible behavior ever since he had first set foot in the room she longed to flee. Instead she gulped down her emotions and forced herself to meet his stern, disinterested gaze. "Yes," she said, for there was no point in trying to be evasive. "Please forgive me." Despite all she could do, her eyes strayed back to his gloved hand resting lightly upon the damask-covered table.

"Ah, I see." An exaggerated expression of comprehension crossed his face. "It is my hand which concerns you. *Voyons,* a matter of no importance at all." Graciously, he pretended not to notice Julia's bafflement and returned his attention to Lady Elizabeth. "Milady, forgive this small instance of curiosity, but may I ask why two bereaved ladies are abroad?"

"You mean, jaunting about the world in a highly improper manner, don't you?" asked Julia in a sweetly dangerous voice, not at all mollified by his refusal to capitalize on her embarrassment.

He frowned. "I would never express myself so rudely, mademoiselle."

"Julia, dear, you needn't poker up so," put in Lady Elizabeth, flustered. "I am sure his lordship only wishes to maintain civil conversation." Turning to the marquis, she said before Julia could stop her, "You mustn't mind her, my lord. Indeed, she is not herself, having lost her dear papa only this morning to celestial hands." She paused, frowning in some distress. "At least, I hope his soul went in that direction."

"Milady." He turned to Lady Elizabeth after refilling his glass from the bottle the waiter had left upon the table. "*Pardon,* but since you are bereaved, will you go back to England soon?"

"We sail tomorrow," said Julia in a flat voice before her aunt could answer. If he had had any intentions of pestering them further, that should depress them.

But Du Vallon merely lifted cool brows. "*Très bien!* And you reside in London?"

"Oh, yes, indeed we do, my lord," said Lady Elizabeth in a chirp of good spirits. His gaze returned to her, and she flushed a rosy pink that made her rouge quite unnecessary. "In Swanton House on Clarges Street."

"The street of the moneylenders?" He looked a bit surprised.

Lady Elizabeth pretended to pout. "My dear sir! Of course we have no associations with *that* end of the street, although poor Sir Geoffrey used to make no end of dreadful jokes about it. He was much addicted to their aid, I fear." She put a corner of her handkerchief to her eye for a moment, then rallied. "But I don't mean to dwell upon him, poor thing! We are going to be very gay this season and accept all the invitations. Perhaps you are shocked and think us most *unfeeling,* but indeed no one's sensibilities could be more guilty! Yet there are Julia's chances to think of. Really, she has no time to wait out another—"

"Aunt!" cried Julia in as damping a tone as possible. She caught a gleam in Du Vallon's eyes and could not be sure if it was amusement or censure. But she did know, with a tortured inner wriggling of embarrassment, that she must prevent her aunt from continuing these reckless disclosures. Of course a gentleman in France could pose no threat to her plans, but this looseness of Lady Elizabeth's tongue was most alarming.

Julia put out a hand. "I really doubt that his lordship is interested in all these details."

"*Au contraire*!" he interjected swiftly, his sardonic amusement quite plain now. "I am all attention. Please continue, milady. In my boyhood, *tout le monde* was in continual mourning but those were times of great trouble. I am *enchanté* to learn this custom is to be abolished."

Julia's hand clenched hard upon a fold of the tablecloth until her glass was nearly overset. So he *was* laughing at them! Insufferable! She rose to her feet, intending to prevent any more jests at their expense by sweeping from the room, and incurred a look of the deepest displeasure from her aunt.

"My dear child, whatever are you doing? I have barely begun on my tart. No, no, my lord! Please do not rise. Julia, pray sit down at once. You are causing the greatest inconvenience."

Nonplussed, Julia sank back into her seat, her face scarlet at having erred again. But if she could not escape, then she must conquer her embarrassment enough to change the subject. "Forgive me. We have seen so little of your country, my lord. Is Paris very fine at this time of year?" As she spoke a vast roll of thunder jarred the house, making her flinch.

A faint frown of distaste crossed his face as he, too, glanced quickly at the lightning outside the window. "Paris is filled with blood and terror and false gaiety, mademoiselle. And now that there is this fiasco of a divorce, the Imperial Court is a travesty." He shrugged his elegant shoulders ever so slightly. "*Enfin,* all is confusion with the *beau monde.* One knows not whether to make one's bow to the Impératrice Joséphine or to the Impératrice Maria-Louise." His thin lips curled as if to say that is what one must expect when a Corsican commoner is crowned. "Be glad, mademoiselle, you are not going to Paris. Me, I will be happy to be in London, where the princes exhibit only royal vices and do not consider themselves gods."

"You are going to London?" Lady Elizabeth beamed and clapped her pudgy hands like a child. "But how marvelous! Tell us when."

Julia thought she murmured something, but she

never knew what it was. A band of alarm had gripped her to the point of suffocation, and for a dreadful, endless moment she could do nothing but think of all the horrid implications. It would of course explain his presence in Calais—but *going to London*! The very thought drove her mad. And after Aunt Beth had prated out all those indiscretions! Julia's heart dropped in a sickening fall, all the way to the toes of her soft kid slippers.

"Tomorrow, *aussi,*" he was saying in reply to Lady Elizabeth's question. His glance in Julia's stricken direction was quite without expression. "Mademoiselle looks overcome. But I am transported with delight to think that it will be my privilege to watch Mademoiselle Swanton have her last chance." With incredible, insufferable audacity that made Julia's hands clench in her lap until her arms shook, he leaned toward Lady Elizabeth and asked in the most innocent fashion, "But what is this all about? My curiosity is of the most aroused."

Julia drew in a quick, furious breath. If Aunt was foolish enough to answer *that*, she—

"Why marriage, of course, my lord," said Lady Elizabeth with a giggle. Blushing again, she put one plump hand to her face and peeped out between her fingers in a manner that made Julia long to box her ears. "The poor child is quite penniless, you know, and now that dear Sir Geoffrey is gone, leaving her destitute, she must contrive to gain a suitor before her situation is made known. I am sure you sympathize."

"*Naturellement,*" he said, while Julia sat frozen in her chair, torn between the desire to strangle her aunt and the longing to crawl beneath the rug. He eyed her as though she was some oddity exhibited in a Piccadilly freak circus. "But why is mademoiselle not already wed? There is an expression of the English, to call the lady an 'apeleader.' Are you such a one, mademoiselle?"

For a moment Julia could not speak for the outrage strangling her. How dare he, a perfect stranger, have the audacity to tease her? Oh, if she were a man she would gladly cast aside all her objections to physical violence just for the supreme bliss of running him through and through and *through*!

Ignoring him with all the hauteur she was capable of, she looked at her aunt. "I suppose you do not realize, ma'am, that by blurting out these private matters you have brought about our failure before we have even begun?" It was impossible to repress the intense bitterness in her voice. Coldly she watched dismay crumple Lady Elizabeth's rosy features. "I will ask Madame Chérare if she has any black crepe we may procure."

Quickly, to hide the sudden hot tears blinding her, she rose and started to leave, for she could not bear to remain here among the ashes of her hopes another moment. Du Vallon, however, was swifter and stood up to block her path.

She threw up her chin, lips trembling, eyes on fire. "Please have the courtesy to move out of my way."

"I think you can be of use to me." He eyed her in a manner so peculiar, she blinked and backed up a step. "Yes." He seemed to make an abrupt inner decision, and the gray eyes with their devastating clearness were suddenly veiled. He smiled ever so faintly, the short dueling scar on his lean cheek white and narrow against his skin. "It is rare to find a *demoiselle* so daring of purpose. Let us bargain. *Voyons,* I will say nothing of your *bon papa,* and you will open the doors of English society for me. You do enter the better circles, *n'est-ce pas*?"

Julia was bewildered, but she could throw up her chin with pride in answer to that last question. "The best, my lord."

"Bon." He held out his gloved right hand. "We are agreed?"

She held her arms stiffly at her sides. "I think not." It was a simple enough request to meet, but she could not forgive him nor would she give way out of gratitude for his offer of reticence. "I refuse to subject my acquaintance to your odious advances. Come, Aunt. I do think it is time we parted company with this gentleman."

"Julia!" said her aunt, scandalized. "Oh, my dear sir, I do apologize for the poor child. She is still overwrought!"

"Apologies are not a necessity, milady," he said, but with a faint snap in his voice. The thin nostrils flared. "If this is what mademoiselle desires, I will not press her again." He shrugged and moved languidly out of her way, the diamond stud in the folds of his cravat flashing a thousand shades in the candlelight. "Go, Mademoiselle Swanton, and find your black dress. You are *charmante* in pink guaze; it is a pity the gentlemen of London shall not see you so attired."

Everything wrenching within her, Julia halted and whirled on him. How had he perceived that she still hoped to carry it off despite him? "That is blackmail, sir!"

"Exactement." Unperturbed, he brought out an exquisite Sèvres snuffbox and opened it with one hand with an elegance of manner rivaling Brummell's.

"I am all at sea," declared Lady Elizabeth with a frown. "What has blackmail to do with Julia's raiment? And, really, my dear, if his lordship desires our help in gaining a few invitations, I am sure I would not begrudge him so small a favor. What he must be thinking of your churlish behavior I cannot contrive to imagine."

"I am sorry," said Julia in a flat voice. "But I think my lord marquis can gain entry by his own endeavors."

"Ah, *oui,* but not as quickly." Du Vallon finished helping himself to snuff with a graceful turn of the wrist and snapped shut the box. "I will not be in London long; time is important."

Julia stamped her foot. "Well, I shan't help you!"

"Julia—"

"No, no, milady, do not scold her," broke in the marquis with a measuring glance at Julia. "It is entirely her choice."

"Fudge and feathers!" said Lady Elizabeth roundly. "If she must act like a hoyden, one can but hope a measure of self-disgust will soon bring her back to her senses. But in the meantime, my lord, I am perfectly willing to do all that is necessary to assist you."

"Merci." He bowed. "Madame, I am at your feet. But the hour grows late; I must not detain you from retiring." He glanced at Julia, who trembled with rage at his smug triumph. *"Alors,* mademoiselle, you do not have to wear black after all. I will be most discreet. *C'est un promis!*" Arrogantly he gave her his faint smile and headed for the door.

"One thing," said Julia, refusing to let him leave a total victor. "Why is it that you desire to go to London and sample its gaiety? After all, we are at war."

Standing with one hand upon the doorknob, he allowed his courteous expression to become very cold. "That is not your concern, mademoiselle. *Au revoir!*"

"Well!" said Julia as the door shut behind him, and promptly rounded on her aunt. "Aunt Beth, how could you? I have never been more thoroughly mortified in my life! Do you mean to discuss our affairs with every stranger we encounter? Because if so, I—"

"How dreadful you are, to scold me!" cried Lady Elizabeth, beginning to weep a little. "Anyone with the least discernment could see at a glance that Lord du Vallon is to be trusted. A gentleman of the first head, *obviously*. Why you had to be so crossgrained I cannot imagine, but if you were mortified by my behavior I certainly was by yours. Arguing and glaring at him like a perfectly *brazen* savage without manners or breeding; I shudder to wonder what he thought."

"I do not care a fig for what he thought. Nor should you." Julia ground her fine white teeth together. "A rude, overbearing, arrogant, conceited *beast,* who is intending to use us shamefully to his own ends. How can you possibly make sheep's eyes at him?"

"I beg your pardon!" gasped Lady Elizabeth, going quite scarlet. "That is a cruel thing to say, Julia, a most cruel thing to say. I should never have suspected you would turn out to be such a—a viper in the bosom!" Her chins began to quiver. "I trust you will be contrite in the morning. Goodnight!" And with a suppressed sob, she rushed from the room, leaving Julia in angry but unvictorious possession of the field.

Despite her hopes, Julia saw Lord du Vallon succeed in securing passage upon their packet boat. He came with a veritable mountain of luggage and a small wiry valet dressed in strict, serviceable black. Julia's fingers tightened upon the weatherbeaten rail out of her dread lest my lord join her with more of his brutal comments, and she was greatly tempted to hide below in the stuffy confines of the cabin where Lady Elizabeth had already retired, quite overcome by the noisome smell of the debris swept into the harbor by the storm. But Julia loved the whip of the brisk sea air with its sting of salt against her cheeks and, since she never suffered the malaise of the sea, she had planned to keep her place at the rail and glory in the rise and fall of their progress upon the waves.

She would not let him rout her from her pleasure, she decided with a firm set of her mouth. She would stay right here, and if he had the effrontery to come up to her she would cut him dead. Someone so rude and overbearing did not deserve courtesy.

But other than tipping his hat when she glanced in his direction, Du Vallon paid her no attention at all. Instead his interests were directed in giving a great many instructions to his servant and in standing near the vessel's stern to watch the shores of France fade to a purplish-gray haze upon the horizon.

Gulls wheeled overhead, squawking in a terrible din before diving back to fight over the dead fish floating here and there upon the gray surface. Their clatter recalled Julia from her momentary spell and she realized with a little start of self-annoyance that she had been gazing at Du Vallon's back like an infatuated schoolgirl. Of course he was rather a striking figure—with the drab folds of his ankle-length caped driving coat billowing about his erect frame—but not one that could at all appeal to her. Resolutely she turned away to gaze in the opposite direction, toward England. How glad she would be to get there! She was tired of listening to French spoken all around her, French which she did not understand because her father had detested its accent and would not permit her to "learn how to speak through her nose."

The thought sent a pang through her. Indeed, Sir Geoffrey had never lavished much affection upon any of his three children, considering Gaylord to lack style and polish, Sophie to exhibit too much interest in geegaws and furbelows to the exclusion of all else, and Julie to have betrayed him by refusing to learn how to play cards. But he had always shown her a breezy friendliness tempered with awe that she should resemble her French mother so closely, and Julia could not help but miss that now. Nor could she quite dismiss the last shreds of guilt at having laid him to rest on foreign soil, although she knew it would not have mattered one jot to him. She knew, too, that he would cheer her daring, and the knowledge bolstered her drooping spirits a fraction.

Irresponsible and devil-may-care as he was, Sir Geoffrey had indeed taught her to appreciate the best of everything, whether it be clothes, company, or possessions. Her previous tastes of life in the *beau monde* had been too deep; she had been raised in circles too high for her now to countenance falling from that dizzy plateau into the mud of a dreary existence. The very thought of draping herself in drab merino and taking up a post as a governess or as a shop clerk just to eke out a bare living made her shudder with horror. Although she had long criticized her parent for plunging them into the deepest debt, she had to admit, in this moment of self-honesty, that her shame could not erase her pleasure with the luxury they had enjoyed. She must succeed, however vulgar and mercenary her plan might be. Shrinking at such a time achieved nothing; it was necessary to take firm grasp of her admittedly wild Swanton heritage and accomplish her goal.

If only this Frenchman were not in the way! She sent him another glance, but he had disappeared and was no longer to be seen on deck. For a moment she was cheered by the notion of so elegant a personage being vilely sick into a bucket, then she spied a slim cutter slicing through the waves across their path. A tricolor flag fluttered arrogantly from its highest mast, and she thought she understood the reason for Du Vallon's sudden absence.

Hope surged up through her as she craned her neck to watch the cutter heave-to smartly alongside. Some distance away, two larger ships—frigates perhaps—waited on the alert with their guns run out and a great deal of activity upon the deck. It was the notorious French blockade, that practice which deterred smuggling of fine French wines to British tables, thwarted mail and the majority of visitors to and from the Continent, and jealously regarded any individual of French nationality attempting to escape the iron, bloodied grip of Napoleon's empire. Suddenly she longed to throw back her raven-black curls and laugh. How silly of her to be so angry at Du Vallon and his threats to put a spoke in her plans. In a matter of minutes he would be hustled aboard the cutter by that officer swaggering about with his men, and taken back to France where he certainly belonged.

Despite her pleasure at this prospect, she could not like the officer of the cutter nor the way he bullied the packet's captain with all manner of questions in rapid, shrill French while his men searched the cargo and peered insolently over the passenger list. These were her enemies, the men who were killing and maiming the brothers of her friends. She glared at the tricolor as it streamed out and snapped in the freshening breeze. Gray, sullen clouds still rolled overhead, making the colors brighter than ever, and she found herself hating them and all they stood for.

Then the search was over and the cutter reboarded, the officer leaving last. He passed Julia and halted to ogle her in a manner that made her blood rise until she had magnificent color. He tipped his hat in the continental manner. *"Bonjour, mademoiselle."*

"Good-day," she said firmly, and turned her back on him.

She continued to stand there at the rail, pulling her chip-straw hat off to dangle it by its ribbons and allow the wind to ruffle her curls. She smiled faintly to herself as the cutter heeled over and pulled away, the detestable flag flopping about the mast. A single beam of sunshine pierced through the grim clouds, then another, breaking them apart to reveal the azure sky above. At once the sea lost its dull pewter hue and sparkled into blue-green life. Julia smiled, delighted with the beauty around her. That the sun had so gallantly appeared just as they left the French blockade behind seemed an excellent omen, and she laughed as she caught herself already foolishly looking ahead in hopes of a glimpse of the cliffs at Dover. She could not wait to get there.

"Mademoiselle looks *ravissante* in such light," said an increasingly familiar voice without warning.

Startled, she whirled, and the wind snatched her hat from her fingers. "Oh, *bother*!" Doubly furious to find him still about, she lunged over the rail for her property and would have fallen into the sea after it had his hand not seized her arm with unexpected strength and hauled her back. "Let me go!" she cried, wrenching free and stamping her foot at him. "That was my newest hat—my best one in fact—and it is quite your fault that I have lost it!"

"Quelle horreur, the loss of this bonnet." He snapped his long fingers with a shrug that infuriated her. "Now you shall have the pleasure of shopping for a new one. You should thank me, *peut-être.*"

She gasped, quite outraged at his effrontery. "I think not, my lord. How on earth did you escape the blockade?"

"Ah." A faint smile of amusement curled his lips, and the clear gray eyes regarded her in a lazy way which made her stiffen. "So you had these hopes, mademoiselle. I am sorry to dash them, but bribery is the best means to many ends. *D'accord?*"

For answer she turned her back on him, her hands gripping the rough railing as though they would throttle it.

He touched her elbow quite gently, and sighed when she jerked away as though burnt. "I came, mademoiselle, to offer you one of the Italian peaches I brought with me. They are of an excellence exceptional."

Julia did not even trouble to glance at him. "No, thank you, my lord."

"As you wish." He hesitated a moment until she sent him a quick, fulminating glance of dismissal. Then he permitted his clear, fiercely cold eyes to soften ever so slightly. "When we arrive in London, I shall—"

"Please!" she said stiffly. "I do not wish to discuss it. Your methods can only arouse resentment, my lord. Do not ask—or expect—anything but the most unwilling cooperation."

"I see." He stepped back a pace and bowed, his features once again haughty. "But I *do* have the cooperation of yourself and your *tante,* mademoiselle. When we arrive in London take care you forget it not."

Turning sharply on his heel, he strode away, his natural grace lending itself superbly to the dip and surge of the deck. Her violet eyes stormy with scorn and disappointment, Julia glared out over the water at the sodden wreck of her hat still gamely bobbing along in the white froth of their wake. Her hopes of being so easily rid of this arrogant stranger, whom she could not bring herself to trust one jot, were as mangled as her bonnet, and her early jubilant hailing of a good omen meant nothing to her now. Du Vallon and his unexplainable meddling had made sure it brought her nothing.

Chapter Two

Before ten days were out, Julia's activities of settling in at Swanton House had—as she knew they would—drawn Lady Lewing to call, with Gaylord Swanton reluctantly in tow.

Julia was trying on a quantity of new dresses—bought on the credit after her trepidations against running up further debt had fallen before the argument that a few more bills could make little difference—when her visitors were announced, and thus, in a walking dress of primrose muslin, she was able to descend to the drawing room with no delay other than the few moments required to thread a matching ribbon through her raven curls.

"Sophie!" she cried, trying not to appear nervous. Stretching out both hands briefly to clasp her half-sister's, she sent a smile in Gaylord's direction and begged them both to be seated. "How long it has been since we were all so agreeably together! I'm sorry to tell you Aunt Beth has not yet left her bedchamber, but—"

"That is fine," broke in Sophie in her imperious way. "We do not require her muddling things up." Beneath an enchanting white plume curling down over the brim of her hat, Sophie's green eyes fixed themselves upon Julia and narrowed. "Rutledge tells us Papa did not return. Now, what *are* you up to? Opening Swanton House at the height of the season and running up goodness knows how many dressmaker's bills as though—" She stopped and regarded Julia for a moment in open speculation, her mittened hands smoothing a crease from the skirt of her fawn-colored dress. "Has Papa enjoyed an extraordinarily fortunate run of luck? Is he back in funds?"

Beside her, Gaylord's vague hazel eyes produced a gleam. Of small, almost girlishly slim stature, he looked the picture of an idle Tulip in his high shirt points which served as blinders on either side of his pomaded head. His spangled green coat was waspwaisted and injudiciously padded at the shoulders, and he affected ankle boots so narrow and pointed she wondered how he managed to take a single, unencumbered step. One soft, white hand toyed with the collection of seals and fobs dangling from his waistcoat, broidered in violet, as he sat sprawled at his ease on the cherry-striped settee, looking more than half foxed despite the mask of affected boredom he was careful to keep in place.

Disgust with both her siblings rose into Julia's throat, making her throw out one hand in denial. "Good heavens, Sophie!" she said sharply. "I can understand Gaylord coming to ask such vulgar questions, but *you* surprise me."

"Lewing makes me a handsome allowance," replied Sophie in her aloof way, hiding a tiny yawn behind her hand. "But I must admit it is excessively disagreeable in my position to be obliged to own a father in such constant straits with the creditors. If he is to return soon and pay off his debts, however, I will be able to hold up my head to society once again."

Julia knew very well that her half-sister's golden head had never bowed to any circumstance, ever. Angered, she gripped the arms of her chair until her knuckles whitened and vowed neither of them deserved to ever know the true fate of Sir Geoffrey. He would never be mourned by his two eldest children, that much was certain. *And the youngest*? asked a barbed conscience, making her wince inwardly. No, she was hardly mourning him, was she, sitting here with as many schemes in her head as a Machiavellian intriguer. But at least she *missed* him a little.

Still, this was hardly the time for introspection. She must put these two off, and speedily, before she lost her temper and said something rash. Lifting her head, she permitted herself a small, quelling smile and said, "Why, if Papa has regained a fortune I should be astonished to hear it. And he certainly has no plans to return and waste money paying off debts."

Gaylord loosed a small sigh and stood up. "That's it, then," he said with visible annoyance. "I knew I shouldn't let you drag me here on this fool's errand. There shan't be a thing for me out of this, and I could have been entering a few bets at the Fives-Court to better effect."

"Don't be such a dolt," said Sophie. "Sit down and do try to remember that Julia is here and living in every evidence of abundance." Having seen her brother throw himself back down onto the settee, she turned her gaze back to Julia. "Let us have plain speaking, my girl. Someone is paying for your dressmaker, the servants, and that new pair of bays I saw pulling your barouche yesterday. If it is not Papa, *who*?"

"What a wretched mind you have," said Julia with some sharpness of her own, but it was a sharpness born more of fright than of indignation. She must convince Sophie, or the game would shortly be up. Drawing a deep breath, she tried to feign annoyance. "You are the most *prying* person, Sophie, but if you must know, I have come into a little trust fund left to me by one of my maternal relations."

"The Clembeau family?" Sophie's green eyes widened in her exquisitely featured face. Then she gestured with impatience. "What fustian! You don't know any of them."

Julia raised her brows, hoping she had a natural talent for being a fibster, for it would take audacity to pull the wool over Sophie's eyes. "And what, pray, do you imagine I have been doing while in France? Sketching the scenery?" She smiled with all the smug complacency she could contrive. "The present Comte de Clembeau is a person of excellent address—"

"Stuff and nonsense!" Sophie shook her head. "Papa regretted his union to your mother from the hour he married her. And I will never believe him willing to let you associate with those French people."

Julia's eyes flashed at this slur, but with a supreme effort of will she held back her temper. "Nevertheless, whether you believe me or not, I am in funds," she said as mildly as her vexation would permit. "And I decided it was such a bore to sit in those stuffy lodging places when Aunt Beth and I could be here, enjoying ourselves."

"Well, look here," put in Gaylord, sitting up from his indolent, sulky pose. "Don't you think you could extend a small loan just till the end of the month? May is coming up, and my luck always runs sweetest then. I should pay you back in a thrice."

Julia had never in her life been touched for money, but she had watched Gaylord wheedle pound after guinea from Sir Geoffrey, who had in turn gone to his friends for the same type of assistance. It was a vicious, loathsome cycle, and even had she been in possession of the wealth she claimed, Julia found herself too revolted to have any mercy. Her eyes grew a bit cool, and she shook her head. "I am afraid I cannot help you," she said firmly so that he should detect no signs of weakness and return another day to pester her. "Seasons are very expensive, you know. One of your friends must suffice to help you." She put out a hand. "Gaylord, if only you would cease frittering your life away and come up with some scheme to make your way in the world."

He struggled to his feet and swept a bow, a sneer spoiling his pleasant, if weak, countenance. "As a matter of fact, I do have a scheme. All my funds have gone into a partnership for a gaming salon, and a fellow does need a bit extra to fly on now and then."

"A gaming salon!" Julia gasped, quite horrified. "Gaylord, how could you bring yourself so low? Next, I suppose, you will be telling me you are a dealer at a faro table. No! I shall never consent to helping you with anything so horrid."

"As you like," he said with a huff. "Only do recall that it's always Sophie who makes the cutting remarks, never me. I've never done a thing against you."

"Nor have you done anything for me!" she retorted, too annoyed to remember to curb her tongue. "Ever!"

"No, and I shan't, my miss. Good-day!" And he minced rapidly from the room in something very near a flounce.

Not bothering to look up, Sophie helped herself unasked to a bonbon from the chased box at her elbow. "The fool," she said contemptuously beneath her breath, then glanced at Julia. "So you mean to have another season. May I ask why? You shall refuse any suitor who does come up to scratch. You always have."

"Do not be so sure of what I will do," said Julia, with Du Vallon's taunt of "apeleader" echoing in her ears. She had thought at first she would be able to persuade her aunt from lending him their assistance, but in these past days she had not bothered to try. There was something in the air when London was in season, something quite special and undefinable which had caught at her with its excitement, making it impossible for her to don weeds and turn her back on the temptation of having this last chance to make a splendid match, even if it meant remaining beholden to that odious Frenchman for his discretion. Now a fresh tingle of eagerness sent her more erect in her chair. Sophie might be induced to help if her whims were correctly applied to. "I suppose," she began carefully, "what with Wellington's campaign on the Peninsula and now this silly talk of war with America, London is woefully thin of company. Have all the gentlemen bought their colors? Lord Garde surely has. As I recall, he was always a fire-eater."

"Garde?" Abruptly Sophie loosed her silvery laugh which had enchanted so many suitors before her marriage to the Viscount Lewing. "I should think not. He lost one brother at Brussels, and the other is now in Spain. Dick is hardly such a fool as to jeopardize the title by playing soldier, as Lewing persists in doing with his stupid talk of honor and country. What honor, I ask you, if he is killed and so fails to inherit the earldom from his uncle? No, Dick is much more sensible."

A slight chill ran down Julia's spine. Last year Sophie had not been on such familiar terms with Garde. Abruptly cautious, she decided to make no further mention of her interest in his lordship. If the man was among Sophie's court of admirers, she would have to tread warily indeed to avoid offending her half-sister.

Sophie began gathering up her reticule and a small parcel she had brought with her. "A new toy for Edward," she explained, smiling. "You must come, I suppose, and see your nephew. What a bore it is, enduring a baby in town! But it was impossible to leave him behind in the country, with only the servants to look after him." She affected a yawn. "Oh, and tomorrow night is my rout. Do come, if you want. The Jerseys and Seftons shall be there. And Brummell too, unless he decides to be odious and snub me. Dick, of course, always comes to my little things to give me support." She smiled with the satisfaction of a woman whose world is arranged exactly as she wants, and a pang of envy shot through Julia at that smile.

"And won't you tell me *exactly* what Papa is doing?" asked Sophie, standing up so that her Junoesque height towered over Julia. "I should like to know where he is, so I may write him. He mustn't be made to feel we have all forgotten him, no matter how much he behaves like a shameless scapegrace."

Still occupied with wondering how devoted Garde was to her half-sister's circle, Julia almost fell into the pitfall. Just in time, however, her quick wits saved her from biting her lip and stammering in dismay. Not for nothing was she a Swanton. Copying Sir Geoffrey's most innocent expression, she met Sophie's observant eyes without flinching and said the first thing that came to mind. "Oh, he is languishing very comfortably in the company of an Italian countess. They met at one of the Empress Josephine's—no, I suppose I should call her the Duchess of Navarre. It's so dreadfully confusing, even after all this time. So wicked of Bonaparte to go on having two empresses, don't you think? I daresay Papa has left Paris by now. He mentioned Milan, but you know how erratic his plans can be."

Sophie gave her a rather small smile. "Yes. I shall write to him at Milan then. Is this countess a widow? No, do not tell me. I couldn't bear to think of him returning with yet *another* wealthy foreigner on his arm." Julia stiffened, and Sophie paused to wrinkle her forehead into a frown. "No, forgive me, Julia. That sounds unkind, and I did not mean it so. Your mama was very sweet, but I do not think an Italian would suit any of us." Turning back from the door she sat down again in her chair. For a moment she seemed very young and uncertain.

"Julia," she said in a tone which caught Julia's curiosity. "I could use some advice."

"Oh?" Surprised, Julia lifted her brows as she tried to remember whenever Sophie had made such a request of her before. "Concerning what?"

"Concerning—oh, why wrap it up in clean linen?" Sophie jumped to her feet. "Of late I have found myself regretting my marriage."

Now Julia came to her feet. "But you adorc Lewing!" was all she could immediately say.

"Yes, yes." Sophie gestured with impatience. "He is gentle and kind, all that anyone could wish for. But . . ." Her eyes fell before Julia's. "There is another who makes me feel as I have never felt before. His compliments set me as high as though I were a queen, and when his hand touches mine I could swoon in delight."

Shocked, Julia turned her back. "Sophie! You—no, you could not—" She stopped, unable to say it.

"No," said Sophie with quiet firmness. "I couldn't. But, Julia, though I shall always have a steady regard for my husband, he . . . well, he is away and I cannot help liking Dick more! I cannot!"

The oddest sensation flashed through Julia. She whirled, but even as she demanded the question she already knew the answer. "Not Lord Garde? Oh, Sophie!"

"If I am thought wicked, I cannot help it," said Sophie, drawing off her gloves then pulling them on again. "He is quite devoted to me, and that is such a comfort since I am stranded without Lewing's escort." She laughed a bit self-consciously. "In fact, I dare not deny it. I am exhilarated at the compliment of his attendance. He is such a man of standing."

"Yes, I know," said Julia, though the words nearly choked her. How could Sophie? Why must she feel the need for flirtation *now* when so much depended upon marriage to Garde?

"Do you?" Sophie laid a hand on Julia's arm, and it was all Julia could do not to jerk away. "I remember you casting sheep's eyes at him last year. It's just as well that interest came to nothing. He is quite a man of the world, and you are such a green little dab. Even I cannot see my way clear. I only know how fine it is when he is quick to perform some trifling service on my behalf." When Julia neither moved nor replied, Sophie dropped her hand and drew away with a sigh.

"Perhaps I have shocked you," she said. Julia crimsoned, and Sophie laughed. "Yes, indeed I have. I am sorry for it. But I thought I must speak to you before some gossip-tabby came round to give you her account. You see, Julia, Lewing hurt me dreadfully when he decided war was more important than Edward or I. I have no assurance he shall ever return, and so I cannot deny myself the compliments of other gentlemen forever. It is pleasant to flirt a little. Julia? No, do not give me your comments now. I do not require them. Good-bye, I will tell my friends you are back and wanting invitations."

Julia wrinkled her nostrils and whirled round to glare at her half-sister. Vile, wicked creature! How dared Sophie lay claim to Garde? Word of this must eventually reach Lewing's ears, and would Sophie expect him to receive it with calm? Worse, why need Sophie, who had a husband, stand in the way of those who did not?

"Sophie," she said with considerable sharpness, causing her half-sister to halt in the doorway and glance back. "You made a good match. How shall I have any hope of doing the same if you mean to attract all the gentlemen to your side?"

Sophie whitened and something blazed hard in her green eyes. "I had thought you would understand, but I see you are still too ignorant to do so. Let us forget this conversation. It should not have been uttered, least of all to you."

With a slam of the door she left, and as soon as Julia heard the sound of her departing carriage she dashed the nearest vase to the floor and ground the heel of her slipper upon the fragments. *That* for Sophie and her instructions to stay away from Garde! Julia had not the least intention of obeying her. If Sophie came to grief over this it would be her own fault entirely. And her rout would serve very well as an opportunity of meeting Garde again. With a decisive set of her chin, Julia ran upstairs to begin laying her plans.

Chapter Three

Lady Lewing's rout fell on an unusually warm evening for early May, an omen promising success for her assembly. Enlivened by the blithe temperature, which did not require even the lightest of wraps, and excited to such a degree she was almost feverish, Julia alighted from their carriage in the wake of Lady Elizabeth and passed up the gracefully appointed stairs to her half-sister's salons. Upon first entering, she was surprised to find the rooms redone in a different style and color from when she had last seen them a few months past, and paused a moment to survey her surroundings, unaware of how coolly confident the action made her appear. Attired in a simple gown of celestial blue silk with Juliette sleeves and a white sash caught up high under her bosom, and her black hair dressed *à la Sappho*, she looked and felt entirely at her ease among Grecian chairs, rosewood tables, and a cream carpet which had eradicated the crocodile-based sofas and Egyptian ostrich fans upon gilded bases presiding there before. She exchanged a perfunctory kiss of greeting with her half-sister. Then, gliding into the room on new sandals, which had been extravagantly dear but showed glimpses of her feet to exquisite advantage, she moved forward to join the other guests, eager to pick up the old threads of her life among the circles of the *ton*.

Lady Sefton was the first individual to seize upon

her, professing that she was positively *dying* of curiosity concerning Sir Geoffrey. "Has he returned to town incognito?" she asked almost at once and, rather to Julia's discomfiture, tittered like a schoolgirl. "Such a dear, *roguish* man," she gushed on with a glance over her shoulder at her amiable husband. "You mustn't let Sefton hear me, but I vow I could almost be swept off my feet like the silliest green girl. Sir Geoffrey has such ramshackle charm." And, peeping through her fingers at Julia, she tittered again.

Swallowing down her irritation, somehow Julia found a civil smile for her. "Indeed, ma'am, I am sure my father would be flattered by your praises *were* he in London. But he is not. My aunt and I are here without the support of his company."

"Do you find a constant attendance on all the gambling salons *supportive*?" inquired a languidly caustic voice over her shoulder.

Startled, Julia turned to find a pair of hazel eyes regarding her from above a classical, albeit slightly crooked, nose. At once she relaxed, even chuckled, for no one could take offense at such a remark if it were uttered by this gentleman. "Mr. Brummell," she said, holding out one slim hand with unfeigned pleasure. "How pleased I am to be hearing your odiously sharp remarks once more."

His brows swept up, but a faint gleam in his gaze told her he was not unappreciative of her spirited reply. A faint sigh escaped his lips. "Yes, I daresay the overbred formality of French salons does become tedious after a while. I, at any rate, am delighted to see you return—*sans parent,* of course."

"Of course," she murmured, her violet eyes alight with mirth. She understood very well how much the Beau disapproved of her rakehelly father and his carefree ways—especially after Sir Geoffrey in a decidedly castaway condition had nearly run him down while engaging in a curricle race up Bond Street with Sir John Lade—and could laugh because she had very often found herself in perfect accord with the first gentleman of fashion on this matter. Then with a breath caught sharply enough to hurt, she realized she was actually making jokes about the dead. For a moment she was appalled at her own lack of proper feeling, then common sense righted itself enough to enable her to see she had been right, after all, to concoct this pretense. For as long as no one knew of Sir Geoffrey's fate, she, too, was able to forget it. To think of him abroad somewhere and up to all his usual tricks was much, much easier to bear.

The momentary sadness in her small face was replaced by a glow of fresh confidence and renewed spirits, and she was able to make a remark which set the Beau laughing. This feat was remarkable enough to send Lord Alvanley sauntering over in hopes of joining their amusement. Brummell gave him a careless wave.

"My dear fellow," he complained in his soft but devastating way. "Miss Swanton was merely favoring me with a highly original observation on Monsieur Talleyrand. Pray, let us not sour its bite by repeating it over and over."

Alvanley begged Julia's pardon with his usual good humor, and she was about to ask him whether Lord Garde was yet arrived when Brummell snorted. "Miss Swanton, I fear my opinion of your sister as a hostess has plummeted." He nodded to point out the arrival of Lord Byron. "She may consider his presence a coup, but with Caro Lamb already here, I am soon likely to be nauseated by a public display fo that damsel's emotions. Excuse me." Turning on his heel, he left them.

Alvanley chuckled. "That has said it neatly, I must admit. Lady Caroline is rather a headstrong miss; sometimes I wonder how her people bear her tragedies.

But you must give me a little account of how you enjoyed the Continent. France can't be very jolly with this war on."

Julia, however, had spotted an auburn head towering above the rest now, and with a pulse hammering at the base of her throat from a breathless sensation of sheer nerves and excitement, she pried herself free and sought out her quarry. It took an exasperatingly long time to merely cross the room, for there was nearly everyone to acknowledge. But at last she reached the edge of the circle surrounding Garde—only to see him spy the exact instant when Sophie abandoned her duties at the door and at once excuse himself to escort her in search of a glass of refreshment.

Someone provided the same service for Julia, but her spirits had plummeted to the soles of her new sandals. Good heavens, the man acted devoted to Sophie! And if he genuinely was, what hope had Julia of diverting his interest? She must find out.

At the first opportunity for a private word with Lady Jersey, who could be counted on to know every *on-dit* and crim. con. story in current circulation, she brought up the matter of the two—delicately.

But Lady Jersey was in quick-witted form that evening and gave one of her rich, rippling laughs. "How sharp you are, to notice so quickly," she said, her eyes alight with amusement. "Lewing is pleasant, but such a pattern-card of virtue as to be positively dull! I daresay when he returns from fighting in Spain he shan't be at all willing to set up a little *ménage à trois*. So dog-in-the-mangerish of him, don't you think?"

"It is the fashion for married ladies to have their cicisbei," said Julia with some difficulty, determined not to betray her anger with Sophie.

Lady Jersey's face softened. "Oh, my dear child, how foolish of me to forget that you have yet to cut your eyeteeth." She patted Julia's arm and shrugged. "I do not truly believe there has been any conduct beyond the bounds of propriety," she said in a significant way. "Their friendship is so very—public, you see. And her ladyship seems a bit immature . . . still, it occasions a certain amount of gossip, and I should not be recounting it to you as though you were a matron."

With a little dignity, Julia rallied enough to lift her head. "Not at all, my lady," she said with as much composure as she could muster over embarrassment at having her feelings mistaken for missishness. As though she had not the least bit of town polish at all, she thought with a stab of vexation. "Surely you know I have not been raised in cotton wool."

"No, I believe not." And the amusement returned to Lady Jersey's eyes, thus ending the awkward moment for both of them.

Though she continued to keep up her end of various conversations, Julia's thoughts remained in a turmoil. She knew she was far from being plain, but Sophie—despite her marriage of five years—was still a diamond of the first water. Julia knew she could not hope to steal any gentleman's attention away from her half-sister. She was defeated before she began, and should be better spending her time finding someone less attached in the petticoat line.

Then with exasperation she caught herself up. What a dolt she was, to be forgetting about her strongest asset! After all, Sophie *was* married. No matter how strong her sister's preference for the Earl of Garde, there was Lewing between them. It was absurd to give up so easily. From what she knew about Garde, Julia was certain he was not the sort to pursue an unfruitful dalliance indefinitely. His interest must eventually wane, and Julia meant to make sure such an event happened as quickly as possible. Stifling any doubts concerning such ruthless measures, she lost herself in speculations and thus did not immediately notice the couple that had come to stand before her chair.

"Poor Julia," said Sophie with affected concern. "Are you so bored you must sit by yourself and glower in a brown study?" She performed her silvery laugh, which the Prince Regent had once claimed sent shivers of delight up his back. "I hope you remember the Earl of Garde? He says he made your acquaintance last year and was struck by what a pretty child you are."

"Very pretty," corrected Garde at once, his murky, deep-set eyes not leaving Julia, "but hardly a child." The eyes roved briefly over her person in an arrogant way which made her shiver with a chill of excitement.

With her most enchanting smile, she sought to press her momentary advantage of having engaged his interest. "Yes, my lord, I recall you quite well," she said. "You were gracious enough to partner me through a country set." Then she dared send Sophie a sisterly look. "I thought I would visit my nephew tomorrow morning—that is, if you have not planned an outing with him yourself." It would do no harm, she reflected, for Garde to be reminded of Sophie's status as a wife and a mother.

Lady Lewing's green eyes blazed. "No," she said as though struggling to hold back something sharper, "I am sure Edward will be delighted to see you."

Garde's heavy lips twitched into a smile appreciative of this exchange, and Julia had her reward. She found she did not remember him being such a large man. He was quite tall, especially so in regard to her diminutive height, and strongly muscled. A noted Corinthian, he was obviously vain about his auburn hair, which was thick and wavy, for he wore it long against the current fashion. His heavily featured face was coarsened from dissipation; when in repose its expression was harsh and scarcely lightened by his frequent, careless smiles. Yet, he had smiled now, and whether it was for her or at her did not matter since Sophie's nose had been put out of joint.

"Will you be at the Devonshires' ball?" he was asking, putting an end to her dizzy thoughts.

Swiftly she pulled herself together and nodded, unable to keep from smiling as Sophie began to fidget. "Yes, I received an invitation only today, my lord." And one for that dreadful Frenchman as well, she thought with a prick of annoyance, remembering the lengths she and Lady Elizabeth had gone to in procuring it. He had best be satisfied with this morsel, for she would not put herself out on his behalf again. Toadying favors for people who were impudent and in the way was not her notion of a pleasurable activity.

But Garde's lips were curving back in a wide, insolent smile, and she must pay attention to him or else consign herself forever to the rank of peagoose. "I am going to be very unfair to all the other gentlemen," he said, exhibiting a rather wicked charm. "Will you promise to save a dance for me, Miss Swanton?"

Her heart skipped a beat, and only at the last moment did her natural sense of justice prevent her from glowing in arch triumph at Sophie, who looked to be finding this conversation hard to endure. Instead, she permitted herself a gracious curtsy. "Your lordship does me honor," she murmured. "I should be delighted to do so."

"Dick! Look there!" interrupted Sophie in an eager tone which did not quite conceal her irritation. "I have not seen Lady Cowper for an age. Take me to her at once."

Fancying she saw a hint of impatience in Garde's face as he complied, Julia did not mind this abrupt end to their meeting. Despite her half-sister's ill-advised jealousy, she had recaptured the interest he had been all too willing to bestow upon her last season. And at the forthcoming ball, she had little doubt of succeeding in winning him away entirely. Julia laughed to herself, much too pleased to heed the rancor which lurked in Sophie's eyes.

"I still think, Julia, that it was unhandsome of you to put down my suggestion of asking Lord du Vallon for his escort," said Lady Elizabeth in an injured tone as their carriage turned into the sweeping drive at Devonshire House.

Julia sent an annoyed glance in her aunt's direction and gestured. "Nonsense! Wanting escort when there is not the least reason to require it. Besides," she could not forbear adding as the footman jumped down from his perch to open the door and let down the steps for them, "say what you like, I cannot like the tone of his mind, nor do I approve of his lack of sensibility. He is not a proper companion for us at all, and I wonder at your persistence in this matter."

Leaving her aunt in crushed silence, Julia descended from the carriage—a lovely vision in her ballgown of white spider gauze and French slippers of matching satin. She realized, as she rearranged her lace scarf to drape more gracefully about her elbows, that perhaps she had been a bit too harsh with Lady Elizabeth. Her aunt was ever easily stricken to the point of tears, which would certainly mar the powder and Bloom of Ninon so carefully applied to her countenance, but at this moment Julia was too vexed to be contrite. Lady Elizabeth was on the deplorable verge of conceiving a *tendre* for a gentleman almost young enough to be her son, and for it to be Du Vallon was doubly reprehensible. He had been brought into every conversation for the past week, and Julia desired to hear no more of him. Nor did she intend to show him more than the barest civility at this function, for that man sorely needed his pretensions depressed.

But she was not permitted to carry out this resolve, for while she was laughing in the center of a small group of youthful gentlemen, a few of whom she had known ever since leading-string days, their number was parted by his grace, the Marquis du Vallon, a resplendent figure in pearl-colored satin breeches and a coat of pale apricot, his chapeau bras held at an angle more elegant than anyone else's.

Seeing him, Julia gasped, the laughter draining from her face to leave it cold and rather set. Du Vallon swept a graceful bow. "*Enchanté,* mademoiselle. I am in a transport of delight to see you again."

Young Mr. Wrexham, quick to sense an undercurrent of hostility in Julia, shouldered his way forward with all the finesse of a dog in the manger. "I believe you have the advantage of us, sir."

Ever cool, ever insufferably correct, Du Vallon begged pardon and raised his brows at Julia, thus reminding her of her duty to make the introductions. She did so coldly, determined not to give way an inch more than necessary to his unscrupulous methods.

"I say!" Mr. Wrexham, a fashionably dressed young gentleman sadly inclined to a bit of rotundity toward the middle and more determined than successful in escaping the leading-strings his mama was still inclined to employ, now blinked and promptly gave up his championship of Julia to beam at the marquis. "Du Vallon, yes! I knew the name was familiar. You're the great duelist, aren't you? The best marksman in Europe. Jupiter! I'm deeply honored, my lord, to make *your* acquaintance."

A duelist! Startled, Julia's eyes flew to her tormentor and took new meaning from the thin scar on his temple, the steely quality of his keen eyes, the close-fitting glove he habitually wore on his right hand. She had heard of European gentlemen who made themselves notorious by performing other men's duels for a fee, but somehow the thought of the elegant, graceful marquis following such a revolting course was incongruous to the highest degree. Unsuccessfully she tried to fight off a sinking of dismay. Her every suspicion concerning him was true then; he was an adventurer and, as such, no fit companion for either her or her aunt. How was she to escape his coils?

She was still asking herself that question when he led her away in search of punch. "But I do not want any," she said with a great deal of crossness, resenting the masterful way in which he held her hand entrapped in the crook of his arm.

He sent her a flicker of a glance. "*Tiens, tiens!* Then you may have a glass of orgeat."

She frowned, determined to resist these overtures. "I do not want anything to drink!"

"But I do." His voice remained soft, even mild. "Do not be rude, mademoiselle. It is so unbecoming."

She gasped at his effrontery, her steps faltering to a halt. How dare he call her such an unkind thing, when his behavior was equally bad! She drew in a deep, scorching breath, but before she could speak, he pulled her to one side.

"Come, come, *ma bonne fille*. We cannot stand in the way of the dancers." And thus unscrupulously employing the aid of Mozart's minuet, he obliged her to continue toward the long refreshment table.

Still suffused with indignation, she permitted her eyes to flash magnificently with anger over the rim of her glass. "I think it quite unhandsome of you," she said, "to repay me in this Spanish coin after I had to positively cajole her grace into issuing you an invitation."

His gray eyes lightened with laughter. "*Chérie,* was that a snub?"

Furious, she rounded on him, fingers clenched hard on the glass she wished she could hurl at his head. "I resent your jests and your ill manners, sir!" she said in a low, rapid voice, every line of her body stiff with outrage. "You will cease at once to treat me upon such familiar terms."

The amusement faded from his countenance, leaving it suddenly pale and pinched with an emotion she could not name. Perhaps it galled him to be chastened like a schoolboy, but she did not care. He deserved a set-down.

For a moment she thought he would leave her, and a bit of hope fluttered to life within her breast. Looking past him, she glimpsed Lord Garde and his brilliant leonine head towering above the rest of the company. If this arrogant, meddling Frenchman would but accept his *congé*, she would be free to go about her own pressing concerns. In the background a waltz was being struck up. Garde lifted his brows, and she smiled acceptance, happily remembering her promise and pleased that he should claim it now instead of for some dull country set. She was so intent upon what she was doing, she passed completely unaware of Du Vallon's intrigued observance of this communication.

Garde started in her direction, but by now Du Vallon, with every evidence of his sangfroid regained, was sweeping her a bow. "My apologies, Mademoiselle Swanton. I was *injuste* to forget the dictates of formality. I beg *mille pardons* for provoking you."

She frowned, unable to help being slightly mollified by so neatly spoken an apology, but before she could excuse herself he had captured her hand again and given her half-finished orgeat to a passing servant. "I beg this waltz, if you please."

Annoyed, she tried to snatch her hand away. "I do

not please!" she snapped, then bit her tongue in chagrin over her vanishing command of good manners. "I—I mean, I am already promised." Where *was* Garde, she wondered impatiently, and could have stamped her foot to see him halted in conversation with their host.

"But your partner is not here, and the dance is starting." The gleam in the marquis's clear, cold eyes was challenging. "And I do not think mademoiselle has fear of so improper a dance."

Her spirit leaped in ready answer. So he thought she was some shrinking miss afraid to permit his arm around her waist. Well, she was not, but though she longed to tell him so, she fully intended to join the other couples with Lord Garde.

Du Vallon, however, had seen the initial flash in her eyes and took this for his answer. Before she could protest further, she was swept off her feet by a very strong arm and plunged into the midst of the twirling couples. Snatching up her train in a haphazard way, she sent him a muted glare as her feet found the steps.

"If I did not desire to become this week's leading *on-dit*, I would leave you to stand no-how in the midst of everyone," she gasped, trying rather desperately not to be overwhelmed by the air of authority and masculine power emanating from him at such close quarters. She had danced the waltz countless times before, but this was the first occasion she had been so . . . so aware of the intimacy of the exercise. Du Vallon's arm held her quite correctly and made no effort to draw her too near, but the fact that he was holding her at all seemed to be oversetting her every sensibility. A crimson blush burned up her throat to the roots of her hair, and out of resentment over her discomfiture at being in the hands of one she had come to view as her enemy, she snapped, in quite a heartfelt manner, "You, sir, are nothing but a vile, unhandsome toad."

At once she was gripped by dismayed horror. Surely she had never intended to say anything so stupid! Why did she always permit him to bring out the worst in her?

With a little sigh she looked up to apologize—certain she must confront his annoyance—only to blink with surprise as she saw him struggling to hold back laughter. And how impishly those gray eyes could gleam! A little taken aback, she stared at him for a moment, unable to deal with the sight of someone usually so stern and odious now suffused with mirth. Then in relief, and also because it was all so terribly absurd, she relaxed and began laughing herself. For that instant it was easy to enjoy the lilting melody, the fragrance of hundreds of lilies arranged throughout the festooned ballroom, the fact that she was partnered by a personable gentleman—if not precisely the one she had desired to be partnered by.

"I *am* sorry," she made herself say, and smiled a bit wryly at the thought of it. "I should never have called you such a thing."

"*Vraiment?*" He lifted his thin brows, grave again. Or was he? "I admit, never have I been compared to such a creature. It is a crushing moment."

"I am regretful of it," she hastened to say, lest he conceive the mistaken notion that she was apologizing, "only because it is such an unimaginative term. You have provoked me most severely, you know," she went on, warming to the theme of her scold. "I would have done so much better to have employed the label of brute, or carpet-knight, or even unmitigated shabster!"

"Shabster?" He frowned delicately over the word. "I do not know this *mot*. But no matter. I see I am crushed again by mademoiselle's so formidable tongue." His gaze quizzing her until her eyes fell, he asked, "Am I so abhorrent you cannot bear to dance with me? Is that why you are so provoked? Please remember you are the only *demoiselle* of my acquaintance in this company. Have mercy, *s'il vous plaît*!"

"You could have been more gracious and waited until I had an unclaimed dance," she began severely, then stopped, vexed to find she was sounding like a prim governess. "I was looking forward to waltzing with Lord Garde, and you spoiled everything."

"Ah." Another of his unreadable expressions appeared. "You are perhaps betrothed to this gentleman?"

Again, much to her mortification, she crimsoned. "No," she said bluntly, but a suspicion that he already knew the answer and was merely baiting her made her add, "But you appear to know that."

He inclined his head, eyes hooded and now unreadable. "But of course. Mademoiselle forgets I have been in London nearly a fortnight. And I am never idle."

Did she hear bitterness in that last remark? No, surely not, she decided, and dismissed the notion. The music ended with a flourish, and he swept her a bow.

"Now," he said, "I shall escort you to the hand of this lord and explain how it was that my lamentable command of English prevented me from understanding you were not free to dance with myself."

"Thank you!" she said, unable to forbear sending him a wry glance. "But you speak English very well, my lord."

He almost smiled. "He need not know that, *d'accord*? Come."

But the musicians had halted for a brief respite, and in the crush of guests Garde was not to be seen. At last Du Vallon sighed. "Your so pretty gown is becoming harmed. Let us go onto the terrace for a moment until there is room to breathe again."

Uncertain of what this suggestion might entail, she was hesitant about agreeing, but thankful for the cool air once they were away from the overheated ballroom.

She stood beside the stone balustrade, gazing out over the gardens dimly lit by paper lanterns. The thick scent of honeysuckle seemed to hang in the air like a soft blanket, wrapping about them with its lazy fragrance. Du Vallon leaned himself against the balustrade and took a pinch of snuff. Tired of his banter, Julia was glad he made no further effort at conversation and left her free to watch various couples promenade off into the darkness of the shrubbery with muted trills of wicked laughter.

Then she saw one couple returning, and her hands clenched down hard upon the gritty stone railing, the blood in her veins draining away to ice. She made no sound, but at once Du Vallon was alert beside her.

"What is wrong?" he asked.

"Nothing." Her voice came out too crisp and emphatic. Unable to watch Sophie strolling along with her lips parted in a blissful little smile while Garde—Garde!—murmured in her ear and deliberately kissed the tips of her fingers, one by one, Julia whirled to put her back to the sight. She trembled with fury at having been so neatly cut out. "I see merely that my half-sister and Lord Garde have been enjoying a *tête-à-tête* in the arbor."

"Which are they?" Du Vallon's voice was disinterested, which reminded her with a painful stab of self-recrimination that she was fast making a cake of herself.

"There." Without much success she attempted to reply calmly in an imitation of his tone, but her fists remained clenched and shaking at her sides. It was maddeningly unfair! If she had danced with him, Sophie would not now be enjoying his favor! Of course, thought Julia as her heart thudded a bit uncomfortably, she could not be sure she would have desired to go off in that naughty way, but at once she dismissed these undermining notions and allowed her resentment against Du Vallon to come boiling up again.

"Your sister is *très belle, ravissante*," remarked the marquis after a pause, with an appreciation in his tone which flayed Julia's already lacerated temper.

Her lips compressed. "Sophie is also married, and she has a four-year-old son."

In the gloom, Du Vallon's laugh was a soft, mocking murmur. "Can mademoiselle be so prudish, to set her face against a little lovemaking? The night is very fine."

It was not the sort of comment, somehow, she had expected of him, and it served to fan her anger. "Yes, my lord, I respect fidelity, and if that is prudish so be it," she retorted and sent him a defiant look.

But he was gazing elsewhere and did not observe her expression. "Or perhaps mademoiselle has jealousy over Milord Garde. He is the best shot in England, I have heard. Quite a distinction."

"Yes, he is a notable Corinthian," she snapped, completely uninterested in such considerations at the moment.

Now Du Vallon turned his disconcerting gaze full upon her. "Mademoiselle has perhaps a *tendre* for this gentleman?"

Julia stiffened. How dare the man be so perceptive! "I cannot with propriety answer such a question, my lord, since I have not made Lord Garde's acquaintance long enough for the consideration to arise." It was a very stiff and proper answer, but she had the uncomfortable suspicion that Du Vallon was neither fooled nor approving. Her chin came up; it was none of his business whatsoever.

"In the circumstances, I think we may not seek out milord's company just yet," was all the marquis said, however. He toyed with a lacquered snuffbox between his long, shapely fingers, and kept his gaze upon it.

"*Voyons,* let us discuss other matters instead. There is an establishment *très cher* to English society." His eyes lifted coolly to meet Julia's smoldering ones. "I wish you to procure vouchers for me to the assembly rooms of Almack's. Not a task *difficile* for a young lady so charming as mademoiselle."

Her eyes flashed with incomparable brilliance. Perhaps now he expected her to blush behind her fan and beg him not to be so ardent with his compliments. "I shan't lift a finger to help you again," she said with a snap. "The entree given you tonight is enough; if you desire more, it must be from your own efforts." She started to walk away, but he caught her arm with his gloved hand. Even as her temper flared at his effrontery, she wondered again what that glove concealed. "Please be good enough to unhand me, sir!"

"But should I when mademoiselle appears to need a reminder of our agreement?" he asked, his previous friendly tone vanished.

She ceased struggling at once to regard him with a frown. "You cannot be so shabby as to expect us to continue opening doors—"

For answer he released her arm and stood implacable before her with his stern lips compressed and his arms crossed over his chest. She tried to outstare him, but failed to her chagrin. Not did it help to admit that he was right in this matter; she certainly was in no position to indulge in a show of defiance.

She sighed and gave in with a reluctance she did not bother to conceal. "Oh, very well, I shall try. But I can make you no promise since everything depends on the whim of the patronesses."

"I understand this," he said, almost with impatience, and gave no sign of triumph. "You will be asked questions, and you may tell them I am wealthy and of impeccable lineage. As a child I served as page to Louis of France. My father lost his head, his property, and his *duché* during the Revolution. *Ainsi*, I am left with but the title of my birth." He shrugged, a hard light glittering in his eyes. "It serves me well enough. Once I am settled here, I wish to bring my sister to England." He smiled unpleasantly. "All this you may tell to your patronesses, if they wish to know."

"Thank you," said Julia, put off by his disagreeable manner. She wondered if this tale of his past was true. Probably not, but sometimes gentlemen of birth and breeding did turn out to be rogues. She had almost liked him during the waltz, but he was detestable and arrogant for all his grand airs and façade of elegance, and if she had not been convinced he would slander her name right through the mud she would have asked several gentlemen of her acquaintance to make certain this—this *adventurer*—never invaded England's shores again. "I shall see what I can do, since you insist in this brutal way of yours," she said with all the stiff dignity she could muster. "But again, I make no promises."

His countenance was a cold mask, the finely etched features showing no expression at all. "I require none, mademoiselle. You—"

"Oh, Julia, dearest, here you are!" Lady Elizabeth came fluttering up in a hapless manner calculated to entangle her fringe in the shrubbery and sketched Du Vallon an out-of-breath curtsy. "Why, it's the Marquis du Vallon! How delightful to see you again, my lord. Are you finding our society to your taste? I do hope so, for it was the greatest pleasure to be able to persuade the duchess to invite you. And do call on us. We are on Clarges Street, do you remember? I confess I was quite crushed by your absence, but perhaps you are still finding your feet and were reluctant to intrude. Not at all, I quite assure you! But I must *not* forget why I am here." Flushed and still out-of-breath, she turned back to Julia, who could not help but regard her with impatience at these ploys.

"The Earl of Garde sent me to find you, lamb. Is it not excessively romantic?" She laughed in her flustered way. "He says he is dying to stand up with you, and *such* hair, Julia, as you cannot imagine. It quite set me aflutter, like a silly schoolgirl again. And Mr. Wrexham—what a pity he has inherited his poor father's nose—wants to dance with you too, although at first I thought he was going to be too shy to say so with Garde standing there."

"I must not keep you from your admirers, mademoiselle," said Du Vallon, with that peculiar coldness of his still in evidence. He turned away, leaving Julia free to try to dismiss him and his arrogance from her mind.

She could not, of course, for she was still seething over the indignity of being bent to his commands and wishing she might do anything rather than accede to them. But it was a relief all the same to be gone from his company at last, and she returned to the ballroom to join a lively reel with Garde, who politely inquired about the gentleman who had stolen her for the waltz.

"Lord du Vallon," she said somewhat shortly, weary of the marquis. "He is newly here from France and would not understand that I was already claimed for the dance. I hope you are not annoyed."

"Not at all," said Garde with the faintest hint of displeasure beneath his wide, careless smile as he prepared to lead her onto the floor. "One can only deplore the encroachment of these *émigrés;* if the fellow was rude to you—"

"Nothing of the sort," she was obliged to say, hating having to lie for the marquis's sake. Du Vallon and his meddling had managed to spoil her carefully contrived plans; she could not help but be displeased because all her anticipated pleasure at being in Garde's company was now gone and simply would not return. The name of Du Vallon seemed to tremble upon every thread of her anger and would not be banished. "I am previously acquainted with him, you see," she added, a bit unwillingly.

"Ah." And the music began, leaving no more time for conversation with Garde, who, much to her chagrin, looked politely bored. Julia passed up the line with every appearance of being merry, but she knew that for her the evening had gone amiss, perhaps even to the point of losing Garde's interest entirely. Catching a glimpse of Sophie flirting on a sofa with an extraordinarily handsome officer in regimentals, Julia was stricken with dissatisfaction. Indeed, she was the object of Garde's rather lazily impertinent smile now, but Sophie had already proven her claim on him for the evening with that revolting little excursion into the garden. It was rather as though Sophie had thrown her cold scraps, and Julia could not find it anywhere in herself to be grateful.

Chapter Four

The following morning she arose in a leisurely fashion and, after consuming a breakfast of rolls and chocolate, donned a bronze-colored riding habit and small hat with a jaunty pheasant feather sweeping off the brim, and ordered her mare brought round from the stables. Another daunting expense, she could not help thinking as she descended the stairs and paused to rearrange a bowl of fresh hyacinths on the hall table. But although the amount of oats her spirited mount consumed in a day was considerable, Julia forced herself to dismiss the worry. After all, she must cut as dashing a figure as possible, and her riding ability *was* one of her most notable accomplishments. Therefore, a mare was necessary, as well as the new pair of bays to pull their town carriage. But she did heartily wish the need to avoid looking shabby in any way did not require the services of a butler, cook, two maids, groom, stableboy, and coachman—not to mention that terribly expensive footman and his livery as well. Moreover, tallow candles were all very well for the servants' quarters and her own bedchamber, but wax ones must be seen elsewhere, and at a dear price too. And she must remember to send to Swantoncourt at the first opportunity for the gold brocade draperies hanging in the library there. While not precisely new, they weren't as worn as those here in the drawing room and would at least create the illusion of new furnishings.

Her thoughts were abruptly interrupted by a loud pounding upon the front portal, startling her into dropping a bloom. "For heaven's sake, do they think we are deaf?" she exclaimed with a wince to Rutledge, who had appeared from the nether regions.

"It would appear so, Miss Julia," he replied in his grave tones. Without pausing, he trod across the polished Persian marble of the hall and opened the door to reveal a man, obviously a servant, upon the steps. Beyond, a carriage with garish yellow wheels waited in the street.

On instinct, Julia was certain she did not wish to receive the visitor, whoever that person might prove to be. But she could not help but be dismayed at her presence an awkward five feet behind Rutledge. The servant's quick eyes traveled to her as he made his inquiry as to whether Sir Geoffrey Swanton was in.

Julia took a swift intake of breath as a spurt of anger clenched her hands upon the edge of the table. So her suspicions had been correct; it *was* a creditor. Conscious of the prickly sensation she usually experienced when facing any of several species of vermin, she lifted her chin.

"Rutledge," she said in a commanding tone calculated to rebuff her unwanted visitor with that indefinable air of quality so daunting to the lower orders, "please ask the man to inform his master that Sir Geoffrey is not at home. He is visiting—acquaintance abroad," she went on, annoyed with herself for allowing that brief catch to appear in her voice.

Rutledge relayed the information to the servant and was preparing to turn him away when the door of the carriage flew open with a force explosive enough to rattle the panels, and a short man, very richly dressed and tending to corpulence, thrust himself out. Puffing at an alarming rate, he came hurrying up the steps with such natural velocity, Rutledge, despire years of dealing admirably with the worst situations, gave way.

Outraged by this intrusion, Julia drew herself up and started to deliver a severe setdown to this incredibly rude, encroaching man, but he cut the ground from beneath her feet by thrusting his heavy jaw forward in a bulldogish way and saying, "I heard every word in my carriage, missy, and I believe not a word of it!" Still puffing from his exertion, he brandished his stick. "Look at the place," he commanded in a bluff, gravelly voice which grated on Julia's ears. "Out of dust covers. Mark my words, that Sir Geoffrey is here, and I'm not fool enough to believe anything else."

Julia boiled to hear herself and her parent spoken of in such a manner by a person of this kidney. Up came her chin. "You may address me as Miss Swanton. Who are you?"

"Robert Duffy," he said, jerking a short bow, and wagged a blunt finger at her. "Now, Sir Geoffrey if you please."

Accepting a situation threatening to get out of hand, Julia controlled herself with as much grace as was at her command. She awarded the man—gentleman was certainly *not* the term to describe him—a very tight smile, and took him to the small drawing room, where she might deal with him out of the hearing of the servants.

Turning haughtily to Rutledge, who had followed, she said in a firm manner, "Ask the stableboy to bring Temptation round in *ten* minutes, please."

Rutledge's stony countenance twitched ever so slightly to indicate he understood the order and without changing expression even a fraction, sent the unwanted guest a look that conveyed crushing disapproval.

Julia was satisfied at having so neatly provided herself with the means to terminate this interview in short order. For a moment she indulged herself in watching her guest's prominent but shrewd eyes assess every object in the room; he even permitted himself a brief caress of a particularly fine Sèvres figurine. Julia's hands tightened on the silver-handled whip she was gripping. Insolence! No doubt he was calculating how many of these objects were going to pass into his possession since Sir Geoffrey could not meet his debts. Her determination to rout this mushroom of a fellow heightened.

The subtleties, she immediately decided, would be lost upon him. Her chin came up as she prepared for battle. "This intrusion is to be answered for. Immediately," she said in a forthright manner, refusing to sit down despite the looks of longing he was expending upon a winged armchair.

Her challenge brought his blunt head up and around like an old hound's, and an appreciative gleam shone in his eyes. "Aye, you're your father's daughter, buckle and strap me if you ain't. I admire that."

Revolted, she took refuge in freezing hauteur. "I am under no obligation to grant you this interview. If you wish it to continue I strongly suggest you address me with respect." And her furious violet eyes dared him to do otherwise.

"Very well," he said with some coldness in return. "If you don't choose to share a bit of friendliness, we'll get down to it. I refuse to be gaped by your father any longer. He can stop hiding behind women's skirts, for it won't do him a mite of good. That, I promise you!"

Julia had disliked this man on first sight without bothering to question her immediate impression, but now certain details began to come to her notice—the strongly scented oil with which he pomaded his hair, the collection of heavy rings on his coarse fingers, the garish note struck by a bright yellow moleskin waistcoat with pewter buttons. For a moment the horror of thinking how it had been her parent's frequent habit to deal with this sort of person threatened to nauseate her. How could he have brought himself to beg from a cit? Then with a savage little wrench of will she brought her offended sensibilities to heel. This was hardly the time to stand on her niceties. She had need of wits, not feelings, to get rid of this man.

"How much does Sir Geoffrey owe you, Mr. Duffy?" she asked in a quiet voice, standing erect with her hands demurely folded and the gaze of steel in her eye.

"Aha!" His eagerness seemed almost to pounce, making her hard put not to shrink back in distaste. "Now we come to it, eh, Miss Swanton? Twelve thousand pounds, plus accumulated interest."

Something in the way he added that last remark sent a wave of color washing through Julia's cheeks and she could not keep from faltering back a step, one hand gripping the froth of lace at her throat. "A moneylender!" she gasped, feeling quite undone. And she had been thinking this merely an irate tradesman who could be fobbed off. Moneylenders were quite another matter indeed. The dizziness of dismay swirled through her.

"It's a necessary service, Miss Swanton," he said in an aggrieved tone. "You needn't look at me like that."

But Julia was fast recovering as her courage came bounding back to give her support. How foolish of her to react thus, she thought with exasperation, and let her hand fall away from her throat. The whip she was holding gave her a momentary temptation to bring it down across this fellow's shoulders, but she resisted the urge, knowing it was futile. For one thing, this was a man of some importance and wealth, not a common lackey; and for another, if he did indeed have such a horrifying sum coming to him, she dared not antagonize him. It must be his vulgarity rubbing off to even make her consider such a thing, she thought distractedly. Oh, why had her wits gone begging? She must think of what to do and say next.

Again her gaze met his squarely. "I must have proof of this debt, Mr. Duffy."

His look was surprised but approving. "Well, you're a miss with an uncommon head on your shoulders." And without fuss, he pulled out a paper from his pocket and handed it to her.

She read it once, twice, then found it necessary to sit down. Mr. Duffy settled himself on the sofa and thrust out his short, bandied legs in their expensive boots with a snort of relief. But Julia paid him no attention. Carefully she folded the heavy paper, its stiff crackling loud in her dazed ears. The terms of usury were quite simple, certainly disastrous, and she had no doubts whatsoever concerning the authenticity of her father's looping scrawl of a signature. The existence of the debt was incontestable, but . . . *she* did not owe it, nor did she intend to pay it even were she able. This determination sent fresh strength through her, enabling her to meet those shrewd, bulging eyes.

But he spoke first. "No doubt you've never heard of Duffy, the moneylender. Jew King's the popular fellow with the Quality, but I'll tell you to your head that he wouldn't pay out a shilling to Sir Geoffrey—considers him a bad risk. He laughed at me when Sir Geoffrey fled the country, and said I'd been bubbled, but I *will* get my investment back. I always have." His heavy jaw thrust itself out to underline the menace in his words, and he leaned ponderously forward, one hand set on each knee. Julia heard his stays creak, but could not bring herself to be amused for the sick sensation spreading within her of being cornered. "Now, missy," he said in a manner which sent a chill coursing up and down her spine. "Let's have done with these games. You just step along and tell your pa I know he can't come up with the money. But I am willing to accept in its stead a certain paper." He looked at her from under his brows. "Aye, the letter he used to persuade me into giving him a loan. He has a week to produce it. If he doesn't, he will find himself in hot water, very hot water indeed."

Julia gasped. How dare he threaten them! "I have not the slightest conception of what you are referring to," she said coldly.

"No, I expect you haven't." He leaned forward with a grunt and wagged a stubby forefinger at her. "Quality holds with hiding everything under the tablecloth, but I don't. No, indeed. Your pa possesses a letter written by a reckless peer to the wife of another gentleman. I don't know how he got it, but I could make dandy use of it."

"How dare you imply my father is a blackmailer!" Furious, Julia rose to her feet, gripping her whip with hands that shook. The notion was so horrible, so impossible to contemplate she could scarcely believe this man had actually made the accusation. "You may go, Mr. Duffy," she said. "You may go at once!" And she placed her hand on the silken pull.

His florid countenance turned livid. "Have me thrown out by my collar, would you?" He drew himself up as much as his bulk would allow. "Let me remind you, Miss Swanton, that I'm no common gutter cleaner brought in off the street. I'm worth a great deal, enough to do as I like. You pa can hide in his house today, but I know he is here."

He let out his breath heavily, and the shrewd eyes no longer held the least trace of friendliness. "I have eyes all over London. Sooner or later Sir Geoffrey will come out of this house, and when I have proof that he is in this country I promise you the watch'll be pounding on your fine door to arrest him."

Her eyes flashed scorn. "So you would dare set spies upon us! By heaven, sir, if there were a gentleman in this house I would have you soundly dealt with for such impertinence." As she spoke she tugged on the bell until it pealed through the house.

Mr. Duffy's eyes narrowed. "We'll see who comes out ahead on this. The crime of evading debt is something even the finest airs of Quality can't—"

The door opened to reveal Rutledge. Her cheeks a battleground of color, her eyes flashing sparks, Julia made an imperious gesture. "Show Mr. Duffy out, if you please, Rutledge." Her shapely bosom swelled. "He can have no occasion to call here again."

Rutledge bowed, observing the livid countenance of Mr. Duffy with dispassion. "Very good, Miss Julia. There is a *gentleman* waiting in the library to see you." He extended a salver containing a plain card.

Julia took it between her fingers and stood to one side, every line rigid as Mr. Duffy was escorted out. At first she could spare no thought for her other caller, not even to read his card. She was too overcome by disgust and revulsion at that beastly moneylender, and too horrified to think of Sir Geoffrey—charming, debonair Sir Geoffrey—going hat-in-hand to that vile affliction of a fellow, that parasite upon society. It nauseated her, infuriated her, and filled her with a burning desire to see Duffy horsewhipped in the street.

But then the first edge of her anger dulled enough for her to remember that after all, her ramshackle parent had willingly put himself into the sucking clutches of this form of financial disaster. A little pang wrenched through her. "Oh, Papa," she involuntarily said aloud. "Why were you so irresponsible?"

As for this claim that her father had held any such paper, it was nonsense, utter nonsense. Dissolute though he had been, Sir Geoffrey was a gentleman. He would not stoop so low. In a moment she was able to straighten her shoulders and dismiss the unpleasant scene from her mind. Sir Geoffrey was forever beyond the reach of his creditors, and she need not worry further about any of them. Shaking away a sting from her conscience over the way she herself was running headlong into debt despite all her fine principles, she now recalled the card she was holding. She read the florid script and was galvanized by a thrill of excitement. Lord Garde had actually presented himself upon her doorstep. How wonderful!

Exulting, she hugged herself, then flew to the gilt-edged mirror to check her appearance. Her color was too high, and now from the fast beating of her heart, she suspected it was not likely to recede at once. Frowning, she adjusted the delicate lace at her throat and wrists, trying to convince herself it did not matter. But everything mattered; every detail must be perfect. Briefly she wondered about her poor mare, saddled and waiting, no doubt, and about to be unsaddled and put away again. But Garde here, to see her of his own volition! A smile lit her face, and she hurried from the room with the train of her habit over her arm.

Reaching the library, her impetus carried her well inside the rather dim, musty interior, one slender hand outstretched in greeting, before Garde could rise in his lazy way from a deep leather armchair. But his bow was all that could be asked for, and his clasp swallowed hers for no more or less than the correct moment of time.

His careless, wide smile, showing a quantity of large white teeth, spread over her. "How charming you look in that habit, Miss Swanton! Perhaps it is forward of me to be calling upon such short resumption of our acquaintance, but I dared think you might wish to accompany me for a drive round the park."

The words were deferential, but his murky eyes, so alight today with interest and charm, told her of his confidence in her answer. They were impetuous, daring eyes, though she could not decide on their color, and their reckless gaze quite took her breath away. She gasped a little and looked down, trying to dispel the tremors he aroused in her.

"Indeed, my lord, you do not presume at all," she said, striving to sound normal. Why must she stand blushing and simpering like some wretched schoolgirl? Angry with herself, she lifted her gaze to his and made herself keep it there, despite the tumult in her blood. "I should be honored to drive out with you—that is, if you are not now quite shocked with me for receiving you alone. My aunt—" Despite her intentions, his little smile made her gaze fall again. "My aunt does not rise so early, you see, and—"

"My dear Miss Swanton," he broke in, sounding so amused the hot color sprang to her cheeks again, and she was certain, with a rush of embarrassment, that he must be thinking her the veriest green chit. "You may be assured I am no stickler to the proprieties. But you have been riding and are perhaps too fatigued to come out again?"

She shook her head at once, relieved he was not turning in disgust from her naïvete, and found it remarkably easy to take her lead from his casual dismissal of the need for Lady Elizabeth's presence. Indeed, it was so silly to expect poor Aunt Beth to rise a full hour earlier than her custom just to watch Julia go out on the arm of a perfectly respectable gentleman.

Giving him a shy smile, she explained, "No, I was about to go for my daily ride, but a drive would be equally pleasing. You are very kind to think of me, my lord."

His brows quirked up, and the ready smile appeared again on his heavy lips. Picking up his leather gloves of York tan, he cocked his auburn head to one side. "Kind? Miss Swanton, you do yourself an injustice. Shall we go, then?"

Pausing only to leave word to her aunt through Rutledge of where she was going, Julia allowed Garde to escort her outside to his waiting curricle. He spoke a word to the tiger holding the heads of a team of restive bays, and Julia took her opportunity to draw on her gloves and study the equipage before her. It was of the lean racing variety, new and well sprung. The body was painted black and the tall wheels white, to make a splendid, showy contrast. And Garde in the gaudy attire of white corduroy small clothes, blue-and-yellow striped kerseymere waistcoat, spotted cravat, and ankle-length driving coat with some sixteen capes making his large shoulders seem vast indeed—all of which proclaimed to the world his membership in the Four Horse Club—left her in no doubt of his ability to handle the ribbons. He helped her up, and as she settled herself upon the box and watched him ease his fiery team out into the street traffic with a dexterous looping of his rein, she realized she must be glad after all of that odious Mr. Duffy's visit. For if he had not come and delayed her, she would have altogether missed this opportunity to be with Garde.

Too happy to chatter, she soon discovered Garde himself was not naturally disposed to excessive conversation. But he did tell her how glad he was she had decided not to miss the London season. "You have grown up since last year," he went on, his laughing eyes seeming to invite her to share some joke she could not grasp. But determinedly she pushed away the impression that most of his meanings and implications were going over her head. She need only grow better acquainted with him to understand, to be able to share in the laughter which lit in his eyes so often. For now, she would let nothing spoil this time in his company, *nothing.*

Daring to quiz him, she asked, "Was I such a child

then? Yes, I daresay I was, but I promise not to stamp on your toe as I did before when you vexed me so."

He laughed in his loud, unrestrained way. "I perceive the lady is still a minx, with a tongue full of wit and mischief. And you may be sure I will hold you to your promise. Shall you be attending Almack's like all the other damsels? Such a dull place. Masquerades are much more lively."

His casual mention of Almack's left a dark reminder in her thoughts, but she tried to keep her attention on the conversation rather than on how much she despised Du Vallon. "I am sure they are," she replied, "but I have never attended a ridotto."

"Then you must," he said, his muscular arm brushing hers as they negotiated a tight corner in prime style. "I can procure an invitation to any number of them for you."

Without much reluctance, for she was fully aware of this man's reputation as a notorious flirt, she shook her head. "My aunt would never permit me to go," she said sunnily enough to show him she had no intention of making any clandestine excursions and promptly changed the subject. "What sweet goers you have."

"Yes, I am pleased with them," he said, the corners of his mouth quirking to show her he was aware of her tactics and amused by them. "They're darker than I like for true bays, but Alvanley is so mad to have them I shall have to make sure I don't find another team more to my fancy."

"Why?" she frowned, puzzled by his statement. "Are you and Lord Alvanley rivals, sir?"

"Hardly," he said with a good-humored snort of contempt. "But it pleases me to keep the little popinjay dangling. I can't imagine why your father should want to linger in France," he added, taking his own chance to alter the topic once again as she seemed inclined to defend Alvanley. "Nothing could be worse than the company of a lot of dashed frogs."

Julia, who had started to reply with her little tale of the Italian countess, now shut her mouth and frowned. Of course Garde did not know she herself was partially of French extraction, but she could not quite dampen a spark of annoyance at so broad a statement. Because she was a little vexed she changed what she had intended to say. "Do you think so?" she asked sweetly, forgetting for the moment that the last thing she desired was a disagreement between them. "My mother was French, and though she died before I could come to know her I have heard it said she was very charming."

He frowned at the backs of his horses. "Forgive me. But your parentage is hardly your fault, is it? And I am fully aware that you've been raised in a thoroughly English manner. A born Frenchman is someone I can and will not abide. My brother James was killed in a sea engagement two years ago, and George is now off in Spain like a young idiot, full of enthusiasm for this bungler Wellington."

Subdued, she forgot her resentment and stared down at her hands clenched loosely together in her lap. "I had not realized you had such tragedy in your family, my lord. I spoke out of turn."

He took one hand from the reins to lift her chin. "Good Gad, you needn't be cast down about it. We all make our mistakes. Now, would you prefer to join the morning promenade in the park, such as it is, or visit the lending library?"

"The park, please," said Julia, intrigued by the new custom of going to the park in the morning as well as the afternoon. A fellow named Barrow had set the style, which was in general not expected to last. She straightened her shoulders and forced herself to be pleased with Garde's heavy-handed attempt at reconciliation. "I am not bookish," she added with a slight smile.

"Gad, neither am I," he said with his loud, reckless laugh. "The park it is!"

But once they had swept through the gates of Hyde Park, Julia had cause to regret her choice despite the treat of seeing the regent—grimly up and about at so early an hour—tooling along with his phaeton-and-six, a royal prerogative that had every other whipster in the realm chaffing at being allowed to drive no more than four horses. Garde had not joined the procession of carriages and yawning riders for more than a few minutes until they encountered Sophie in her landaulet, looking the very picture of angelic motherhood in a ravishing carriage dress of pale celadon-green silk with the Honorable Edward at her side in stiff nankeens and clean lace collar. It was he who saw Julia first and broke into sudden animation by jumping onto the seat and waving.

Alarmed lest a jerk of the carriage make him fall, Julia gasped and threw out a hand, thus directing Garde's attention to the difficulty. He drew rein at once, and Sophie put an end to Julia's fears by seizing her small son's arm and pulling him down to a safer position. Her green eyes raked Julia before she pinned on a faint smile of cordiality. Young Edward, who was never permitted to speak when his mama was conversing with friends, satisfied himself with stealing surreptitious grins at Julia, his long blond curls enchantingly disordered by the May breeze.

"Julia. Dick." Sophie nodded. "How pleasant to see you *both.*"

Julia stiffened at her acid tone, but Garde merely laughed, showing his large teeth, and winked at Edward. "So this is Lewing's heir, is it? He favors you more, my dear."

Sophie's smile became warmer. "Make your bow to Lord Garde, Edward." The child obeyed, and Sophie cast up her eyes at Garde. "His manners are becoming quite pretty, I think. Do you like him, Dick?" She widened her green eyes as he looked down into them, and Julia was left completely out of the conversation as though she were no older than Edward.

It could hardly please her, but she held down her annoyance and tried to be patient by responding to Edward's game of peeping at her through his fingers. After all, it was petty to wish Garde and Sophie had nothing to discuss. Despite Sophie's foolishness in the matter, Julia did not want to make an enemy of her.

"I looked for you at Vauxhall last evening after the ball," Garde was saying to Sophie. "But you did not come. The rest of us had a splendid little party, but for me the enchantment of the night was lost."

Sophie's eyes glittered like hard emeralds as she fiddled with the catch of her sunshade. "So lost, my lord, that you were obliged to seek new companionship today?" Her gaze shifted to Julia and blazed scorn.

Julia gripped the edge of the box, barely able to restrain her temper. How dare Sophie—a married woman, a mother—show jealousy of Garde so openly! Did she not realize how swiftly gossip could embroil all their names? And what concern was it of hers in any case if Garde chose to turn elsewhere? Sophie was a fool if she thought she could dismiss her marriage ties on a whim. Julia longed to give her half-sister a snub, but before she could invent anything suitably crushing, Garde murmured some light remark and drove on with a laugh.

"What a pretty temper my lady has," he said quite cheerfully and tipped his hat to another beauty trying to engage his attention. Putting his horses to a spanking trot, he continued, "So quick to take offense at the slightest occasion. But I'll bring her around to her usual sweet self soon enough. Don't let her upset *you*, Miss Swanton!"

To be civil, Julia was obliged to laugh and deny her half-sister had affected her in any manner, but inwardly she seethed at Sophie's luck in having the last barbed word. Nor did she at all appreciate Garde's remarks! He was the least observant man she had ever seen. Really, as though she cared to hear his plans for cajoling Sophie into accepting him back into her good graces! Again, as it had been the previous evening, Julia found her satisfaction in being in his company quite spoiled and could no longer be at all sure about his reason for seeking her out.

They had paused to speak to a group of Garde's acquaintance, whom Julia was not familiar with, when a soft, *most* recognizable voice near her sent her turning in startlement. She found herself on a level with the piercing gray eyes of Du Vallon, their depths so clear in the radiant sunlight one could almost believe one saw to the farthest corners of his inner self. But of course that was nonsense.

Abruptly, she shook herself out of her surprise enough to note he was sitting astride a gray stallion with dappled flanks and a neat head proclaiming Welsh breeding. Its clean hocks had the look of power and long endurance rather than showiness, and its chest was of proportions noble enough to ensure the creature's heart would go to the utmost in giving whatever was asked of it.

"What a beautiful horse!" she said with involuntary admiration, quite forgetting to greet him properly.

He smiled a bit wanly, his thin, chiseled features showing fatigue. "Do you like him so well? I have but bought him and came here to try his paces." The marquis gave a little shrug of his elegant shoulders encased in finely woven Bath coating. "*Mais, peste!* The park is so filled with these persons we can do nothing."

For a moment Julia took pity on him. Indeed, if she owned such a magnificent animal she, too, would be longing for a good gallop. "You must wait until an unfashionable hour, I'm afraid," she said, unconsciously smiling as she again ran her gaze over the stallion's lines. "Before nine o'clock in the morning is best—if you can bring yourself to rise that early."

"Oh, yes, of a certainty." He made a gracious inclination of his dark head. "Such good advice is so obvious to me now. I am grateful, mademoiselle."

"I beg your pardon?" Garde turned then and regarded Du Vallon with a frown.

Recalling his previously voiced aversion of anything French—and Du Vallon could never look anything else despite his Weston-tailored coats—Julia hastened to make introductions and could not banish a chilly anticipation of something dreadful about to happen. Knowing the marquis's excessive pride, she hoped Garde would say nothing inflammatory, for if there should be a scene here before half of the *ton*, she would certainly sink into the ground with mortification.

"*Enchanté,* milord," said Du Vallon with a civil nod. "You are the famous marksman, *non*?"

"Yes, I can shoot a pistol," replied Garde coolly, the laughter completely absent from his gaze.

They were something alike, Julia realized, although the similarity was not a physical one. Garde was heavier, more muscular, while Du Vallon must ever appear willow-slim and lithe. No, if they were alike at all, it could only be in the authoritative personalities of each. Both were men of violence and hot tempers, only in Du Vallon these tendencies were concealed behind a veneer of grace and elegance. At once Julia sensed a natural hostility snap into a barrier between them. Their eyes—one pair dark, the other clear—met and held, and in her fancy she almost could hear the tumult of battle.

She blinked suddenly, the absurdity of her thoughts

jerking her free of the spell. What foolishness was her too vivid imagination leading her into now? They did not even know each other; there was nothing for them to fight over. But even as she attempted to convince herself of that fact, she knew she was wrong. For these two gentlemen would never be friends in any way. And after all, why need they be? With a mental shrug, she gave up her thoughts.

A very few more remarks passed, in which Du Vallon contrived with devastating subtlety to remind her once again of her obligation to procure vouchers for him. Then Garde was whipping up his horses, much to her relief. She sat in careful silence, wondering why the marquis must persist in plaguing her at every turn just when she managed to forget his existence for a moment, and hoping Garde would show no curiosity concerning her acquaintanceship with the French stranger. But this last desire was doomed to disappointment.

"That is the fellow who waltzed with you last night," said Garde in a thoughtful tone which shot involuntary guilt through her.

"Yes," she said, chin up in a bit of defiance. No matter how much she wished to maintain good terms with Garde, she would not consent to being grilled concerning her actions. "You have an excellent memory for faces, my lord."

"He's a frippery-looking sort." Garde frowned. "And what the devil is he doing in England?"

Julia longed to echo the question with matching exasperation, but dared not. "I believe he desires to make his home here," she answered in a quiet manner.

Garde snorted. "Indeed? Bonaparte granted the royalists amnesty years ago. He's a bit late to play the refugee, don't you think?"

"I couldn't say," she demurred, refusing to up in his displeasure. What, she thought, wc if he knew how Du Vallon was using her?

toyed with the notion of telling him, knowing Garde would deal effectively with the marquis. But although it was a way of escaping, it would also oblige her to betray her secret, and that of course was quite impossible. Pensive, she said nothing more until he put her down at her door, when it was necessary to thank him for the outing.

"My pleasure, Miss Swanton." He smiled, then gave her a significant look. "If this Du Vallon should ever annoy you with his attentions, I shall be happy to put myself at your service." And with a casual tip of his hat, he was gone.

Julia was thoughtful throughout a cold luncheon of burnt ham shavings and cucumbers with sauce; so thoughtful Lady Elizabeth at last inquired if she were feeling ill.

"For you do look pale, lamb. And with all the excitement lately I shouldn't wonder if you are inclined to be under the weather."

Thus adjured, Julia roused herself to smile and shake her head at the vague anxiety in her aunt's eyes. "No, I feel perfectly well," she said, putting down the fork she'd been toying with. "I believe you mentioned the desire to shop for a new scarf. Would you mind if we call on Lady Jersey on the way?" The chore, she thought wearily, might as well be done as soon as possible. Then perhaps Du Vallon would cease his irritating tendency to meddle in her affairs. "I promised someone my help in getting vouchers."

"That pleasant French marquis?" asked Lady Elizabeth with unexpected astuteness. "Oh, I *am* glad you are beginning to like him, Julia! Such pleasant address, so charming of manner. It would be wonderful if we could persuade Sally to let him into Almack's."

Since Julia wanted her request refused, she was pleased to see Lady Jersey look doubtful later when they were seated round a tea table in her ladyship's gracefully appointed library. "Indeed, ma'am, he is hardly more than a cap-acquaintance. Still, when one is cajoled into promising assistance . . ." Letting her voice trail off, she permitted herself a small, eloquent shrug.

"I see," said Lady Jersey, pursing her lips.

"Oh, pooh," broke in Lady Elizabeth with unwonted spirit. "How hoity-toity you do sound, Julia." She swallowed down another biscuit before sending her hostess an earnest look. "Sally, *pray* don't climb onto the peaks of disapproval. Such a handsome, polite man, always feeling just as he ought without being a dreadful milksop of a creature. You should adore him, for he waltzes beautifully."

Just in time Julia curbed back a reproving frown. Why must she be reminded of how splendidly he danced, or how much she had enjoyed her waltz under his expert guidance? It was all an unwanted distraction. But Lady Jersey was still frowning, and Julia took heart.

"But *émigrés* are so boring these days," sighed Lady Jersey, ringing for a fresh pot of tea. "They have gone quite out of fashion."

It was a golden opportunity, and Julia plunged to take advantage of it. "That's very true, isn't it," she agreed, already savoring Du Vallon's chagrin when she told him of his denial to Almack's revered portal. "Lord Garde remarked only this morning on how odd it was for him to come here *now*. I suppose he isn't truly an *émigré* in the sense we are used to thinking of. He certainly had no difficulty in passing through the blockade."

"How very intriguing." Lady Jersey's lips curved into an amused smile. "Jersey's newspaper from Brussels *never* arrives. It's exceedingly droll to think a royalist can get here more easily than a journal."

Julia joined in polite laughter, but Lady Elizabeth frowned and leaned forward, to the endangerment of dipping her fringe into the sugar. "Fudge," she said in round accents, her soft blue eyes flashing in mild championship. "How can you know he is a royalist? He never has claimed to be, has he? After all, he has wealth and position—things not so easily come by in France these days. But for goodness sake, who could possibly care about the poor man's politics? My father was sadly addicted to political discussion, and you cannot conceive how dull we all found him! Lord du Vallon is gracious and rather charming, and I cannot see why he should fail to make a welcome addition to your assembly rooms, Sally. His bow is perfection, and he has a nice eye in waistcoats. Julia does not like him, and if you permit her to influence you against the man—"

"Very well!" Laughing, Lady Jersey threw up one well-shaped hand in appeasement. "Gracious, my dear Lady Beth, I had no idea you were so partisan toward the gentleman." She shrugged easily, her rich dark eyes gleaming at Julia, who had sat back in her chair with a little frown of unconcealed disappointment. "By all means we shall let this paragon in. I'll convince Emily; she is ever agreeable toward a personable gentleman, quite *unlike* Mrs. Drummond Burrell, who can be so tediously difficult at times and for the least comprehensible reasons." Again her eyes slid to Julia in a sly manner which was not lost upon that young lady. "You do dislike him, Miss Swanton. I can see it plainly. As a rule, your taste is so impeccable." And she laughed in her slow, confident way. "Can there be a *tendre* in the shaping?" Much to Julia's annoyed discomfiture, she laughed again. "Indeed, I cannot help but wonder."

It was left to Julia to take her leave in as civil manner as was required, and ride seething all the way home. Moreover, her aunt's smug little smile of complacency did nothing but lacerate the offense. Julia sat rigidly against the velvet squabs, one small hand gripping the leather hold with throttling intensity, one slender foot beating a silent but furious rat-a-tat upon the carriage floor. Oh, it was too horrid of Lady Jersey to go making such an implication! *Tendre*, indeed. As though any properly brought up, *sensible* young lady would let her head be turned by that disagreeable man. She was quite well aware of the old adage about love and hate going hand-in-glove, or some such stuff and nonsense. But she did not hate the marquis at all; she merely detested him. And had he not the gall to be blackmailing her, she supposed she might like him well enough. But if Sally Jersey dared be cruel enough to set any such beastly *on-dit* about town—Julia's hand flew to her flaming cheek, and her even teeth ground fiercely together. It was simply not a thing to be borne!

Chapter Five

Eventually her resentment dimmed, and common sense convinced her Lady Jersey was merely quizzing and had little reason to be voicing such unfounded gossip; by the time she set out the next day to the lending library to return an armful of the lurid novels Lady Elizabeth had an especial fondness for, Julia was calm enough in her mind to be able to direct the coachman to make a detour by way of Chesterfield Street. Of course, as a young lady with a strict regard for her reputation, she could not call on the marquis. But there was nothing which could be said against the plan of halting her carriage at a corner and sending her footman to the door with a message.

It was an especially fine day, with the sun shining brightly enough to oblige her to open up her frilled sunshade which so prettily complemented her walking dress of pale pink cambric. She knew perfectly well she could have waited until she encountered him by chance somewhere, but the notion of doing so displeased her. She was determined that her behavior should encourage no more speculation such as Lady Jersey's. If her dislike of the Marquis du Vallon showed itself suspicioully violent, then she must alter her ways and endeavor to emit one degree more warmth toward the man.

Her gloved fingers fiddled with the shaft of her sunshade. Surely there could be nothing more he might ask of her. He had such odd notions of how to proceed in English society, but with the opening of Almack's doors to him he need not consider himself an outsider any longer. Still, she could not be easy knowing he had possession of the secret which could ruin her. He *seemed* to be a man of his word, but he was a stranger, a foreigner, a man she knew nothing about. That suavity of manner could conceal an unscrupulous heart, and indeed, she had already savored more of his ruthlessness than she cared to. Try as she might, she could not shake off uncertainty regarding him.

Her uncertainty, however, seemed to be wrong. Those who liked him liked him well and with little reservation. A doubt shook her. Was she being too willful in trying to resist helping him? But, no, she must question herself no further on this lest she end up convinced she ought to like the man simply because everyone else did.

The slowing of the barouche brought her attention back to her surroundings. She looked up and around to see they were approaching a tall narrow house with a Georgian façade. Its door was open so that she could not read the number, but she was certain this was Du Vallon's lodging. And in the next instant she was proven right as the marquis appeared in the doorway. Carrying his hat and Malacca cane, he was obviously about to go out, and Julia had opened her mouth to instruct the coachman to hurry when the small, black-garbed servant who had accompanied Du Vallon on the crossing appeared at his master's side. He carried a fawn driving coat and with an obsequious bow draped it across the marquis's shoulders. But to Julia's surprise, Du Vallon's patrician features suddenly snarled and he struck the man a blow across the mouth with the glove he held.

Julia blinked, unable to believe what she had seen. But, yes, there was Du Vallon turning curtly on his heel and striding down the steps without a backward glance at the servant cringing back with a hand to his face.

Her coachman looked over his shoulder as she sat there, benumbed with shock and revulsion. "You said to stop here, Miss Julia?"

"No!" It was out before she realized it, but at the moment she did not care how much she contradicted herself. "No, I gave no such command. Drive on!"

Puzzled but obedient, he whipped up the horses. "Miss—" began Julia's abigail, but was quelled with a fierce gesture.

Rigid, Julia brought her sunshade round to the side to conceal herself as the barouche passed Du Vallon striding down the walkway. For an instant she caught a glimpse of his set mouth and flaring nostrils. Then they were ahead of him and she could see nothing more.

Still shaken, she loosed a sigh, barely able to collect herself enough to nod at Mr. Brummell, who paused in the act of descending his steps to do her the honor of making an acknowledgement. Complexion forgotten, she fumbled to close the catch of her sunshade and let it fall unheeded in her lap. She had seen Du Vallon clearly when he first appeared, and she could swear he had not been in the least way vexed until the appearance of his servant. The blow itself had been so sudden, so unexpected, so *cruel*, she could scarcely credit having witnessed it. Even now she was disposed to tremble, and there grew an awkward lump in her throat, which would not be swallowed away. Perhaps she did not particularly like Du Vallon, but until now she had always regarded him with a measure of respect, for despite the arrogant way in which he was accustomed to treat her there was an excellence in carriage and address which held him a cut above most gentlemen of her acquaintance.

But his charm, his elegance, were all a carefully calculated mask. No *true* gentleman would forget himself and lash out at a menial in that manner. If the servant had been out of place, a sharp word would have been sufficient. For all her dislike of him, she had never once thought him capable of such low behavior, and she was ashamed both of him and of herself for having believed better of him.

Clutching ineptly to her sangfroid, she completed her errands as hastily as possible and fled home to the privacy of her own chamber, where she paced for a full half hour, frowning in turmoil. Her perambulations settled none of the chaos within her, but eventually she was able to sit down before the corner escritoire and take up a pen. Then she paused, chin in hand, to glare at the wall. No, how could she write him felicitations on his acceptance to Almack's when the very thought of his name sent a quiver of revulsion through her? But she must do it, just as she must make sure she kept him firmly at a distance in the future. Too many people were misjudging his character, and while he had not committed a crime in striking his servant, it had been a despicable act. He should continue to find coldness from her, and if anyone chose again to remark upon it she would have no hesitancy in explaining herself. That should put him in his place.

Taking up a sheet of ivory paper, she scratched out a short note telling him of Lady Jersey's promises. She did not deign to reread what she had written, but instead shook a bit of silver sand over her composition and sealed it with a savagely crooked wafer. How doubly sorry she was now to know she had helped this creature gain admittance to the most exclusive doors of the *ton*. But it was done, and her only hope lay in enough other people seeing through this—this churlish fortune-hunter with his silken tongue and his adderish designs. Oh, how she despised him!

Slamming shut the lid of her writing desk, she dispatched her note by hand before marching herself off to the library to sit down with a quelling book of sermons lest she weaken and give way to a bout of silly, excessively unwanted, certainly unjustifiable, tears.

But she was not long embarked upon her volume when Lady Elizabeth came wandering in to rescue her with aimless discussion concerning the Countess of Menton and whether she was going to present her lord husband with a second set of twins. Julia, who had not the slightest interest in ladies who were breeding, and indeed could not be brought to consider such a subject suitable for her maidenly ears, attempted to change the topic without success until Gaylord Swanton was ushered in. Since he rarely came round for purely social reasons, Julia could not decide if she were sorry or glad to see him as she gave him her hand to bow over.

"You look ravishing as usual, Julia," he said in his bored, affected way and bestowed a kiss on Lady Elizabeth's cheek. "And how is my favorite aunt?"

The acid comment that Lady Elizabeth was his *only* aunt rose to Julia's lips, but she bit it back at seeing her aunt flush with pleasure and fuss over him, insisting he have the most comfortable chair and getting up herself to ring for a glass of madeira for him.

"*Dearest* Gaylord," she said, beaming upon him as though he were the most cherished treasure on earth. "You come so rarely I declare it must be an age since we saw you last. But how fine you do look. As fine as fivepence, isn't he, Julia? Oh, but how wicked of me to employ boxing-saloon cant! I can't imagine where I heard it. But such a sweet boy—I recall how pretty you looked on the day you were breeched. My dear, dear sister's first child. I was so giddy with delight I indulged in a bit of dissipation and drank a blueberry cordial afterward to celebrate."

She went on in her confused, reminiscent way, but

Julia no longer heard the words for the sorrowful disgust welling up through her. How could Gaylord sit there—no, *sprawl*—in that indolent manner and smirk at such drivel being lavished over him? It was revolting; Julia was convinced he actually enjoyed the attention. Her lips primed up. She had always tried to be fair with her half-brother, but to her way of thinking, anyone who could saunter about in the public eye dressed in a coat so monstrously padded as to make him appear grotesque must be labeled a fop. Indeed, she quite failed to understand how he stood the discomfort of a starched cravat at least a foot in width swaddled about his neck in such rigid, intricate folds he could neither lower his weak chin from its haughty position, nor turn his head more than an inch to either side.

He sent her a sweet smile. "Do I detect admiration for the arrangement of my neckcloth? It's my own invention, perfected just this morning, so you are among the first privileged few to behold it."

After a brief struggle with herself not to laugh outright, Julia managed a faint smile of what she hoped was interest. "How clever of you, Gaylord," she said, trying, for his sake, not to snap at him. "What do you call it?"

"Oh, something really smashing," he said, affecting a yawn as he took the glass of madeira Lady Elizabeth poured for him. Raising his glass as though to toast his own powers of creation, he said: "I call it—why, I call it the Avenue of Delight. Pretty, don't you think?" He tossed down half his wine in one gulp. "You may despise my gambling establishment all you like," he went on complacently, "but it is doing very well indeed. I hope you notice the improved quality in my coats."

She had no idea of what she might have said then in an effort to keep the impossible conversation going, but Gaylord chose that moment to recall the purpose of his visit. "Well, I didn't call for an afternoon of idle chitchat," he said, abruptly looking put out over something, and drew a carelessly folded note from his pocket. "Sophie appears to have taken leave of her senses. It's probably only last night's lobster, but one can never tell. Here." Negligently he thrust the letter at Julia. "That's for you."

"But, Gaylord, you alarm me!" cried Lady Elizabeth, turning pale. "What can have happened to upset her so? Is it serious? Oh, dear, I see my duty is to go to her at once. She cannot truly have gone mad, can she? Lewing would be so vexed to come home and find it all at sixes and sevens. Can mental disorders run in the family? Grandmother was a bit peculiar, it's true, but then she lived in those days of shocking turmoil when the Hanovers were brought over, so I daren't wonder. Thank goodness Julia is of different stock! It would sadly reduce her chances of contracting a splendid match. And asylums are said to be wildly expensive."

"Devil take us, how you do run on," said Gaylord with a quelling frown her way. "I meant only that she's having a fit of hysterics. And you needn't blame me, because I wasn't the cause of it," he added with defiance as Julia glanced up from her letter. "I was merely there being agreeable in the midst of a half-dozen other callers and hoping to catch her ear in private to ask for a—er—paltry loan." Again his eyes shifted away from Julia's. "Can't dip from the business all the time, you know. She got a message of some kind, brought round by post, and climbed into the boughs at once. Well, you know how white she gets when she's in a passion and must bottle it up on account of guests. So here I am, playing messenger boy, and dashed disagreeable it is too." He shook out his cuffs with fastidious care. "I can see it'll be all for nothing. No money to be wrung—er—coaxed from her in this state." His hazel eyes fixed themselves on Julia with wary hope. "I daresay you could spare the funds if you took a fancy to. It's rather shabby letting your half-brother languish in dun territory, you know."

Pointedly Julia ignored this broad hint, for she was reminded too much of Robert Duffy's visit, and turned to her aunt with a slight frown. "She says the worst has happened, Aunt, and desires me to come at once. Look how distracted her hand is."

"But I don't understand," said Lady Elizabeth plaintively as she read. "What can she mean?"

Julia's frown deepened. "I fear it must be bad news from Lewing." She hardly knew her brother-in-law, save that he was a pleasant, taciturn gentleman. How horrible to think he might be dead. And poor Sophie, having to receive such news when she had a house full of callers and could not give way. Differences forgotten, Julia's heart went out to her half-sister, and abruptly she stood up. "Let us hope he is only wounded. But I must go to her this instant. She will need support."

"Yes, indeed." Lady Elizabeth struggled up, her skeins of yarn rolling from her lap in a tangle, and her plump face growing splotchy with tears. "Oh, Julia, how dreadful to think we must be plunged into mourning again."

"Again?" Gaylord frowned. "When the devil were we last—oh, surely she's gotten over Léonie's death by *now.*"

"Silly boy," retorted Lady Elizabeth, helplessly hunting through her reticule for a handkerchief. "I was not referring to Julia's poor mother, but—"

"Aunt!" A spasm of alarm convulsed through Julia, and putting her arm about the plump shoulders she hurried Lady Elizabeth to the door. "Now, dearest, it is out of the question that you should come with me," she said in a low, rapid voice. "You are too overwrought. What help, pray, could you be to Sophie? She will want you a little later."

"Yes," quavered Lady Elizabeth with an uncertain

nod. "I suppose you are right. Oh, dear, and just when we were all so happy." And sobbing into her scrap of handkerchief, she disappeared upstairs.

With a sigh, Julia gave orders for her bonnet and gloves to be fetched down and turned back to Gaylord. She was still a bit shaken at how close her aunt's heedless tongue had brought her to disaster.

Gaylord was standing in the center of the room, his hazel eyes narrowed. "Gad, what a scene!" he said, forgetting, as usual whenever annoyed, his affectations. "Did you find out whom she was speaking about?"

Julia's heart contracted all over again, but she forced herself to give a casual little shrug. "An old bosom-bow she knew as a girl. Do you mean to escort me to Grosvenor Square?"

"What, and watch Sophie have histrionics?" He shuddered delicately and raised one pampered white hand in denial. "If Lewing *has* cut his stick, no wonder she was in such a taking. She had her heart set on becoming a countess."

Julia's eyes narrowed in contempt. Because Gaylord was weak she had taught herself never to expect much from him. But really, to think Sir Geoffrey had sired this mincing little toad! Such hard statements were going too far. "If you realize what you have implied," she said scathingly, "I hope you are properly ashamed. I do not deny Lewing's position was a factor in Sophie's decision to marry him, but she also—"

"No!" he cried out with a sneer. "Do not be stupid enough to say she loved him. For that, you know, is sheer drivel. I can't exclaim at scandal, for Papa keeps our name well in it and I'm no saint, but Sophie's been running pretty free lately." His face grew thoughtful. "Though if she is to be a widow, I must say she'd do very well to marry Garde. And he isn't one to begrudge laying down a few pounds here and there to new relations. He might even be persuaded to pull Papa out of the basket, though I doubt Golden Ball himself could cover that many debts." Gaylord drew out a scent-lavished handkerchief and waved it in Julia's face. "Go and comfort Sophie, and then we shall set about celebrating."

Shaken, Julia was left to tie on her bonnet with trembling fingers. As the barouche took her through the streets Gaylord's words haunted her the entire distance. Of course she knew she would not find Sophie in such a callous state as Gaylord claimed, but indeed when it was time to lay aside mourning how could her half-sister not turn to Garde? If their feelings for each other were sound, then Julia knew she was the one out of place instead of Sophie. For a moment rebellion shook her. Why should *she* be expected to give up all she had hoped for? But she quelled the thought. Garde had little interest in her. She needn't be a fool over him. If it was to be him and Sophie, so be it. Just now it seemed a cruel turn of fate, but in all fairness and decency she could not scheme to stand in their way merely for her own gain. And if Gaylord was right about Garde's generosity then perhaps it could be all for the best. But poor Lewing!

Upon her arrival she was ushered at once upstairs to Sophie's boudoir, where she found her half-sister pacing about the floor, weeping, and constantly dashing the tears away with her hands. She whirled at Julia's entry, her face white and drawn so tight it looked as though she might shatter at any moment. "Julia! Thank God!" She gasped and held herself tensely until the door was closed behind the liveried flunkey, then grasped Julia's hands and sank to the floor at her feet. "Oh, Julia, I thought you would never come! It's Lewing. I am undone. Oh, dear heaven, what shall I do?" And throwing herself down, Sophie began to sob.

At first Julia hesitated, for although she had expected Sophie to be distracted, she was not entirely certain of what she could do for someone in such violent grief. She had never been able to effectively calm her aunt's nervous spasms without losing her temper, which, at the moment, would *not* do at all, but casting off her bonnet she knelt and put her arms tenderly round Sophie's shoulders. Such wrenching tears must not be allowed to continue unchecked.

"Sophie, dearest, you really mustn't cry," she murmured over and over again, amazed by her own calm but grateful for it. "We shall all miss John terribly, for he was very fine, but at least we may be sure he was brave and courageous at his end—"

"What?" Abruptly Sophie raised her drenched green eyes in a flash of astonishment. Her fingers clenched hard on Julia's wrists. "What are you saying? Lewing dead? No! I should be mad if he were." A laugh, wild with bitterness, escaped her. "What shall I do? There is Dick, and I cannot bear to give him up now."

"Sophie!" cried Julia in alarm, wondering if Sophie had lost her senses. "You must not say such things."

"I shall say what I please!" Clenching her fists, Sophie jumped to her feet and stood glaring down at Julia. "How dare he wait until he is in Dover to tell me he is coming home! He will be here tomorrow, and I have no warning, no time. Everyone knows that I—oh, how could Lewing do this to me? I need time to arrange a cooler understanding with Garde!"

"Nonsense," snapped Julia with a gasp of relief, but certain it was time this wild talk were stopped. "You must be glad to welcome your husband home. Give up this reckless infatuation and be sensible."

Sophie made a despairing gesture and began to pace again. "You are not the least help, Julia. You do not understand what it is to be caught in such a situation. I should have known John was inconsiderate and selfish after he left me for that ridiculous war. I hate him! I do!" She snatched up an exquisite hand mirror and hurled it to the floor.

Seeing it was impossible to remonstrate with her, Julia got to her feet and stepped over the shattered glass to pick up the crumpled missive from the floor. Written in a boyish, firm hand, it was short but cheerful, the words of a man done with bloody carnage and eager to be rejoined with family and friends. His few, shy endearments made Julia's throat constrict and with a burst of anger she tossed the letter aside. "What a heartless creature you are, Sophie," she said in a cutting voice, her relief that he was indeed unharmed making her sound even sharper. "He has been away over a year and yet you cannot summon up the least gladness for his safe return. Do you really wish he had been cut in half by a cannonball?"

Sophie jerked to a halt and whirled with a cry of horror. "No! Of course not. Julia, how can you think such wicked things of me? Why will you not understand me? I should love more than anything to have him home again, but not now, not when I am guilty of having lost my regard for him." She put a hand to her lips, weeping. "I am so ashamed of my feelings for Garde, but I cannot lose him."

"Sophie, no!" Julia took a step back with one hand held out in distaste. "Don't make me hear such things from you."

"But you must. You must help me. My own common sense has failed." She paused. "If only I could depend upon Lewing to be reasonable, but I dare not trust him. Do you realize what would happen if he calls Garde out?" She shuddered. "Oh, God, to be dueled over. I shall die of shame."

"Then for your own sake, practice a little sense," said Julia, placing a pleading hand upon her half-sister's shoulder. How dreadful it was to see Sophie, normally so clever, lost in the clutches of infatuation!

Beginning to feel as though she were gripped by a nightmare, Julia frowned and sought some way of shaking Sophie free of her trap.

"Sophie," she said with deliberate quiet, "will you let your reputation fall to become *the* crim. con. story of the season? Will you permit a passing, foolish fancy to render you that low? I beg you not to become despicable, at least for Edward's sake. Do you want him to grow up hating you for this moment of folly?"

That got through. Crimson, Sophie drew herself up to her full queenly height. "How dare you say such a thing to me?" she demanded coldly. "I am no fool. Rest assured I know how to practice discretion." She laughed then, unpleasantly, and Julia almost wished for the wildness back. "That is why I sent for you, Julia. You must help me."

"Do what?" asked Julia, on fire with suspicion at this change. "I shan't help you betray John."

"Don't be childish," snapped Sophie with enough impatience to quell Julia. "You are to go to Mrs. Wrexham's al fresco party tomorrow, are you not? Dick was to escort me. But that must be changed now." The hot color ebbed from her cheeks, leaving them deathly pale again. There was a forbidding set to her flawless lips, and her eyes continued to glitter like emeralds on fire. But she was in control of her emotions now, in strangling control. "I will not be able to go at all, I daresay. Lewing is selfish enough to insist I be on hand to greet him." Her lips tightened until their ruby color was lost. "All I ask of you, Julia, is to tell Dick what has happened. I daren't trust these stupid servants to carry a note to him." Then she glanced at Julia and frowned. "Stop looking so shocked and stubborn! It's an easy enough thing to do. Promise you will do this, Julia. Promise!"

But Julia stood on the other side of a frozen wall, too appalled at her half-sister to speak. How could Sophie make such a mistake? How could she be such a fool? Did she not realize she was going to ruin her life? And worse, to dare play upon Julia's affection for her by demanding she help in this wickedness! Julia's eyes began to flash, and her chin lifted. "Sophie," she began, but before she could continue Sophie had stepped back with narrowed eyes.

"I see what it is now. Oh, Julia, you poor, dewy-eyed little idiot. Have you really been mooning over Garde since that ball last year when he terrified you out of your wits by flirting with you? But having got a taste of it, you now think you must catch him for yourself. So!" Her lips tightened in unconcealed anger. "And I have been stupid enough to pour out my confidences to you, hoping you would help me. But nevertheless you shall do as I have asked of you. Your little machinations will be so inept I need not fear you as a rival." She waved a hand as her laugh rang out in free mockery.

Julia frowned, her violet eyes stormy as Sophie's words scraped her raw. Sophie was so wrong, but that was no excuse for such jealousy. She need not be cruel; she need not blame Julia because she had decided to take the path to her eventual ruin. A rival, indeed! How dare Sophie look at it that way, when she had a husband and Julia did not. Julia clenched her fists. This season she *must* bring a suitor up to scratch, and Sophie's folly would not be permitted to stand in the way. Julia's cheeks suddenly burned as she vowed to learn how to flirt as wickedly as anyone else. If that was necessary to lure Garde away, she would do it, and then let Sophie call her inept. Besides, Lewing's return would certainly get in Sophie's way, and as long as he did not kill Garde he would be a definite advantage.

Chin high, Julia met the challenge blazing from Sophie's eyes. She even managed a small smile. "Of course I shall do this one favor for you, Sophie," she said, knowing that to relay the message would give her an excellent excuse to approach Garde. Sophie had made her first mistake.

"Thank you," snapped Sophie coolly and tossed her head. "Be sure I shall ask nothing more from you. You may go."

Furious at being dismissed like an abigail, Julia swept out and, as she went home to tell her aunt there was no need to mourn anyone, thoughts of revenge ground through her heart. She would teach her sister a much-needed lesson. She would indeed.

Chapter Six

"Well!" said Lady Elizabeth with a huff as they clipped sedately along the lane toward the Wrexhams' river villa. "I can only say I think it extremely shabby of Gaylord to tell us that fib about Lewing being killed. Extremely shabby. I quite cried my eyes out, for he is such a dear, pleasant man—Lewing, I mean—and did you know 'twas I who encouraged him and Sophie to make a match of it? I knew he should make an unexceptionable husband, and so he has."

At that point, Julia found herself obliged to come out of her own dark thoughts and be fair. "Aunt, really I think you're being too harsh upon Gaylord. He never said—"

"Perhaps he did not come out and say it," interrupted Lady Elizabeth with a firm nod that bobbed the three jonquil-colored plumes atop her bonnet of puce basket-straw. "But he quite left us with that impression. No, lamb, I do adore your attempts to take up for him, but it's all in vain, I assure you. I am vexed with Gaylord, deeply vexed, and I intend to stay that way until I am otherwise." She said this all with perfect seriousness, but it sprang up a bubble of laughter in Julia and raised her clouded spirits.

"What a pretty May we have this year," remarked Lady Elizabeth after a pause, and indeed Julia could do nothing but agree. Great puffy clouds wheeled and frolicked like a collection of oversized lambs through a sky almost as blue as her eyes. A light rain the night before had served to make the surface of the lane springy and dust-free, and it was pleasant to ride along in the open carriage through sparkling country air. A row of stately oaks and elms bordered one side of the lane, very free with their dappled shade, while on the other side marched a tall hedge where blooming cow parsley and red campion peeped out with shy heads. Jaunty bluebells lined the ditch for the most part, but here and there honeysuckle sprawled, filling the air with its heavy fragrance. A multitude of birds provided them with song over the steady clop of the horses, and once a plump squirrel paused on an overhanging limb to scold at them, going so far in his displeasure as to drop his nut squarely in Julia's lap. Laughing, she tossed it back at him with a cry of "Jackanapes!" and found her tension melting away as the countryside took over her senses with its gentle spell. She was reminded of Swantoncourt, her beloved country home not more than ten miles from here. For a moment she was tempted to cast off obligations and responsibilities and change the coachman's orders, but she refrained. Swantoncourt must wait till another day, when she could be more assured about her future.

The Wrexham house was a rambling Tudor structure set high above the river on a gentle yet imposing bank, with smooth lawns running right down to the water's edge. Fragrant lilies were planted there, and shy swans swam with dignity through the quiet eddies. Julia had visited before and so knew her way about without being obliged to view the Grecian temple or gaze into the ornamental pond. Arranging herself upon a chair in such a way that the playful breeze fluttered her mint-colored skirts of jaconet muslin in the most becoming manner, she set her small face—enchantingly framed by raven curls and a broad chipstraw hat—to gaze out over the other, perhaps fifty, guests. There was Amelia Cunningham, the notable eccentric who always went about dripping with paste jewels, and Lord Petersham in an odd double-breasted coat of his own invention, who was said to possess a different snuffbox for every change of clothing, and Miss Charity Timmons, the little dab of a cousin everyone thought young Wrexham would soon offer for. But Garde's tall, striking figure was not to be seen.

When she first came to this realization she experienced much disappointment, but it gave way to the indignant suspicion that Sophie had decided to send a note round to Garde, who had then stayed away out of deference to her absence. Julia's fists clenched in fury at having the ground cut out from under her feet. Her pleasure in the outing was destroyed, and she knew the day would drag interminably until she could take a reasonable leave of her hostess.

Glancing up with a frown, she spied young Wrexham coming toward her with two croquet mallets in his hand and an expression of hope upon his boyishly round face. Dismay leapt into her throat in trampling panic. No, she couldn't! To stand around idly whacking at balls when she longed to tear up the earth in a fury was too much to be borne. But even as her every feeling rebelled, prudence calmly took up the reins and made her see that she must school herself. It was pointless to throw a tantrum like a spoiled child.

Resignedly, she stood up and was about to go forward to meet Wrexham, who was no more than her own age and rather tedious at times. But before she had time to take a single step or even smile, a deep voice behind her said:

"Miss Swanton? I believe you would like to feed the swans."

Startled, she whirled to face Garde standing with his broad back to the shrubbery, the careless smile upon his wide lips. "Lord Garde!" was all she could gasp for a moment. Then she regained her composure and smiled. "Yes, indeed I would like to."

And with a pretty smile of apology over her shoulder to Mr. Wrexham, she permitted his lordship to lead her away.

Procuring a silver bowl of crumbs, they turned their steps toward the river, she having a little difficulty in keeping up with his long strides which he neglected to shorten. In other circumstances it would have annoyed her, but she was too occupied with wondering how best to relay Sophie's message. As the bearer of bad tidings—traditionally an unrewarding task—she realized she could see her own hopes scorched.

"Banty Wrexham was quite bent on attaching you to his side," said Garde with his rather loud laugh. "Aren't you glad I stole you away?"

She looked up to meet his murky gaze with a smile. Perhaps it was cruel to cut poor Mr. Wrexham off like that. But she could not afford to indulge in his attention if it meant whistling Garde down the wind. Laughing a bit self-consciously, she said, "Yes, my lord, quite glad."

And still there was the decision to be made on how to approach the subject of Sophie. The problem fretted her as she paused at the very edge of the bank where the water lapped just inches away from her sandals, and began to toss crumbs from the bowl he held for her. One of the swans bowed his graceful neck and sailed up to take her charity, one of the most dignified beggars she had ever seen. How was she to put it? she wondered, keeping a smile on her face as they chatted in a desultory fashion. It was not enough to merely say Sophie was not coming; Julia ached with the need to turn this all to her own advantage. If only she were more clever and could think up something! But the idyllic moment lingered on like a caress, and she could not help but be conscious, despite her preoccupation, of how encouraging Garde's dancing attendance upon her was. It was impossible to blurt Sophie's name into the middle of things.

"I hope Lady Lewing has not fallen out of sorts," he said at last, making her bite her lip as her heart hammered in dread. "Mrs. Wrexham was wondering aloud what had become of her."

"Oh?" Still tossing crumbs rather more rapidly than the swan could gobble them up, Julia repressed a violent little spurt of annoyance over his continual preoccupation with Sophie. Collecting her thoughts, she hesitated once more, still seeking a bit of cleverness within herself, and when she still did not find any, gave up and blurted it out. "I suppose I shall have to make excuses for her. Lord Lewing is arrived home today." And she held her breath, waiting for an explosion of wrath or acute disappointment.

Instead, his reaction was a laugh that sent her turning to him in amazement. "That *is* a rich joke," he said when he'd caught his breath again. "I daresay she's no end put out, for he is certain to cut off her extravagances. Still, it's just as well, for I've little patience with these dashing young matrons who turn into paragons of timidity at the last line of propriety. Pity." And with the most unconcern in the world he turned the subject to other things, asking Julia any number of questions about her mare and whether she'd ever hunted, even going on to invite her to join him for a gallop through the park.

A bit overwhelmed by the picture he painted of Sophie, she accepted with every evidence of pleasure even as a part of her marveled at him. Either he was a consummate actor or else extremely volatile, and she was inclined to believe the latter was true. It was hardly a point in his favor, but it went with the rest of his reputation. She told herself firmly it did not matter, nothing mattered as long as she found herself comfortably married by the end of the season.

Some minutes later, Wrexham, looking not at all vexed over having been cut out, and a friend of his from Oxford days came rushing up to eagerly demand an account of Garde's duel last Sunday with the Hon. Rutherford Bentley.

"Nonsense," said Garde with his careless smile, eyes flicking to Julia as if to seek her approval for his prowess on the field of honor. "I can hardly go puffing off in front of a lady without appearing a veritable Captain Johnny-raw. Excuse us. I think the sun here is becoming too warm for Miss Swanton." He led her away from the two plainly crestfallen youths with a murmur of: "What a bore these young chubs are! You'd think they'd realize when a man is agreeably occupied."

But some of her pleasure in his company had been shaken. Dueling alone horrified her, but that he could present himself on the *Sabbath* to commit a bloodletting made it all doubly reprehensible. Now as she glanced at him, she saw again her father, brought in bloody and swooning, to be put away in that shabby bed where he had died. The whole story of that tragedy had never been explained to her, but it was enough that she knew the end. And Garde was another who lived by such violence. If she attached herself to a man of his stamp, would she eventually be left a widow as she had been left an orphan? Could she bear to go through such a nightmare again? She was not sure, and did not yet know how to seek reassurance from him.

"This man you fought with," she said in a low, troubled voice she could not disguise. "Will he die?"

Garde stopped and turned to her with a sudden eagerness lighting his heavily lined face. "My dear child, can you be afraid I shall have to fly the country?" He caressed the curve of her cheek with one finger, and still afraid, she quivered beneath his touch, using all her willpower not to flee in confusion.

Cheeks flaming crimson, she let her eyes fall away from the searching in his, thinking bitterly as she did so that Sophie had been right in saying she was ignorant in the ways of dalliance. She was conscious of somehow failing to seize the chance just opened to her, and loosed a miserable sigh. "Will you have to leave?"

Laughing, he shook his auburn head, the sunlight striking golden sparks in all directions. "I am never so careless as to kill my man, now that the law is so strict. He will be a bit late in joining his regiment, that is all, although I can tell you the beggarly little cur deserved far worse."

The sudden hardness in his voice, the grim narrowness of his dark eyes reminded Julia too much of Du Vallon in one of his freakish humors. Both these men were too old and too ruthless for her, she thought. She sighed, helpless as though sinking into waters far too deep for her capabilities. "Please," she said faintly. "I'd rather discuss something else. Duels are so horrid!"

"Quite so," he agreed, his grim expression softening. And at once she was conscious of some subtle pressure slackening from between them, giving her time to catch at her breath and pull her teetering wits back into some semblance of order. "I ought to take that young idiot Wrexham to task for bringing up the matter at all. But, may I tell you something, Miss Swanton?"

She looked up, eyes wide, and did not quite dare to smile. "Yes, of—of course, my lord."

He grinned, teeth gleaming. "In a way I'm rather grateful to Lewing for popping up again. This country setting really shows me just how lovely a little thing you are." And with a loud laugh, he led her blushing and overwhelmed back to the others.

* * *

A few days later she did go riding in the park with Garde, although it took the utmost of her skill in horsemanship to keep up with him and his rawboned sorrel. And there were times when he called to take her driving, offering even to teach her how to take the ribbons. She declined demurely, preferring to let him remain enchanted by her timidity, instead of telling him she had been handling a whip and pair since childhood.

It was on one of these excursions when they encountered Lord and Lady Lewing in the park, and Sophie turned so white Julia thought she must swoon before Lewing finished exchanging a cool word with Garde and drove on. Garde glanced after them a moment while Julia clenched her fists tightly in her lap, waiting in dread to lose him back to Sophie.

"What a tiresome woman your sister can be," he said at last, shaking out the thong of his whip. "She simply will not understand how I refuse to dangle after her beneath the nose of her husband. It would be shocking bad *ton* to fight a duel with him, don't you think, my dear? Especially since the outcome would be so unworthwhile." And he laughed so freely Julia's tenseness faded, and she could join in with a smile.

It seemed he was indeed finished with Sophie, and Julia's gratitude to her brother-in-law and his timely arrival grew as the days brought either Garde's company or a posy with his card attached. He even overcame his boredom with the theater to escort them to Covent Garden upon one occasion, leaving Julia's attention torn between Mrs. Siddon's enthralling performance in *Macbeth* and Lord Garde's presence between her and her aunt. Inevitably, their names were linked, and rumors began to fly round. The desperate drive to succeed eased its pressure upon Julia, and she grew more confident and at her ease, worrying less about their dwindling finances and the continual need to guard her aunt's heedless tongue as she grew more certain that

Garde would come up to scratch. There was a great deal of satisfaction to be derived from such thoughts, for not only would it mean the end of her troubles, but it would also be quite a feather in her cap if she succeeded in snaring one of the *ton*'s most eligible bachelors. Her contentment with her world increased daily.

Then a note from Sophie was brought round by messenger, asking if they might ride together *early* some morning when they could have a private conversation. Julia read the curt request perhaps a half-dozen times, resentful, inclined to refuse, yet seeing no civil way to get out of it. And, too, it was not her way to back away from challenges, as she sensed this was. Confidence raised her chin and sent her dashing off a reply of acceptance. Why not see Sophie? Her half-sister had lost, there was no question of that, and it might do Sophie some good to be gloated over just a trifle. Julia dismissed the instinctive unease the note had aroused in her with a snap of the fingers. At this stage, there was nothing her half sister could do.

Sophie met her on the morning of the following Wednesday just inside the east gates of the park. She looked rather tense in her severely tailored habit of bronze green, a short crop clenched in her hands, but that could perhaps be attributed to the weather. Julia could not forbear another glance up at the clouds which rolled across the sky in a solid sullen mass. The blithe sunny days were gone, swept away by this ominous change, and it was cold as though the fitful breeze dared threaten them with winter again. Julia shivered, though in her pale velvet habit with its jaunty lacings of silver she was not really chilled. Dreadful weather for any sort of outing, she thought as she dismissed her groom and trotted after Sophie, but at least it ensured them privacy. She glanced around, curbing the skittish black mare she called Temptation. No one else was even in sight. Yawning, she frowned to herself.

"Surely," she said, smothering another yawn with the back of her hand as a muted growl from the heavens sent her mare dancing, "a comfortable coze in your Gold Salon would have served the purpose just as well." She tried a smile, but the taut expression on her half-sister's face did not change. Julia tried again. "I feel so much like a conspirator, skulking round through the trees at seven in the morning. If we stumble onto a duel I shall account it your fault!"

It was a gay little attempt at a joke, but Sophie frowned. "Don't be absurd," she snapped. "Not even a flat would have a meeting with pistols in Hyde Park. And do see if you can't hold in that wretched brute of yours. It's making mine shy at everything."

Julia's lips tightened but she apologized for Temptation's bad manners. How easy it was to be kind and patient now that she had the upper hand! "She is terrified of storms, you see. I hope we shan't get a dousing."

"I intend to be brief." Sophie drew rein deep within a copse of beeches and gave Julia a long, hostile look. "At least five people—one of them Lewing—has seen fit to throw your flirtation with Garde in my face." And now she let some of her rage and humiliation show. "Scheming little wretch! How *dare* you turn him against me!"

Julia's head snapped up, color surging into her cheeks as resolution not to quarrel died. "You are beyond your place, Sophie," she said curtly. "If I were attracting John Lewing's attention it would be a justifiable matter for this disgusting scene of jealousy, but—"

"Don't read me a homily, you impertinent little half-breed!" Sophie made a vicious gesture with her crop, startling both mounts. "Thanks to you I have lost John's trust, and now there is not even Dick to turn to. Now that my every happiness is being destroyed, are you satisfied?"

Julia had whitened, and rage struggled to gain possession of her senses, but she fought it back, realizing that to let herself go out of hand was to give Sophie complete advantage. Still, Sophie had no right to humiliate her like this, and to slur her breeding was more than vile. Her hands tightened on the reins, and she sent Sophie a black glare.

"You have only yourself to blame. Remember that I tried to warn you," she said through gritted teeth. "But you would not heed me. And why should I honor any illicit feelings you have for Garde? Your disloyalty to Lewing can only sicken and disgust me!"

With a breathless gasp Sophie snatched at Temptation's reins, preventing Julia from riding on. "I shan't let you steal the man I love, Julia!"

"Love?" Julia laughed harshly, incapable of feeling pity. "My dear Sophie, you wouldn't know love if it came begging to you. Now, drop my reins, if you please!"

But Sophie continued to hold Temptation's head round short, although the mare sidled and jerked in protest. Sophie's lips were a thin, bloodless line beneath her blazing green eyes. At that moment there was not the slightest vestige of beauty in that flawless face. "There is no cause for you to do this, Julia," she said, the words reasonable, but the tone wild. "Can you desire to put my nose out of joint so much?"

Again Julia laughed, despite her urge to throttle her half-sister. She had not asked for this hideous quarrel, but she would die first before she showed any mercy now! Deliberately, Julia said, "I think you forget Garde's own interests have changed. At least he is not bacon-brained enough to continue a casual dalliance in these circumstances."

Sophie gasped again, looking as though she'd been slapped. "Casual dalliance! Oh, how *dare* you! How dare you!"

Heady with the savage thrill of victory, Julia pressed

for her home thrust. "Yes," she said with her chin high. "And what is more, my dear, I very much plan to bring Garde to the point of declaration, which is something you can never do, is it?"

"No!" A brand of scarlet seared Sophie's cheeks. She released Temptation's reins as though burnt and shook her head violently. "I hate you!" she screamed, causing Julia's already nettled horse to rear. "I hate what you have made me do!"

Fool! Julia thought, fighting to keep her seat and fearing to be swept off by a branch. But before she could bring her mare back under control again, Sophie raised her crop and slashed it across Temptation's throat. Now it was the mare which screamed in protest, plunging back and whirling so quickly Julia was almost flung from the saddle.

"Sophie!" she cried out in fury, not yet able to be afraid.

But Sophie's crop whistled down yet again, this time across Temptation's plunging hindquarters. With a kick and squeal, the mare bolted headlong through the stand of trees, dodging and twisting, the bit between her teeth.

A lesser rider might have been thrown, but Julia had an excellent seat and she hung on grimly, dropping her beloved silver-handled whip and half her reins, yet not considering herself lost. She dared glance back once and was infuriated to see Sophie wrench her mount around and trot out of sight in the opposite direction. It was obvious her half-sister had no intentions of seeking assistance. Then a branch whipped across Julia's face, stunning her so that she fell forward on Temptation's lathered neck; the pungent smell of wet horsehair rose sharply into her nostrils and revived her somewhat. She kept her balance by she knew not what, and the need to cling to her runaway mount grew suddenly too desperate to leave time for anger and hatred against Sophie's cruel action.

Julia might have regained control in a few more minutes, for as she fought to draw in her shattered breath and blink away the tears of pain from her welted cheek, she could feel the mare's speed diminishing. Hope renewed the energy and strength in her limbs, and she had just leaned forward, striving to catch the dangling right-hand reins when a smoking crack of lightning and thunder directly overhead set Temptation rearing and darting off again in a wide-open gallop Julia knew she could never stop.

Terror seized her now for the first time, snatching away what breath was left to her and constricting an iron band round her throat. Dimly, through the haze of fear smothering her, she heard a strong drumming as though all the drummers in Wellington's armies had been assembled in the park. Then with a final bound, they had left the dubious shelter of the trees and were racing low to the ground at a dangerous pace across the clipped grass. The rain poured from the sullen sky in great, drenching sheets, and as she struggled to lift her face from the pungent-smelling mane, Julia realized the drumming was only the sound of the downpour. Deafened, numb, her muscles jerked and aching, still she could think and her thoughts brought her a fresh fear. They had no footing in this kind of weather. At any time Temptation could slip and go down.

Galvanized into action, she forced her trembling body as erect in the sidesaddle as she dared, wishing with all her might she had not been such a gudgeon as to drop half her reins. But if she could she must try to turn Temptation in a short circle and perhaps stop her that way. Biting her lip against the effort and hardly able to see for the rain lashing into her face, she gripped her left-hand reins with both hands and tried to pull the mare's head around to one side. Plunging and slinging her head, Temptation fought her, stumbling so that Julia was almost dislodged, then galloping on.

Julia could have cried aloud with frustration, for her wet gloves could not keep sufficient purchase on the reins. But she tried again, and again the mare fought her, squealing as the thunder roared over them. Then Julia felt herself slip a little more from the saddle and knew with a quake of horror that she was losing. Furious with the elements as well as with her own inability to control her mount, she flung away the useless reins and twisted her fingers in Temptation's sodden mane, having to face the bitter, horrifying prospect that despite all her vanity in her skill as a rider she would soon go off in a rattling fall and probably break her neck. A scream rose in her throat, sour and loathsome in the hysteria it brought. By a supreme effort of will she held it back behind clenched teeth, refusing to give it utterance, refusing to break down wholly to panic. She was a Swanton and a Clembeau, and no one would ever say she died screaming her head off.

Then there was a stern shout, very near, which startled her as much as it did the mare. A large pale shape closed in beside them out of the gray sheets of rain, looming so near, her leg was crushed between the horses' sides, racing with her mount, then gaining. Through the blur of water she saw the man reach dangerously down and snatch up the dangling reins. Then abruptly they were halted, mercifully standing still with only her heart racing on and on. She swayed and was draged down from the saddle into strong masculine arms.

"Are you hurt? *Mon Dieu,* are you all right?" he was saying urgently, but she merely closed her eyes against the rain beating into her face and could not answer. She had neither the breath nor the strength to speak. The world slipped a bit around her, only to right again in a few moments as she discovered her rescuer's lips upon hers. Startled, she jerked open her eyes and looked too deeply into clear gray ones.

"Bah, this madness, this rain." Du Vallon dropped his gaze first and carried her inside a nearby glass pavilion. He set her down upon the bench there, but before she could gather her dazed wits together enough to demand an apology for his liberty, he had plunged back out into the tempest to lead up the horses—Temptation lathered and spent with her fine head down—and tied them to the shrubbery by the entrance.

Gasping, Julia sat with her hands to crimson cheeks. Was the man insane to be kissing her? And she hardly knew what to think of being here with him in this scant little shelter. Since the day when she had seen him strike his servant she had not exchanged above a dozen words with him, and yet now here he was, her rescuer. She must cling to that fact, if only to save her bewildered wits.

Desperately she sent him a wan smile as he reappeared in the doorway, pausing there to slap the water from his clothes and remove his hat. Shortly cropped hair curled across his high angular brow, and his eyes were upon her, cool as ever and yet widened a bit with concern.

"How—how very glad I am you chose to heed my advice and ride early," she said, breathless. Stripping off her wet gloves with difficulty, she held out one trembling hand as he moved to meet her. "Thank you."

Instead of taking her hand, he reached out and gently ran his fingertips across the rising welt on her cheek. *"Ma pauvre,* does it hurt?"

It stung fiercely, but in confusion she shook her head and rose from the bench to go and look out at the rain. It was pounding down just as hard as ever, isolating her from the rest of the world in this shelter with a man who could be kind or horrid, as the fancy struck him. The fact that she was trapped here alone with *any* gentleman was enough to send crimson staining up her throat in another embarrassed surge. No, her thoughts corrected her at once, not trapped, for he had rescued her at some risk to his own person and now his anxiety on her behalf was plain. But she dared not trust his erratic, mysterious personality despite the certainty stealing over her that the time they must spend here would be unguarded minutes, which would refuse to heed the usual barriers of hostility dividing them.

Alarmed by her own thoughts, she let a hand steal up to rub at her smarting cheek. She must, she decided, be more shaken from her narrow escape than she had first supposed. She was still trembling and chaotic in thought. To break the rather dreadful silence lengthening between them, she glanced nervously back over her shoulder and said, "It isn't bad. A cold compress shall deal with it nicely once I am home."

His expression, as usual, was hard to read and haughty, but the faint smile he awarded her was warmer than his custom. "*Bon.* You have a spirit to be admired, mademoiselle. Many other *demoiselles* would be having an indulgence of the hysterics, and I would not know what to do."

Julia was diverted into a small chuckle. "I admit the temptation to go into a spasm is strong. But I am recovering speedily." Her amusement did not relax her jangled nerves, but it did serve to make her want to chatter rather than think of Sophie, of Du Vallon, of—of anything. She sat down again and removed her ruined hat with its bedraggled plume. Wrinkling her nose at it in a silent grimace of distaste, she dropped it on the floor beside her. "Do you think, my lord, we shall be here long?"

"A while." Unclasping his hands from behind his back, he lifted his brows. "Is mademoiselle alarmed? She need not be." He brushed some of the water from his face and sat down with a sigh. "Attempting a seduction when one is wet and cold is *très désagréable, non*?"

His clear eyes were veiled, but Julia suspected he was

laughing at her. Nettled, she started to make a tart reply when her gaze fell upon his right hand, ungloved for the first time since she had encountered him in Calais. She was surprised to see it neither malformed nor maimed as she had let her curiosity previously suppose. But a deep, ugly scar disfigured the back and ran across the palm and on up inside the wrist. She frowned, puzzled as to why he should feel the need to hide it. It was hardly a pretty sight, of course, but certainly far from shocking.

She did not realize she was staring until his soft voice broke in on her thoughts. "Mademoiselle is possessed of an osbervant eye."

Mortified, she glanced up with a look of contrition, but his gaze was resting pensively on his hand and he did not notice. Her hostility toward him softened for a moment. "What happened?" she asked.

At first she thought he would not answer, then he gave a little shrug. *"Eh, bien.* I was once among the ranks of the best swordsmen in France. Long ago, when the rapier was still the *arme d'honneur,* and not the clumsy pistol." A look of disdain flitted across his chiseled features, then he smiled at her in his faint way. "The sword must be wooed, mademoiselle, before she will fight for you. She must be grasped as lightly as a bird, so she will not choke." He flexed his hand with some effort, and the frown returned between his brows. "At Austerlitz, I lost the lightness of touch *nécessaire.* So . . ." He shrugged.

It was her turn to frown now, for she was caught up in his story with her own problems forgotten. "Austerlitz? Then my lord is a soldier?" She could not help but sound disbelieving; he seemed too fastidious for the role.

But he gave his chestnut head a shake. *"Non.* I will not lie to you, mademoiselle." Throwing back his head, he grimaced. "I was never a soldier. To fight my country and my people—no matter how despicable both have become—would not be a *geste noble.*" A sigh escaped him. "You have no approval of me, yes, I know it. But there are worse men in this world than I, and the first I would name are those who ordered my hand to be maimed."

She exclaimed, but he silenced her with a glance. "No pity, *s'il vous plaît.* It was asked of me to spy."

"But you could not!" she said involuntarily. "No gentleman—" And then she stopped in confusion, a blush staining the whiteness of her face as she remembered what she thought of him.

"Merci," he said with a slight bow. "Then I was young and headstrong. I was proud to refuse, to insult Monsieur Talleyrand, as though it would atone for the murders of my parents during the Terror." His face very cold, he stood and turned his back to stare out at the rain. "I have learned to be wiser since then," he said, almost in a whisper, and there was something dark which haunted his voice. *"Mon Dieu,* but I have learned. And the cost is too high."

She could make no answer to such statements, and so she sat in silence, listening to the rain lashing about and thinking on what he had said. Why, she wondered with impatience, was it so impossible to pierce through the mystery which hung about him? She fully believed he had suffered as he said, and yet how odd it was that he should be free and alive and wealthy. She wondered if one could amass a fortune as a professional duelist and doubted it very much. But there were many avenues to wealth—or at least a semblance of it—known to the unscrupulous adventurer. Yet even as her mind moved to condemn him again as an undesirable sort, her heart was stirred by sympathy. Something within him still suffered; memories of a terrible past, or perhaps a secret so horrible he could never escape its clutches. She was growing fanciful, but still she knew she could never again blame him so harshly for his ruthlessness. Today he had shown her a side of him which denied condemnation.

"Thank you," he said, breaking the long silence.

Startled, she looked up. "For what?"

He neither met her gaze nor answered her question. "It was madness, to talk to you in such a way. I should not have done it." And then he did look at her, and his clear gray eyes flashed to the depths of her soul with a strength that hurt. "You are so *belle,* so frivolous, but when you are still as you are now and thinking, how could I resist confiding?" He walked straight up to her and stood there to gently cup her chin in his hand. "Such eyes of beauty; could I help but kiss you before?"

She sat there breathless and unmoving lest the least thought break the spell. It was as though they had been taken from the world and set apart in a magical place, where the rain outside guarded their isolation. Something very queer fluttered through her, like a sensation of fainting, only it was not that at all. She did not know what to call it and indeed was afraid to examine anything about this moment lest, like a butterfly whose wings are touched, it crumble into dust and the enchantment be lost.

"In words and thoughts we comprehend each other not at all," he said, frowning. "But it seems as though our souls would speak if we let them." His frown deepened and he released her, breaking the spell into a hundred pretty fragments that fluttered about her like flakes of ash then faded away. "How can you look at me sometimes with such sympathy as though you had walked at my side through the past? *Peste!*"

Despite her puzzlement she had to smile at his. "I have the answer," she said suddenly. "My mother was

French. And so sometimes I perhaps understand the feelings in your country even though I am not acquainted with the events."

"What nonsense," he said, but mildly, and she nodded, feeling rather foolish.

"Yes," she said with a sigh. "I suppose it is."

He smiled. "Your *maman* is French. But how *charmante*!" Interest gleamed in his gaze, and he looked animated, even young—she doubted he was yet thirty. "Of what family is she? I am sure to know it."

She smiled at him in shy eagerness, pleased even with a question so terribly *grand seigneur*. Most persons deplored the Gallic half of her ancestry; it was delightful to meet someone—even someone as naturally prejudiced as a Frenchman—who did not.

"I'm afraid she died when I was born, and put an end to Papa's hopes for a son more . . . personable than my half-brother Gaylord. Papa's first wife died in childbirth too. He grew very disgusted about it." Julia shrugged, trying to rout the old sense of guilt which had briefly reared up after having been dismissed years ago by a combination of defiance and common sense. After all, she really could not be blamed for her mother's death, and even had Léonie Swanton lived to a ripe old age it was doubtful she could have prevented Sir Geoffrey from falling into ruinous debt. "But *Maman* was the daughter of the Comte de Clembeau—"

"Clembeau!" An expression of startlement and pain flashed across Du Vallon's face, destroying the interest which had shone so keenly. He glanced away, his fists clenched until the knuckles whitened.

At a loss, not knowing whether he was a sworn enemy of her relations or suffering a more private agony, Julia stared at him in dismay. "Do you know the family, sir?" she asked, certain she must say something, and was rewarded by seeing his fists slowly unclench.

He glanced back at her, his features remote, and inclined his head in that manner of stately graciousness he had. "There is some acquaintanceship," he said stiffly. "My sister wed the present comte several months ago. She had great happiness then. Now—" He broke off with a gesture and seemed unable to speak for a moment. Julia was conscious of having been cut off, as though he had switched a curtain of hostility between them to prevent her from learning anything else. His head came up, and he went on fiercely. "We speak of trifles. I must ask, mademoiselle, now that you are not so pale, what you were doing in a violent storm on a horse running away without even a lackey or a groom in pursuit?"

She gasped in surprise at his attack; this sudden switch when she was just beginning to regard him with warmth was too much to comprehend all at once. "But you make it sound all my fault," she said with a frown and pushed back a ringlet drooping over her eye. "It wasn't. I—"

"When riding, mademoiselle," he said with clipped sternness, "you are fully responsible for the control of your animal. To let it run away is a carelessness which could have seen you killed. *Mon Dieu,* I am of the opinion you need a horse of less spirit."

She still could not understand why the mention of her relatives had put him at once into a beastly temper, but she did know that this scold was unjustified and not to be endured from anyone, least of all from a man she hardly knew. Very much on her dignity, she rose to her feet and gave him a direct look. "I am quite grateful to you, Lord du Vallon, for having rescued me, but I shall not let you dictate to me in this manner. Never has my mare gone out of control before, and she would not have done so today if it had not been for—"

Abruptly she stopped and bit her lip. Injured pride would not let her tell him how her own sister had committed such a vile act. The horror and rage of her experience swept again over her, gripping her so with the fear of what had nearly happened she could think of Sophie only through a haze of fury. "I shall never forgive her," she declared with an emphatic gesture, not conscious she spoke her thoughts aloud. "Never! How could she have done such a thing to me?" And abruptly Julia burst into tears.

It had never been her way to cry, and indeed she could not understand why she must needs break down when her adventure was over. But the warm tears did not stop, and they left her wracked and helpless in misery caused by the hatred forged between her and Sophie. Worse, she expected Du Vallon to sneer at her for this show of weakness. Instead he took her arm and guided her back to the bench, sitting down beside her and gently patting her hand.

"Mademoiselle must not cry," he said quietly and offered a handkerchief she was forced by necessity to accept.

"Don't you dare try to soothe me!" she said with watery fierceness, blowing her nose. "You are impossible to deal with, or to understand."

"But of course," he said and gave her one of his faint smiles. "You must tell me what happened. Who is this person you can never forgive?"

"Sophie," she said without thinking, then, to cover her mistake, thrust his handkerchief back at him. "Thank you. I shall not need it further."

With lifted brows he declined to accept it. "Who is Sophie?"

She tightened her lips, then sighed, knowing it was useless now to hold anything back. "Lady Lewing, my half-sister," she said with more calm than she felt. "We have not been on good terms lately, and when she asked me to ride with her this morning I thought it was an attempt to patch matters between us." She paused, her fists clenched in her lap as she strove for words to describe the meeting without experiencing its sting again.

"But you quarreled," he said, taking snuff gracefully.

She nodded. "We—oh, indeed it is not pretty of either of us, but she is so wrong! And to strike my horse to make it bolt—" Julia turned her head to blink back fresh tears of fury. "I cannot forgive her for it, ever! She must not expect it." She looked up at him, seeking sympathy, and was jolted to find mockery gleaming in his eyes. Her hand stole up to her throat. "Why do you look like that? Do you not believe me?"

He shook his head and started to speak, but she was on her feet in an instant with indignation quivering through every line.

"How dare you call me a liar! Everything I have told you is true. And I would not have told you about it at all except that you pried it from me." Julia's chin rose. "Sophie did strike my horse."

"That is not in question," he said, his calm tones rather bleak against her impassioned ones. "*Voyons,* would she do such a thing without reason? You wish me to think so, to be all on your side." He shrugged and shook his head. "But this cannot be true."

Julia stamped her foot. "You are horrid!"

To her utter outrage, he applauded with a brief smile. "But mademoiselle is so *charmante* when she has anger. *Très belle. Ravissante!*" He held out a hand to her. "The rain begins to stop a little, I think. Come and see."

But she drew back from him, unwilling to let such deliberate mockery pass. She did not like this man whose personality was as ungraspable as quicksilver. He charmed her one moment and humiliated her the next. Such treatment, coming after she had experienced the fright of her life and a devastating quarrel with Sophie, was too much for her to bear, and her self-control went down before the onslaught. Rage took mastery of her, searing her through with white heat, so that she neither heeded nor cared what she lashed at him.

"Lord du Vallon—if you really are a nobleman—I find you despicable! A barbarian would show more consideration to a lady than you have done. Every act you perform is conniving; I shudder to think of what you will demand of me now that you have saved me from a runaway. What business is it of yours if my father is dead and I am penniless, thrown on my wits to survive? I have no one to help me, no one to care whether I achieve the security of marriage or must end out my days as a poverty-ridden spinster. You certainly do not care; in fact, you thrive on my straits. I hate you and your cruelty, leaving me in constant dread lest your whim lead you to betray me. I suppose it can hardly matter to you, can it, if my reputation is left in shreds. But it is not just me you choose to pick on, my lord. No, you must also abuse your position by physically striking your servants. I daresay the poor man must be French; no Englishman would stand for such treatment, no matter how handsome his wages—"

"Enough!" White to the lips, Du Vallon seized her by the arms with a grip so painful it jerked her back to herself with brutal immediacy. "I think now, mademoiselle, you go too far. *Oui,* you are upset today, and I make allowances. But no further!" Giving her a single rough shake, he thrust her away with force enough to make her stagger. *"Voyons,* I agree I have had no scruples in knowing you do not mourn your papa. I have no approval of such disrespect, but I have not intruded into your reasons, mademoiselle."

"No, but you make use of them all the same," she retorted, shaken by his show of anger but still clinging to her spirit.

His smile was so chilly it turned her seared veins cold, and she shivered. *"Oui, c'est vrai.* But mademoiselle must remember that I could not were she observing the proprieties. Oh, *mais oui,* I am vile. I am cruel. I am one of no heart. Do I care what you think? I dare not." The horrible smile faded, leaving his lips thin beneath pinched nostrils. How white he was, and how grim! The light in his clear eyes blazed a ruthlessness that was like a blow against her, crushing her rage until she was frightened and left without even anger as a defense to cling to. "Your sense of wrongs is too keen, mademoiselle." Suddenly his voice sounded overloud, and it was with a shock that she realized the rain had ceased. The desire to flee seized her, but she could not move. She was trapped by the relentless chill of his voice, by the steely flash in his eyes.

"Let me go," she said, her voice a quaver.

"Go?" He waved a hand with fierce grace. "But of course go. Rejoin your silly games. Forget to think of all save your own pleasures. I asked little of you, mademoiselle. A waltz, an introduction. Nothings." He snapped his fingers, and she flinched. Then he glanced at her with the centuries-old arrogance of haughty blood-lineage. "I could have demanded much, but I am not sunk to such lowness. No matter how many threats hang over me, mademoiselle, I am still the gentleman." She made an involuntary movement, and his brows drew together.

"You disagree, but that is because you judge by conventions I am not permitted—I cannot—observe. Beyond that," he continued in that same cold, level tone which seemed to slice through her, "I need not explain or excuse myself."

"How cold and disagreeable you are," she said in frustration and stamped her foot because she could not find words to answer him. "Oh, I do not understand you at all!"

"When I tell you my only sister is kept a political

prisoner, can you understand?" he asked. "I am powerless to help her. Do you understand that? No, of course you do not. *Sang de Dieu!*" His eyes fell, then flashed back to her. "It does not matter. I am of course lying to you. Why do you say I beat my lackeys? Where do you get this information?"

Never had she seen anyone so angry, so cold. His abrupt switch of questions left her more at a loss than before. Her wits were scattered by the mere glance of his eyes. She could not think. He frightened her with his fury. She drew back, wishing she had never spoken, but when he threw out one hand in impatience for her answer she had to obey.

"I—I was driving past your house. I meant to tell you Lady Jersey had agreed to send you vouchers; only, you were coming out, and as you did so, you struck a servant for bringing you a coat." There, it was out, and for some reason, the telling seemed to shrink her until she felt small and somehow in the wrong for having seen.

Though it did not seem possible, his expression grew colder and more menacing. She was shocked to see hate glitter in his eyes as he nodded in remembrance. "That would have been Baptiste, my *valet de chambre.*" The thin lips curled in a sneer. "Someday I shall cut out his treacherous heart and burn it on the grate!"

She saw he was serious and not merely dramatic, and gasped. "Good God, but you *are* horrible!"

Immense bitterness crossed his face. He stared at her for a long moment with his gaze as sharp as a rapier point before bowing. "*Oui,* I am horrible. The fact has been clear to me for too long."

"But what has this poor man ever done to you?" she could not help asking, although his flat agreement of the accusation made her head reel.

The smile he gave her was infinitely worse. "That, *ma petite sotte,* I do not tell." Turning on his heel, he strode to the doorway, then glanced back with a harshly expelled sigh as though to speak again was against his wish. "Will you dare judge, mademoiselle? You are yet a child."

Vaulting into the saddle, he kicked his mount into a gallop which sent mud and chunks of lawn flying. Temptation jerked at the shrub she was tied to and nickered after them, but horse and rider were already out of hearing. Julia remained standing in the pavilion, one hand to her sore cheek until the hoofbeats could no longer be heard. She was completely exhausted; to think was as much an effort as to push herself outside across the squelchy ground to the mare. He was wrong, so very wrong. He had insulted her, mocked her, twisted her words into accusations against herself—but he had also rescued her from certain death and treated her with a gentleness that could not be denied. She blushed and tossed her head at the quick memory of his lips upon hers, bringing her out of her swoon.

And then suddenly she was ashamed, both of herself and the things she had said to him. None of the hurtful words need have been uttered. She realized she had failed to understand something within him which needed desperately to be understood. For a moment he had opened himself to her and been other than a remote figure with graceful manners. But she, in her stupid anger, had made certain he would never do so again. Perhaps she ought not to care, but she found that she did care, terribly. And so miserable and guilty did she feel, that once she had managed to mount Temptation she was too depressed to search for her lost whip, and instead rode home to the anxious bosom of her aunt—wet, draggled, and very low indeed.

Chapter Seven

There was nothing Julia desired to do more than lock herself into her room and wallow in a sea of self-pity, but it was impossible to cry off from the evening's plan of going to Almack's. She had persuaded Garde to look in during the course of the evening and knew, for the sake of everything she'd worked for, that she dared not give away to strain now. Certainly such trifles as violent quarrels with both Sophie and that dreadful marquis could not be permitted to overcome her spirit. To do so would be a kind of defeat, and she could not countenance that. Thus, after letting Lady Elizabeth pet and fuss over her, applying cool, scented compresses to her cheek and even permitting her to wear a *très décolleté* gown, Julia stepped across the threshold of the assembly rooms on King Street in the wake of her plump aunt—a very cool expression upon her prettily *gamine* features, as though she had spent a day no more eventful than a session with her needlework in the cosiness of the drawing room.

Dressed in a narrow Empire gown of white tulle with its exquisitely daring bodice, she wore a spray of natural violets in her raven curls and another clutch of the flowers tied round her wrist with a matching ribbon. It was a simple, fetching costume which, when combined with the lift of her chin and the flash of her dark blue eyes, contrived to say its wearer was very much a woman. Greeting Lady Jersey, who was standing at the door with the vivacious Princess Esterházy, Julia was delighted to find her entrance had coincided with an interval between dances, thus permitting every eye to turn upon her.

"My child, you are ravishing tonight," cried Lady Jersey with one of her rich laughs. "Every other lady shall be your enemy, myself included."

This pleasantry made Julia smile in reply and return a pretty answer, but as she passed through the crush of guests to help Lady Elizabeth find a comfortable sofa, her lovely eyes held a hint of a frown in their depths. It might be *fast,* she argued with herself, but she simply *had* to look round the lofty ballroom with its spartan festoons and meagerly laden refreshment table in hopes for a sight of Garde. His large auburn head was not evidence, however, as to be expected this early in the evening, and she sat down with disappointment raging beneath her pose of demure elegance. A short distance away a matron tittered behind her fan to another, and supremely conscious of the slightest thing, Julia straightened her slender back another impossible fraction. Were they discussing her, she wondered, then impatiently dismissed the doubt. It was absurd to be so self-conscious.

"Miss Swanton?"

The pleasant, somewhat diffident voice broke gently into her thoughts, and with a slight start she looked up to see Mr. Wrexham's youthful features smiling at her. Her glance seemed to confuse him, for he turned bright red above his cravat tied in an impetuous Trône d'Amour. But after an alarming fit of coughing he stiffened up. "You're looking much too pretty to be sitting out this waltz, Miss Swanton."

At her side, Lady Elizabeth glowed and rapped his hand with her fan. "Delightful boy, you will quite turn my lamb's head with those compliments."

With such a warm sanction from her chaperone, Julia stood up with her admirer in the doubtful hope that he would not tread on her toes in his nervousness. Then her sense of fairness made her admit that Mr. Wrexham was an unexceptionable young man after all, and she found a smile for him.

"I believe your dancing has much improved, sir," she said and was rewarded by a self-conscious beam.

"Do you honestly think so? Lord knows I've been at it hard enough with the plaguey caper-merchant my sisters call a dancing master. Waltzes are such queer see-sawy tunes, though, it's devilish hard to get the knack of 'em." Turning red again, he cleared his throat. "Er, I daresay there won't be many more chances to stand up with you now that Garde is about to cut the rest of us fellows out."

Startled, her gaze fell in confusion, and she nearly missed a step. Did the *ton* think matters were so nearly settled between her and his lordship? A singular little quiver of triumph and relief set her pulse beating more rapidly. Oh, how she hoped it were true! After her horrid experiences today she was more than ever convinced Garde was the one she should always turn to, for at least he had never betrayed or abused her. It would be such a blessed relief to throw all her worries onto his more capable shoulders.

Raising her eyes with a little flush of excitement, she made herself cling to the proprieties. "I am afraid you know more than I in this instance, Mr. Wrexham."

"Oh!" He grinned at her in a conspiratorial manner so broad she was hard put not to let her lips quiver into an answering smile. "Quite right, Miss Swanton." Then his youth took over again as he exclaimed, "But I say! You can't think how dashedly swell it is."

She frowned, unable to like the introduction of cant into their conversation. *"Swell?"*

"Yes, wonderful," he explained, unabashed. "I

mean, Garde is jolly well the best man at pistols in the country. I've seen him aiming at wafers, foxed to the brows, and never missing. He can even shoot the dead center out of an ace of spades at fifty paces. I know, for I heard Barrymore held the card, and that, you must agree, is *something*!"

It was indeed, she thought with rising pique, for Cripplegate Barrymore and his set were surely the most wild, degenerate libertines in England and no gentleman who joined their circle ever emerged untainted. But with some effort she forbore to inform her partner he was thwarting his own endeavor to raise her estimation of Lord Garde's notions of amusement and managed another, less radiant, smile. "Do go on, sir."

"Well, don't you think it of all things marvelous that not only do you know the nonpareil of English marksmanship but the master on the Continent as well? Garde and Du Vallon," he repeated reverently, worship in his naïve blue eyes. Galled by the mention of the marquis's name, Julia barely held back a comment which would have been unflattering in the extreme. "It's really the most capital thing," continued Wrexham, failing to notice the new set to her mouth. "They ought to have a contest, by Jove!"

Alarmed, all resentful thoughts flew out of her head, and she faltered. "Good heavens! You don't mean call each other out, surely?"

"No, no!" He looked equally alarmed. "Gad, what would that serve? I meant, they ought to pit their aim at wafers against each other. It would be a splendid show, I should say. Everyone would turn out to see it."

"Yes, I think you are right," she said, but without much conviction. The end of the music saved her from any more of his rather unsettling conversation. Although it was better than murdering each other, the idea of grown gentlemen taking such keen interest in blowing tiny wafers to bits seemed to her utterly ridiculous and a waste of time. And she could not see Garde submitting himself to the indignity of performing for public entertainment. The notion smacked strongly of vulgarity, and she was almost inclined to be vexed with Mr. Wrexham for having brought it up at all.

She stood up with several other gentlemen after that, including the Beau himself, who complimented her on her dress but failed to appreciate the style of her French kid slippers. Then Garde arrived, very tall and striking in his blue coat, pale breeches, and chapeau bras, and thoughts of every other gentleman in the room flew out of her head. She stood up with him for the minuet, her limbs tingling with weakness, her eyes brilliant with heady excitement, and her thoughts whirling over everything from memories of Sophie's stinging words to considerations of his admiring gaze. In effect, by the time he had procured a glass of orgeat for her, then led her back onto the floor for a lively waltz, she hardly knew whether she was on her head or her heels.

She had been strung with anticipation since her arrival, but Wrexham's artless comments had set her hopes flaming, and now there was something about Garde's tone whenever he spoke and the way in which his murky eyes gleamed which told her she had succeeded very much in capturing his fancy, and perhaps to the degree necessary to persuade him to abandon his bachelor status. She knew she would make him a worthy wife and countess, one who would not foolishly try to change his dissolute habits and thus alienate him. And in return he would take care of her mounting debts, protect her from Sir Geoffrey's creditors, and surround her with ease and security for the rest of her life. Tonight, while the music soared and his muscular arm was entwined about her waist, the fears of an uncertain future and the worries of being penniless without daring to let it show could fade to the far reaches of her mind and let her sail along on a wave of giddiness.

Somehow he contrived to maneuver her so that they were near the card rooms when the music ended. He smiled, showing all his large teeth. "Let us have some quiet for a moment, my dear."

Without protest, she allowed him to escort her past the dowagers playing cards with ferocious concentration for penny stakes into another, smaller room—hardly more than an alcove—where they sat down *tête-à-tête* upon a curved-back sofa. Stroking the fronds of a fern positioned beside her, Julia sought to stem the roar through her ears so that she might hear the tender words of flirtation he was saying, but she could not succeed. This vexed her, for she knew she must be calm if she was to accept his proposal with a gracefulness that would delight him. But for once practicality was lost upon her. She glowed with anticipation, and her eyes flew constantly to his face as she waited for him to speak. Instead, he swept her into his powerful arms and crushed her close. His lips burned with passion that made her tremble at first. The man was wicked to kiss her so when she—when he—she closed her eyes and did not care. This was a more masterful declaration than any words.

"Milord! You forget yourself, I think."

The voice came from nowhere; the words were hard, cool, and so unexpected, Julia jerked free of Garde's embrace with her cheeks ablaze in a mortification no hastily collected sophistication could dispel. How dare it be Du Vallon standing there before them in such elegant black, with such a stern set to his mouth and such a gleam in his eye! She fumed, unable to keep from putting one hand to her fiery cheek and the other to her panting bosom. It was too much. Just when all was perfect, this wretch must interfere! Oh, how could he dare plague her so!

Garde, however, was unperturbed and turned to Du Vallon with an easy laugh. "Why, we have met before, haven't we? Lord du Vallon, I believe." He laughed again, but this time in a less friendly way. "The lady does not need rescuing, sir."

It said no very pretty thing for Julia, and she had to bite her lip to keep silent despite the indignation which reared up within her. Garde need not imply to the world that she was as melting butter in his arms. She could not repress a glance of reproach his way, but he did not see it.

"Is there something you require, sir?" Garde's tone was growing colder by rapid degrees, and despite her annoyance with both men Julia's heart faltered a bit in alarm lest Du Vallon's quicksilver temper be set off by Garde's manner. The last thing she wanted was the supreme embarrassment of two men coming to blows on her account in a public assembly.

"Please—" she began, but Du Vallon was already making his graceful bow.

"I am *sans doute* resented greatly for my interruption," he said with a mocking curl of his lip that had Julia hating him more than ever. "I beg your pardons. But there is one Lady Jersey who craves a word with you, milord."

"Oh?" Coldly, Garde rose to his feet, easily taller than the marquis by several inches. His face showed disbelief plainly enough but he merely bowed in return. "I am indebted to you, sir. Excuse me, my dear Miss Swanton." His dark eyes flickered to her and lingered for an instant in a way that snatched her breath. "It shall only take a moment for me to deal with my summons."

As soon as Garde was gone, the marquis permitted his cool façade to vanish, leaving his nostrils pinched until they were white. His normally clear eyes smudged dark with angry intensity. At that moment he looked as though he could almost throttle her.

Fresh annoyance stirred within her as she gazed up

at him. Not only had he managed to interrupt the most glorious moment of her life, now he dared linger as though he would scold her. The dog! Her hands clenched.

"Thank you," she said with the coolness of dismissal. "Your lordship need not stand guard over me."

Restraint seemed to snap within him. He gestured. "What type of little fool are you, to let that—that *petit-maître* make love to you?" His bloodless lips sneered so scornfully she flinched. Have you a *tendre* for him? The *roué* is twice your age."

She whitened with rage. "How dare you make such remarks to me! Impertinent beast, this is none of your concern!" Jumping up, she would have run past him, but he caught her roughly by the arms.

"I asked, mademoiselle: Do you love this man?"

Her head lifted; she was proud to answer. "Yes. Yes. I do, if you must know." Seeing something flicker in the depths of Du Vallon's gaze, she added with vicious imperiousness, "Nor do I see why you must take it upon yourself to act like a jealous suitor."

"Do you not?" He gave a low, mirthless laugh which dashed a chill over her anger. "*Peut-être ou non*, one may take pleasure with little fools." And before she could retort, he crushed her already bruised lips with a kiss that sent a rapier plunging to her depths.

The fire of his embrace was quite a different matter from Garde's jaded passion. Fire, yes, but so clear and swift it was as though ice sealed her veins. Breathless, stunned, she was snatched away from herself and from the sultry caress of Garde still lingering upon her senses. A wind lashed through her every corner, sweeping away every thought and desire until she was bare and clean with a small new fire being kindled—*No!* In sudden desperation she fought to escape the danger which was rising to bear her to the swooning point. She managed to free one fist, but beating upon his chest was to no avail. He was ruthless . . . magnificent. No, no, how could she . . .

Then he released her so suddenly she stumbled back and half fell against the sofa. There was none of the triumph she had expected to see in his face as, breathless and trembling, she gazed up at him, the back of one hand pressed against her burning lips. But instead, he looked colder and more scornful than ever, setting the seal upon her humiliation.

She struck the satin seat with one wild fist, not knowing whether it was the tumult he had stirred in her shameless veins or his cold contempt of her which drove her to such distress. "I hate you! I *hate* you!" she cried beneath her breath, eyes blazing blue fury in her frustration.

"But of course, mademoiselle," he murmured. Raking her once more with scornful eyes, he left her.

And that seemed worst of all to bear. Trembling, she gasped and pressed her hands to her fiery face, hating him and hating Garde and hating herself. Du Vallon was a horrid, horrid beast to have condemned her so; but she also knew, with a desperate writhe of shame, that she could never again be able to dismiss him from her mind. The wretch, what did he mean to do? Worse, she was at least experienced enough to realize Du Vallon's kiss had been more punishing than amorous. And that morning when she had fainted and he had kissed her, it had been nothing like this. Oh, it was awful, *awful*!

Garde returned before she had time enough to compose herself, and with a frown he drew her to her feet. "What has happened?" But he gave her no chance to reply. "Damn the cur! If he has dared be impudent to you I shall heave him out of here by his collar!"

Julia laid a swift hand on his arm. "Pray, hush!" she commanded, unable to think or know what to do. "I will not let you quarrel over me. I could not bear it!"

A slow smile replaced the thunder on Garde's face. Taking her hand, he kissed it between the knuckles. "Why, my dear, he could not bring me to harm. It is because he shoots with the left hand that he is counted so deadly, but I am accustomed to the trick and know how to deal with it."

The blood seemed to drain from her. Again she saw her father, the soaked linen, death. "You mustn't," she gasped. "Promise me never to duel. If you knew my horror—"

He frowned in some concern. "You look and speak as though you have watched one. Surely not—"

"No, no." She shook her head, troubled. "But I once watched a man die, my—" Biting her lip, she stopped. The subject was growing dangerous. In a moment she would be telling him about her father, and that must not happen.

Though certain that if she took a single lively step she would be sick, Julia managed a smile. "The music has begun again. I very much like this tune."

"Then we shall dance to it," he said, tucking her hand within his arm with the amused gleam back in his face. But his murky eyes were still narrowed, and he stopped at the sight of Du Vallon *tête-à-tête* with the Duke of York, who seemed quite vehement on some point of discussion. "But what the devil is the man up to in any case, lounging about town and poking his cursed nose into everyone's concerns? He says he wants to bring his sister over, but that's obviously gammon. Men of that ilk do not give a thought for their sisters. He isn't an *émigré*, so what the deuce is he doing here?"

"I do not much care," said Julia, growing rather petulant at this lack of attention. Garde laughed and led her out to join the set, but though he finished the evening by being as attentive as anyone could wish for, he did not again press her hand or take her anywhere to be alone. She supposed it would be quite scandalous if she slipped off with him twice in one evening, but nothing could alter the fact that her chance had come and been spoiled and looked as though it would not return.

Afraid, she clung to Garde's arm as he handed her into her carriage after Lady Elizabeth and searched his face more openly than she had ever dared to before. With amusement he bowed and stepped back, although she knew with a flush that it would have pleased him more to have kissed her before the others assembling outside for their carriages. But her heart failed within her, for there was nothing to be read in his features but flirtation. No impatience, no eagerness to speak, no look of significance. Stung with disappointment, she fell back against the squabs of the seat as their carriage rolled forward. He had stood there and let her depart without a word spoken of his intentions.

Suddenly exhausted, she pressed a hand to her mouth and did not hear one word of her aunt's chatter. Good God, did he have no intentions that were honorable? Was he but trifling with her as he had with countless others? No, no, it could not be! But her heart was thudding, and she felt sick with despair. He had had every chance to speak of marriage, but he had not done so. He had not even hinted at it. Oh, the shame! She had been a fool to let herself believe Wrexham. Look at her hopes. Ashes! Garde thought no more of her than he had of Sophie, and like her unfortunate half-sister, Julia now realized she had fallen into the trap and become enmeshed in the man's spell. It was too late. Du Vallon's brutal intervention had saved her tonight from goodness knew what folly, but that would never happen again. She began to shiver. Oh, why, why had she lost her senses *now* with success almost in her grasp? If she was to melt every time Garde even glanced at her, how would she ever be firm and clear-witted enough to bring him to marriage?

The condemnation she had read in Du Vallon's eyes haunted her. He was right, curse him! But why had he seen fit to interfere? She must not let him do so again, for she could not give up the hope that, had she been left uninterrupted with Garde this evening, she might have come home betrothed and safe. But indeed, she was ashamed of herself. Was she going so far beyond the line in her scheming that every gentleman thought he could get away with kissing her? To have been embraced by two different men in the same evening was enough to sink her to the depths of shame. Thank goodness no one had seen her. If she was not careful she was going to end up with a reputation of being fast.

But she *was* fast, and a man-chaser as well. A sob broke from her, and then another, and suddenly she was weeping uncontrollably. Before tonight it had all seemed so clear what she must do to save herself from poverty and debt. Now nothing was clear save the fact that she was brass-faced and had no principles. She had gambled, and tonight she had lost. Garde and a chance of a comfortable future had been illusions. Besides, she suspected her days of credit from the best dressmakers and milliners were not to be continued much longer. Then the duns would descend upon her and her secret would be made known and she would die of the shame.

"Julia, dearest!" implored her aunt with a helpless quaver in her voice. "Please, *please* tell me what is wrong. Oh, dear, I knew there should only be disaster when you came in from your ride soaked through and without your hat! Did Garde not come up to scratch?"

"No, he did not," said Julia, choking, and turned her face away. She wanted no comforting and no sympathy. She deserved nothing but scorn for the rest of her days. "Oh, I hate myself! I hate myself!" And she fell into a fresh bout of weeping.

Chapter Eight

Lady Elizabeth gave strict instructions that Julia was not to be let up from her bed all the next day, declaring such a fit of hysterics was not to be dismissed lightly. But these intentions were thwarted before eleven o'clock by the arrival of Lord Lewing and his subsequent demand to see both ladies of the house. Supposing this to mean that Sophie had eloped with Garde, Julia was at first inclined to hide from news of any such calamity. But anything was better than confinement in her room with only her wretched thoughts for company, and she gave the order that his lordship be received in the drawing room.

Wan and drawn after a sleepless night battling with herself over whether she should admit defeat fully by announcing her parent's demise, she met her aunt on the stairs in a dark blue dress of Indian mulled silk, made up high to the throat with white ruching there and at the wrists, which showed she had decided nothing at all. But to her aunt's anxious scrutiny she returned an expression of perfect, if pale, composure, and together they went down to confront their visitor.

At first sight of his frowning but calm countenance, Julia experienced a pang of relief so sharp it caught her breath and she could only nod mutely in response to his greeting. He would not look like that if anything awful had happened. This must be a purely social call, but if so, where was Sophie?

A small, well-proportioned man with somewhat too regular features, Lord Lewing stood before them attired in a coat fashioned by a good but unpretentious tailor. Fawn Wellington trousers were buttoned over his shoes in a manner which set well with the plain fob dangling from a quiet kerseymere waistcoat. In fact, the only fault to be found with his appearance was the celadon-colored neckerchief knotted round his throat Belcher style and a complexion burnt startling dark by the fierce Spanish sun.

Seating herself and folding her hands in her lap, Julia gave him a wan but friendly smile. Perhaps it would help if she engaged her mind with his reasons for calling alone in this unexpected way; she must have some relief from her own relentless round of thoughts. "We are delighted to see you safely home again, John," she said with as much warmth as she could muster. "I was thinking of how well and yet how unpretentiously you dress."

His smile was rather sweet in the stern lines of his face, and he accorded her a bow. "Thank you. Sophie tells me I look more like a bumptious country squire than the heir to an earldom, but perhaps now that I am done with the army I shall have an opportunity to catch up with the current modes."

"You've sold out?" Delight surged through her, making her whole face light up as she clapped her hands. "Aunt, is it not wonderful? Oh, I am glad, John. You have been absent far too long."

The soberness returned to his face, and clasping his hands behind his back, he gave a short nod of agreement. "Yes, I fear so. My household is not at all in the state it should be."

Dismay clutched at her like a sharp dousing of icy water—dismay not for herself, but for him. She had always liked her brother-in-law although he was quiet and she hardly knew him, and now she wondered how deeply he had been hurt by Sophie's flirtation with Garde. Dreading to hear, but at the same time impatient with his dramatic pause, Julia sent him a swift but direct glance. "What has happened?"

"Dear me, yes! We must know," put in Lady Elizabeth, her mild eyes agog.

But Lewing was still silent, the frown deeper between his brows. Julia was obliged to prompt him again, and he came out of his brown study with a start.

"I *am* sorry," he said with a self-conscious smile. "Perhaps I should not have come, but I felt I could not do otherwise than speak to you both." He bit his lip, then continued in a stronger voice of decision, which Julia thought of as his parade-ground manner. "We are leaving this afternoon for a repairing-lease in the country. Town air is making the child sickly; he is not permitted outside enough. And then there is Sophie."

Yes, Sophie. He had, of course, come for no other reason. Still bitter against her, Julia looked away. His disappointment with his wife and her flighty conduct was all too apparent in the tones of his quiet voice, but Julia could not bring herself to comfort him, for that would mean dredging up all of Sophie's finer points. Every feeling of decency urged her to do so, but she resisted, unable to forget how her half-sister had deliberately left her in the park to break her neck.

"I find her changed," he said, circling the room with a pace as deliberate as his words. "She is no longer light at heart. She seems burdened by my presence and yet I am sure it is not that."

Julia put one hand against her lips, forbidding them to speak lest they bring him more unhappiness, but she could not stop the words. "She has not acted very prettily of late. Surely you must know of—"

"Garde?" Lewing gave a short laugh. "The danger of having a beautiful wife, I suppose. Thank God that folly is passed."

"Is it?" said Julia too sharply.

His glance flew to her and read—what? She flushed and dropped her eyes, unable to understand why she must act like a shrew today. If only defeat were not so bitter within her. If only she had not been so stupid to think she would not get scorched as Sophie had.

"Julia," he said quietly. "You need not fear Sophie shall ever come between you and his . . . lordship again. She and I have had a long talk since yesterday morning. I know all now. It could have been worse." He came to Julia and took her hand. "Perhaps there is blame to lay all around. She is deeply unhappy. She wished me to tell you that and also that she is sorry for losing her temper with you."

"I see." Julia swallowed hard, unable to look up into his gaze. What was she to say? Indeed, it was dreadful being at such outs with Sophie, but her anger was not assuaged by what she saw as a lukewarm apology. Sophie should have come herself. If she was sincere she *would* have come. Julia's lips tightened.

"Oh, dear!" Lady Elizabeth turned a pink, flustered glance Julia's way. "I did not know you and Sophie had quarreled. How dreadful! Now I see why you have been so distraught."

"Will you not help her make amends?" asked Lewing.

Despite the resentment in her heart, Julia put out her hand to him in sympathy. "Poor John," she said with an unsuccessful smile. "How you must wish this family at Jericho." And as she spoke she knew she must tell him of her own difficulties. Matters could not continue as they now stood. With her hopes gone she was a fool to go on pretending her father was alive and riches resided in her pocket. How she hated the thought of charity. But she felt so pressed by guilt she knew she must speak. "John—"

"No, no, how could I fail to like you all?" he said with a gallant smile. "Though I cannot approve his faults, Sir Geoffrey is not without charm. Gaylord is a bit of a bother with his requests for money. How I wish he could learn to stand on his feet and make a man of himself! But as for you, Julia, and Lady Elizabeth—why, I could not ask for sweeter relations. At least the two of you are untouched by problems you wish me to solve." His smile faded a bit. "I am troubled by all of this, of course, but not cast down. I feel it is much my fault for having gone to Spain. Sophie is yet so young in many ways. We are not well enough acquainted, not sure enough of each other. But I hope to rectify this by taking her away. It being the middle of the season, I don't deny she is disappointed. That's why I came here, to be sure I am doing the right thing."

"Whatever you decide is certain to be the proper measure," said Lady Elizabeth with a nod for him. She was still pink. "A military man can always be depended upon to make decisions. And I hold a very high opinion of your powers of judgment."

"Thank you, ma'am," he said, laughing a bit, and pulled out his watch. "There. I suspected I was running late. We shall never get off by noon if I do not hurry. Good-bye to you both. We shall expect you for a visit in June."

He paused and looked hard at Julia, and she thought, he is waiting for me to give my forgiveness to Sophie. But how could she? And after all he had said, she knew she could not begin to approach him for assistance. There was no doubt he would be gentleman enough to help her, but the poor man was burdened enough with the scandal his wife had wrought. Could he be expected to take on more? Julia bit her lip and dropped her gaze to her hands clenched in her lap.

With a bow he turned and left, and she sighed, knowing that eventually she and Aunt Beth would have no avenue left to them but his aid. What a fool she was, to be so stubborn over a quarrel! It would only deepen the rift between Sophie and her. Small wonder he had looked displeased. Julia imagined the probable tears and recriminations that had raged in Lewing House to bring Sophie to the point of reconciliation. Julia sighed, conscious of another chance lost, of another mistake made. Why did life seem to be growing increasingly unbearable?

That afternoon Julia had no desire to go out, and they were playing a rather sad game of backgammon, instigated by Lady Elizabeth in the hope of diversion, when Lord Garde was announced. Julia's hand inadvertently upset the board, but she took advantage of the search for scattered counters as an opportunity to calm the jarred pounding of her heart. Her mouth was so dry she feared if she spoke it would be a meaningless croak, and she struggled with trembling hands to readjust the board, letting Aunt Beth see to the task of properly greeting their visitor and offering him refreshment.

Conversation while they waited for the madeira and tea cakes to be brought was desultory, mostly polite inquiries concerning Julia's health and remarks about the fineness of the weather. He scarcely looked at her, for which she and her tense nerves were grateful. She could not imagine why he had come, but she did know that if he expected things to continue in their old vein after the events of last night he was very much mistaken! She was too ashamed of herself, and sat rigid and confused, her cheeks scarlet, her composure lost to the four winds. It was almost beyond her powers to make the simplest answer to his remarks, and thus she sat like a wilted heap of clothes, despising herself for acting like this but unable to do anything about it. He must be thinking her a perfect nodcock, which was exactly what she was.

Then Garde set down his glass and went to Lady Elizabeth's side, where he took her hand with his indifferent smile. "My dearest ma'am, I fear I must ask a favor of you. Now, don't deny me, I beg!"

Flustered like the merest schoolgirl, Lady Elizabeth gave a nod. "Why, of course, my lord. Whatever you like. More madeira? Another macaroon?"

"No, no." His loud laugh rang over the room as he drew her from her chair and led her to the door. "Leave us for a moment, please?"

"Oh, my goodness!" Open-mouthed, Lady Elizabeth peeped past him at Julia, who was suffused with the greatest agitation. "I'm sure I don't know, my lord. She has been so distraught, I think I dare not."

"But you did promise, ma'am," he said with the smooth insidiousness of Eden's serpent, much to Julia's mounting panic. What, she wondered frantically, gripping the arms of her chair in acute indecision whether to rise and flee, was the man up to? Did he mean to offer her a *carte blanche*! How could she have possibly led him to believe she was that sort? But what else was he murmuring into Aunt Beth's ear? Julia strained to hear without success.

Lady Elizabeth broke into a smile and patted his arm. "Yes, of course, my lord! Julia, the most delightful thing. Oh, but I mustn't give it away." She put her plump hands to her mouth and giggled. "Fifteen minutes, my lord, and I must leave the door just a tiny bit ajar."

By now there could be no question of why Garde was here. As Lady Elizabeth bustled out with a coy wave, Julia came to her feet with such relief and joy she could scarcely stand. Gripping the back of her chair, she watched him approach her with his long stride. Something in his expression stripped the misery from her and left her violet eyes wide and the pulse at her throat flying. It was true! She could read his purpose in his face. Dear heavens, she did not know what had brought this about when all had seemed so lost, but her happiness unfolded in a glow of warmth.

"My dear."

She blinked and came down to earth enough to realize he had taken her hands. And why was he looking so serious? Was this not a proposal of marriage after all? She gasped and could not get her breath. Surely she had not misread the situation yet again! "My lord?" she faltered.

He pulled her from behind the chair and drew her near him. "How lovely you are," he murmured, his voice a rasp of huskiness. "So tiny, so enchanting." His arms went around her, and her heart thudded until she thought he must surely hear it. How magnificent he was! His very presence overpowered her senses.

He kissed her throat and chin with a tenderness that already seemed to own her. "I must have you"—he kissed her lips, her shut eyes—"for my countess. Marry me, precious one. You must marry me. I cannot bear for another to claim you."

She trembled and opened enormous eyes. "My lord!" she cried aloud involuntarily. Then shyness dropped her gaze from his. "Yes," she whispered, blushing scarlet in her delight. "Yes, of course I will." She tilted up her face for another kiss, but instead he released her from his hold.

"Good," he said and went to lean his shoulders against the mantel.

Astonished by this abrupt change, Julia could only stare at him for a moment. Then, flustered, she sank down onto her chair.

"I received grim news this morning," he continued

with a frown and looked at her as though he expected a response.

She struggled to pull her wits together. Hurry, she scolded herself, fearing she looked green not to have better command of her emotions. But once stirred so fiercely, it was not easy to dampen them again. This time embarrassment reddened her cheeks. "I am sorry," she said, striving for conversation. "The war—your brother?"

It was a guess, spoken without the least thought, but Garde nodded. "Yes, I've just one now. He has been seriously wounded."

For an instant anger flared within her. How dare he spoil the grandest moment of her life with tiresome war talk! But at once she was ashamed of the thought and stamped her baser self into submission. "That is terrible," she said, breathless, but able to sound concerned now as her senses recovered. "He—will he be sent home?"

"Yes. I'm sailing my yacht round to Portsmouth to fetch him." Garde clenched one powerful fist and struck the mantel with it. "First James had to go and lose his life in these stupid European skirmishes. I thought that would stop George, but, no, it only seemed to whet his desire for soldiering. If he should cut his stick now, there shall be only my elder sister's brat—a milksop of a boy who fancies himself to be a parson someday—to stand as my heir. Good Gad, what a mull he should make of being earl." Garde's murky eyes flicked to her, and he smiled. "I have thought hard on the matter today, my sweet, and to be frank, I have never wanted to saddle myself with the restrictions and duties of married life. I always intended my brothers to carry on the title. Now I can't depend upon them. And so I—"

But Julia was on her feet, fists clenched, eyes snapping. "You give this as your reason, my lord? You wish to marry me because you must meet a duty and not because—because you hold any regard—"

"No, no!" Quickly he came to her, but she saw the smile lingering in his eyes, upon his lips, and stiffened.

"Do not touch me!" She whirled away from him and hurried to the window, unable to dare glance back at him. "I—why did you not tell me this before—before—" She choked and could not say it.

"Before I declared myself?" He laughed, openly amused now. "My dear Miss Swanton, such dry disclosures are hardly romantic. Would you have accepted my suit if I had laid it before you in such a prose-bag way? But I am honest, in my fashion. I prefer that you know my reasons from the start, that we may avoid misunderstandings in the future."

But she had not known them from the start. He had tricked her. She started to speak, then bit her lip. Was she mad, to throw him away in a fit of pique? Oh, it hurt, it hurt indeed to learn he cared so little for her. He had chosen her as one would a bolt of cloth in a linen-drapers; he had chosen her because he thought her young and innocent and easily handled. But he *had* chosen her, of all the damsels in the realm. Need she be greedy enough to want more than that? Her eyes flashed in determination. She had him; she loved him. That was enough. She could not bear to lose him now.

"I am sorry," he said. She glanced over her shoulder in dread lest he be mistaking her silence for rejection, and saw him still amused in an arrogant, *conquering* sort of way, as though he were confident she would not refuse him. Her eyes widened with indignation. "You are not one to bear frank speaking. I see a bit of wooing would have been more to your liking." He shook his large head. "But, my dear, I know what is best for us. We shall have our household, and we shall be happy. I will make you happy. There need not be sighs and excessive clinging, however." This time his glance at her was sharp. "The settlements shall be generous. I am aware your father cannot give you a dowry."

Julia swallowed hard, suffering under this speech. But her English sense rose to squash French pride. He was right. She much preferred the cards laid upon the table, as much as it might hurt. She had longed for him to turn to her, and now he had, but for his reasons and not hers. Reluctantly she hardened her heart. Very well, if this was to be a marriage of convenience, so be it. She would be his countess, his ornament, the mother of his heirs, and he would wrap her in security and luxury. For the moment he was charmed by her, but all he said implied he would never give up his vices for her sake. She need not wish for it.

Slowly she turned to him and managed a curtsy. "My lord, forgive my youth," she said in a low voice, the clenched fists hidden within the folds of her skirts showing what it cost to maintain her composure. "I am deeply honored by your proposal. I shall do my best to be the kind of wife you desire."

"Sweet Julia," he said and kissed her brow. "Don't sound so determined. You are an adorable chit. We shall have a splendid time. I promise you that." Then his smile faded abruptly, and he kissed her full on the lips with such hunger it frightened her into stiffening. With a laugh he released her, then appeared to hesitate. "There is your—er—father and his consent. Will you be so good as to give me his direction?"

He was looking away from her or she was sure he would have seen the alarm that gripped her. "No!" she said, then gasped in dismay at her own vehemence.

It certainly startled him, for he sent her a peculiar look and started to speak, but she rushed on.

"I don't have his direction, you see," she said breathlessly, hoping he would think her flustered because of his bit of lovemaking, which certainly had done nothing for her composure. His very presence stirred her, sometimes more than she preferred, but she must keep her thoughts on what she was saying! "To write him is quite useless because he can't abide to take a pen in hand for even the most trivial note. We should have to wait ages and ages for his reply, provided he ever bothered to make one at all." She bit her lip and stopped, knowing she was not handling this with enough nonchalance.

The strange look on Garde's face was replaced by a smile. "A careless parent, is he not?" he murmured with a smugness that seemed to have little to do with their discussion.

But Julia was too concerned with maintaining her deception to heed him closely. "Yes, he is. Of course my aunt has full responsibility for me as long as Papa is . . . gone. And then, there is my half-brother Gaylord. Papa, poor thing, cannot be depended upon at all since no one knows whether he shall ever be able to return home." She nearly broke then, for she had hoped to tell Garde the truth concerning her father. It was becoming almost impossible not to confide in someone. But, no, she could not do so, not after he had made his proposal in that way. He would not understand.

To her relief, Garde was satisfied and lost no time in broaching the matter to Lady Elizabeth, who granted her consent in a voice incoherent with delight. "My dear, dear child," she cried, casting herself upon Julia's neck. "I thought I should never live to see you happily wed. And a countess as well! It puts me quite in alt. I wonder if the children shall be dark or Titian-colored? Such a contrast as to leave everyone in doubt, I am sure." Then before a mortified Julia could put an end to these speculations, Lady Elizabeth's vague blue eyes suddenly filled with tears. "Oh, if only your dear papa could be here."

This ground was far too dangerous. Julia gave Garde a curt look of dismissal. "I shall deal with her, my lord. Perhaps you should—"

"Yes, of course," he said. "I'm no good at dealing with watering-pots. Good-bye, my dear. Lady Elizabeth." And he took his leave without further delay.

By the time Julia had dried her aunt's tears, seen her laid down upon a day bed upstairs with a handkerchief sprinkled with lavender water to clutch, and drawn the draperies, Julia's nerves were completely frayed. Going downstairs again, she was met by Rutledge, who took the liberty of an old retainer to wish her every happiness. She thanked him as calmly as she could, then fled to shut herself away in the musty refuge of the library, where she burst into tears.

Chapter Nine

"Mademoiselle, I have learned the word for you. Watering-pot, *d'accord*?"

Startled so thoroughly she nearly choked, Julia rose up to glare at Du Vallon over the back of her leather armchair. *"You,"* she said with a blink and sniffed.

"Permettez-moi." Quickly he put down the long slim package he bore and came forward to hand her his handkerchief, a piece of the finest cambric with his initials embroidered in one corner.

She made use of it, a little surprised to discover she was pleased to see him again despite his treatment of her the evening before. Bracing herself up, for she knew she had no explanation she could give for her tears, she folded the handkerchief neatly and faced him with a bare bit of composure. "Thank you, my lord," she said, wondering if he had come to apologize. "I—I am sure I must look dreadfully splotchy and tear-ridden. You must forgive me," she went on, struggling a little for words as he continued to gaze at her with that faint frown between his brows. "I was *not* expecting visitors."

"Pauvre enfante." The gray eyes swept through her as though she had no face to hide her soul, and for one wild brief instant she knew the longing to cast all of her troubles upon his sympathy. He was too often a horrid, supercilious creature, but when he looked at her like

that it was as though he were the one person in the world who could understand her.

Slowly, with exquisite male grace, he seated himself and rested his gloved right hand upon the arm of her chair. "Mademoiselle's nose is red, but that, I think, is because she has blown it so hard. Otherwise, she is *très belle.*"

The compliment, coming so gently after Garde's shattering proposal, cheered her into attempting a smile.

"Bon," approved Du Vallon, and now he took her hand. "But tell me. You are miserable today. Why? Is it me? *Peut-être.* Or is there another quarrel with milady, your sister?"

Julia shook her head. "No, she has left town."

"O le bon Dieu!" he exclaimed and rose impatiently to his feet. "In the middle of the season? And with the husband I desired to meet? Milord Lewing is an adjutant to General—ah, bah!" He snapped his fingers violently.

Julia eyed him in puzzlement. She had seen him angry, yes, but never exasperated, especially over something as trifling as a missed introduction. "I did not know John was such an important figure in your opinion."

Du Vallon's head came up, and his eyes snapped back to her warily. "Not at all," he said, and the exasperation was veiled at once. "And now you will explain this trouble within yourself."

She frowned. "What a curious creature you are. Like a cat with its whiskers in every corner."

He shrugged. "There is a time when everyone needs a confidant." Reseating himself, he took out a Sèvres snuffbox. Once more he was inscrutable and very much at his ease, but also intent upon her and the answer he desired.

She bit her lip, pride refusing to let her give way to

her desire to do as he said. What a goose she was, wanting to tell a gentleman that the person she loved was capable of caddish behavior! Lifting her chin, she said with spirit, "I do not confide in you, sir. There is nothing to confide."

He sighed a bit wearily. "I am not a good person; my temper escapes me. Last night was an unfortunate event. It is not my place to keep you in the bounds of proper behavior. Forgive me." He eyed her in an odd manner of appeal. "Please?"

"Subjecting me to your embrace can hardly be called reminding me of the proprieties, sir!" she said with a flash of her eyes. But then she relented. "Oh, very well, of course, I shall forgive you since you have apologized so prettily. But I am not troubled, not at all," she said with force. Sudden pride lifted her. "In fact you may felicitate me. I am betrothed to the Earl of Garde."

He had been helping himself to snuff with an elegant turn of the wrist, but at her statement his hand arrested in mid-motion and he shut his box as though he would crush it. *"Mon Dieu!"* he said harshly beneath his breath. Abruptly he was upon his feet, and bowing. "Your happiness, mademoiselle. I must go; I have appointments." Picking up his package from the rosette-carved table where he had laid it, he handed it to her. "For you."

She did not take it. "Thank you, my lord, that is very kind, but the proprieties forbid my accepting any such—"

He made an impatient gesture. "It is no gift, suspicious one, but your own property."

Though puzzled by his reaction to her betrothal, she was diverted enough to take the package. Then suddenly with a spurt of excitement she guessed what it was. Tearing away the paper, she ran relieved, loving fingers over her silver-handled whip, and jumped up to press his hand. "You found it! How good of you! And

I thought it was lost forever." Delighted, she showed him the engraved crest. "See, my lord? It was *Maman*'s. She brought it with her from France when she married Papa. This and her pearls are all I have of her."

He traced the outlines of the crest with a well-shaped forefinger. "*Alors,* it is a treasure. I am honored to be able to restore it to you. It was lying beneath a tree when I rode this morning, and I knew the crest of Clembeau could only be yours."

She smiled, quite happy now, and ran to ring the bell for refreshments, which he tried to decline. "Nonsense," she said roundly, directing Rutledge to pour his lordship a glass of the best claret. "You deserve a reward."

The frown deepened in his gray eyes, but he gave in, seating himself once more and taking an appreciative sip of the wine. Finishing it, he settled back in his chair with an expression not quite a sneer, and began to polish the quizzing glass which hung round his neck by a narrow black riband. "Is the betrothal why you were weeping out your heart?"

Her chin came up in haughty denial. "You have the most *odious* notions. No, I had a—a bit of dust in my eye."

He inclined his head in a remote manner. "*Pardon,* but this grain of dust must have had the size of a pebble."

Outraged, she started to retort, then saw the absurdity of argument. "You are too astute for your own good, sir," she told him.

He nodded in agreement. "Shall I make another guess? It is because you have stolen milord from your sister that she struck your horse to make it bolt. *C'est vrai, non?"*

"Yes," she said with reluctance. "It is true. But you are wrong to say I stole Garde's attentions. She has no right to claim anyone's but her husband's!"

He smiled briefly at her indignation, leaving her in doubt of whether he considered her notions stodgy. "Milord Lewing is a little of a fool to not claim so *belle* a wife's devotion. He could make her love him. There are ways," he said rather as though discussing the best means to bone a fish.

"He is trying to win her affection," she began, but Du Vallon frowned with impatience.

"Bah! Win it? Milady must be mastered."

Affronted, Julia stood up. "I shan't have you discussing my sister as though she were a horse that needs breaking to bridle!"

He shrugged, unimpressed by her show of temper. "That is a metaphor most appropriate, mademoiselle. *Mais, tiens,* why champion her? You have anger for her, *non*?"

"Yes, but just because she has acted badly toward me does not mean I shall permit you to—"

He stopped her by rising and taking hold of her arms. "Ah," he said as though having solved some puzzle. "When we discuss Milady Lewing you are all fire, all temper. When that English cur Garde is mentioned, such misery comes into your eyes, though you think it does not show. I have found you out, mademoiselle, and now I have hope. Let us go for a drive in my new phaeton."

For a moment astonishment warred with indignation. Really, how dare he read such things in her eyes! It was not true, not at all. He was saying that to please himself. Her chin came up in decision. She would most certainly not go anywhere with him. But he had already rung the bell and, when the footman appeared, ignored her dagger glare as he requested mademoiselle's bonnet be brought to her at once. Responsive to Du Vallon's authority, the fellow was gone before Julia could countermand the order.

Frustrated, she stamped her foot. "Your impudence

knows no bounds! I have no wish to go driving with you."

"So you may cry the rest of the afternoon because you are so happy?" he asked unkindly. "Bah! I am breaking an appointment of the most importance to take you out." He accepted her hat and gloves from the returned lackey and thrust them into her hands. "Please have the courtesy to accept my kindness."

And after that there was really little choice but to go to the mirror and don her bonnet, which had been refurbished with a new ribbon and would—she very much hoped—look new. By the time she was ready, his equipage stood at the front steps, and she was delighted, in spite of her annoyance with his highhanded tactics, to see it was a phaeton with a very dashing perch, and drawn by a handsome team of matched blacks.

He must have noticed her eagerness as he helped her up, for when he joined her on the box and gave the nod for the boy to stand away from the wheeler's head, he smiled at her and said, "Mademoiselle approves?"

"Of a perch phaeton-and-four? Certainly!" she said, all admiration for the way in which he held the spirited horses well up to their bits at a clipping, yet superbly controlled speed. "You're quite a top-sawyer, my lord," she added, honest enough not to quibble over giving merit its due.

"I have learned the meaning of that expression from milord Alvanley." He seemed genuinely pleased by the compliment, although being French, he could not admit it. "Is this not better than a house all stuffy and dark?"

It was indeed. Never one for preferring to languish indoors despite the freckled nose she invariably gained, Julia could already find her oppressed spirits opening up. He was right—insufferably so, of course—but quite right. It was better to put up one's chin and face the world than to sit moaning and wailing in a dismal corner. She was ashamed of herself for acting like such a wet goose.

"Good horses and sunshine always put me in high grig, sir," she admitted at last, beginning to thaw ever so slightly toward him. She could like him if only he were not always doing something to set off her temper. "Thank you for—"

"*Non.* Do not be polite. Tell me of yourself. Of your papa," he commanded, tipping his hat to the occupants of an antiquated town barouche. "Sometimes it does good to talk. I am a lonely man, mademoiselle. I wish you would talk."

Startled by the appeal, she found herself relaxing, unable to be stubborn and angry any longer. Indeed, it was something of a relief to be with him, for since he knew the truth about her father she was not obliged to hold up her pretenses before him.

In a low voice she began: "You have undoubtedly heard my father was a scrambling, ramshackle fellow without a feather to fly with. It's true, just as it's true he was obliged to flee the country because of debt. He promised me I should sample the delights of Paris, and since it sounded so exciting, I made the crossing with him. We never got farther than Calais." Her voice faltered, then hardened as she braced herself within to deal with the hurts and disappointments time had not yet been able to totally dispel. "I daresay we could not afford to go on. Then Papa made some acquaintance—he was always good at that—and began gambling with them. His vice," she said, unable to really hate him for it, yet resentful too.

She sighed, realizing she was saying too much, and hurried on. "We had a fortune when I was small. I suppose it was *Maman*'s dowry. But he went through that just as he went through the money he inherited. He could never resist a game of hazard, even when in the basket."

"How did he die, mademoiselle?" Du Vallon's voice was soft, almost gentle. "A fever? Calais has too many dirty streets—"

"No, no!" She shook her head. "I almost wish it had been. I wish—" She looked up at him in agitation, but his gaze was calm and somehow steadying. She bit her lip and gazed out over the horses' backs. "He dueled with someone at the gaming hell. The men who brought him back to the inn were kind, but since I don't speak French well I never could clearly understand all that happened—only that it happened before anyone could stop it. Papa caught his opponent cheating and lost his temper. I know he always carried a firing piece upon his person because he did not like the Calais streets at night. He drew it and accused the man, who wasn't a gentleman but some sort of scruffy captain-sharp. And the fellow had a pistol too, and he rose up and fired it without warning, and—and then claimed self-defense." Her voice rose despite all efforts to maintain her composure, and she stopped to swallow back tears. "It wasn't really a duel. I—there was no hope of recourse. No one knew the villain; they thought he was not French. He helped them put Papa into a carriage and then vanished."

Du Vallon quietly put his whip in its bracket and placed his gloved right hand over her clenched fists. She threw him a wild, shattered glance. "This is not what you asked to hear, my lord."

"It is a sorrow which should be talked away, *au fond*," he answered, his eyes shuttered and watchful. "But please go on."

"You know I am quite penniless, but I need not tell you the means by which I have contrived to gain myself this season." She frowned, pulled in two directions again, as she had been since starting on this entire mad escapade. "If it were known Papa is dead, his creditors would descend like a ravenous horde. I should be confined in strict mourning, unable to go out or meet anyone." Now she sent him a fierce, defiant glance. "Do you understand? To survive, I *must* marry."

"Yes, I understand." He frowned, delicately. "Now that you are betrothed will you admit the death of Sir Geoffrey?"

"No! Never until my vows are said," Her violet eyes flashed with spirit. "I dare not take the risk of some obstacle arising until I am *safe*."

"Safe?" His thin lips turned down in marked disapproval. "*Sang de Dieu!* Marriage is not meant to be a haven, but—" Quite abruptly, he halted himself before her astonished gaze and looked very severe, as though castigating himself against delivering such opinions. "*Pardon*," he said stiffly after a pause. "For females unmarried, life is—" His shrug finished his sentence eloquently. "And your sister, she will not help you? Or you will not permit her?"

"Yes, she would take me into her home," said Julia, frowning, "but—oh, what does it matter now? I have got what I want. I am betrothed. Soon I shall be married. And then I shall pretend to hear word of Papa's death. He will be mourned properly. I only mean to delay it a little. He would not mind, I know he would not! What harm can I do?"

Du Vallon was silent a long moment, and when at last he spoke his voice was very low. "I am not a hypocrite, so I cannot speak to you of what is honest. But your sister and your brother, do they not have the right to say how their father is—"

Defiant, Julia raised her chin. "I have no choice but to be ruthless."

"*Quel dommage*," he said dryly with a shrug. "But you, Mademoiselle Swanton, have a conscience as well. *Ainsi*, you weep."

"I suppose that's so," she said, stricken by this bald assessment of her besetting weakness. "Oh, if you only knew the number of times I nearly fail with doubts and tiresome attacks of principle." Tears of self-pity stung at her eyes, but she forced them back lest Du Vallon see them. Then with a start of disappointment she realized they had completed their circle and were already upon Clarges Street. She found herself dreading to pass back through the portals of Swanton House, for then she would be on her own resources again with no one as astonishingly sympathetic as Du Vallon to hear her problems. In any case, she knew she should never have spoken at all, but now that she had, she did indeed feel restored and was grateful for his persistence as well as the trouble he had taken on her behalf. "Lord du Vallon," she began, wanting to thank him properly, but he reined the horses to a halt and put up a hand to silence her.

"Have you fear of Garde? Why did you weep over this betrothal you want so much?"

At once she stiffened, the warm words withering on her lips. "I am glad of your kindnesses today, my lord, but some questions are too personal."

"Bah!" He gave an impatient shake of his head. "Are you afraid to admit you love the man?"

"No, of course not!" she said, hot with indignation. How dare Du Vallon ask her such a question! "Would I accept his proposal if I did not love him? Lord Garde is a man of great personal courage. He has charm to his manner. I am pleased to become his wife, and I intend to be all that he wants."

"Bah!" Something flashed in the gray depths of Du Vallon's eyes. "Does he not like you as you are? Must you change to suit him? Then you do not please him now, and you shall not please him ever." Flushed, she started to interrupt, but he grasped her hand in his free one and clenched it hard. "*Ma pauvre, ma pauvre,*" he said in appeal. "You do not see. You do not understand. I beg you not to sacrifice yourself until you do."

She shook her head. "No, I—"

But he frowned to silence her. "Does he know I kissed you?"

Her indignation faded, and she blushed, hanging her head at the reminder of that dangerous moment. "Yes, he guessed it."

His horses grew restive and stamped with a jingling of the harness, but he ignored them. "And is he á fire of jealousy? Did he claim you lest I should, *peut-être*?"

"Not at all!" Her eyes flew up in startlement. "Of course he does not like you, but—no, he had no such reason." Suddenly as she met the austere, yet steady gaze of the marquis, she knew she could not champion Garde further.

"I—he told me he must begin to think of setting up his nursery." Her pride stopped her a moment but the words burst out: "I am to be a bride of convenience! It is so humiliating."

"*Peste.*" Du Vallon's thin, dark brows drew together. "He said this, and yet you agreed? Mademoiselle!"

Her violet eyes were wide in an effort to hold back involuntary tears of frustration, but her head lifted. She knew she owed the marquis honesty. "Fiddlesticks!" she said as much to brace herself as him. "I wish to wed him and I will not let silly pride stand in my way."

He made no answer, but instead chirruped to his team and drove her the last remaining feet to her door. There was no choice except to climb down, but she hesitated upon the front steps, one slender hand gripping the wrought-iron paling. In some indefinable way she no longer saw him as she had. He seemed less remote and more human, not because he had cast off his austerity but because he had stood by her in some way which Garde had failed to do. She realized that just because Du Vallon was not always pleasant did not mean she must go on disliking him. After all, she loved Garde and *he* was not a model of perfect behavior.

Julia drew in a deep breath, conscious of Rutledge holding open the door but not permitting it to distract her. "Lord du Vallon," she said, looking up at him rather wistfully. "I— please do not think me forward or insincere, but I see I have judged you wrongly in the past. Could we—might we be friends?"

As she spoke a glow spread within her. She was right to make this step. Surely they could like one another. He could be kind when he wished, and he was someone to talk to freely, and she need not go on being so critical of him.

But he frowned, and his thin lip curled into an unmistakable sneer. *"Friends?"* he repeated with hauteur. "*Mon Dieu*, but you are a child!"

Never in her life had she felt so humiliated. After being so kind this afternoon how could he sneer at her? He had gone to such trouble to restore her whip to her, he had neglected his own business to play her confidant, and yet when she tried to repay his kindness in turn he flung it back in her face! The man was impossible, completely impossible.

With a crack of his whip he was gone, leaving her flushed and chagrined beneath the gazes of Rutledge and a man in a frieze coat lounging across the street. The latter gave her a coarse wink, and with a gasp she whirled and fled into the house.

Chapter Ten

But she had other things as well to drive her to distraction. The following afternoon, as she and Lady Elizabeth set out to Gunter's for an indulgence in fruited ices—partly because a newly landed cargo of the purest Greenland ice was making such a treat available for the first time in a fortnight, and partly because of a desire to show herself after the formal announcement of her betrothal to the sixth Earl of Garde in the morning's *Gazette*—she observed the man in the frieze coat lingering across the street again. Worse, he had the actual impertinence to lift his shabby headgear and grin when he saw her eye upon him.

Flushing with vexation, she gave a sharp order for the coachman to drive on, and continued to seethe over the severe indignity of enduring such harassment. The knave could only be one of Mr. Duffy's detestable spies, and despite the knowledge that he was doomed to failure, she found it insufferable to be forever stared at, with all her movements noted, by that vulgar fellow. Worse, she hardly knew what she could do to rid herself of this surveillance; she had sufficient pride not to go with her complaint to Mr. Duffy. He would be sure to be odiously condescending and not the least bit compliant to her wishes, and she just simply could not suffer his presence again.

Knowing she was helpless in this matter did nothing to bring her high color down during their promenade through the rooms at the confectioner's, but she hoped her lack of composure would be put down as the natural confusion of a bride. It was very crowded, with any number of her acquaintance waylaying her with warm wishes and greetings. Finally, in the midst of such a convivial atmosphere, her anger began to play itself out and it grew less difficult to smile with interest in the conversations around her. But just when she began to take pleasure in this outing, another small incident occurred to mar the day's success.

Beau Brummell, lounging in the midst of the small group gathered round her and Lady Elizabeth's table, gave her one of his ironic glances when called upon to present his well-wishes. "Garde, is it?" he said in the dry fashion which had withered many seeking his approval. "I daresay it was the color of his hair which clinched the matter." And she was left to smile in unconcern while gritting her teeth at his unexpected malice. Repressing the desire to hurl what was left of her ice at his retreating back, she made a very pretty little shrug *à la français* to quiet the cries of dismay around her. "What a pity," she said, "that the dandies must needs be so jealous of the Corinthians."

This sally was hailed with laughter and acclamation, received everywhere as a very neat setdown to the Beau, quite daring of course, but at least it helped prevent society from following his lead in sneering at her choice of a *parti.* But Julia was too annoyed to be pleased at her own adeptness of wit. Tomorrow she would in all likelihood be hailed as the goddess ideal of the Corinthian bloods, but she cared not a snap for that. She and Brummell had always got on very well with one another. Now she was hard put not to consider this piece of unkindness an active betrayal. Of course everyone knew her father could give her no dowry, but she did not see why she must be looked at with condescension for accepting Garde's suit. Any girl with the least sense would have done so, and besides, Julia was sure even the haughty Brummell would have pursued a marriage with an heiress had he not possessed sufficient funds to enable him to remain independent. The man ought to understand that some people could not afford to snap their fingers at a marriage which was vital.

Arriving home again, she was faced by the diffident announcement of her abigail that another household had promised a higher wage. Since Julia would not—indeed, could not—raise the girl's wage herself, Lucy was resolved to go and better herself, as she put it. That meant she must be paid now instead of at the end of the quarter when Julia had planned to be married and in funds. But there was no help for it—especially since cajoling the wench seemed only to make her more determined to go—and Julia reluctantly dipped into the ever-dwindling supply of money kept locked in the library strongbox. By the time she arrived at Lady Sefton's soiree in a simple muslin gown the downstairs maid had pressed, with her jet hair in a mere cap of ringlets she could arrange herself instead of the mulberry silk and dashing coiffure *à la Charybdis* she had intended, she was far from in a compliant humor when Garde suggested a promenade upon the terrace.

But she went. He looked so handsome and worldly in his dark blue coat, broidered waistcoat, and pale satin breeches, she was comforted, especially as his presence reminded her she could soon be a heedless, carefree creature as in the old days when Sir Geoffrey had not been so encumbered with debt and she had run as wild as a hoyden at Swantoncourt.

"I must say, I never thought to see such a slip of a girl best Brummell in a bandying exchange," said Garde with loud approval. "The popinjay shall think again before he crosses wits with you. Fredericks told me all about it. A capital remark, my dear."

She lifted her prettily *gamine* face, not altogether pleased with the subject he had chosen. "I expect we shall be enemies from this day on," she said with some tartness, "for Mr. Brummell cannot bear cuts at his expense. I can only regret this falling out with him."

"But it was not his place to be denouncing you, my dear," said Garde with too much complacency for her taste. "It's high time he had his comedown."

Julia made no reply. Tonight she was not particularly eager for Garde's company, although he apparently meant to show the world how pleased he was with her, and she could think of nothing she desired to say to him. He was loud tonight as always and, as she soon discovered, a trifle on the go. Weary of the terrace and the company, she sighed and wished he would not hold her arm so closely entwined with his or speak so closely to her ear. Already his pride in possessing her was making itself keenly felt, chaffing at her fierce spirit of independence until she could take little pleasure in her coup at having brought him up to scratch.

Then all at once the fragrance of the late roses spilling over the low terrace wall was pleasing again; the starry sky became a wonder as it grew from dusky purple to black. She had thought of something which would give Garde pleasure in performing for her.

After all, had he not once offered to come to her aid should Du Vallon grow offensive? Why then, would he not perform the same office in ridding her of a true pest—that horrid spy of Mr. Duffy's? Of course he would, she knew, glancing up at his rugged profile from beneath her lashes. He would enjoy a helpless appeal from her. Naturally she dared not speak to him of Mr. Duffy, lest he decide to confront that piece of vulgarity in person and thus learn more than he should. She detested the necessity of yet another little deception, but her apparent lack of a proper reason for wanting rid of the surveillance would, her womanly instincts believed, appeal to Garde more than anything else. And what pleasure it would be to get rid of that moneylender's henchman! He would learn she was not lightly to be dealt with.

Hesitating a moment to summon her resources, she sent his lordship an uncertain little smile. "I fear I am snappish and but poor company tonight, my lord."

"Not at all." He was all politeness in his usual careless way, and it infuriated her to see him coarse enough to ogle a pretty damsel standing nearby as he spoke. "But I confess, my dear, I have been wondering at your abstraction."

"Oh, dear," she said in soft distress, irritated sufficiently by his poor manners to perhaps overplay her part a bit. Did he think her such a ninnyhammer she could not see the dallying he was trying to effect with that silly Kitty Wrexham? Julia paused to send a fulminating glance the chit's way and was pleased to see her too shy to be more than confused. But at the same time Julia knew alarm. Garde had a decided preference for pursuing green girls and inexperienced matrons, who too often could be coaxed into little acts of imprudence. And his volatility was an established fact. She could still lose him!

Julia put her hand quite firmly on Garde's arm to reattract his attention. And when he glanced blandly at her—confound him!—she was all melting appeal and trustfulness. She looked down with a show of demureness she was far from feeling, and let her fingers tighten on his muscular arm. "My lord, I fear I have let my distress make me a displeasing companion. Forgive me!"

"Distress?" He was listening now, and his instant clasp of her hand was reassuring.

With a nod, she said, "I hesitate to trouble you with

so slight a matter, but indeed it has quite cut up my peace."

His fingers tightencd, almost crushing her hand, and there was suddenly an ugly scowl on his countenance. "Some impudent puppy here has been annoying you, has he? You have but to point out the cawker, and I'll—"

"No, it is no one here." She peeped at him through her lashes. "It is the most revolting brute in a frieze coat. He stations himself across the street from my door *every* day, and every time I emerge from the house he—"

"I see." Garde's voice was quite hard, and the violence to be read in his narrowed gaze was all she could wish for. "No doubt the fellow is a scout for a band of footpads, hoping for a chance at your jewels."

Involuntarily her eyes widened and one hand stole to the necklet of pearls at her throat. Was it possible? But, no, it must be Duffy's man. Garde, however, could believe what he pleased.

"I have frightened you. I'm sorry," he said, lifting her chin and giving her a confident smile. "Tonight I shall escort you and your aunt home. And tomorrow—" His eyes narrowed again. "Tomorrow my groom—an ex-pugilist, very useful fellow—shall be waiting to trounce this interloper when he appears." Garde laughed and flicked her cheek with an arrogant finger. "Don't worry. You shall be freed from this annoyance." Plucking a few roses for her, he bowed. "I am delighted you turn already to me for these things. It will always be my desire to protect you from harm and distress."

His flirtation with Kitty Wrexham had already slipped her mind. How good and kind he was! Julia was confident his regard for her would soon grow into love. She took the blossoms and thanked him in her prettiest manner, her thick lashes drooping shyly onto her cheeks.

* * *

Garde kept his promise. In the morning when she finished her chocolate and arose at a leisurely hour, the watcher was gone. Nor did he or a replacement appear throughout a day spent rather drearily with an agent from Smythe's & Cates' Employment Service, who produced for her selection six capable girls deserving excellent pay, and one scrawny wench, country-trained and so new to London she was still awed to incoherence. In the end, Julia had no choice but to take the least desirable one, whose wages could be fixed very cheaply, and pretend she was doing so from purely philanthropic interests. Thus she gained an unskilled abigail, who was underfed, hardly more than a child, and gave every appearance of being less than bright.

But Nan, as her name proved to be, was quite intelligent and quick-witted once she overcame her terror at waiting upon so grand a London lady. Moreover, she was pathetically eager to please, already showing signs of strong devotion to Julia, and willing to learn all that was taught her. She was distressingly greedy about food, but Julia gave orders to the cook to be lenient in this regard until the girl should show signs of filling out a bit.

On the whole, after initial disappointment, Julia was rather pleased with her bargain acquisition of Nan's services and set out with her in tow early Sunday morning for chapel. It was a fine morning for walking, and the absence of any spy of Mr. Duffy's put extra jauntiness into her step. Then she saw Du Vallon strolling along the *trottoir* toward her. For a moment she faltered, glad to see him, but not certain she wanted to deal with this difficult gentleman today when one's attention should be focused on higher things than cap-pulling. But at once she was ashamed of this unfair attitude and juggled her prayer book and reticule to free a hand to extend to him.

Removing his hat, he bowed in his particularly elegant fashion. "How pleasant to see you this morning." Then his fine eyes fell on her book and seemed to light up. "You are going to chapel *aussi*? Bon! May I have the honor to escort you?"

She knew it was the most errant stupidity to stand and stare at him like a gapeseed—besides being rude—but she could not help herself. Then impatience clawed through her astonishment. Surely his gallantry was carrying itself too far. "But you are French!" she protested, hardly caring if she was tactless. Really, this was all quite absurd. "My dear man, *Maman* changed her religion to marry my father, but you need not do so merely to seize the chance of carrying my prayer book for me."

A flicker of something flashed through his eyes before the shutter of aloofness banged shut in his face. For a moment he stood glaring at her in icy disdain. She thought he was going to turn on his heel and leave her as he had before, but he did not.

Rather grimly, he said, "Perhaps mademoiselle chooses to forget her history. There have been Protestants of good birth in France for several centuries. But since you prefer to walk alone, I shall not intrude again into your privacy. *Mille pardons*."

And that was when she first realized, with a shock, that this man had his spots of vulnerability just like any other person. He could be hurt, for all his sangfroid and hauteur, and she and her stupid remarks had been far too cutting. Ashamed, she put her hand quickly on his arm before he could completely turn away.

"Please, my lord," she said in appeal, her small face troubled. "I was most unkind, and do sincerely apologize." The cold look of rejection still on his face made her hesitate and bite her lip. "It was a stupid, base remark, quite unworthy of being uttered. I don't know why I let my tongue run away with me like that. Please forgive me."

"*Eh, bien.* I shall." The tense set of his shoulders eased, and he took her hand into the crook of his arm with something approaching his usual faint smile. With ease he adjusted his stride to the pace most accommodating to her—so unlike Garde, who always led her about gasping for air like a stranded fish. "I am a little reminded of my sister Thérèse in you, mademoiselle," he said, glancing at Nan in a silent command not to follow so closely. "She is full of the most heedless chatter, always making *gaffes énormes*, but so *gaie*, so *charmante*, no one can blame her for long."

There was a particular warmth in his voice Julia had never heard before. Glancing up as he spoke, she saw his face animated and free of its usual hauteur. He obviously loved this sister dearly, and Julia was intrigued enough by this softer facet to ignore the implication that *she* was equally a silly widgeon who always fell into scrapes. "Your sister sounds like a delightful creature," she said by way of encouragement and saw him smile thoughtfully.

"*Oui, elle est absolument ravissante.*" He glanced down at Julia good-humoredly, their poor start apparently forgotten. "You do not mind if I speak of her? It is so boring for you, but there is no one in London with whom to discuss her—except Baptiste."

His face darkened, alarming Julia, who at once decided she far preferred him in a happy mood. To divert his mind from the servant he hated to such a degree yet, for no discernible reason, refused to turn out, she shook her head quickly. "No, no! I am excessively diverted. Have you a miniature of her? I should love to know what she looks like."

"Ah, she is taller than you, a little." He thought a moment as though gathering the best details to mind.

"And has nineteen years. She was a *bébé* when we fled." He laughed a bit wryly. "Such lungs she had, always howling at the worst moments until I half-believed she was a revolutionist herself and set on bringing discovery to us. But now she is grown into a creature of the greatest delight. Her hair is gold—pale, *comme du soleil.* And her smile has spoiled her too much; no one can resist it! She is like the quicksilver, always here, then there, impossible to be still. The bucks of London would be killing each other for the love of how neatly her ankles are turned. Oh, she is a treasure, mademoiselle, the one light of my heart."

"I should love to meet such a paragon," said Julia, smiling. "Why didn't you bring her to London with you? Everyone should adore her! Does she stay at Paris?"

The shadow returned to his face at once, leaving Julia puzzled as to how one of her innocent questions could have offended this time.

He cleared his throat after a too lengthy pause, and replied with a great deal of constraint, "Yes, she is in Paris—at the Tuilleries."

Julia's eyes widened. "But that's—"

"Yes, and yes." The coldness was back, but this time Julia knew it was not directed against her. He ran a nervous hand over his brow, brushing the short scar. "She serves as one of the ladies-in-waiting to Madame l'Imperatrice. At first to Joséphine; now to this Austrian."

"A position of some honor," said Julia with care, realizing they had ventured onto treacherous ground.

His brows lifted in scorn. "It has been called so. I give thanks she may soon escape. Her husband—your cousin De Clembeau—has sent me word of a plan." He sighed and seemed to hesitate. "It is not fair Thérèse should be imprisoned because of me! Will you pray for her release, mademoiselle?"

By this time they had reached the chapel and Julia had just time to answer that she would before he left her to take her customary pew with an open-mouthed Nan, who was undoubtedly unused to so finely carved an altar. He seated himself closer to the back, where the worshippers of less regular habit and punctuality were wont to duck in late. Impatient of the separation, for it left her with a hundred unanswered questions, Julie settled herself to attend the sermon. But try as she might to concentrate, the words of Saint Paul were constantly ousted by an image of fine gray eyes, very clear, but far more haunted and bitter than any ought to be. What drove the man? What did he mean about his sister's imprisonment? She remembered he had made mention of it before but she could not recall what he had said. Why should this Thérèse be in prison? A mere girl could surely be no harm to Bonaparte's government, and yet for some reason she was suspect. Or Du Vallon was. A pang of sympathy touched Julia. Little wonder he was cross so often! He must be mad with worry. But why did he leave his brother-in-law to rescue his sister? Why was he here in England and so very far from her? Julia frowned, determined to question him more closely.

It seemed Du Vallon's concentration had been totally unimpaired, for during their stroll back to Clarges Street he discussed various points with her, showing a nicety in his tone of mind and an ability to quote properly various Biblical verses, which could only increase her estimation of him. In such an area, she valued sincerity above all things, and it was a refreshing change to talk with a gentleman who had not found the sermon too long, the singing too shrill, or the style of his neighbor's hair too exceptional.

But of course she had lost none of her curiosity, and

as soon as the conversation permitted a natural change in the topic, she brought it back to Du Vallon's sister.

"Indeed, sir," she said, laying one hand upon his arm. "I confess I would like to understand better what you mean when you say your sister is held at the French palace against her will."

He shrugged. "Mademoiselle is too kind, but I do not need a confidante."

"Nonsense!" she said tartly, refusing to be put off. "You are always encouraging me to lay bare my soul. I do not see why you should not do the same upon occasion." Then she softened. "Come, sir, I can see you are unhappy. Is there nothing anyone could do to help?"

"*Non,* no one." He sighed, his dark lashes dropping to veil his gaze. He was pale. "Thank you. All that can be done is being attempted. Next week I shall know if Rupert is successful. He has tried twice before and failed. This time we are sure there is hope for success." Du Vallon looked up, and a fierce light shone in his face. "And then, *parbleu*, there will be no more of this degradation intolerable! They will have no more ways to force my obedience."

"I hope she does escape," said Julia, troubled as she tried to figure out the full meaning of his words. Something hinted itself, but she could not grasp it. "But again, why is she in this situation at all? Surely she has done nothing wrong."

He looked bleak. "No, but she is my sister. That is enough. *Peste!* To think of the years I struggled to raise her, to keep her safe, and me a child barely able to survive myself. The Terror was a hard thing, but we lived, and we escaped. And now when life should be safe at last . . ." He drew in a long breath through his teeth. "But as long as I stay in England they will not harm her. And now, mademoiselle, you know my secret. Of all the acquaintance here, you alone can I count upon to keep it." They had returned to Clarges

Street, and this time as he left her at the steps and handed her prayer book to Nan, it was he who made the appeal. "Please, I am often unkind to you and selfish. I beg pardon. Pray for the safety of Thérèse. She is your cousin by marriage. A plea from you may avail in heaven." He bowed. "*Au revoir*, mademoiselle. Till next week."

"Yes, of course I shall. Indeed, I—" But he was already gone, nervous quick strides taking him up the street. He turned the corner and vanished, leaving her disappointed that they must part so soon and upon such a sad note. But how agreeable the outing had been, and so different from their usual times together. They had not wrangled once—except for that bad moment at the very first—nor found criticism in one another, and it was as though no few hours had ever been spent more pleasantly. It began to seem as though she had known him forever, and that was rather delightful. She smiled to herself as she went inside, wishing he would have stayed to luncheon, wishing he were not so distraught over his sister's well-being, but happy all the same. Of course she would be seeing him again, perhaps tomorrow, or in a few days, and already she could hardly wait to experience this contentment in his company again.

Then her gaze fell idly on her left third finger, and the heavy cluster of diamonds there made her stiffen. Garde's diamonds. And she had not spared the man a thought all day. Stricken, she ran to the mirror surmounting the mantel to stare at herself. It had been singularly foolish of her to have spent this time today enjoying the company of a gentleman who was not her affianced. A blush of shame crept into her cheeks and made her squirm a little. If she meant to make a success of her union with the earl—which, for the sake of her future happiness, she must—then she could never dare be quite so careless again.

But even as she made the proper resolution, rebellion

flared within her, sharp and bristly. She had a right to certain friends, didn't she? And besides, if Du Vallon's sister was married to her cousin, that made them almost related. Here her thoughts paused guiltily. No, of course she could claim no such thing. Her mind was quite correct to dampen her feelings. She owed Garde her fidelity at every point. Still, it was impossible not to look forward to seeing the marquis. And no number of resolutions could alter that.

Chapter Eleven

Although her conscience might render her discomfited, she continued to sweep it aside and waited in a fever of impatience to hear from Du Vallon concerning the Comtesse de Clembeau's escape. When the last post arrived on Monday, bringing the usual spate of gilt-edged invitations and letters from various acquaintance, Julia thought she must die of anticipation. Surely by now Du Vallon would have *some* word. Catching her lip between her teeth, she thrust all the invitations at Lady Elizabeth and searched through the letters.

"Gracious, child, how eager you are today," remarked Lady Elizabeth. "I'd heard Kitty Wrexham has come down with the measles and been carted off to Bath. So disappointing for the poor thing, especially since her mother's hopes are quite pinned on bringing an eligible gentleman up to scratch, though I think she is casting her garter at the moon with her hopes to find a peer. Kitty's dowry is said to be paltry, and I can't think why her brother doesn't do *something* to ease her way. Do you expect a letter from her so soon? Oh, dear, measles are so very *dull* a malady."

Julia plumped the bundle of letters down in her lap. "It isn't here," she cried aloud, so steeped in disappointment she heard nothing her aunt had said. Then with a sigh and a little vexation against the marquis for having so many other appointments her own commission had quite slipped his mind, she held out a rather plump packet. "Lewing has franked this, so I daresay it is from Sophie."

"Sophie! Why didn't you say so at once?" Going pink with such delight her chins were set quivering, Lady Elizabeth pushed all the invitations back to Julia and held out her pudgy, beringed hands for the letter.

Julia cared little about hearing her sister's news. It was certain to be a string of complaints against the rustic life. Besides, that dreadful incident in the park still rankled in Julia's breast like a live coal, requiring only the merest reminder to fan it into a blaze. It would be a long time before she could forgive Sophie for all but seeing her killed—a very long time, if ever.

In some dissatisfaction Julia began picking through the invitations, bored with the old round of amusements. Most of them would be refused; her calendar of obligations was already filled to overflowing. Then she spied one addressed in a spidery, elegant hand unknown to her and opened it with interest merely because it hinted at something different. It was so short the signature *Vallon* seemed to spring at her. Excitement bounced up, knocking her breath away. It took a moment to regain control of herself, then she read swiftly.

It said nothing about his sister. For an instant she was let down, then she reread it and was diverted enough to chuckle wryly. "Look, Aunt," she said with no compunction against interrupting Lady Elizabeth's avid perusal of several heavily crossed sheets. "Lord du Vallon has invited us to a little gallery party Thursday afternoon." She chuckled again. "Gallery party! How quaintly he phrases things."

Lady Elizabeth allowed herself a frown, looking as stern as an adorable bunny. "Dearest, should you criticize the poor man? He is very well-received these days.

The Regent has asked him to play cards at Carlton House; such an honor, don't you think? I am sure whatever sort of entertainment he is planning in his gallery will be perfectly splendid."

"Yes, Aunt," said Julia. She hadn't been speaking critically at all, but it mattered little if Lady Elizabeth had misunderstood. "He explains he has recently hung several paintings. I should love to go. May we cry off from that tedious Venetian breakfast the Lambs are giving?"

Lady Elizabeth expressed herself willing to go, and at the proper time Thursday they arrived at Du Vallon's spacious town residence, which he had rented from an elderly peer who no longer cared to endure the fashionable bustle of Chesterfield Street. Julia was pleased when the marquis singled her out to escort her round his modest gallery, leaving a vexed-looking Garde to give his arm to Lady Elizabeth. There were perhaps ten or eleven other guests, including the minister of foreign affairs and the regent's secretary, a repulsive little man often referred to by the less patient as one of Prinny's fawning bootlickers. It was said the regent had wanted very much to come since he adored art, and had actually thrown a fit of temper because a prior engagement could not be broken, going so far as to hurl his boot at his valet and offending that august person very much.

The company ranged itself agreeably round Du Vallon as he pointed out each painting with much charm and elegance of manner. There was a delightful collection of Watteau's renditions of the formerly idyllic French countryside, as well as a Rubens which set the regent's man scribbling madly in a notebook. Everyone exclaimed over the English landscape especially commissioned by the marquis for his own pleasure, which was so new the paint was not yet satisfactorily dried. But Julia was most taken with the exquisite family portrait, painted—according to Du Vallon—when he was nine, to celebrate the birth of his sister Thérèse.

"Behold," he said, and she thought she heard a hint of pride beneath his formal tones. "Here is *mon père*, Duc de la Cuillé. *Maman, la duchesse.* And *le bébé.*" He paused, then flashed a humorous glance round. "Myself—I leave you to discern from the dog."

Everyone laughed at this sally, which so neatly set the tone for how the marquis wished this reminder of a happier time in his past to be dealt with. Julia realized anew exactly why he was so well-received among the *ton.* He was no *émigré* bemoaning the past in a tiresome manner to people who could do nothing to bring back the old regime. Nor did he rant against that dreadful oppressor Bonaparte or appear to support him. In short, his manners were faultless, he was affluent, and he made good company in whatever circle he was in. The bitterness haunting his eyes was kept to himself. Now the guests surrounded him with compliments, the secretary going so far as to dash back down the length of the walnut-paneled gallery to take another scrutiny of the Rubens.

Julia unobtrusively slipped her hand from Du Vallon's arm and stood a little apart to study the portrait at her leisure. The artist had executed his work with a clear, decisive brush, and the likenesses had survived the onslaught of time and abuse quite well. There was a noticeable but carefully mended rent in the upper corner of the canvas. The family was grouped upon a spacious country terrace overlooking an ornamental lake where swans glided in sedate dignity. Julia was at once impressed with the imposing features of the duke, who stood behind his wife's chair with the hauteur of an eagle. His hair was dressed and powdered, and the quaintly old-fashioned clothes of maroon velvet breeches and skirted coat laced with gold upon the elaborately wide cuffs did not in any way make him look ridiculous to Julia's modern eyes. The duchess sat serenely beautiful in her chair, holding the baby, which reached up a chubby hand to grasp one of her blond, undressed curls. But it was the young marquis who held most of Julia's attention. Even in his child's costume and long chestnut curls, he stood as imposing as his father, the hauteur already forming upon the youthful features. One hand rested upon the greyhound's slim head as lightly yet as possessively as the duke's beringed fingers fondled the hilt of a gilded small-sword. Again Julia smiled, delighted to see how much Du Vallon was his father. Those arrogant features could almost put her in a flutter.

"Mademoiselle?" came Du Vallon's soft voice over her shoulder. He sounded distinctly curious. "What engrosses you so much with my *famille*?"

She laughed a bit self-consciously and turned away to cock her head at him, determined to betray no secrets. After all, one could not very well inform one's host that one had just conceived a *tendre* for one's host's father! How incredibly silly! "Why, my lord, I was struck with admiration for your bold sash."

He grimaced, then smiled with a hint of embarrassment. "Ah, *oui*, what must the *imbécile* do but paint it red. Red! I was horrified when I saw it. The sash was really dark blue, but *monsieur l'artiste* decreed red to be better for his scheme of color." Eyes alight, he affected a shudder. "*Quelle horreur!*"

"Not at all," she said, quizzing him. "Crimson is a noble color."

"Bah! Exactly what *Maman* said to console me. For years I detested it." Then he laughed and tucked her hand in his arm. "I am *enchanté* that you like my people. But come, the others are eating the refreshments away while you admire."

She cared not a jot about food. "Has there been word?" she asked, eager to see him happy, really happy, and not merely hidden behind a façade of pleasantness.

He shook his head. "Nothing. But at times news comes slowly. Come, mademoiselle, let us speak of you. Now that you are betrothed, you are safe from the creditors, *oui*? Or do they come for Milord Garde to pay?"

Flushing, she drew back from him a little. "No, I am untroubled by Papa's duns, except for—" She broke off, not thinking of what she was saying but of the fact that she ought to be with her aunt and fiancé rather than alone in this gentleman's company.

"Then you do have trouble." Du Vallon's brows drew together. "How may I help?"

"What?" She started, then shook her head. "No, no. A moneylender by the name of Duffy plagued me for a time. For some reason he was convinced Papa was in London and hiding from his creditors in a priest's hole or something equally absurd." She sighed, so weary of her deception she was tempted to give it up. "Poor Papa. I have gone through my whole life thinking I cared little more for him than he cared for me, and yet it is a constant surprise to me . . . If you only knew how much I—I miss all the exasperation he caused—" She faltered, but he smiled, and she went on. "But Lord Garde has convinced Mr. Duffy to cease setting his spies about the house." Her nostrils curled. "Filthy creatures. It is very comforting to know I have someone such as his lordship to turn to in times of need."

He agreed readily enough, but at once withdrew back into his formality, with a stern expression which daunted her. "We must return to the Blue Salon, mademoiselle, before you are missed," he said, proffering his arm. "I promise you the delicacies are superb."

But she stood where she was, eyeing him with puzzlement. "Why don't you like Garde?" she asked, deciding to employ his tactic of the devastating question.

He was more adept than she, however. "Why don't *you* like him?" he shot back.

Her face flamed scarlet beneath the flash of his gaze. How could he say such a thing? Why did he persist in seeking to destroy her happiness with Garde? She turned to go, but Du Vallon seized her wrist and held her prisoner. Heart hammering, she forced herself to look at him. Her pride would not let her struggle against his hold, but as his gray eyes swept into the violet storminess of hers she was certain he meant to kiss her.

Fear shook her as she had never been shaken before, a fear which tore at the safeguards of her soul. For if he dared touch her, she knew she was likely to lose Garde and all she had struggled to gain. She gasped, still not trying to pull away, but so terrified it seemed she must soon shatter. Why must Du Vallon do this to her? She loved Garde; she could not love another. Good heavens, she must not fall into the snare of loving them both!

"No!" she whispered and shut her eyes, but after an uneventful moment she found her wrist released and Du Vallon taking snuff. Her eyes widened. "You!" she exclaimed, but his glance silenced whatever she had been about to say.

"Mademoiselle Swanton," he said in a clipped cool voice which nevertheless did not quite conceal a roughness to his words, as though he did not completely have command of them, "do not ever think you must have a fear of me. I wish to see only your happiness."

"Then why do you provoke me so unfairly?" she burst out.

His brows lifted. "Almost, I could ask you that question. Shall we go?"

Subdued, she accompanied him as far as to the end of the gallery, where the door opened just as Du Vallon reached for it and his hated servant entered.

Du Vallon's brows swept together. "Yes?"

"*Pour vous, monseigneur.*" Baptiste bowed and extended a slim letter. Excitement quickened within Julia. Perhaps—but she put a halt to her speculations to frown at Baptiste. Why was he smiling in that unpleasant way? He looked malevolent. Suddenly she did not like him or his insolent air.

Du Vallon's hand was quite steady as he took the letter. Without glancing at it he said, "*Merci, Baptiste. Allez.*" Only a faint quiver of his nostrils gave him away.

As soon as the servant had bowed himself out with his furtive, unpleasant smile, Du Vallon threw a curt glance at Julia. "You must excuse me," he said and tore open the heavy seal.

She smiled as she watched, certain the news would be happy. No doubt he would prefer to be alone now, and she was just about to slip out when she saw an odd gray look pass over his face as though he had been struck. His eyes stopped in midline and reread it. Then abruptly he crumpled the letter and flung it on the tiny blaze which had been kindled in the grate to keep the damp of a rainy day away from the canvases. The blaze leaped, devouring the paper in two greedy gulps, but Du Vallon gripped the mantel with one tense, white-knuckled hand, his fine head down, the elegant shoulders drooping.

There was no need for him to speak. Sympathy sharp within her, Julia came up behind him and laid a hand upon his arm. "I am so sorry."

Startled, he glanced up and around, despair in his eyes being masked at once by chilly hauteur. He took up the mask too easily, she thought. He had been forced to conceal disappointment so often it had become a habit.

"It was from Monsieur—the man who sometimes permits her access to the letters I write to her." Du Vallon's voice was heavy, low. Suddenly he looked too weary to go on. "He wished to inform me that Milady Thérèse has not escaped. Her carriage was turned back at the gates of Paris. *Morbleu!*"

Her grasp tightened on his arm. "My lord—"

"*Bon.* I am well." He patted her hand; he even summoned a faint smile. But his eyes did not see her.

The door flew open with a bang, startling her so she whirled, her hand still on Du Vallon's arm. Garde glared like a rampaging bull, his bright head thrust forward, and his vast muscular shoulders hunched ominously. "So this is where you've gone off to!" he snapped at Julia, his dark murky eyes blazing at Du Vallon.

Stricken, she let her hand slide limply from Du Vallon's arm.

The marquis was still very pale, but he managed a bow. "I see I am making a neglect of my guests." He strode out without a glance at either of them.

"Damn the fellow!" Garde glared after him, then turned on Julia. "And you, ma'am! Are you dead to the proprieties? Do you have no thought for your reputation or for my pride? By God, I'll teach that frog his lesson. There shall be an end to these *tête-à-têtes*!"

"Hold up, sir!" commanded Julia with a snap that halted him. Defiant, she faced his anger without a qualm, too furious with his brutish reaction to care that she was having her first quarrel with him. "I suppose you mean to stamp off like an impudent donkey and call him out. Well, I won't have blood spilled for this! I won't! It was not my contrivance that brought Lord du Vallon to come searching for me. *You* might have done so. But, no, you preferred to neglect me and come charging in now just when his lordship has received bad news of his sister. How dare you have the poor taste to cause a scene!"

Garde reddened beneath her scorn, but he did not back down. "The fellow is an oaf and a scoundrel. I do not trust him and his careful friendships with every high-ranking member of our government, and I shan't stand for his nose in my personal business either."

Julia drew herself up, white to the lips. "He is *not* seeking to claim my interest, if that is what you are implying! You might have the decency to trust me, sir. And you might have the decency to act like a gentleman in my presence. I ask nothing more of you than that. Surely it is not so difficult."

Suddenly she realized as she faced his set, furious gaze where sharp words were taking them. Tears stung her eyes, for she feared she had lost him. He was standing aloof with his auburn head high and his lips held very tight. The admiration she was accustomed to seeing in his murky eyes was gone, as though it had never been. She made a blind, frustrated gesture. "Oh, go then and call him out. And when he has killed you and I am left to face the scandal I suppose you will be satisfied." A sob broke from her, and the fury faded from Garde's features.

"My dear, I am sorry." He drew her into his arms and kissed the top of her head. "You are right. I am not thinking of you. Besides, the knave doesn't deserve my pistol ball in his heart. I shall see us rid of him in a more effective way." Taking out his handkerchief, he dried her tears, then gave her a grimly sardonic smile. "With my resources it shan't be difficult to find a way of discrediting him. And then he shall be out of everyone's way."

Julia sighed, letting him comfort her. She had managed to curb his anger and save Du Vallon from certain death. For this moment that was all she desired, and she paid no heed to the latter part of Garde's promise.

Chapter Twelve

Then for a sennight Garde was away settling in his wounded brother at their Devonshire estate to convalesce, and Julia, caught up as she was in a head-spinning round of routs, Venetian breakfasts, and balls, had little time to think of him. The date of their wedding had been set for late June after the close of the season, and the banns were soon to be read. She saw nothing at all of Du Vallon either for several days, which surprised her, for he was used to being at the center of all the most exclusive activities. She did not see him, but she began to hear about him in the form of an ugly little rumor. It first came to her ears the afternoon Mrs. Wrexham—who had shamelessly abandoned Kitty to the dull company of measles, a deaf Tartar of an aunt, and Bath's antiquarian society—and Lady Maxwell called together for tea and dived into encouragement of Lady Elizabeth's notion about holding some sort of entertainment.

"Yes, indeed," said Mrs. Wrexham, to Julia's alarm. "But you shall have to plan something *unusual*, don't you agree, Hermione? Everyone seems to be jaded already, with the season hardly more than half gone. It's so provoking." Affecting a pout, she accepted yet another macaroon from the plate passed to her by Julia, who was trying to calculate how much of a strain an *unusual* assembly would place upon their straitened finances. Although her betrothal to a wealthy peer of the realm had extended her credit limitations, some things simply could not be charged. Besides, every new debt oppressed her as though another stone was being added to the laden basket already borne on her back.

But Mrs. Wrexham was chattering on: "I am sure card parties have palled. The regent's was a success, but then at *his* tables the play is so deep one may as well be in one of those gaming establishments." She passed along a refilled cup for Lady Maxwell, clattering the spoon. "My own this week was sadly flat. Even Lord du Vallon did not come, and he promised me he should be there!"

"Yes, but how fortunate for you, dear," said Lady Maxwell, leaning forward with a look of concern. "Have you heard the *on-dit* about him? So wicked, don't you think? And I cannot possibly invite him to Sir Victor's name-day celebration *now*, which is distressing because I am left with odd numbers." Ever inclined to droop at the least exertion, she sank back in her gold-and cream-striped chair and had recourse to her vinaigrette.

Never very astute, Lady Elizabeth began some soothing remark, but Julia knew the signs of fledgling social ostracism. She set down her cup abruptly. "I fear I haven't heard the latest piece of news," she said as pleasantly as she could manage, trying not to betray the rather cold gleam in her eye. When betrothed, one must be careful not to betray too much interest in another gentleman, especially in front of two gossip-tabbies such as these.

"My dear," gushed Mrs. Wrexham, her eyes lighting with ill-suppressed eagerness. "It is all very terrible. Lord du Vallon is a *spy* for that dreadful Bonaparte. Such an insinuating creature; he had me quite adoring his charm. But now we all know of course that he is a viper of the lowest sort." She gave an exaggerated shudder.

Julia frowned with an annoyance she could not suppress. "Fudge!" she said forthrightly. "I'm surprised anyone would listen to such a round tale. His lordship is an exemplary individual."

"Yes, but he is *French*," said Lady Maxwell in quite innocent deprecation. As though that signified anything, thought Julia bitterly, and all but blurted out a reminder of her own origins.

"I was terribly shocked," proclaimed Mrs. Wrexham, laying one hand upon her scrawny bosom. "My son is utterly cast down to find out his idol has feet of clay. He had been nourishing such hopes of seeing your dear Garde and Lord du Vallon engage in a shooting exhibition to discover which of the two nonpareils was the better shot. But of course that is now completely out of the question."

"But how distressing!" cried Lady Elizabeth, pulling her handkerchief to tatters. "I so like the young man. Is he really a spy? It's said Bonaparte prefers English children for breakfast instead of ham, and although I am inclined to believe that all a hum, one can never be *sure* in times as troubled as these. But Du Vallon? No, I cannot think it of him! Indeed, I cannot!"

Julia averted her face and longed to walk out and escape these nasty creatures. That anyone could indulge in such a worthless, malicious pastime which would only result in an ineradicable slur upon a gentleman's honor was unthinkable, and horrid besides! How she hated having to listen to such twaddle! And how she would dearly love to set the house burning about their ears, but she had no choice but to sit quietly, smothering in outrage, and trapped by the tea service which comprised her responsibility.

"It is being talked about a great deal now—ever since this morning when the regent gave him the cut direct on Bond Street," continued Mrs. Wrexham, flushed with success at having aroused such shock and dismay in her audience. "No one credited the story until then, but *well*! It must be true, mustn't it? There are spies everywhere, all terribly clever and horrid. And he has been received through every portal—"

Unable to bear another single word, Julia swept the sugar bowl to the floor. Its crash silenced the tirade, but she suspected they knew her action was deliberate. Turning scarlet beneath their gazes, she murmured, "I am so sorry," and rose to ring the bell in an effort to hide her confusion and guilt. But indeed, how could she be expected to endure any more of this denunciation?

While the footman cleaned away the mess, she stood apart, trying not to accept the horrible tale as fact. Her every feeling must say he was innocent of so nefarious an accusation, but her belief was shaken by the regent's action. Surely that easy-mannered and gracious prince would never cut an acquaintance without justifiable reason! Of course Mr. Brummell had called the regent a jealous, puffing blow-bag upon one memorable occasion when deep in his cups, but His Highness and the Beau no longer got on well, and that comment could hardly be taken as a dependable judgment of the regent's character. No, she must trust His Highness to do what was right.

Unwanted recollections began to rise like bubbles to the surface of her thoughts: Du Vallon's ease in passing through the French blockade; his unexplained desire to join the best ranks of society *at once* rather than going through the more orthodox channels; his curiosity and knowledge concerning everything which went on around him; and a dozen more incidents which could be innocent or damning, depending on the truth.

Bewildered and swept with horror, she had one clear certainty. Garde had made a threat to blacken Du Vallon's character; it could only be he who had set this suspicion about. For an instant she was blindly, furiously angry; then, nibbling at her fingertips, she grew calmer by slow degrees, and eventually determination formed crystal hard within her. She would believe nothing yet, either way. She had come to think of Du Vallon as a friend, and one did not throw over one's friends on the mere basis of a bored woman's gossip. Garde was to go riding in the park with her today. She would ask him about this and his part in it then, and if his jealousies and prejudices had caused him to spread about a lie, she would never forgive him for it.

And if it were indeed true—undeniably, inescapably true? She squirmed a bit, then made herself face what would have to be faced in such an event. She must remain grateful to Garde for his better judgment, and she would have no choice but to cut herself off from Du Vallon's friendship forever. This last seemed hardest of all to think about, for he had become her one confidant, and she did not know how she was to manage once his sympathy and support were lost to her.

When their guests were at last gone, Lady Elizabeth crumpled into tears. "I shall never like that Wrexham woman again!" she wailed. "I don't believe dear Lord du Vallon could be so infamous as she says. I'll never believe it!" She jumped up from her chair and ran to clutch Julia's cold, comfortless hands with unusual purpose to be read in her eyes. "Whatever society may say, I am on his side!" she declared, her chins joggling resolutely. "And I shall do something to prove it! We shall hold that shooting exhibition, although it will be frightfully noisy and bring on my nerves. But I do not care," she went on doggedly, dabbing at her eyes. "Everyone will be curious and come. And we will have it at Swantoncourt, on account of it being an out-of-doors activity. Now, don't give me any reasonable arguments, lamb, for I am quite determined to be obstinate." She met Julia's eyes, and Julia's protests against so daring a function died unspoken. "Now, when Lord Garde comes, you must persuade him to agree to it. I shall go upstairs and start making lists immediately."

And clutching her scrap of handkerchief with great firmness, she bustled out, leaving Julia convinced she could not face Garde just now with any sort of equanimity. The possibility of having her newly established trust and regard for the marquis destroyed overset her every sensibility, making her pace about the room in an agony of frustration over her helplessness to do anything about the whole mess. Then she drew herself up sharply, marshaling her rampaging thoughts into the strictest order. One simply could not thrash about in this futile way; it achieved nothing. Before she permitted herself to go into tragedies she must first ascertain whether this sordid tale were true. That should be found out first, and she must in no wise—if her pride were to remain intact—allow Garde to see how distraught she was over this. He must have no more cause for his unreasoning jealousy of Du Vallon, lest he do worse than set about rumors.

She was standing magnificently at the window in dull gold satin when Garde was ushered in some forty minutes later. The narrow mullioned window made an enchanting frame for her slender, petite figure, and the gown set off her raven curls and flawless coloring to perfection, but she was not thinking of how she looked. All her thoughts were revolving around that dreaded question: *Is it true*? She had to know before she could dare let herself remember how she had let Du Vallon's charm win her from her dislike of him, or how nobly he had rescued her that terrifying day in the thunderstorm. She must *know*, before she could think of anything.

Facing Garde with an unusually challenging gaze, she suffered her hand to be kissed, but swept aside the careless gallantry of his greeting. "I have no patience to ride today," she said without preamble, dispassionately thinking how well his riding attire of fawn corduroy breeches and boots with the newly fashionable white tops set off his impressive, muscular figure to advantage, then she dismissed the consideration as of no importance. She gave him a level look in response to his frown. "I wish to discuss something I won't deny has distressed me." She gestured in distaste of the whole business. "This rumor that Du Vallon is a spy. Did you set it about?"

His frown deepening, he hunched his shoulders until the muscles strained at the fabric of fine Bath coating. "Yes, but it is no rumor, my dear," he said at last, looking a bit sullen and displeased. As usual, the murky hue of his eyes hid his thoughts from her.

She took a step toward him, trying to ignore the numbness threatening to envelop her. "I know you dislike him, and I remember the threat you made." He started to speak, but she hushed him with an uplifted hand. "In recent days, I have come to consider Lord du Vallon a friend of some reliability. If I am to deny any dealings with him in the future I must be convinced he is not the gentleman of honor I thought him. I will *not* give up a friend merely because of a sordid little *on-dit*."

"I see." He sighed. "I cannot imagine why you must needs be so distraught over this, but there's no denying the fact, my dear. I've suspected the fellow for some time. And there have been others who had similar doubts of his *bona fides*. William Lamb, for one." He loosed his careless, meaningless laugh. "I shan't say there's any incontrovertible proof; he hasn't been caught redhanded at poking through a dispatch box, but he has charmed several fools into talking more freely than they should. Why people must fall all over themselves to adore a conceited coxcomb who graces himself with airs just because he is French, I will never understand. You'd think someone would remember we are at war. But, no, even York has blurted out the most—"

"Very well." It was not necessary for him to go on. She believed him. Biting her lip to hold back any sign of her distress, she turned away from Garde to stare blindly out the window. For a moment her surroundings did not seem real. It was too ordinary a setting, this room with its restrained furnishings, herself, and Garde standing firm and honest in his English nobility. They spoke of spying and intrigue, things that had no place in this room, things she knew nothing of, and yet were so dark and nefarious she shrank inside with distaste. But beneath her shock hammered grief. She had been betrayed. She had come to trust the marquis. She had permitted his charm to win her affection, and this was how she was repaid!

Worse, the things he had confided in her now made sense. No man could have come closer to confessing his dastardliness outright, but she had been blind, wrapped in her own concerns, too stupid to understand. He had even dared to play upon her sympathy for his sister!

And then all at once her thoughts halted and her anger died as she finally did understand. Of course! He had been forced into this. As a gentleman with royalist sentiments he would die before he worked for the present French government, but he would not jeopardize his sister's life. No wonder the poor man was so unhappy! Every principle had been violated for the sake of his sister's safety. He could do nothing else.

Garde stirred, and she had the urge to whirl and tell him of how Du Vallon must not be blamed. But even as she did turn, she knew she dared say no such thing.

No one would believe her, least of all Garde. Thanks to him, she must close her friendship with Du Vallon. The man was guilty and she could not deny it. His reasons would weigh with no one in a position to help him. If only Lady Thérèse had escaped!

With a sigh she managed a smile for Garde and indicated the sofa for him while she seated herself upon a narrow chair of Chippendale creation. It was time to redirect the conversation.

"You must forgive my making this next request of you, my lord," she said in a hushed, deprecating voice, hoping desperately he would understand, as Du Vallon would have understood, at once, with little explanation necessary. Already she missed the swift preciseness in the way he dissected her thoughts and emotions and told her exactly what she needed to be told.

With effort, she shook away these reflections. Du Vallon must be as an ended chapter in her life; and never mind about his exasperating tendency not to remain where her thoughts designated he should go. She sighed. "My aunt has decided she must champion Du Vallon and wishes to sponsor a shooting exhibition between him and yourself at Swantoncourt." His raised eyebrows made her blush, but she struggled on: "I know how fantastic it is for us to have a sporting event. Most improper, and indeed I do not like it because of the talk it will occasion, but when Aunt Beth sets her mind on something she can be obstinate to an unreasonable degree."

"Say no more, my dear." With an eager gleam upon his heavy features, Garde leaned forward. "Nothing would give me greater pleasure than showing up his skill—if he can shoot at all. But as you say, it would be highly irregular for you ladies to play hostess to such a thing. I will issue a public challenge to test skills with him and name Swantoncourt as the ground. A meadow will do, and then you need not be expected to offer refreshments or go to any trouble. Your aunt will still think it her affair. Now that's a splendid plan, is it not?"

It was indeed, and she told him so with genuine relief. She had not expected him to take charge so neatly, but he merely laughed when she tried to thank him.

"All I ask is your championship, my dear. With those fetching eyes for me, I shan't miss a single wafer." She blushed in confusion, and he laughed in his loud, ringing way. "Run along now and change into your habit. Exercise will do you far more good than moping about this house."

"Yes, my lord," she said meekly and hastened upstairs to obey. It was, after all, easier to get out into the fresh air even if it did mean enduring one of those exhausting long gallops Garde was so fond of. Anything was better than sitting and thinking about Du Vallon.

She was tying on a fetching hat with a short veil to protect her cheeks from the wind and dust when a tiny sob broke from her. At once, however, with the haste of desperation, she locked Du Vallon back into a tight little compartment somewhere deep within her, determined more than ever not to let him escape to trouble her again. He was not worth weeping over, not now, not ever. Let Aunt Beth champion him; Julia could not. She dared not, for she knew with a miserable rush of warmth she was no longer indifferent to him. She also realized how disastrous a partiality for him was, especially if she meant to keep her relationship with Garde intact. But strong resolutions or none, it was hard—unbearably, incredibly hard—to convince herself to be careful, and prudent, and not make matters worse than they already were. Still, as she stood there, breathless and flushed before her looking-glass, rebellion and defiance joined hands in an effort to overcome her.

If Garde thought he had increased his estimation in

her eyes, he was decidedly wrong. To put the matter in vulgar parlance, he was nothing but a common tattler, and as such, to be despised. Yes, yes, his judgment of character was excellent, but misplaced. One must simper and hold oneself obliged to the man for having rescued one from the clutches of a treacherous enemy to the nation, but one was not obliged to respect the means! Gazing at herself in sudden dislike, she spoke aloud to her reflection: "You are a fool, Julia Swanton, to be throwing your cap after a man you can no longer admire. A marriage of convenience is a high price to pay for the loss of your self-respect." With that, she slammed herself out of her chamber, keeping her feet planted firmly upon the path she had set for herself. Nevertheless, it was immeasurably difficult to prevent herself from running straight to Du Vallon with the demand that he flee the country and save himself.

For two more days, Du Vallon continued to be the name on everyone's lips, but when that elegant gentleman continued to attend the functions to which his invitations had not been hastily withdrawn and to act quite in his normal, cool fashion, rampant speculation suffered a check and was all but stifled to extinction when Mr. Brummell was heard to declare at White's, "The man has a nice eye in waistcoats; why need I trouble myself with his politics?" Society heaved a collected sigh of relief at having the acknowledged arbiter of the *ton* at last set some tone of conduct to be followed—although a few persons of perception believed this support to be caused by nothing other than the Beau's desire to continue his rivalry with the regent—and many of the hostesses who had been too quick to snub Du Vallon actually reissued invitations, which he then declined. While he continued to enjoy the treatment his rank and breeding seemed to demand, he was nevertheless viewed with considerable doubt and suspicion behind the displays of good manners. Then Garde's challenge was issued and accepted publicly, although it was noted with great interest that Du Vallon did not seem eager to take it up. Tremendous enthusiasm went into the laying of bets as the gentlemen prepared to hail this as one of the sporting events of the age, comparable to that last mill of Belcher's when he lost to Cribb.

Certain she was standing too close to the scandal surrounding Du Vallon—since she had introduced him to the *ton*—Julia was terrified of encountering the marquis. She had not the least idea of how she should speak or act toward him. She hated this craven side of herself and sought to whip up her courage time and time again without success. Certainly she could not take as much delight in Garde's escort as she once had, and too often for peace of mind she dreamed of gray eyes rather than brown ones. She also knew she should make the effort to seek out the marquis at some gathering and tell him she did not blame him. Still, how could she when his guilt remained unproven?

But it was silly to hope she might bury her head in the sand and ignore everything if only she were not obliged to encounter Du Vallon, for eventually she tripped on a loose board in the lending library while rounding a bookshelf and fell into his startled arms in the most mortifying manner conceivable, sending her own selection of books—and his—sailing in every direction. She remained rigid with embarrassment, her eyes clenched shut, her face inflamed, her heart thudding, and dared not make the slightest move out of an overwhelming dread of this confrontation, which had happened at last. Surely everyone was staring and whispering, and she longed to sink right through the floor.

"Mademoiselle Swanton?" he breathed into her ear, his placid tones somehow managing to instill some calm into her. "It is delightful to hold you, but we are crushing your bonnet, I think, and I do not want to be responsible for the ruin of another. *Voyons*, stand up, and I will get the books."

It was exactly what he *would* say in such a situation as this! Vexed right out of her paralysis, she pulled away and straightened her headgear with a jerk, glaring at him while he returned the volumes of Miss Austen's newest novel to her.

She thanked him curtly. "I suppose you think I contrived to stumble against you, you beastly man, and if you—" Suddenly it was all right. Her annoyance was passed, and the uncertainty beneath it. She began to laugh. It was all so terribly absurd.

He smiled in his faint manner, his gray eyes watching her. "*Merci*. Mademoiselle does not treat me as a leper or with politeness oppressive."

Her amusement checked. Did she hear mockery? But when he took her arm and said, "Come, you are doing errands perhaps, and I will help you," she was too pleased at being in his company again to lend much heed to doubt. How silly she had been to fear meeting him, as though the controversy raging about his head would have wrought any change in him.

"Thank you," she said. "Nan and I were going next to buy some ribbons."

"Ah." He dismissed the maid and escorted Julia outside to his perch phaeton. "I am *désolé*," he said, joining her on the box, "to not have seen you for so many days. All is well?"

"Why, yes." She bit her lip, then decided the subject might as well be broached now and finished with. "That is, with me. But you, my lord, are in a rather distressing position. I—please do not think too harshly of Lord Garde. He does not understand."

The phaeton surged forward sharply enough to make her clutch hold of the seat. Du Vallon's face was stone hard when he glanced at her and lifted one brow. "So I am to think of Garde with kindness. And what of yourself, mademoiselle? Do I remember that Garde knew no suspicion of me until I confided in you? Or do I forget it?"

So sharp and sudden was the attack she could not at first answer. What was he saying? Oh, no, how could he possibly think that of her? Her hands clenched in dismay. "No, I would never—"

"Mademoiselle, you need not have distress," he broke in coldly. "*Naturellement* I do not think you wished to betray me. But if Garde questioned you, you were bound to answer. He is to be your husband. One expects no less. But I am the fool to have spoken so much to you."

"No!" she cried, her eyes enormous at his mistake. "No, you are wrong, my lord. It was not—I have said nothing, even when I wished to clear your name."

He threw her a glance one would use to silence a child. "It need not be discussed more. Where do you buy your ribbons?"

"At the Pantheon Bazaar," she answered. "But please, you need not trouble. I wish to go home. I cannot believe you think this of me."

He shook his head. "Since I have meddled into your expedition of shopping, I will see it finished. Surely my advice on ribbons is as good as that of a *bonne*."

She sat in constrained silence, thinking it did her little good now to recall how pleased he had been to see her until she had been stupid enough to render him so angry. Or had he sought her out with the intention of accusing her? She sighed, concluding she dared not offend him further by making a fuss of protest over a mere ribbon.

"Very well, my lord," she said a bit stiffly, looking straight ahead at nothing.

"For what purpose is this ribbon?" he asked, looping his rein smartly to avoid a landau which seemed bent on coming to a halt in the middle of thronged Bond Street.

She stared down at her clenched hands, beginning to resent his arrogance in dragging her about. No doubt he was not interested in serving her at all, but was trying to use her company to affect popular opinion as he had done before. "Nan is to make me a simple gown of blue cambric for this shooting match between you and Lord Garde," she said, her violet eyes flashing slightly behind their veil of dark lashes.

"Ah." He nodded and drew to a halt before an expensive linen-draper's shop.

Annoyed further, she turned on him with heightened color flying in each cheek. "I believe my lord did not hear correctly. I asked to be driven to the Bazaar."

He shrugged dismissal of the request. "To rub shoulders with the *canaille*? I think not."

Her mouth set itself. She would not get down from the phaeton. If he desired her to enter that shop, he would be obliged to drag her by the hair on her head! "My lord," she said, "ribbon here costs five times as much. I do not wish to buy from this establishment. Let us not be arguing in the street."

"My hostess shall not appear looking like a shabby milkmaid," he retorted. With lithe grace he climbed down from the high perch and reached up his hand for her while a street urchin darted to hold the horses' heads. "I may be harmed socially, mademoiselle, but at least my finances are in order. I will buy your ribbons."

"You shall do nothing of the sort!" she snapped, quite outraged. "How dare you insult me in this fashion, sir!" Her eyes flashed. "I am not a *kept* woman, to be receiving my geegaws at your hands! No gentleman would ever dare presume—oh, I hate you!"

He gave her a cool, mocking sneer. "You sell yourself to Milord Garde, mademoiselle. What is the difference?"

Shaken to her depths, she could only gape at him for a moment, then terrible, terrible fury possessed her, raking across her wounded pride with searing, bloodied claws. He had no right to say such a thing! No right at all! She would humiliate him as he had humiliated her. Without an instant's hesitation, she seized up the reins and whip and sent the team stepping out at such a vigorous trot, the urchin barely had time to jump aside. There was a shout behind her; she did not think it was Du Vallon, but really she cared not a fig for who it was or what people were going to think at seeing her driving a difficult perch phaeton-and-four up Bond Street at such a reckless clip, her face alternately pale then crimson with anger.

She was convinced he had deliberately set out to cut her to the quick with this insult as a means to avenge the wrong he thought she had done him. She would never forgive him, and she hoped with all her being that Garde's skill with a pistol would make him look like the veriest green boaster. She hoped Garde would contrive some means to run him out of the country in the most shocking disgrace. She hoped someone with a great deal of sense would someday shoot him and thus silence him and his mockery forever.

Reaching Clarges Street, she drew up with a flourish which left Rutledge considerably startled, and threw the reins at the groom who came running out from the stables.

"This is Lord du Vallon's conveyance," she said, coolly drawing off her gloves while the boy gaped at her. "You may return it to him at once. But first see that my books are brought in."

Chin high, eyes glinting steel, she swept inside and upstairs to her room without a backward glance. Let any who had seen her driving Du Vallon's well-known phaeton be shocked if they chose. Missishness might go to the devil! She was a Swanton and she had the Swanton pride. No one who insulted her so deeply need expect anything but the swiftest retribution, and so she had dealt it.

It took many more minutes of rapid pacing about her chamber to restore her to a semblance of calm. One thing at least had been achieved by the day's encounter: she no longer felt sorry at all for that despicable Frenchman. Garde had been very right to protect her from his clutches.

Abruptly reaching a decision, she rang the bell for Nan, and when the abigail appeared, informed her that her sewing services would not be required. The gown of Egyptian gauze would be worn at Swantoncourt. Let the other ladies think what they liked; she would not honor the occasion with new attire. Her fists clenched. Garde must win! He must set the seal on that blackguard's ruin. She could not be happy or rest until it was so.

Chapter Thirteen

The hour of the match was appointed for three in the afternoon, but Julia and her aunt arose early and set out not long after nine o'clock in order to take the ten mile drive slowly enough not to arouse Lady Elizabeth's dreaded carriage sickness. With them went a small mountain of luggage, for Lady Elizabeth had decreed a repairing-lease in the country would do both of them a world of good. They were to stay at dear, musty old Swantoncourt, with its overgrown gardens and neglected ivy for two days and return to town at the first of the week.

Julia, who had gone about for the past few days in what could only be described as a simmering, foul sort of humor, found herself emerging into an increasingly sunny-tempered creature as they left the outskirts of London and began to venture more deeply into the verdant countryside. She had to admit she was childishly eager to see her beloved home again after an absence of months and found herself privately wishing, as they turned at last into the weedy drive lined with stately oaks of Cromwellian girth, that their stay could have been prolonged enough to warrant bringing her black mare along. Nothing delighted her more than a brisk gallop across the rolling meadows when the night mists were just retreating before the smile of dawn. But she promised herself, just before they pulled to a halt at the steps of fine, hand-quarried stone, that she would find time to walk out to the bottom meadow where the brook meandered so lazily. All her life she had gone to the old sleepy willow standing in gnarled solitude on the bank to hide herself behind the curtain of branches and let the brook babble her troubled thoughts into some kind of order. She needed to go there now, she realized, as the shabby but blissful peace of the estate came enfolding her from all directions. The last month and a half had proved an incredible strain; she must go out to the willow tomorrow when this dreadful sporting event would be over and everyone gone, and calm all the lingering doubts and guilts in her conscience once and for all.

Although set out so far in the country, it was to be expected that a sizable crowd would come to watch England versus France. In any other circumstance the audience would have consisted entirely of male spectators, but Julia's and Lady Elizabeth's presence encouraged the appearance of those ladies who thought their nerves could withstand the excessive noise of pistol reports. As a consequence of the feminine presence, the wagers were laid with more decorum but with no less enthusiasm, and gentlemen spluttered in attempts to explain sporting cant to their fair companions.

Julia was warmly greeted by several local landlords whose inns were full to overflowing, while the sporting bucks of Mr. Wrexham's cut gathered in fierce groups to discuss the merits of rifled barrels and precision firing caps, and constantly repositioned their equipages to obtain a better view. Tigers stood importantly at the Welsh heads of their charges, craning their necks and occasionally daring to climb atop the traces for a quick glimpse of the doings. And coachmen and footmen clustered in their respective groups here and there, laying their own bets and arguing just as fiercely as their masters over the likely outcome of it all. The local squire, very redfaced and hot in his starched cravat, and the owner of one of London's finer shooting salons were to preside over the contest. A silversmith had fashioned a cup and engraved it with the date and occasion. Rather to her embarrassment, Julia was induced to be the one who would award this prize to the winner.

She sat with the thing at her sandaled feet, a fetching picture in the soft Egyptian gauze which fluttered in the breeze. Her violet eyes were shaded by a broad-brimmed hat of willow straw, and its ribbons, tied in such a pretty bow beneath her left ear, rivaled the meadow flowers in hue. The honeysuckle overrunning the bank behind the targets triumphantly conquered Lady Elizabeth's scent of lavender and Hungary water and mingled nicely with the starched smell of Garde's cravat as he bent over Julia's shoulder to hand her a clutch of dog-violets.

He smiled carelessly as she looked up. "May I have a token from you for luck, my dear?"

It was a romantic moment, in a romantic setting—despite the noise—but Julia's heart did not melt with tenderness as it should have, as she wanted it to. Du Vallon's bitter, cutting words fell between her and Garde's face, haunting her and infuriating her as they had done since the marquis had uttered them. Selling herself, indeed; the man was mad.

Garde's eyes softened as he gazed at her, and confused by the involuntary shrinking she had to struggle to hide, she averted her eyes quickly and found her lace-trimmed handkerchief to knot around his wrist. It was such a frivolous, dainty scrap for a man so muscular and virile to be sporting. People glanced their way and whispered, smiling, but Julia was miserable.

Out of a desperate need to distract her thoughts, she glanced past Garde, who was enduring a burst of questions from a callow youth without the least bit of town bronze about him, to observe Du Vallon leaning against the trunk of a twisted elm, alone, pale, and a bit haggard in the clear light. He was frowning into the distance in abstracted thought. Near him knelt his obsequious servant Baptiste, priming one of a fine set of silver-mounted dueling pistols, the long, slim barrel flashing whenever a ray of sun streaked across it. Julia frowned at the sight. Du Vallon loked drawn into himself, miserable perhaps behind that careful façade of sangfroid; he looked as though he expected to lose, so unlike Garde, who was laughing and jesting in a radiance of confidence. But when Baptiste handed his master the firing piece for inspection, Du Vallon's lean, shapely hands and his gaze were capable and steady. Julia saw him examine the weapon with a bored, cold-blooded competence which chilled her and made her glance quickly at Garde in alarm.

Reluctantly she recalled the marquis's reputation, as notorious as Garde's, the thin dueling scar, the utter ruthlessness which could make his gray eyes so bleak. No, he would not be easily defeated, and her desire that he should be fired up anew, making her hands clench in determination. Silly of her to be thinking she did not know her own mind—of course she did!

She pressed Garde's hand, startling him out of the comment he was making to that dreadful boy. When he glanced at her, she smiled, tilting up her face so the sunlight could dance in golden skips over her cheekbones and firm little chin. "I insist that you win," she said with an intensity heightened by her anger with Du Vallon. Anyone who had dared say such horrid things to her deserved a trouncing.

Garde's eyes widened, gold flecks showing today in their murky brown depths. Above her, his auburn hair was a blaze of copper highlights, and his vast shoulders blocked away the sun. "Do you care so much, my dear?" he asked as though a bit surprised.

She nodded emphatically, trying to ignore the feeling that she was casting herself over a precipice. "Yes! Yes, I do. Win for me!"

He caught his breath audibly and with a swift movement, kissed her hand. "Then I shall do my utmost to please you."

Suddenly her handkerchief fluttering from his wrist did not seem so ridiculous. Relaxing a little, she was diverted from further comment by the sight of a small gig drawing up.

Garde laughed. "That couple has cut it pretty fine. We'll be starting with this shortly."

But Julia had stopped listening. Something about the uncertainty of the lanky, angular gentleman and the searching glances cast about by the young lady caught her curiosity and held it. She was certain she had never seen them before. Who were they?

She stood up with the intention of going to her aunt—who had wandered away to speak to Lord Holland—and asking, but before she could take more than two steps, the gig had jerked to a halt, and the young lady was stumbling out and running to Du Vallon with both hands outstretched. "Lucien!" she cried quite clearly. "Oh, Lucien, *mon cher*!"

Her own breath caught, Julia saw the marquis whirl, so pale he looked bloodless, then he and the girl were embracing, laughing, chattering madly in French as though the rest of the world—especially the gaping spectators—did not exist.

Garde cleared his throat at Julia's elbow. "Good Gad, who is that? His wife?"

Julia shook her head, certain she could see a resemblance of features beneath the girl's dowdy bonnet. "No, his sister, I should think." The absolute transformation in Du Vallon's face and manner held her astounded. His bleak air, his fatigue, his cynicism which he had held to him like a mask and domino now were ripped away; a much different creature emerged forth. Watching, Julia stood apart, gripped in the conviction that she had been left behind and forgotten. She could do nothing but stare like everyone else as the lanky gentleman, a Frenchman as well from the cut of his clothes, came up to shake hands with Du Vallon, who was still gripping his sister's shoulders and paying not the least attention to Baptiste's furtive slipping away.

Then with a stunning flash of white teeth, the marquis smiled at Julia and came towing the two strangers in her direction with an impetuous stride so vastly different from his usual step of ennui. "Mademoiselle Swanton!" he said almost jauntily as she continued to stare in amazement at him. "Please, I must present my sister, Milady Thérèse, and her husband *aussi*, Monsieur le Comte de Clembeau."

Their quarrel was forgotten as though it had never occurred. Warmth spread through Julia. "I am so glad," she said, pressing Lady Thérèse's hand. "How wonderful it is you have escaped after all." She turned to the comte with his long thin face and black hair, now ruffled in the breeze as he removed his hat. "And I must welcome you as well, my lord—"

"Rupert, you fool," said Du Vallon when De Clembeau raised his brows in puzzlement. "She is your relation! Do you not guess?"

"Swanton." The comte frowned a moment, then grinned. "Aha! This *fille ravissante* is the daughter of Tante Léonie. I am ecstatic, me, to have so *belle* a relative." He swept a bow. "*Petite cousine*, I am of a delight to meet you at last."

Julia laughed, charmed with him. "But you must tell me of your escape. I thought it had failed."

The comtesse hesitated, glancing at Du Vallon, who nodded. "She knows all. You must fear nothing here, nothing ever again. *Sang de Dieu*, when I think of that letter I received—"

"Calculated lies," said Lady Thérèse with a shrug that set off her shoulders. She was as fragile and as lovely as a rainbow, with an exquisite delicacy of feature beneath her cap of golden curls. "Written to trick you. Poor Lucien, how you have worried!" For an instant she laid a hand upon his arm, then turned back to Julia. "But of my escape? It was all Rupert, *naturellement*. He gave me money to bribe my *bonne* to pretend to be me, and I walked out in this *chapeau affreux*." Laughing infectiously, she untied the ribbons and tossed it onto the ground. "*Voyons,* Lucien! I am free, and you do not have to make spying again. *C'est merveilleux, non?*"

Garde pushed forward, looking arrogant and skeptical. "I'm afraid, my lord, we don't understand all of this." And there were various shouts of agreement from among those crowding around.

Du Vallon flushed, then his chin lifted and that haughty eagle look came into his face. "My friends, it is a thing of simplicity. Because my sister was a prisoner of the French government, I had no choice but to come here under pretenses false." He hesitated, his vulnerability at that moment very plain. "I have done wrong. I ask your pardons." Then he snapped his fingers with an exclamation. "A horse, *tout de suite*! I must go to London and beg pardon of *le roi anglais*."

"Nonsense!" snapped Garde angrily. "You shan't forfeit this contest so easily, sir. Or is your skill as a marksman just another Banbury tale?"

Julia gasped and frowned at her betrothed as shocked murmurs ran through the crowd. What a brute Garde was, to fling down an insult at such a moment. It had taken much of Du Vallon's courage to make this public explanation. At the moment no one cared about something as unimportant as a shooting match!

Lord Jersey stepped forward with a placating gesture.

"Surely, gentlemen, a postponement could be arranged."

Lady Thérèse turned pale with fright. "*Y a-t-il un combat d'honneur?*" she gasped. "Rupert, stop it!"

"No, no!" Du Vallon smiled for his sister's sake, although Julia could see his teeth were clenched with annoyance. He made a swift explanation in French, then turned coolly back to Garde. "Milord Jersey makes a suggestion excellent, but I have no intention of committing the forfeit," he said with an icy hauteur that made Garde appear more churlish than ever, and bowed. "Shall we commence?"

Garde inclined his head and turned on his heel to finish preparations, while Julia found chairs for herself and Lady Thérèse. She was glad of the diversion, for she needed time to think. Of course, all of her resentment and anger with Du Vallon was gone as if it had never existed. There was a release, a freedom to be read in him which caught at her heart. Garde's skepticism was becoming a bore, and if he chose to continue his attack on Du Vallon's veracity she would lose all patience with the man.

Why, she asked herself, fuming a little as she arranged her skirts, must he trample about in that overwhelming way of his, plunging in straight off to try to discredit Du Vallon all over again? Surely he was far too intelligent to let his passions carry him beyond the line of permissible jealousy, but the glimpse she caught of his clouded, thunderous countenance as he reprimed his pistols made her more uncertain than ever of what he might do. She wished now she had not encouraged him so much today, for she could no longer desire Du Vallon to lose.

"We hurried to London to give Lucien the surprise," whispered Lady Thérèse with a flash of dimples as she glanced at her husband standing nearby with an expression of frank interest in the proceedings upon his face. "And then, *peste*, he is gone into the country for shooting. Rupert wished to wait, but I could not sit in a salon. So, pouf, we hurried to come here and give Lucien the surprise all the same. *Quel aventure!* But this big *bête* of a man, he will not shoot better than my Lucien, oh, *non*!"

Amused by this opinion, Julia had no time to explain *who* the big beast of a man was, for just then there was a shout and the contest began.

There was a great deal of crashing noise, smoke, and the acrid smell of burnt powder. Each man would discharge the brace of pistols he held, then hand them to his servant to be reloaded while scores were recorded. Only, Du Vallon's servant seemed to have vanished without explanation, and an elated Mr. Wrexham was performing the service of priming the marquis's pistols. But Julia wasted no thought on Baptiste's absence other than her recollection of having seen him slip away. No doubt he had gone off to sample some pleasure of his own and would be soundly thrashed upon his tardy return. Indeed, she was too overwhelmed by the noise of the reports, which deafened her aching ears and gave her a frightful headache. And the smell of sulfur had her cowering behind the handkerchief she was obliged shyly to borrow from cousin Rupert. But mercifully it was all over at last, with the whole business declared a draw. That of course threw the laid bets into confusion, but the judges remained adamant that both their lordships had equal skill despite a bit of harsh badgering on the part of several partisan gentlemen who had plunged heavily on the outcome. The notable exception was Poodle Byng, who capered about with the cry of: "I knew it should be a draw! Ha, ha, Sefton, you old thing! Pay up, man. Pay up!"

Garde all but flung his weapons at his man and strode away in search of his coat, a scowl still blackening his coarsened features, then he turned about and came tramping up to Julia, who was sitting like a limp rag in her relief that it was all over at last.

He made a rather curt bow and thrust her handkerchief back at her. "It seems I have failed you, ma'am. Your property."

She frowned at this show of ungallantry and accepted her handkerchief with reluctance. "A draw is hardly a failure, my lord," she managed to say through the pounding at her temples. "I thought you did very well."

"Thank you," he said, still in no pleasant humor. "But not well enough. And now that damned fellow has gained everyone's sympathy with his tragedy-acting."

He started to turn rudely away, but Julia's hand was on his arm to detain him, despite her excessive consciousness of his poor manners at this moment. What a churl he was! "My lord, may I present my cousin, the Comte de Clembeau and his wife, Lady Thérèse?" she said politely, but letting a faint rebuke appear in her tone all the same.

Lady Thérèse inclined her head rather coldly, but Rupert flourished a grand sort of bow with his dark eyes twinkling out of ready friendliness. "So charmed, so pleased to have your acquaintance, milord."

Garde eyed him stonily. "I daresay." And without further ado he shook off Julia's grasp and strode away, leaving her gasping with indignation.

"Oh, how rude!" she cried. "Forgive me, please, both of you, for having subjected you to such indignity. He is Lord Garde, my—my betrothed, and I should quite like to box his ears for being such a poor loser!"

But Rupert disarmed her by laughing. "*Petite cousine*, it is nothing. And Thérèse is all eyes for her *bon frère*. I think she could never be angry today."

Reluctantly Julia relaxed, so charmed by this tall awkward gentleman with his beaky nose and long, humorous mouth she felt she had known him forever. Impulsively she smiled and put out her hand. "How glad I am, sir, to find at least one representative of my French relations after so many years of wondering what *Maman*'s family was like. You must stay with us here for a while."

"*Oh, mais non, non!*" cried Lady Thérèse with a wave of agitation. Tears welled up into her pretty eyes, and she clutched at her husband's sleeve for support as she faced a discomfited Julia. "Mademoiselle is so kind, *mais* Lucien is one I must be with for a—a time." She wrinkled her nose in helpless distress. "*Pardon,* I have made you offended. Rupert, *chèri*, explain for me."

"But I do understand," said Julia at once. "Of course you must also visit me in London. Please do." Her eyes moved up to meet those impish dark ones of her cousin's. How young his eyes made him appear, although he must be near Garde's age. Garde. Involuntarily she frowned. He had no need to be so top-lofty, and she would take him to task for it at the first opportunity. Or did she dare, mocked some despicable inner voice. She quelled it at once, but the damage to her resolve was already done. At once she was irritated with her own craven impulse, but she knew she must keep silent, for Garde was not one who could accept rebukes. Still, it was hard to think she must stifle her frank tongue yet again for his sake, and she was obliged to struggle with her own sense of rebellion before she could dismiss this instant of soul-searching and rouse herself back to the conversation. "Lord du Vallon knows my direction—"

"Number ten, Clarges Street," said that gentleman's soft voice as he came up from behind where Julia was standing. "But why?"

The content, quizzical look he sent her threw her into confusion, for it was as though their last quarrel had never occurred, and she was not sure what ground she stood on now. In any case, she did hope with all her might that they could be done now with those tedious battles and stand on excellent terms. But there was a hint of impatience about his eyes as if he really did not desire to linger here with them and her, and she knew a rush of disappointment.

"We are to visit her, Lucien," said Lady Thérèse, gaily slipping her arm through his. "Already invitations to call. Is that not *merveilleux*? *Mais, quel dommage*! She is to marry that big man *terrible*. Lucien, is there no one better?"

Julia tried to look severely polite, but it was impossible not to be amused by these artless remarks. Her lips twitched despite all she could do as Du Vallon cast a glance her way, and the frown he had been wearing when he approached cleared away at last.

"*Tais-toi,*" he told his sister sternly, but with such tenderness in his voice no one was in the least bit quelled. "Milady, your tongue is a naughty one. De Clembeau spoils you too much."

She sighed happily. "I am made to be spoiled, *non*?" And somehow the innocent manner in which she said it made such an outrageous statement seem not at all conceited. Rupert said something witty in response which made them all laugh, but Julia again noticed Du Vallon's impatient glances about.

"If you are wondering where that atrocious silver cup has gone to," she said lightly, "the silversmith has taken it home with him. And very disappointed he looked too."

"Oh, Lucien, you were excellent!" cried Lady Thérèse with a clap of her hands. "But I wish you had given that bad man a defeat."

He frowned with an uncomfortable flicker of his eyes in Julia's direction. "*Ma chère*," he addressed his sister.

"You will not call Milord Garde names. He shot *très bien.* I am honored to have made his match. No, mademoiselle," he added, turning back to Julia, who was thinking if she sat down again her head might ease. "I am seeking Baptiste."

"That *coquin*!" exclaimed Lady Thérèse with an angry gesture. "How I wish for you to shoot him, Lucien. *Immédiatement!*" She saw Julia's expression of frank bewilderment and added, "He was to report all the time what Lucien did. If Lucien did not spy, then he would write Monsieur Gueran, who was to take me to the guillotine." Her fastidious little nose wrinkled up. "Bah, pigs, all of them! I am so glad to be free."

Julia swallowed down a peculiar little lump in her throat and looked desperately about for a chair, but they were all too far away. How horrid it was, and how brave of Lady Thérèse, no older than herself, to speak of such infamies, of such personal danger and hazard, with that casual air. And no wonder Du Vallon's eyes had shown a lust for blood each time his servant's name was mentioned. A despicable little *weasel* of a man! Julia could not believe she had once felt sympathy for him. Her misjudgment of character was appalling, but before she could make any sort of shocked comment, Du Vallon was throwing up his shoulders in a show of resignation.

"But he is gone. *Sang de Dieu*, if I could have thought at the first moment—" He broke off, shaking his head, then sighed. "I must go *immédiatement* to the king—ah, no—the regent, I mean, and cast myself at his mercy for a pardon. Milord Jersey"—he nodded at that gentleman, who was some distance away chatting happily to some acquaintance—"goes with me *comme un homme juste* to swear I speak the truth." He stopped, frowning a little, to caress his sister's pale cheek. "*Ma chère*, if he is lenient, *Dieu permet*, we will all make our place here in safety with these *anglaises*.

Hein? I will find a little estate to buy." He flashed a steady look at a rather grave De Clembeau. "No, no, we will not discuss this now. I must seek the mercy of the prince, then we will hope for our happiness. *Au revoir.*" Swiftly he kissed his sister's hands. "Follow me to London tomorrow. Mademoiselle Swanton will be kind, *peut-être*, and lodge you tonight." He seized De Clembeau's hand and shook it firmly. "*Merci, merci*, for all you have done. You have saved us all; I would have gone mad soon, I think."

And then he was gone without a glance or a farewell to Julia, who was standing there numb and ill and very much left out of the intense joy of these people. Somehow she managed a response to Rupert's amused comment that he had been too hasty earlier to refuse her hospitality and continued to stare blankly after Du Vallon's retreating figure. The world was his again. His sorrows could be forgotten; the shadow hanging over him was cleared away. Julia supposed he had been kind to her upon occasion as a sort of substitute for the beloved sister which had been snatched from him. Now Lady Thérèse was safe, and Julia knew, with a sharpness of disappointment she'd not expected, she had lost his friendship. She was forgotten as a part of his life better ignored, and while she had never supposed his occasional attentions mattered all that greatly, she now realized differently. She had in many ways depended upon him as a rescuer as well as her confidant—functions Garde did not perform. Du Vallon had been a source of refuge—sometimes unwanted, admittedly, but nevertheless there. Now there was only Garde to turn to. And as she forlornly went about gathering up her gloves and frilled sunshade, which Rupert offered to carry for her, she could only see she had built her house upon the sand and was left with nothing but an ineffective little hope that such a foundation would not begin to crumble. Short of throwing herself at Du Vallon, there was nothing she could do to regain the friendship she had at first assumed would naturally fall into place; how she wanted to be saved from her own follies! But he could no longer be expected to have time for her, and she must not hope for it.

Her head began to pound more fiercely than ever, making her long for a bit of solitude, but of course there was no question of excusing herself since she had Rupert and Lady Thérèse to get better acquainted with. And keeping up with their merry banter and frequently erratic English left her no opportunity at all to think upon what she should do.

CHAPTER FOURTEEN

It was with considerable startlement that Julia awoke early the next morning to find Lady Thérèse sailing in, looking considerably freshened and quite charming in her simple muslin dress and golden halo of curls. "You are awake? *Bonjour!*" she said in sunny tones. Coming up to the bed, she subjected Julia to a swift scrutiny, then nodded. "*Bon!* You look much better today. I had fear, me, that you would swoon yesterday, you looked so ill."

Julia frowned with impatience. "What fudge! I've never swooned in my life. I could not do so."

Lady Thérèse's dimples showed. "Oh? But it is *très facile*. Everything grows dark, and you wake up in the arms of a handsome man." Her eyes twinkled. "Or upon a sofa, which is too dull, *n'est-ce pas*?"

Julia smiled, giving in, and nestled back against her pile of soft pillows. "At least we do not have to endure a second day of that contest. It gave me such a headache!"

"*Oui*," agreed Lady Thérèse. "Billiards is much more *amusant* than pistols. Bah!" She rang the bell for Julia's breakfast, then seated herself on the bed with a gay little bounce. "Your *tante* is so kind. I adore her! And Rupert, he prowls the house like a shameless one and says his Tante Léonie's portrait is *très mal*."

"I think she is beautiful," said Julia in quick defense and received a shrug.

"That Rupert, he must make an opinion of everything. *Mais*, I am in your way now? You wish me to go away, *peut-être? Non?* Then I will stay and practice my English upon you. Please?"

Helpless before this onslaught, Julia nodded. "Very well," she said as a laden tray was brought in and put before her. "What shall you talk about?"

"*Moi-même*—myself." Again the dimples peeped out, and she helped herself to a hot croissant dripping with butter. "It is the subject I have best. Do you like Lucien?" she asked, changing the topic with disarming rapidity.

"No." But Lady Thérèse looked so crushed, Julia was ashamed of her cowardly denial and hastened to make amends. "I—I daresay upon occasion we have dealt very well together."

Lady Thérèse plucked at the coverlet until the lid of the chocolate pot rattled in warning. "I hope Monsieur le Prince will forgive him," she said, her lovely features shadowed. "Lucien is very brave; he deserves not to be hung as a spy."

"Hanged?" Julia almost dropped her cup as agony shot through her. This possibility had never occurred to her. If it had, she would not have been able to have slept a wink. Small wonder Du Vallon had been so anxious to be on his way. Hanged—in public, like a low scoundrel for all to gape at—it made a curious shrunken sensation go through her, shriveling up her complacency like an apple left too long in the sun. How horrible! Oh, why had Garde gone stirring things up? He must surely have realized the consequences of his mischief. And then she was galled by the answer which came to her thoughts. Of course he had realized what was likely to come about. Of course he knew. And as he had no love for the French, she could not dare show much support for Du Vallon. Somehow, in some way, she had failed in her dealings with these two men, and if Du Vallon swung, or if he was drawn and quartered with his fine head set on a pike upon London bridge, *it would be her fault.* Shaken, she put down her cup with a clatter of the saucer, and looked up in desperation. "Surely you are dwelling upon too pessimistic a possibility."

Lady Thérèse looked at her with an expression too wise and mature for her years. "How pampered you English are! Did you not think of this before? In France," she said flatly, "It would be the guillotine. But we will hope your prince is *un homme juste.* And Lucien has his scars to show."

"Scars?" repeated Julia, knowing she was bleating like an idiot and despising herself for doing so in front of this delicate, fairylike creature who was proving so much more resilient than she. "His hand, you mean? But do you think that will weigh—"

Lady Thérèse shook her golden head, the sunlight sparking highlights from it in a hundred directions. "I do not know. He is so proud. Perhaps he will say nothing of it. Oh, Lucien." She grew pale at her memories, and a rather wild look came to cloud her eyes. "They would never have made him spy, those pigs," she said with a proud lift of her head, "if I had not been a great stupid and insisted on seeing Paris. Then I was taken to the Tuilleries to wait on that—that Austrian *souillon,* but really to be a prisoner. No one must blame Lucien; it was my fault. Mine!" And without warning, her happy little face crumpled and she fell down weeping as though her heart would break. "*Mon Dieu, mon Dieu!* He will hang. *Il n'y a pas d'espoir!* We were born to be unhappy!"

And nothing Julia could do or say would comfort her, and it was not until Rupert was sent for that Lady Thérèse could be calmed enough to be led to her room.

One arm about her drooping shoulders, he looked back at a very troubled Julia and smiled.

"It will all be over soon, *je t'assure*! Believe me, *petite*, she cannot make these tears forever. And do not worry for the marquis. The English, they have just governors, *non*?"

"Yes," said Julia slowly, wanting to be comforted by his reassurance. He must know something of what he was saying, mustn't he? "Yes, of course we do." But Lady Thérèse's despair, after her being so bright and courageous at first, had affected Julia's own courage too deeply. Who must she believe? Who must she permit to sway her? Closing the door after them, she could not rid her ears of the echo of those heart-rending sobs. If Du Vallon was put in dock, what hope was there for him? He would be tried by people who had lost sons and brothers in the war; he would have no chance of mercy. Tears stung at her eyes, and without further hesitation she bowed her head to pray, as much for her sake as for his. For if he were hanged, she did not know how she was to bear living with the man who had brought it about.

Back in London, Julia was obliged to occupy herself with wedding details, suffering agonies when no news of Du Vallon convinced her he had been thrown in the Tower. Even Lord Jersey could tell her nothing of the outcome. Then Lady Thérèse called one day to invite her for an impromptu outing in the park, and Julia was all too glad to cast aside everything for a diversion.

They set out in Lady Thérèse's landaulet, ostentatiously decorated with the Clembeau crest upon the panels and with blue paint upon the wheels to match the velvet squabs inside. Lady Thérèse was attired in a fetching walking dress of sea-green piqué which brought out intriguing flecks of green in the eyes Julia had previously thought gray, and a new poke bonnet framed her heart-shaped face to perfection. But Julia, who caught the eye herself in pleated primrose muslin, had little patience today to take note of fashion details. Impulsively, as the carriage started up, she reached out and caught Lady Thérèse's hand.

"I am being driven to distraction by suspense," she said so eagerly she was afraid she might offend, and paused in vain to make herself calmer. "Tell me! I can find out no news of your brother, and not hearing from you either these past four days—"

"Why, Julia," laughed Lady Thérèse, "we but heard the verdict this morning." She flashed her dimples with such wickedness, Julia drew a faint sigh of relief, certain she could not act so carefree if the word was bad. "*Mon amie,* have you a *tendre* for Lucien?" Lady Thérèse asked in her charming lisp of an accent.

Julia drew back at once with a flush of mortification and averted her head. Good heavens, had she been acting in so precipitous a way as to bring on such a question? She must mend her behavior at once. "No, of course not," she said with a great deal of stiffness, deeply ashamed at having been guilty of showing too much interest in the marquis. She could not help from climbing a little onto her hauteur. "You forget I am betrothed."

"Pooh." Lady Thérèse snapped her fingers with a shrug. "Him, I regard not at all. But, *vraiment,* I have been so busy in the hands of a *modiste* I could not come until today." Again her musical laughter rippled out. "Oh, *mon Dieu,* I have made you to be cross. *Pardon,* I will not tease again." She paused to rearrange her skirts, then continued just before Julia thought she should lose all patience and throttle her. "Yes, and yes, Lucien has the pardon of your prince." She gurgled, the dimples appearing again. *"C'est drôle, certainement.*

Monsieur le Regent wanted some painting of Lucien's. Lucien desired a right of citizenship. *Voilà*, so simple to be arranged for all." She made a regal gesture with one of her small-boned hands. "I was a great stupid to cry, and you did not need to worry. *Oh, le bon prince anglais*!" she cried merrily just as they met and passed the Duke of York driving himself as was his habit.

Startled, he blinked and glanced around, then brightened and politely tipped his hat to them. Julia thought she should choke until he was gone on, but at last she could fall back against the squabs and go into whoops until she was limp.

"What is it? I do not understand this joke," demanded Lady Thérèse, pinching at her arm.

Recovering a bit, Julia hunted through her reticule for a handkerchief with which to wipe her streaming eyes. "Oh, my," she gasped at last, most unsteadily. "That gentleman we just passed was one of the royal dukes. He—he thought you were hailing him."

Lady Thérèse's eyes widened, then she went off into a peal of mirth. "*Pardon*, Julia! My tongue, it always throws me into the mischief." Her eyes danced irrepressibly. "But now I shall be a favorite to this duc, *non?*"

Julia's lips twitched. How refreshing this lively creature's company was! It was delightful to laugh until one ached. And really, despite her companion's teasing with the news of Du Vallon's success, Julia could not find it in herself to be vexed. She was too relieved, too delighted, too happily exasperated over the regent's passion for art regardless of what issues were at stake. Suddenly she could not do enough for Lady Thérèse and sought some way to please her.

"By the bye," she said, sitting forward eagerly. "An acquaintance of mine, Mr. Byng, has promised to give me a puppy out of his poodle's newest litter. Shall I ask him for one for you?"

"*Mais oui!*" Lady Thérèse clapped her hands in delight, a pretty sparkle upon her face. "I adore dogs. Will it be little? Lucien and Rupert, they have gone to buy property. I will need little dogs in the country to walk with me, *n'est-ce pas*?"

Julia smiled to mask a fresh pang of isolation. Lady Thérèse looked so happy making her plans for the future; Julia could not understand why she must needs look forward to her own life with increasing uncertainty. If only she could be sure Garde really cared for her, then she would be content. But thank goodness Du Vallon was safe and able again to take his place in society. Beside that relief, nothing else could matter so greatly.

Arriving home again, she took a fond farewell of Lady Thérèse and went inside to the library, occupying herself by unpacking a box of books newly arrived from the publishers her aunt subscribed to, until the footman came to give her a flat, rather heavy package.

"It just arrived by messenger, miss," he said, placing it upon the reading table beneath the arched window for her.

Thanking him, she ripped away the paper in some curiosity, certain it could not be from Garde, who never gave her trinkets, and gasped at the box of exquisite burled rosewood. How pretty it was! Gently she rubbed one hand over the dark, polished lid, then impatience seized her and she turned the key already in the tiny lock and flung up the lid with both hands to gaze in considerable astonishment at a handsome brace of silver-mounted dueling pistols lying upon a bed of crimson velvet. "Oh, bother!" she exclaimed aloud in exasperation. Someone had surely sent them here by mistake. But the bit of folded paper inside bore her name.

Puzzled more than ever, she opened the hastily scrawled note, and read:

28 May, 1812

MADEMOISELLE,

I am overjoyed to say I have been granted both a pardon and the permission to remain in England. In the past, I have not acted the proper gentleman in your presence. For all my wrongs against you, I apologize. As well, I desire you to accept these weapons. They have let the blood of many men, and you will hate them, but I give them to you to say I shall never duel again. There will be no need now that the horrors of my existence are behind me. God keep you, mademoiselle, for your kindness, your beauty, and your setdowns

Yours truly,
LUCIEN AROUET
MARQUIS DU VALLON

Slowly Julia lowered the letter and gazed again at the pistols. They were beautifully crafted things, and as long as she refused to think of their function she would be honored to have them. With a little difficulty, she carried the case upstairs to her room and cleared the mantel to put it there in a place of honor. Then standing back a pace, she surveyed it with a bit of warmth thawing through her melancholy. How like Du Vallon to be so sensitive as to what gesture would most please her. She smiled, comforted, although she very much suspected she would rarely see him again, if ever. She would cherish these pistols always as a whisper of his presence.

A discreet tap on her door preceded the news of a caller awaiting her downstairs. Julia frowned in impatience, hating for this moment to be disturbed. "Who is it?" she asked with a sigh, toying with the notion of asking Rutledge to say she was not receiving.

The footman bowed. "Mr. Swanton, I believe, miss."

"Oh, dear." It was a most inadequate remark to describe her vexation over her half-brother coming yet again to ask for funds, but she could hardly say anything more stringent in front of the footman. "Very well, I'll come at once."

Going down the stairs with her skirts held daintily in one slender hand, she tried to think of some tactful way to put him off. But this resolve flew out of her head the moment she entered the drawing room and saw him leap up to rush toward her with his curled, pomaded locks in disarray and his clothes on anyhow. His eyes flashed desperation, like those of a hunted animal, and the grip of his soft, dead-white hands convulsed on her clasp in a feverish manner.

Julia drew back in revulsion from this wild man. "Good God, what has happened?" she exclaimed involuntarily, then suspicion seized her with a hostile growl right up her spine. "I shan't give you money, Gaylord, no matter how deeply in the suds you are!"

It was his turn to check and move back from her. That terrible clammy grip of his hands fell away, and he shook his head. "Devil take us, it's no amount *you* could scrape up."

"Then it *is* gambling again." Exasperation stung her. "Will you never learn? Do you mean to go the way of Papa, always—" Abruptly she broke off and bit her lip, mortified that she had almost said too much.

Gaylord, however, was in no mood to pay close heed to her words. He threw up his head, his weak mouth trembling a bit. "Lord knows, my luck should have turned this month. If only that devil Garde had not come poking in his nose!" he cried with a bitter gesture, ignoring her start. "What need has a great swell like him got to be fleecing a little place? The Golden Gull's far below his touch." He bit his soft lips, his whole face working. "Looking for variety, I daresay, or else someone bet him to do it. Barrymore's crowd is like that. Oh, *God*, I am ruined!" And he fell into the nearest chair with his face buried in his hands.

After a shocked moment, Julia's temper flared fire-hot. Her fists clenched in a paroxysm of rage, and she struck his shoulder blindly, making him flinch and squint up at her. "You great whining lout!" she snapped, the last frazzled threads of her patience worn through. "How dare you come toadying to me in hopes I'll persuade Garde to tear up your debts! I detest gambling and the ruin it brings! Just because you and Garde choose to rub shoulders with low company does *not* mean you may consider yourself free to drag me into this sordid matter!"

"But—"

"Oh, you are despicable!" And she turned her back on him before her disgust could completely overwhelm her.

He seized her arm, and turned her back to face him, his usual affectations gone and forgotten in the face of his stress. "No, no, Julia!" he said with such earnestness she flashed him a brilliant look of scorn. "Whatever you may think of me, I'm not such a maw-worm as that! No, listen! I came to ask you for Papa's address. That's all. Now, don't be difficult, pray! You didn't know it, but I'm half-owner of the Gull—"

"Yes, I did, for you told me!" she snapped, still scandalized over it. "And how you could—"

"Well, I haven't any expectations, have I?" he asked with bitter reasonableness. "Do stop sneering, Ju! I wouldn't have told you about this if I weren't up against the wall. Garde broke the bank at faro, and I haven't many days left to meet this debt."

"Really?" she said stonily, thinking it served this fool of a brother right. Make a go of himself, indeed. What a scramble-brain he was! And why had he seen fit to inform her it was Garde who had brought him down?

Surely he had sense enough to realize she did not want to hear such tales about her *parti*. "Very well, Gaylord," she said after a moment with a sigh. "If it is your intention to flee the country, I give you my word I shan't betray your whereabouts to Garde." Going to an *étagère* in the corner, she began rearranging the Dresden figurines. "Will that satisfy you?"

"No, dash it all, not a bit!" he shouted, quite out of temper himself now. "Was there anyone who ever had such a goose for a sister? If you would but listen—"

"I have been listening," she cut in severely, without turning her head. "And so far you have said nothing worthwhile. Cut line, sir, and tell me exactly what it is you do want!"

"Papa's address," he said at once. "I must have his permission to sell Swantoncourt. He doesn't care a fig for that humbug tradition of handing it down through generations of Swantons; nor do I. And since it isn't entailed, like this house—which is a puzzle I've never been able to understand—it must go. I think Garde will wait if I put it up for sale."

"*No!*" Julia found her tongue at last. "No!" Enraged past thinking, she whirled and flung a particularly fine china shepherdess, which missed him by several feet and shattered against the door. "You fool!" she said so cuttingly a flush mounted to his face. "Swantoncourt is not yours to dispose of, and never shall be! The day before he died Papa said I should have it as a dowry." Her voice abruptly halted, leaving a terrifying silence in the room. Unable to bear his look, she glanced every which way, then gulped on a little sob and tried to run past him out of the room.

He caught her, however, and shook her until she was dazed by his violence and could struggle no more. "Before he *died?*" he repeated in an ominous tone, his face as white as her own bloodless one. She choked, unable to reply, and he shook her again. "Tell me, damn you!" he shouted. "He's dead, isn't he? And you've been lying—"

"No," she gasped, helpless, knowing she was defeated by this foolish effort to save her beloved Swantoncourt, but unable to give up yet. "I but heard the news today."

"That's a lie!" His soft fingers dug into her arms with cruel strength, making her cry out. "That's why you came back, you conniving little hussy."

Miserable with guilt, she raised drenched, stricken eyes to his burning ones. "I am sorry, Gaylord," she whispered, knowing she had been wrong to deny him his grief. "I had to—"

"Well, good riddance to the old man!" said Gaylord with a sudden laugh, and pushed her away so that she stumbled. "So he's stuck his spoon in the wall at last." Gaylord laughed again. "Fancy that, and here I was at my wit's end. Does Sophie know?" He glanced at her and shook his head without waiting for an answer. "No, I daresay not."

Frowning and quite taken aback by his—his *joy*, Julia clutched at an occasional table for the support she badly needed. "Gaylord—"

"That's Sir Gaylord, my dear," he drawled and put up his quizzing glass to view her flushed face and trembling lips. "I shall have to find a solicitor to take your statement, I suppose." Then he began to swing his glass to and fro at the end of its black riband. "I must thank you for saving me so much trouble. Swantoncourt will go, of course, and no protest about it!" he added sharply as she started to speak. "Lying little jade that you are, you cannot expect any such faradiddles about giving *you* the property to be believed. Furthermore, it ain't legal."

With difficulty, Julia held back the angry, useless words which stung, adderlike, at her lips. Everything he said was true, and there was no hope of changing his mind. She gazed at the oiled parquet floor, stricken by the enormous consequences of having been found out. Now that she had seen Gaylord's reaction she no longer had any guilt concerning the lie itself. Of course her father had never been accused of adoring his children, Gaylord least of all, but there was no excuse for such repulsive, unfilial glee as this. She knew she would despise him the rest of her life.

He smirked at her silence and cast an appraising, proprietary glance about the room. "Tomorrow will see me set up here, in my rightful abode, but of course you and Aunt Beth may stay. I couldn't turn my own relatives out, now could I?" His smile sent a furious shiver through her; she hardly knew whether to hate him or to fear him. As the head of the family, he might still be as weak and degenerate as always, but he now had too much power to be dismissed with disgust as before. He eyed her in an insolent manner which made her hands clench at her sides. "As I recall, there are some smaller rooms up beneath the attic. Those will do, I think."

Oh! To think of herself under the thumb of this coxcomb! If there had been anything immediately to hand she would have hurled it at his head, and it took every bit of strength her common sense possessed to persuade her against the folly of sweeping up belongings and aunt and marching out. Galling though it might be, she dared not ignore the fact that she could not scrape up the price for lodgings at Fenton's Hotel or any other decent place. But she would not give way on every point!

Lifting her dark head with a flash of stormy blue eyes, she said as calmly as she could: "The servants occupy the upper bedchambers."

"What a mind for trivial detail you have!" he drawled in a way that made the flush upon her cheeks deepen. "It shan't kill the maids to sleep in the attic loft. And do stop staring at me with that revulsion on your face! If you are so nice, you may always go elsewhere. I require these lower stories for myself." Pulling out an enormous turnip-shaped watch from his waistcoat pocket, he grunted. "Late, but there's time yet to go round to my club and celebrate after I get a man to put Swantoncourt on the market. Goodbye, Julia."

"Wait!" Dashing round the table, she barely caught up with him at the door and clutched at his arm, heedless of his scowl for the creases she was putting in his sleeve. "Gaylord—oh, Sir Gaylord, then! Will—you won't go spreading this about, please?" It nauseated her to beg like this, but she forced herself to do it. "Only wait a bit longer, until the season is over. I was going to release the news of Papa's death then—when I would be able to escape his creditors."

Firmly he pulled her hand from his sleeve. "My dear child, what a ninny you are. To oblige you means my ruin. I must sell Swantoncourt and pay Garde, or he will call me out. It's very simple."

Driven yet another step toward defeat, she put a hand on the porcelain doorknob before he could. "Very well, you could say that the news but came today."

"No!" he said explosively, pushing her back out of his way. "I'll be dashed before I'll grovel to the dictates of a silly female again! The baronetcy is mine now, and if nothing else it means I shan't be bullied by you and your top-lofty ways. You'll have to think up a new scheme; this one is over!"

She reeled back, her hands at her constricting throat. "But the scandal—"

"Damn the scandal!" he snarled. "What the devil do I care about your reputation?"

"Gaylord! You wouldn't dare—" But the door was slammed in her face all the same. Furious, she kicked at it, only for it to open just before her toe reached the panel. Carried by momentum, she all but lost her balance and had to be steadied by Rutledge.

He bowed respectfully while she struggled to hold back tears. "Excuse my interruption, Miss Julia, but Master Gaylord has given instructions for you and her ladyship to be removed upstairs. Are these orders to be followed?"

Dear Rutledge, faithful to the end. Touched, she lost the impetus of her anger and gave a weary nod. "Yes, Rutledge. I hope the maids shan't find the attic too damp."

His tufty old brows came up in a bit of a huff as though she had slighted his capabilities in seeing the roof properly maintained. "No, Miss Julia, certainly not."

"Rutledge." She met his inquiring gaze with the final dregs of her courage and thought: If I cannot face a servant with equanimity, how will I ever face the *ton*? Oh, why couldn't Gaylord have been kind and helped her? But at once she put an end to the wailing despair threatening to overcome her composure. "You must say Sir Gaylord now. Sir Geoffrey died in France shortly—before I came home." Rutledge was an old retainer; she had to tell him the whole truth if she was going to say anything at all. "I have been very wicked, Rutledge," she said, struggling again to hold back welling tears.

"Yes, Miss Jullia," was all he said, however. "I will instruct the proper rooms to be prepared for Sir Gaylord at once."

She stared after his erect, retreating figure for a moment with a surprised, rueful twist upon her lips. How like Rutledge to take everything in his stride!

The Bible warned about the evils of lying, and now the consequences of her scheming were descending upon her. By tomorrow her reputation would be in ruins, and she would never be able to lift up her head in society again. The last shreds of honor left to her decreed she must release Garde from the betrothal, since it was impossible for him to draw back. She should have realized from the first she would not be able to carry this off. Even Du Vallon had tried, in his own haughty way, to warn her—but, no, she dared not think of him, and his present good fortune lest she begin to pity herself. That would never do.

Unwilling to fall into a black morass of depression, she sought some tiny grain of comfort to ease the pain and humiliation of her downfall. But all she could manage to find was the fact that, from now on, Gaylord should have the responsibility of paying for the candles and the servants' wages, and she doubted he could do so with any less difficulty than she had experienced.

The pain of humiliation wrenched through her again, spoiling her brief grasp at amusement, and with a ragged gasp she cast her pride to the wind. Calling the footman to her, she gave orders for her barouche to be brought round at once. She must go to Du Vallon and—

"I'm sorry, miss," said the lackey, his eyes fixed uncomfortably on a point above her head. "But Sir Gaylord took the carriage. Shall I summon a sedan chair for you?"

"No." It was as though Gaylord had slammed another door in her face. Blindly she turned away. Yes, she could take a chair to Chesterfield Street, but she now remembered the marquis was gone out of town. And she gave way in defeat before it all, unable to bring herself to lay her troubles before anyone else. It seemed she must indeed count herself doomed.

Chapter Fifteen

"But, my dearest, dearest lamb!" cried Lady Elizabeth in that obstinacy peculiar to the vague and amiable, who, when occasionally set upon something, never budge. "I cannot possibly conceive of why you wish to cry off from Almack's. It is quite your favorite assembly."

Julia made a helpless gesture, finding it difficult enough to maintain any semblance of composure without this piece of stubbornness on her aunt's behalf. Every one of her nerves was shattered and raw, making her long for the luxury of simply giving way to violent hysterics, but she somehow found one last dreg of strength and managed to keep her voice calm and reasonable. "Aunt, yes, you are right. But I do not wish to go anywhere tonight. Indeed, my pleasures must come to an end now that Gaylord knows about Papa. He will tell everyone. We are quite ruined."

Lady Elizabeth's plump face worked as she assimilated this dreary statement. Then she jumped up, the voluminous folds of her lace dressing gown all but dragging her chased silver bonbon box from the chair, and began circling the confines of her cluttered boudoir. "How foolish of you to tell that magpie anything," she said in considerable displeasure. "Goodness knows I could never bring myself to utter a reproach against you, dearest, but I cannot like having to go into belated mourning *now* when I have promised to help Emily Cowper hostess that assembly for the Russians that Countess Lieven persists in calling her relations, and I am simply dying to play cards with Evelina Durharvey for penny points tonight. She has beat me three times running and I must break that lucky streak or burst!"

Bitterness twisted a knife inside Julia, making her look away to hide her tears. "Cards," she said in a low voice of loathing. "How I detest them! They have brought every member of this family down."

"Fudge," said Lady Elizabeth stoutly. "I dislike this morbid display in you, Julia, and I wish to see it stopped at once. It is an established fact that no Swanton can live without cards."

"But you are a Pelling," said Julia with a weary sigh.

Lady Elizabeth drew up her plump form as best she was able. "Do not attempt to change the subject. And we *shall* go to Almack's. Gaylord hasn't vouchers. He can't go there to spoil your evening."

Julia bit her lip. How useless it was to say her evening—as well as the rest of her life—had already been destroyed! Aunt Beth simply was not listening to her.

"Besides," added Lady Elizabeth. "Kitty Wrexham is recovered from that nasty bout of measles and is back in town, sporting a monkey everywhere. I simply must see if she shall bring it on her wrist tonight. Such a difficulty for her dance partners, don't you think?"

Julia gave up. "Very well, I shan't try to dissuade you further. But I am not going. If Gaylord is coming here to live, there is a great deal to be done."

"Oh, that. What nonsense!" said Lady Elizabeth with an unconcerned flutter of her beringed hands. "I have always had these rooms. He can have no possible use for a lady's boudoir. Move to the servants' floor indeed." She laughed and patted Julia's cheek. "Poor child, can you not see your brother was feeding you a Banbury tale?"

"No, I cannot see that at all, I'm afraid." Stiffly, Julia rose to her feet. "I have been the greatest gudgeon alive for thinking I could succeed with this scheme. Please do not tempt me into thinking all is as before. And I was wrong to draw you into this when you preferred to do what was right."

"All this tragic talk is going completely over my head," declared Lady Elizabeth, busy readjusting her cap before the mirror held up by bronze cupids. "We get on very well, and if Gaylord wishes to reside with us, I suppose there is nothing so very improper about it. Now come and help me choose which gown I should wear, for I am always so muddled I can never remember what I wore the previous time. And we must do your hair in a new way. Forgive me, but I am so tired of that Diana mode you affect. *À la nymphe de l'eau* will suit those raven locks to perfection, I am persuaded. No more of this nonsense, mind, for I do not wish my enjoyment with the evening spoiled by these Cheltenham looks."

Defeated, Julia went away to submit herself reluctantly to the creative endeavors of her abigail. Somehow the stark simplicity of a narrow gown of white tulle and the straying drama of her hair made her want to laugh in bitter self-condemnation. She ought to be in severe black with her hair arranged in the simplest Banbury-puritan style; she ought to be avoiding the frivolous pleasures of Almack's. Then her chin lifted ever so slightly as a make-do spirit took hold within her. It was bad, yes, but why should she cringe? To go about now in weeds when shortly everyone would know of her duplicity was to be shockingly hypocritical. She could not bring herself to that point of ridicule. Perhaps—and hope leapt up within her at the thought—perhaps if she met the scandal as bravely as Du Vallon had met his, affecting a bit of *faux bonhomie*, then possibly she might weather it with equal success. After all, she moved in the best circles. Surely her friends and acquaintance would not be too harsh or too ready to condemn.

Heartened, she was able to walk outside past Rutledge's extremely expressionless person and enter the carriage with her aunt. Alternately during the ride to King Street, she suffered horrid qualms and rises of spirit. By the time they arrived and mounted the steps, her heart was pounding itself into a frenzy and her mouth was so dry and stiff she could scarcely respond to the porter's courteous greeting. Stumbling a little upon her train, she followed her aunt's blithe entrance with the greatest trepidation mingled with the deepest hope that she might have one last normal evening of gaiety.

Lady Jersey was receiving at the door, with Mrs. Drummond Burrell at her side. Their collective frowns withered Julia's hopes into tiny, shrunken things which scuttled away on the spot.

"I am afraid we must withdraw your vouchers, Lady Elizabeth. And yours, Miss Swanton," said Lady Jersey crisply.

"Indeed," added Mrs. Burrell in her frigid tones. "One can only wonder at your lack of proper feeling, Lady Elizabeth, in letting your charge exhibit such a shocking *want* of conduct."

Lady Elizabeth gazed from one haughty countenance to the other, her own beginning to crumple. "But—oh, dear," she wailed, groping for her handkerchief. "Julia!"

Julia answered this appeal by quietly handing both her and her aunt's vouchers to Lady Jersey. "There, you may burn them or whatever you like," she said in a calm, flat voice, so numb she could feel nothing; indeed, she was thankful for the daze which permitted her to keep her composure in the face of this humiliating public scene. Then her eyes flashed because she dared not let anyone see her tears. "We shan't vex you by coming again. Aunt?"

Grasping a weeping Lady Elizabeth firmly by the arm, she turned and hurried out, her free hand holding her skirts up away from the dirt of the long staircase, her eyes great dark holes of vivid blue in a face as white as her gown. Behind her came Mrs. Burrell's carrying voice: ". . . and not a single sign of contrition—*really* too much!" She faltered, then hurried on almost faster than her stricken aunt could manage. Back in the dark interior of their carriage, Lady Elizabeth collapsed with a wail in one corner, leaving Julia to give the necessary orders to their puzzled coachman. A violent little sob rose in Julia's throat, but she battled it back and threw herself against the squabs to sit in cold, despairing isolation during their journey home. Only her fingers moved, constantly twisting and clutching at each other. Her aunt continued to weep until the sound became annoying and Julia averted her face with a ragged gasp. How useless to say *I told you so*! But the tremendous urge to do so left her hot-eyed and furious at her aunt, herself, her half-brother—everyone, especially her parent, for having, however indirectly, cast her into this imbroglio.

But she was intelligent enough to realize rage helped her no more than tears. And to distract herself she began to mentally plan her move to a chambermaid's garret. She would have all her belongings rearranged by morning, whether she got any sleep or not! And of course she must not forget to write Garde at the soonest possible moment. He had dealt honestly with her; she could not continue to bind him now when a union with her could only be undesirable.

Although she launched herself into a frenzy of activity in order to take her mind off what threatened to overburden it, she was unable to compose herself enough to sit down at her rosewood escritoire and write any sort of a coherent message until the following morning. Garde neither replied nor appeared in answer to her agitated summons for the next two days, in which time she was driven to sore distraction by Gaylord's installation, by the battle which subsequently raged as Lady Elizabeth refused to vacate her handsome apartments and had to be borne bodily upstairs, rigid with hysterics, by the stalwart footman—who promptly resigned his position upon accomplishing this task—and by a curt, derisive letter which arrived from a former friend, who apparently could not wait to tell her what a fool she was. Every line was so filled with gloating, Julia at last lost the frayed shreds of her temper and flung it, half unread, into the puny fire lit to dispel the perpetual damp and sour odor in the wallpaper of her new bedchamber.

She glanced round at her surroundings, and for the countless time told herself she had hardly been plunged into dire straits. The narrow bed, once the cook's property, was filled with uncomfortable knobs and lumps from a mattress which refused to adapt itself to the form of its new mistress. But she was growing used to it, as well as the drab chintz curtains at a window which viewed their neighbor's ugliest chimney. And she had learned which floorboard creaked in the horrendous manner that set her teeth on edge, although she could not quite yet avoid it in the dark. She brightened the room with a rug filched from the cardroom and numerous cushions, but nothing could brighten the tense cloud in her heart, which kept her hidden away despite the fact that she still had free run of the house. The sight of Gaylord was unbearable, and she hated him even more when he summoned her downstairs to face several of her irate creditors.

Grimly, she sat before these representatives of various establishments where she had run up extravagant bills and listened in unprotesting silence as they presented the sums to her with sparse courtesy. What was there for her to say? She hadn't a farthing.

One thin, sallow-faced man, who looked like a solicitor's clerk, gave her a piercing gaze which sent her chin rising haughtily. "Stubbornness will avail you nothing, Miss Swanton," he said in an irritating nasal voice. "Debtor's prison is no respecter of persons."

A jolt of fear made her hands clench the arms of her chair, and she was obliged to look more haughty and contemptuous than ever in order to conceal the alarm spreading through her. Prison! She had never before thought of that possibility. Gaylord would not lift one finger to help her, and she could never go to Du Vallon, or to Lewing, who would be certain to help her out of a feeling of charity. Her every vestige of pride cringed in horror at the prospect of being an object of pity. But it must be Lewing; he would surely come to her aid. And Julia knew she must not care a fig if he pitied her, for he was not—well, he *was* family, and that was a different matter than begging aid of Du Vallon.

Strengthened by this chance of rescue, she rose to her feet and faced the clerk as coolly as she dared. Dignity must help her bluff for time, time enough to write to her brother-in-law before the watch came pounding at her door.

She lifted her brows. "You are precipitate, sir. These bills are not due until the end of the month. I will not be threatened."

"And who is threatening you, my dear?" asked a loud, arrogant voice from the doorway.

She whirled, startled, and could do nothing but send a weak smile of relief to Lord Garde. There was no guarantee that he had not come to revile her, but for the moment his muscular bulk dominated the room and cowed her tormentors. "Creditors," was all she could manage to say and blushed a mortified crimson beneath his gaze.

"I see," he said, but she could bear no more and ran from the room with her hands pressed to her hot cheeks. He looked so cold, so stern. Oh, why could he not have come before, when she was *prepared*?

She paced up and down in the musty confines of the library, which needed a thorough airing as usual, until her embarrassment abated somewhat. She would have to go back and face him; yes, she must. Swantons were selfish, dissolute scoundrels, but they were never cowards.

A faint click of the door interrupted her attempts at self-persuasion. She turned, breathless and pale, and could not speak when he craved permission to enter. There he stood, huge and vast and a stranger, his long auburn hair glinting as sternly as his dark eyes. She had no idea of what to say or do, and stood in frightened silence, her eyes violet pools in her strained face, and the telltale pulse at her throat alive and rapid.

"I have just returned from visiting my brother and came here as soon as I read your letter," he said quite normally, but she flinched all the same.

"Yes, yes," she stammered and turned her back to him in the hopes of being better able to speak if she could not see him. How he frightened her, simply by being here! "I suppose you have heard the gossip, my lord," she said in a sudden rush, determined to have it out and done with. "It's true. I have deceived you about my circumstances and deserve no mercy. I am penniless, dowerless, and an orphan. I hoped to—to marry you so that I might be able to live out my life in comfort and security. So you see how horrid I really am, a brazen-faced little hyprocrite. And of course I cannot hold you to a match you no longer desire." Gulping, she turned back to face him, only to gasp as he swept her into his powerful arms. She stiffened with surprise, but he paid no heed as his hungry lips imprisoned hers.

Her blood was tumbled so by his lust, it was impossible not to respond. But he gave her no chance to do so. Already he had torn a kiss from her, and then stepped back to regard her with amusement as she stood crimson-faced and trembling.

"My precious child," he said. "Your spirit and innocence have put new life into me. Women have bored me for years until I thought of them as mere playthings. But you—you are different." He traced the outline of her cheek a moment, while she closed her eyes with a shiver and wondered what power he had to command her so.

Smiling, he moved away to the window and stood there with his hands clasped behind his back. "And of course the line must be carried on. My brother is no better, and the doctors say his arm must be taken off. It is doubtful a—a *cripple* will ever take a wife of any breeding or intelligence, so I must embark upon matrimony. But believe me, my dear, the prospect of your charms makes it a very pleasant duty indeed. I have dealt with the gaggle of creditors by promising them your debts shall be paid at once. Tomorrow, in fact, when I'll have time to see my bankers."

"But—" She was stunned, hardly able to believe her ears. Could he be so generous, so kind? Could she be saved after all? She dared not think it true. "No, you must not have heard all I said. I—"

"Your past actions do not concern me." He gestured expansively. "Good Gad, do you suppose I have morals enough to condemn you? In the future, of course, your every action shall be accountable to me. Only promise me you will still be my bride. I am mad for you, Julia, as I have not been mad for a woman in a long time. And I could not bear to see that damned Frenchman steal you from me." He clasped her hands between his large ones, heedless of the frown she used to hide her sudden stab of pain; stupid Garde, so jealous of a man who had never tried to claim her! "Say yes again, my dear, and I promise you all the comfort and security you shall ever need."

At once she took herself in hand. She must always remain grateful for this moment of unlimited generosity. He was taking on her scandal without the least sign of reproach and would scotch it by making her his countess.

Looking up into his murky eyes, she smiled, suddenly so weak with overwhelming relief she had to sit down. Her limbs were like water, and she knew without looking exactly how much her hands were trembling. For this, she would adore him forever. How silly she had been to fear he did not love her! This proved he did, and she must never again think of DuVallon. "Thank you, my lord," she said breathlessly. "Yes, and yes!"

He laughed in a way that boomed through the room, and pressed her hand. "Very well. Let us advance the date of our nuptials, shall we? A fortnight from hence, to give you time to prepare. But I warn you, my dear, my impatience will let me wait no longer than that. Given me your permission to announce the date in tomorrow's *Gazette*, I pray! Your situation will be much eased if I do."

"Yes, of course!" she cried. What had Du Vallon said? *Selling herself*—nonsense! She could not repress a flash of resentment against the marquis. Lord du Vallon was very free with his criticism, but it was Lord Garde who cared for her. Impulsively, she laid her cheek against Garde's hand. "Yes, whatever you think best."

He smiled and touched her hair. "Splendid. Shall we go for a drive tomorrow?"

She drew back at once, then her revived spirit sent

her eyes flashing and she gave a decided nod. "Yes, unless you think I should go into mourning."

"Gad, no! The devil with the proprieties; they are for disappointed women. Besides, black depresses me." He smiled, baring his large teeth. "Dress as prettily as you like. And send the bills to me."

With that he was gone. Sighing as a terrible load slid off her shoulders, Julia let herself sag against the door to allow her fevered brow to cool upon its polished surface, then she turned and leaned her back against its panels, hugging herself and smiling up at the creamy rococo ceiling. Just think of it! She was not going to be obliged to pay for her naughtiness after all. Oh, heavenly thought! Her smile widened; silly her, worrying all this time. Garde was a marvelous, generous man.

Then her joy faded a bit, and she frowned. It certainly could not be proper to heed his advice to dress as though nothing whatsoever had occurred. Deep mourning was hypocritical, but light mourning would not be amiss. She thought she must make some sort of amends for her behavior. But when she had done so, the possession of a title as imposing as the Countess of Garde would make an effective shield against the further censure of society.

Encouraged again, she left the library to go to her aunt, who was repining with cushions, bonbons, and a vinaigrette. Julia was eager to tell her all about this wonderful news. Their difficulties were surely over, and soon they could be happy and free of care as never before. Why had she ever doubted Garde? At the moment she could even forgive him for what he had sought to do to Du Vallon. No man, she vowed, hurrying upstairs, would have a more grateful, loving wife. She would see to that. She would never let herself forget what he had done for her.

Chapter Sixteen

Dressed in pearly gray silk, which gave an irresistible iridescence to her vivid looks, she did find the courage to go driving in the park with Garde and his famous bays. It prompted a great deal of excitement, needless to say, and she would have been ready to sink but for his steadying presence. He dominated her, overwhelmed her, encircled her with a vast protectiveness as a sort of buffer against the hostility of the *beau monde*. Trying very hard to appear natural of word and manner—for she was even pointed out in the rudest way conceivable to those dreadful Russians—Julia supposed Garde was proud of his wealth which allowed him to select a dowerless bride if he chose; he certainly mentioned it more than once. It rasped a bit at her temper, but gratitude served effectively to soothe her ruffled sensibilities then and again when he praised her for not trying to coax him to burn Sir Gaylord's IOU.

The very mention of her half-brother was enough to send her into the boughs. "I should never dream of doing such a thing," she said, very much on her dignity.

Garde laughed in his loud, ringing way. "Yes, you're not one to beg. I like that." He laughed again as if it were all a great joke, and she managed to smile despite the strong temptation to seethe.

When he set her down again in Clarges Street, she was surprised and highly gratified to find an invitation to call from Lady Thérèse awaiting her and upon impulse she ordered the closed carriage and the company of her abigail.

It seemed so peculiar to find herself upon Du Vallon's doorstep. For a moment she lingered irresolutely before the portal and did not want to go in. The fact Garde was going to marry her would have to be told, before the portal and did not want to go in. The fact that and while she did not suppose Du Vallon would again accuse her of selling herself, contempt would be in his eyes. She did not want to see it, and she did not want to be reminded of her own disappointment in his failure to—in his failure to come—Suddenly she reminded herself that only Lady Thérèse was here; the marquis, and possibly Rupert as well, had gone into the country to buy property. With that reassurance clutched to her, she was able to shake off her dread and hesitation and lift the heavy knocker.

A liveried footman led her up the hall with its statuary niches into a vast salon, hung with celestial blue satin, where she found Lady Thérèse reclining upon a French sofa and eating Italian grapes with a tiny silver fork.

At Julia's uplifted eyebrows, her dimples peeped out mischievously. "*Voyons,* I am quick to spoil myself, *non*? Come and sit." She waved at a gilded chair. "*Pauvre* Julia, but I am so glad you are here. I had fear you would not."

Julia smiled. "I am brave today. You see, Lord Garde still wants to marry me, in spite of everything."

"Garde?" Lady Thérèse's nose wrinkled with distaste. "Bah! I like him not at all!"

"That is your prerogative of course," said Julia with dignity, hating to be at outs with this merry creature she was coming to think of as a friend. "I will never forget his kind generosity."

Lady Thérèse gestured dismissal of such considerations. "Graditude is *très mal* for—"

"And what is it you are declaring with such passion, *ma chère*?" asked Du Vallon, coming in without warning.

Her heart thumping into her throat, Julia looked up. He was smiling gently at her, and it was so good to see him again. Standing in his erect, elegant way, he looked very fine in a blue superfine coat and silver pantaloons. His Hessian boots could have reflected the snowy perfection of his cravat. As usual, his chestnut hair was trying unsuccessfully to curl in spite of its severe cropping, and his gray eyes shone with utter clearness. He was pale, but she knew she had never seen him look so fine before. Something quivered through her, and she thought of how marvelous it would be to see him come walking in every day in just this manner.

Her smile was quite involuntary as she rose and put out her hand, realizing with a guilty start as she did so that she had been staring in a most ill-bred way, exactly like a besotted creature. Discomfited, she withdrew her hand as soon as he had finished his bow and cast about in her mind for something to say. "I—I received the pistols, my lord. You may be sure they shall always be well cared for."

One fine brow quirked up and he started to speak, but before he could do so Lady Thérèse was rising with a ripple of laughter.

"Oh, Julia, I am so *méchante*. You came to be with me, but I brought you here to be with Lucien. *Au revoir*." Laughing again, she hurried out on twinkling feet before Julia could move in protest.

She stood there, shy in his presence and of two minds as to whether she should run out after her hostess or stand her ground.

"Please sit down, mademoiselle," said Du Vallon quietly.

She obeyed, frowning as he took a chair near hers. "I am afraid, my lord, that I should not stay." She faltered beneath his steady gaze. "I—I don't understand!"

"Ah, but you do, *très bien.*" Suddenly an expression of torment disrupted his sangfroid, and he took one of her hands, in his, tightly. "*Mon Dieu,* I died this morning when I read the announcement of your wedding date in the paper. And when, just now, I entered and you smiled—ah, I lived again. Julia, *ma petite chatte,* why do you turn from me? I adore you; always it has been so, since you first called me a toad. But I dared not love you. I ached to help you, but there were the circumstances . . . *Voyons,* I am free now. I can offer you everything—my love, a home, wealth, horses. Only give me your heart. Tell me I do not imagine what I see in your eyes when you look to me."

Shaking her head in bewilderment at this unexpected torrent of passion, she managed to pull her hand free. "Please, my lord," she said, her emotions in a turmoil. "I think you are mistaken." It was difficult to get the words out for the fiery warmth of confusion engulfing her.

"No, I am not," he said with a firmness that brought up her head. "I know myself. When I am with you, my whole life is—*ah, quel est le mot juste*? My life—is more alive. Each time I must say *au revoir*, I am desolate, of the vilest tempers. This is love, Julia! Do you not have these feelings?"

She was startled by his description. Was he right? Oh, how could it be such a common thing as her simple pleasure in his company and her faint sense of being lost when they were apart? Could *love*—that emotion so praised, so deplored, so longed for—be the peculiar sensation she had experienced when he walked into the room? Could love have something to do with the tremendous dissatisfaction she had been suffering since he left town days ago? No, no, it surely could not be anything so simple, so commonplace.

But if it was, then how much happier she could be, for the clear purity of Du Vallon's passion was like ice flashing in the sun. With Garde she always felt artificial and rather desperate, though sometimes he took her breath away. For one instant she knew bliss at having such a choice laid before her. Two men had offered her their name and their love, and were there any two more magnificent gentlemen in the kingdom? Both were handsome and well formed, with intelligence and wit. Both were peers. Both had affluence. But when she was with Garde, it was always with the aim of having him do something for her, and when she was with Du Vallon it was simply because she delighted in sharing his company. That, surely, should tell her a great deal. And now, at long last, Du Vallon had spoken.

Only he was too late.

For a moment it was as though the world had dropped out of its orbit and left her behind, dangling in the void like a broken and abandoned doll. She did not know what to say or think. Just for an instant she had been so happy at what he was saying, and yet it was all wrong. She had made her choice already. Du Vallon need not have held back because of his problems. Did they not all have problems? Indeed, the notion began to chafe her, for merely because he had felt obliged to hold back his declaration until the most ideal moment for him did not mean she must wait without a word or a hope to encourage her! What conceit! Garde knew her naughtiness and it had not daunted *him.* To love Du Vallon meant she would not have cared a snap for his temporary disgrace. But never mind all the reasons for this and that; she could not bear to examine them again. The fact was, she was betrothed, she was soon to be married, and this tardy declaration could achieve nothing but the guarantee that throughout the rest of her life she would be plagued by the doubt of whether she had made the right decision.

Fury swelled through her, as fierce and as violent as that rage which had gripped her so harshly in the park pavilion. She clenched her fists, hating the expression of tender patience upon his face. He thought he understood her so well, but he had bungled it! He had failed! If he had loved her for such a long time why had he not declared himself before Garde had bound her? Oh, why *now* when there could be no going back?

Catching her breath raggedly, she could have wept in frustration, and flinched when he reached once more for her hand.

"You are silent," he said, a furrow between his brows, and the old unhappiness beginning to form in his eyes. "Perhaps I—"

"No!" In a rush she was upon her feet, struggling to keep her composure. "No, my lord. I—I fear you have spoken in vain," she went on, making her voice very slow and deliberate lest her control slip and she betray herself. "Indeed, you are aware of my betrothal, which has not been broken despite this—this mess fallen down around my ears." Her lips quirked in a desperate, twisted smile. She was suffocating, near to swooning from the violence of her suppressed emotions. If she were not quick about making her little speech and taking her leave, she should never escape. He started to speak, but she held him off with one outstretched hand. "Permit me to finish. I appreciate your declaration, my lord, but you should not have put yourself out so. I am well taken care of and—"

"Oh, sacristi!" he said with such violence she was startled, her heart thundering a din into her ears. In two rapid strides he was far too close, but before she could back away he had her by the arms and was shaking her. "I will hear no more of this drivel!" he snapped so curtly alarm swept through her, snatching away her

strength until she had not the least means of pulling free. "*Morbleu,* you are a stupid. Have I taught you nothing? Are you still so blind and selfish you cannot see beyond these silly plans you have made?"

Her pride rushed up, flinging crimson into her cheeks and fiery sparks into her eyes. "I did not come here to endure any tongue-lashing from you, sir!"

His grip tightened. "It is time someone scolded you. *Oui*, you should be told the truth because you will not learn it yourself! I have tried much to be gentle and to have patience with you, but this is absurdity of the greatest." His lips curled in a sneer. "I tried, with much care, to tell you how wrong it was to not mourn your papa, *non*? And now you creep about weeping and oh, so sorry for yourself because society marvels at you. Bah!" He released her to gesture disgust. "I have shame to see you act like such a stupid. You are made of better stuff than this. You knew it was wrong to make this pretense; you said you did it because there was no one to help you. But did you think to ask anyone for help?"

She eyed him with something bordering on hatred. "There was no one; I had no need to ask. And you do not understand at all."

"*Non?*" His smile was sweetly dangerous. "Why should I not? This is not your first season, mademoiselle. You have had offers of marriage before. This I know. *Mais*, because you were selfish, you would not accept them. You did not want to give up being spoiled by your papa, who let you do as you liked. Then when Sir Geoffrey is no more, you *must* be married because you do not want to give up your fun, your frivolity."

"Beast," she said with loathing, longing to throw something at him. "I told you how I did not want to take charity—"

"Why?" he shot back, equally tight-lipped. "Because you would be expected to perform a few errands or watch after an *enfant*? So difficult, *non*?" He gestured savagely to keep her from interrupting. "No, and, no, mademoiselle! Let us hear no more excuses. The facts are clear. You could be a person of magnificence. You have spirit. You have courage. There is a fire of heart in you that could tame any man. But you choose to spoil it by being petty, and stupid, and selfish. You delight in criticizing your papa, but are you any less irresponsible than he? There are many gentlemen in London who are *enchanté* with you, but, no! You must toss the cap for Milord Garde, a libertine of the worst order. Why? Because you are a hypocrite, and a fool, and though you have love for me you must let pride and stupidity and selfishness make you cling to him, when you know he shall cast you off like an old shoe in a few months—if he marries you at all. But you think you must have him, and so you blind yourself to all that is so obvious and wrong." Frowning, his eyes cold and yet troubled, he drew back a pace from her. "I pity you, mademoiselle."

"Pity!" In a flash, she dropped all stricken consideration of her faults and threw him a challenging glare. "*Pity!* Indeed, sir, and why could you not pity me enough to give me your aid, instead of forever standing apart and giving so freely of your criticism? Do you think I cared a snap for all your advice when I was at my wit's end as to what to do with bills and—and *everything*?" She tossed her head scornfully. "Words are all very fine, but they do not always count for much. And I am very well aware of what Garde is, but I do know that he offered for me—twice. And in the teeth of scandal. He has also paid off my debts. I owe him too much to—" Abruptly she broke off and stamped her foot. "Oh, why did you not come forward sooner? I cannot bear to be reproached now when I have safety in my grasp at last!"

Without warning he gathered her into his arms, tightening his hold when she managed to overcome her natural inclination merely to subside against him. "*Ma petite*," he said so sadly it caught at her, "you did not once come to me for help. I could do so little for you unasked. *Comprenez?*"

She did understand, and was stricken. "But I didn't realize—"

"Then you will give up Garde and marry me?" he asked with a sudden eagerness that threatened to sweep her up and over the bounds of prudence. "I am a strict man; I will not wander. This I promise, Julia." Gently he stroked her hair. "You do not sell yourself to me. I do not ask that price."

The old wound rankled, and she stiffened. She was *not* selling herself! Why must he persist in putting it in such vulgar terms, making her ashamed? Why couldn't he understand how she realized Garde's faults and yet saw good in him for having rescued her from the mire of her troubles? She simply could not, in all fairness, turn about and jilt his lordship. "Garde has done a great deal for me," she said in a low rushed voice, not daring to meet Du Vallon's gaze. "I realize his tone of mind is not all it should be and that he is possessed of gross habits which shock, but he has been kind to me as well as all that is generous. And he did not wish to accept my breaking off the betrothal. I cannot jilt him after that. I simply cannot!" Now she had to look up, and the raw pain in Du Vallon's clear eyes took her breath away.

Slowly he released his bruising grip on her wrists. "I see. The *chien* wants you that much." A bitter smile touched the marquis's lips. "Perhaps I have seen too much good in you, mademoiselle. Perhaps you crave the wicked path he will lead you." He bowed, mockery gleaming in his face as though to belie the agony in his gaze. "As you wish. I shall leave you to be broken to his mastery. It shall not be gentle for you to bend your spirit to his. He will not let you rule him with your little tantrums. But perhaps you shall prefer to become insipid because you fear his temper, and then when you are meek he shall tire of you, and you will languish in the country while he goes back to his dissipation. I describe it well, I think." Du Vallon produced his snuffbox with an elegant flourish and flicked it open. "But you will be safe, mademoiselle. I believe now you really do want to be safe instead of happy. *C'est vrai, non?"*

It was as though he had spoken her every fear aloud, and made her a laughingstock in the process. For a moment she was beset by terror of her future, then rage bolstered her up. How dare he frighten her in this manner simply because of a desire to avenge his disappointment! And then her emotions overcame her completely, and she panicked enough to slap him with all the strength she possessed.

"You brutal monster!" she cried. "I could have been happy, but now—Oh, what does it matter whether I love you or him? I cannot deal him the hurt of rejection, not now when we are so near to the wedding." Sheer despair seized her, and she stamped her foot. "Oh, why will you not understand?"

"I understand *très bien,*" he said softly, one hand to his face. "This Garde is an evil fascination. And, *sang de Dieu,* if you will not free yourself, then I shall do it for you!" Abruptly he swung away, and she had one brief glimpse of his face, terrible and white in its fury, his eyes like burning coals, before he wrenched open the tall double doors and strode out, never heeding her cry to come back.

That evening she sat with her aunt in the drawing room, numbly sorting out yarns and matching colors in her lap. Gaylord was lingering over his port and probably would not join them at all, for his pique over Julia's imminent marriage to his creditor had been plainly evident at dinner. The room stood very quiet with that deep sort of peaceful silence only old rooms can have, the somber ticking of the clock upon the mantel and the purring of the kitten in Lady Elizabeth's yarn basket the only sounds.

Julia's fingers worked steadily while her thoughts revolved round and round that dreadful interview with Du Vallon. She was grateful for the quiet and for the ocher shadows in the corners of the wainscoting where the candlelight did not reach; they helped keep her calm with their sedateness. And she must remain calm, she told herself for the hundredth time. She must not permit herself to fall prey to the doubts and questions Du Vallon had sought to instill in her. There could be no hope of contentment if she did not hold fast to her decision and remain convinced it was the correct one. And as for his threat to break her betrothal to Garde, she could not be less concerned. She knew quite well Garde would believe nothing Du Vallon might say, and would consult her before he took any action. Lord Garde was no fool. Her thoughts shied away from the memory of the marquis's pale, eager face, softened from its usual stern expression just for her. Nor did she dare try to fathom that stirring of her own senses. She much preferred to dwell upon his churlishness in calling her by the most outrageous epithets. In a way it was a pity so elegant a man should have so little control over his temper and manners. She had made the right decision, she told herself firmly, bending her attention once more to her work. Garde had never once shouted at her, much less called her a fool. She *had* made the right decision.

The door opened with a faint click, and she glanced up to see Rutledge advancing with a salver upon which rested a single card. Bowing, he extended it. "The gentleman begs forgiveness for the lateness of the hour. Shall he be received?"

"Who is it, Julia?" asked Lady Elizabeth, who had been cross ever since her nephew had moved in. "If it's one of those horrid acquaintance of Gaylord's I shan't remain downstairs. More repulsive mushrooms and captain-sharps I have never seen, no, not since Sir Geoffrey's salad days."

"No, it's Cousin Rupert," said Julia, dropping the card back upon the salver. She was pleased at the prospect of seeing him, but a small voice of caution warned her he might be here as Du Vallon's envoy. And if that detestable man was desiring forgiveness at this late stage—

"Who, dearest?"

"The Comte de Clembeau," Julia explained, forcing her fists to unclench. She could not go on dwelling over insults to be conveyed to the marquis if she meant to receive her cousin with a fair mind. "Please show him in, Rutledge."

"*Petite cousine!*" rang out a cheerful baritone a moment later. Divested of driving coat and hat, the comte came sauntering in, his angular form attired formally in cream satin breeches, dark blue coat, small clothes of the finest linen, and a diamond of the first cut upon his hand. His cravat, which by its lack of starch revealed he had not yet enjoyed the felicity of meeting Brummell, gleamed beneath his bony chin. "*Bonsoir!*" Gaily he seized both of Julia's hands and kissed them in the continental manner, then flourished a bow in Lady Elizabeth's direction, his sapphire stud glittering among the ruffles of his shirt front. "Madame, you look *ravissante*. And such a cap! I do not intrude?"

"Not at all, sir." Charmed by this entrance, Julia laughed and indicated a chair for him. Her eyes, however, remained wary. "You must tell us to what we owe the honor of this visit."

His heavy brows wagged up, making his nose look longer than ever. "But, *petite*, you begged me to call!

Et violà!" He struck his chest. "We must talk, *naturellement*, of Tante Léonie. I had five years when she married her *beau anglais.* All I remember is she laughed much and stuffed me with bonbons."

"I'm afraid she died when I was born," said Julia matter-of-factly, suddenly wishing, in the light of these past tumultuous days, that she had a mother's advice to seek. "I know nothing whatsoever about her, except I am said to favor her."

"In many ways besides beauty alone, my lamb," put in Lady Elizabeth, readjusting the angle of the Mechlin lace cap which had excited Rupert's fancy, and looking rather pink as usual when she was in the presence of a personable gentleman. "Tell me, my lord, do you mean to take up residence in England or is this merely a visit? I thought your wife a charming creature."

He bowed, looking a little ill at ease. "We must stay in England. It is the only place for Thérèse to have safety."

Julia gave him a polite smile, trying hard not to blame Lady Thérèse for having deceived her into meeting with Du Vallon. "Then I doubly hope you shall like our country."

"Oh, *oui*!" He grinned, his somewhat crooked teeth flashing a brilliant white against the swarthiness of his complexion. "Everyone is so kind. But the food? *Quelle horreur!"* He threw up his hands with a shudder. "I must smuggle a chef from France *immédiatement*!"

They all laughed, and Lady Elizabeth unbent enough from the rather aloof regions she had been keeping since their debacle at Almack's to assure him quite earnestly that he should soon grow to adore pudding. Then, no doubt drawn by the noise of conversation and polite mirth, Gaylord appeared, looking, to Julia's critical eye, as though he had been consuming more than port. Introductions were made, and he promptly horrified Julia by inviting Rupert to accompany him to a gaming establishment.

Rupert shook his head. "*Merci,* but, no. I am atrocious with the dice. And I must sleep well this night." He coughed behind a scented handkerchief. "There is hunting of snipe for tomorrow in the park. But you are most kind, Sir Gaylord, to ask me."

Gaylord affected a bored yawn behind his quizzing glass, looking perfectly absurd in his padded coat of cherry-striped brocade and blue-tinted stockinette pantaloons buttoned over shoes with enormous paste buckles. "As you like. I'm off."

And scarcely was he gone with a final trace of spirits and Scent de Fainéant hanging in the air when Rupert heaved a sigh suspiciously like one of relief and seized Julia's hand with nervous hesitation. "*Petite,* you will perhaps give me a favor?"

"Perhaps," she said a bit coldly and braced herself.

He frowned as though he had not expected such a reaction. "This shooting of snipe, I have not done it before. Lucien says it is best done with pistols. Me, I have none myself, and he cannot lend to me his." He paused and cocked his brows at her.

She sighed and gave her head an amused little shake. So this was all! "How silly you are," she said, but gently, so as not to offend. "You cannot go hunting with a brace of dueling pistols."

He caught the amusement in her tone and grinned. "It is *nécessaire.* Gentlemen have invited me, and I have accepted. But the gunsmith is a *sot* and will not open his shop at this hour. I beg you. And, *aussi,* I promise, me, that I will not drop them in the mud."

"I think I have never heard a more nonsensical conversation," said Lady Elizabeth, breaking into Julia's chuckle. "Julia hasn't any pistols, you silly man."

"Oh, but I do." Smiling, Julia made a graceful gesture and rose. "Cousin Rupert shall explain, Aunt, while I run up and fetch them."

Still chuckling, she hurried upstairs to her room and brought out the elegant rosewood case. But the feel of the smooth wood put an end to her amusement, and she paused, frowning at it. Rupert was very droll and witty, but of course she could not believe any such faradiddle as he was telling. Du Vallon would never degrade his dueling pistols by suggesting they be used in a hunt! Her hands tightened on the case in suspicion. What was Rupert up to?

A bit angrily, she carried the box downstairs, and paused a few steps from the bottom at the sight of him waiting so eagerly for her in the hall. Some instinct made her look sharply at him. "Has someone called you out?"

He blinked. "*Pardon?*"

"Are you planning on fighting a duel with someone?" she asked, more sharply than ever, because if he was, then he deserved the most blistering scold ever delivered. It was illegal, foolish, and would probably oblige him to flee the country, and then what would be done with Lady Thérèse?

His headshake was fervent, and, she believed with a sigh of relief, genuine. "Me?" he asked, brows high. "Ah, *non*! For the snipe, *petite*. For the snipe."

She retreated a step up, almost tripping on her demi-train. "Fudge! You honestly do not expect me to swallow such gammon, do you? I—" Abruptly she broke off as a very hideous thought occurred to her. Du Vallon had been in such a fury; he had given her these pistols to mark the end of his dueling; and now she was being asked to give them back. A queer painful spasm clutched at her heart, and she turned deathly pale. "Good God!" she said, hardly able to keep from dropping the case. "It's *him*, isn't it? He is going to duel!" A fierce whirlwind of horror and desperation caught her up and sent her running down those last steps to Rupert, who was looking so guilty and chagrined she could have no further doubts. "Against whom? Rupert, you must tell me! I will brook no further evasions."

"Milord—" He broke off and grimaced. "But ladies are not to know of these things. Etiquette forbids—"

"Pooh," she snapped without patience. "How am I not to see through such a silly tale as snipe hunting with dueling pistols? I am not such a widgeon as you and Lord du Vallon seem to think!"

"No, no! Lucien said you—" Rupert cleared his throat and tried again. "Ah, yes! I will say it this way. He told me to come and demand the return of his property, *comme un barbare*. But *quelle horreur*! This is not to be done. I thought to spare you."

She smiled rather scornfully, seething at the thought of Du Vallon trying to ride roughshod over her in this manner. "And if I refuse to return them?" she asked, her chin high.

Rupert shrugged. "Then he will employ Milord Garde's."

"Garde!" she cried, and did drop the case then. Only Rupert's quick snatch saved the pistols from the floor. But Julia was standing furiously, battle signals unfurling in her cheeks, and she paid him no heed. "How dare he! Oh, how dare he!" Her eyes flashed at Rupert, who flinched. "If he kills Garde, he shall never have me as his prize! I am not at all impressed by these barbaric tactics. One would think we were living in the Middle Ages. Oh!" She stamped her foot. "It is the most vile humiliation I have ever been subjected to. And I am surprised, Cousin Rupert—yes, and shocked, too—to see you acting as second to—to *that man*!"

He held up a placating hand. "But you are wrong, *petite*! I am refused this honor. He said if Garde dies and he must leave the country, he does not want the scandal to ruin Thérèse and me."

"How kind," said Julia scathingly. "Such a noble gesture." Her fists clenched. "If I were a man I would shoot him a thousand times right through his black, conceited heart!"

"Once would be sufficient," demurred Rupert, but subsided beneath her glare.

She began to pace, clasping and unclasping her useless, feminine hands. If only they were strong enough to throttle Du Vallon for his impudence. "Oh, Rupert, don't you see? He is planning to kill my fiancé. What will become of me if he succeeds? I have never been more infuriated in my life! This is petty revenge, very petty revenge indeed."

"Perhaps Milord Garde will kill Lucien," suggested Rupert with one finger against his long nose. "They are matched shots, *non?*"

"What rubbish you do speak, to be sure," she snapped, that queer spasm clutching her heart again. How dare Rupert attempt to cut up her peace further with such a dreadful remark! "If they slay each other, will that help anything? Don't be such a gudgeon."

"I do not know what a gudgeon is," said Rupert, beginning to frown.

She gave him a long, calculating look. "But you *do* know where this stupid duel is to take place. And at what time. We shall call the magistrates to stop it."

"*Jamais*!" he cried, looking quite horrified. "Such a thing is not honorable!"

"Fustian! I am persuaded you know all about it, and I am quite determined to have the answer from you." He looked stubborn, and she stamped her foot. "Rupert! Don't you dare be such a cloth-headed block! Do you want to see unnecessary bloodshed?"

Abruptly he shrugged and gave in. "Perhaps you are

correct. It is the hour of seven tomorrow on—on Houndslow Heath."

"Ah!" She ran into the library and riffled the mahogany desk for a pen and paper. It took but a moment to scribble down the essential facts along with a plea for intervention, then she affixed a wafer crookedly and dispatched it off by the stableboy. "And you may put those pistols down now, Rupert," she said, suddenly fatigued. "There shan't be any need for them. Were you present when Lord du Vallon called Garde out?"

"*Oui,* I was there, but Lucien did not call him out." Rupert shrugged and put the pistol case upon the desk. "It was at *le club blanc*—"

"White's?"

He bowed. "Lucien walked up to him and said, 'Milord is a scoundrel and a cheat.' Those words exact. Milord Garde bowed and asked if the morning was convenient. Lucien agreed. *Voilà, le duel!*"

Julia nodded. "Well, at least we have foiled it." Impulsively she held out her hand. "Thank you, Rupert. And please forgive me for losing my temper and calling you names."

He demurred graciously. "*Eh bien.* It is to face Lucien with my failure that is hard."

"Stuff!" she said, pleased to have a relation so awkwardly endearing. "You needn't tell him a thing except that I refuse to return those pistols! He knows very well how much I abhor violence and perhaps he will think twice—before he pulls such a stunt as this again," she finished lamely, all too conscious that she was refusing to view Du Vallon in a fair light. How could she after he had—after he had said all those—"Goodnight, Cousin Rupert," she said and managed a smile. "Please call again." Turning abruptly, she gathered up her skirts and the pistol case, and fled upstairs before he could vouchsafe another word. She dared linger no longer lest she do something silly, like burst into tears of self-pity and go running to beg the marquis's forgiveness.

Exhausted, she slept deeply, past her customary hour of rising, until a rough shaking of her shoulder dragged her from that blissful comfort. She opened a heavy, annoyed eye, darkly violet with sleep, and permitted it to glare at Nan. "What *are* you doing?" she demanded with a yawn.

"Please, miss. I'm so sorry. But there's a dreadful gentleman downstairs who's threatening to come up here if you don't see him right away. Mr. Rutledge could barely convince him to let me fetch you down instead."

Awake now, Julia sat up with a frightened jerk, clutching the bedclothes beneath her chin. Surely Du Vallon would not dare! He could not have so completely lost his senses!

"Please, if you wouldn't mind hurrying, miss," begged Nan, quite wide-eyed. "The gentleman said there's been a terrible accident and that you *must* come."

Julia frowned, trying to comprehend this. "Who *is* this man downstairs?" she asked crossly, but when Nan told her it was the gentleman who had called the previous evening, her heart seemed to wither and die that very second even as a bitter sob of frustration escaped her lips. She flung herself out of bed. "Those fools!" she cried, yanking off her cap. "Help me dress at once, Nan! Anything will do, but hurry!"

Minutes later, she rushed downstairs in an old round gown of blue-and-white-striped dimity with her raven locks bound up anyhow by a blue ribbon. She found Rupert pacing up and down the hall with his hat and gloves still on. "What's happened?" she called, heedless of the servants peeping out here and there.

He whirled and hurried to seize her arm. "*Pardon*

pardon!" he said, pale in his agitation. "I was wrong. They dueled in the Marleybone Fields. I have come the moment I learned."

She stood quite still while a cold, slow fury chilled her veins to the bitter ice of sheer hatred. "And he has killed Garde?" she heard herself ask in a distinct but very faint voice as she wondered how she was to go on now. It was true she cared more for Du Vallon, but she would *die* rather than go to him now! She had too much pride ever to go back and try to undo the damage done yesterday. How could Du Vallon be so uncivilized?

"*Petite,* did you hear me?" asked Rupert.

She started, her thoughts scattering. "What? No, I am sorry. What did you say?"

Gently he took her hands, his dark eyes troubled. "Milord Garde is unharmed—a mere nothing of a scratch. Lucien—" His voice broke, and he had to turn away from her with a despairing gesture. "*Nom de Dieu,* he is dying even as we speak!"

She thought she had but closed her eyes against a violent stab of pain, but when she opened them it was to find herself lying upon the drawing room sofa with a cluster of agitated servants gathered around her. Putting a hand vaguely to her brow, she struggled to sit up. "Oh, good God!" she cried bitterly, resisting the attempts to make her lie back. "Why must I faint *now* when—" She started and glanced round frantically. "Where is Rupert?"

"He thought it best that he should go, Miss Julia," said Rutledge gently. "Won't you please lie down and wait for her ladyship to come downstairs?"

"Lie here with burnt feathers and evil nostrums while Lord du Vallon is dying?" she cried scathingly, forgetting she was speaking to servants. "Have the carriage brought round this instant! I must see him before—"

She bit her lip, so shaken with despair she could not go on. The truth was very clear to her now. What a fool she had been! A stupid, stupid fool. She cared nothing for Garde, at least nothing such as this, and she had permitted pride and ignorance to stand between her and the man she could not live without. And now—no! She could not bear to think of what she'd done. All too easily she recalled that dreadful last scene between them, when Du Vallon had rushed out with murder in his eye, and the vow to free her upon his lips. The memory must surely haunt her forever.

But as she hurried outside without waiting even for her bonnet—for what did fashion matter at a moment such as this?—and climbed into the hastily brought-up barouche, she could do nothing else but continue to dwell upon it. She had denied him, willfully rejected his love, and driven him with her brainless obstinancy to the greatest reaches of folly. Why couldn't she have kicked over the traces and forgotten her pride long enough to and driven him with her brainless obstinacy to the have thrown herself into his arms? Why couldn't she have listened to her heart and trusted him? Her missishness was costing his life; how could she ever forgive herself?

As for Garde, why, what could he matter to her now? She would only bring him hurt by wedding him when her heart ached for another. Besides, it was by his hand that Du Vallon now—oh, dear heaven, what had she done? What was she to do?

During the seemingly interminable ride to Chesterfield Street she came to terms with some ugly things about herself, realizing she had been terribly, terribly wrong and wicked to take the course she had. Going the proper route would have been better, even if it had meant giving up most of the gaieties of the season. How could she care about fun and frivolity now when she could see what blindly clinging to it had cost her? In mourning, she still would have met Du Vallon on the packet boat. Everything he had said to her was true, and it was not difficult to understand his contempt for her rash folly. The least thing she could do, now that he hated her, was to let him pass on without enduring the fresh torment of seeing her again, but despite these noble resolves she could not bring herself to order the coachman to turn back. She must see him; she could not bear to do nothing to make a restitution.

Trembling, she let herself be handed out by one of Du Vallon's footmen, and followed him up the curved staircase to a chamber door where he knocked softly once, then swung it open for her. There on the threshold, she stopped, heart pounding so she feared she might swoon again, and could not take another step toward the vast four-poster bed where two doctors were bending over that still form. Oh, dearest God . . . her lips began to tremble, and she pressed one hand to them, unable to bear up in this hushed atmosphere of dread and expectancy.

"Julia?" The whisper startled her out of her ominous fancies, and when she saw Lady Thérèse coming to her, she nearly cried out in relief at there being someone she could cling to. "Come." Lady Thérèse's cold hand took her frozen one and led her forward.

Someone spoke something—the tall doctor commenting to his colleague—but Julia could not take her widened eyes from the bed. Too still beneath the white coverlet, he lay there propped high upon a quantity of pillows. His head was dropped down a little to one side with eyes shut and sunken beneath damp tousled hair, so dark against the pasty hue of his brow, only a faint, shallow flutter of his pinched nostrils told her he still lived.

Lady Thérèse took her hand again and forced her to sit down upon a chair which had been brought in for the purpose. "They removed the ball just before you came. It touched the lung." Then her own composure broke down and she began to weep silently, shaking with the effort not to let her grief disturb him. "Please, please stay," she begged in a broken whisper, clinging to Julia's arm.

Julia embraced her soothingly, her own heart slowly crumbling into dust although her eyes were free from tears. She knew with dreadful, unshakable certainty that his death would take her life with it, no matter if she existed another forty years. Yesterday she had made a dreadful, stupid mistake, and now she must endure the torture of paying for it, no matter how much it had taught her never to commit such folly again. In such a matter there came no second chance. She closed her eyes a moment against the agony within her and listened to Lady Thérèse's faint weeping as it echoed the sorrow in her own heart. "Yes," she brought herself to murmur at last. "I shall stay."

Chapter Seventeen

"*Petite,* you must go," urged Rupert. "It has been three days."

She eyed him mutinously, vexed that he should lead her out into the corridor and then attempt these tactics. Her small, firm chin came up. "No."

"*Pour l'amour de Dieu!*" Trying to swear in a tone no louder than a murmur, he looked strangled in his cravat. "*Petite,* you make the nurse excellent, and we are all grateful, but . . ." he gestured helplessly. "You grow haggard. Thérèse, her I can command to be sensible and rest. You obey nothing."

She gave him a cold-eyed stare, irritated beyond all measure at his acting so utterly devoid of understanding. "I love him, Rupert," she said in a low, flat voice. "I cannot go."

"But you shall." Firmly grasping her arm and ignoring her gasp of protest, he steered her toward the stairs. "Julia, you are an *enfant charmante*, but do not add to our problems with this stubbornness." Indignant, she started to speak, but he frowned in impatience. "Yes, yes, you love him. *Très bien!* But there is talk about this—this vigil."

"I don't care!" she stormed, pulling back against his hold.

"You must care!" He shook her, his long nose looking even longer in disapproval. "There is scandal enough over the duel. *Tout le monde* knows it was for the sake of you."

"You can't keep me away!" she cried, her anger giving way to pleading. It was true, what he said; she was so weary she could barely drag herself about. But she was determined not to give way to her lack of stamina in the sickroom. To do so was to admit she was horrid through and through and could not change herself for the better. No, indeed she could not go away and sit at her ease while there was so much suffering here. And why could Rupert not see her heartbreak would not permit her to rest, no matter where she was? Had she not lain awake last night in the gracious guest chamber provided for her while a capable housekeeper sat with the marquis? Fighting back frustrated tears, she turned to her cousin, her shadowed eyes searching his homely, concerned face. "No, please don't keep me away. Rupert, I cannot bear the suspense."

"*Tais-toi, tais-toi,*" he soothed, enfolding her in his long arms and rocking her ever so gently. "The suspense has no difference here. He does not awake to know or speak to anyone. *Naturellement*, you must come every day. But not to stay. It is not your place, *ma petite.*"

She began to weep, the gentle words cutting right through her, and lost all desire to fight against his comforting. "But it should be my place. I have been such a fool!"

"Yes, yes, *certainement* you have been that." He held her at arms' length and brought out his handkerchief of fine lawn to blot away her tears. "But nothing can be done now. Your carriage is waiting. Go home and pray. You must not make Milord Garde angry."

"Garde!" She jerked away in involuntary distaste. "He could have aimed for the shoulder and satisfied his honor! He did not have to be such a brute and seek to kill!"

"Julia!" It was sharp reproof, and for the first time she saw his dark brown eyes snap with anger. "*Mon Dieu*, I have shame for you. He is your betrothed, and as such, deserves your respect and your loyalty. You must not judge him for this. Lucien would have rendered him dead if he could."

She started to speak, but he gestured for silence.

"You are a woman; you cannot understand this thing which is for men to do. But I will not hear such talk again. No *demoiselle* of the *lignée de* Clembeau ever forgets herself in this way. Were you not betrothed, you could say as you please, but remember your position."

"Yes, of course. Please forgive me." She had herself in hand now, and gave him a resolute nod. Not for nothing had she spent these three days racking her soul. She had prayed for Du Vallon until she was spent, and still the certainty remained that he was going to die. Everyone hoped for his recovery, but no one expected it now, least of all the doctors. But she had come past the first wild urge to play his widow the rest of her life. Inside she might die with him, but the rest of her had to go on. She had let herself be swayed by frivolity and selfish desires; now was the time to look duty in the face and take it up. Rupert was right in saying she was being unfair to Garde. Of course she despised what he had done, but it could not be helped now. It had been her fault for making Du Vallon angry enough to pick a quarrel. If only she had not refused him so harshly! If only she had not refused him! But she still belonged to Garde, no matter how much her wounded heart rebelled, and she must go away from here and seek to begin serving Garde with the decorum he desired in a countess. One had to live with the consequences of one's mistakes, regardless of how much one wished they had never been made.

Meekly she said farewell to Rupert, and let him settle her in the barouche. Because the top was down she was obliged to sit stiffly erect, not giving way to her exhaustion, and appearing to take no heed of the stares she received upon the crowded streets. She knew herself the subject of scandal; she was an outcast to polite society. It was what she deserved, and she must learn to accept cold shoulders and snubs with dignity so as not to offend further.

Lost in her unhappy thoughts, she did not at first perceive she had been hailed until the coachman slowed the barouche to a halt. Looking up with a start, Julia found herself gazing into a pair of ironical hazel eyes.

"My dear Miss Swanton, out at last," said Brummell in his cool way as he bowed from atop his horse. As the white tops of his boots were upon a level with her countenance, she sought to study their immaculate appearance rather than bring herself to face him. Embarrassed by this encounter, she clenched her hands upon the folds of her crumpled gray gown. He was going to make a beastly remark; she could sense it hovering in the air above her, and wished she were brave enough to order the coachman to drive on.

"Come, come," he said with an inflection of surprise. "Do I not get even a nod of greeting, nor a word? I confess I did not realize I had fallen so low in your esteem."

That brought her gaze up, for it touched upon her pride of manners. With constraint she said, "Forgive me, sir. I am pleased to find you willing to recognize me again."

"Oh, tut, how very dull these disagreements are," he reproved her with an airy wave of his hand. Then he took the sting out of his words by awarding her his rare smile. "Where is that flash of spirit, Miss Swanton? I have quite missed it these past few days."

As impatient to go on as she was, she found it impossible not to respond to his raillery. "That is because you have not seen me, sir." Then she sighed, a bit angrily.

"I have seen the papers; they are lampooning me. Must you show me your pity by speaking to me when I am poison to the rest of the world?"

His fine brows rose in a quizzical manner, reminding her of Du Vallon so much she was obliged to bite her lip to keep herself from falling prey to another bout of distressful weeping. "My dear Miss Swanton, I can see you are in a perfectly disagreeable humor, otherwise you would perceive I never pity people. Come, come, weeping is so bad for the complexion. Are you going to let the rest of the world turn their backs on you when *I* find your actions not so very terrible?"

"Don't you?" she said in surprise, the warmth still coming and going in her face. Certainly it did not help her discomfiture to sit before him in her crushed dress and careless bonnet while he was attired *par excellence*. She could sense the reproach he so far had not spoken.

Looking pensive, he curbed a restive movement of his mount. "As a matter of fact, very little. You have shown a ruthless disregard for propriety and convention in concealing the death of your parent, but beyond that I must applaud the original workings of your mind."

She gasped. "But surely you don't approve of what I've done."

"No. But your father died on his own endeavors, not yours. If that were not so, then I should be decidedly shocked. Am I being too frank, Miss Swanton? You were not used to minding before."

"No." She gestured vaguely, fighting to hold back the tears that came too easily these days. "Please go on. I—I am very grateful to find one who does not jeer at me." Her voice dropped. "One may know one is wrong, but it's very hard to go on being told so, isn't it?"

He sighed and frowned at a bit of lint on his sleeve. "You have done wrong, but you have admitted it." His eyes rested upon her attire. "Light mourning is a very acceptable way of showing your apology, both to your father's memory and to the rest of society, although one must deplore crumpled displays of it. No, I should sneer at black, but you have side-stepped that pitfall. Only, do cease hiding and people shan't ostracize you for long." He smiled. "I can see to that, I believe. May I ride alongside? You must agree the day is rather fine."

She could only smile and nod, not trusting herself to speak for the lump of gratitude in her throat. How kind of him! And his escort all the way to her door meant half of fashionable London must see them and take heed of this gesture on his behalf. Although at the moment her worry for Du Vallon was too great for her to be able to consider much else, she realized that shortly she would be very relieved indeed to be taken back within the approval of her class. Garde would appreciate it too. She sighed. Poor Garde. How infatuated she had once been with him! And now when his regard for her appeared to increase daily, her affection in return had cooled. It was a pity, but it could not be helped. She rubbed her temples, paying almost no heed to Brummell's conversation. How tired she was!

But arriving home, she was given no chance to rest. Scarcely had she changed into a walking dress of fresh muslin and sat down for Nan to bathe her temples with lavender water when a summons from Gaylord brought her downstairs.

He was sneering a bit as he looked at her, but she paid him no heed at all. Instead, she saw another sneer, one such as Garde used when he was feeling smug, and it suddenly occurred to her that if Du Vallon died, Garde would boast of it to her. He would probably even contrive it so he would not be obliged to leave the country. A sort of muddiness engulfed her. Indeed, her brief moment of clarity when Rupert had dismissed her was gone now. She thought of what she owed Garde for saving her from financial ruin, and for loving her despite her scandalous behavior. Although he had but professed a fondness for her at the first, he could not go on and on doing these things for her if he did not adore her. He would not have dueled with Du Vallon but for her sake, only she did not want such devotion. She hated him. She wished her father's last word had not been Garde's name, so as to show she should turn to that gentleman. She wished Garde were not so handsome, so fatally attractive he drew all to him regardless of their honest desires. She wished Sophie and she had not quarreled over him, for the break between them suddenly seemed too great a price to pay. And how she wished she need not face her half-brother, who did not respect her or himself and who, with his debts and his gambling, would no doubt meet his eventual end as sordidly as their father had met his, with no meaning to the event, save that it was all a waste.

"Julia! You are not listening!"

She blinked at Gaylord, slowly becoming aware that some moments must have passed. She was now sitting in a chair. She gave herself a mental shake and supposed she ought not to make him cross with her inattention. "I am sorry," she said, her breath unsteady. "I am very tired." Yes, exhausted, as though her life was joined to Du Vallon's and slowly trickling away with his, but she must not think of that now. It led to madness.

"Thank God the sale of Swantoncourt has saved me from Garde." Gaylord sprawled in his chair with his lower lip thrust out. He looked damp and weak, as though his dissipation was wearing out his energies, and even his coat of peacock blue did not blaze as brilliantly as the colors he usually affected. He brought out a handkerchief and passed it over his brow.

Julia eyed him coldly. "Do not expect me to congratulate you. Only a fool throws away the family property."

"You're no saint either, little sister," he said with a yawn, although his eyes narrowed. "Garde has called twice, and your absence did not please him. He's paid your debts, you know."

"Yes, I do know," she snapped, disliking his tone. He need not reproach her for falling into financial disaster when he was in no better shape.

"I wish he would pay off Papa's," continued Gaylord, mopping his brow again. "Damn this fellow Duffy! He does not cease to plague me, even while he knows very well I am run off my legs. Paying my debt to Garde bled dry all my resources."

"I have no sympathy for you," said Julia, standing. If he had treated her and Aunt Beth decently she might have been able to forgive him for losing Swantoncourt, but he hadn't and she could not. "Please excuse me."

"You shan't leave this room until you tell me what has happened to the paper," said Gaylord through gritted teeth.

Her eyes widened, and she remembered her interview with Mr. Duffy. "That again!"

"Yes." He rose so that their eyes were on a level. "That."

"Gaylord, how can you? To believe Papa could be guilty of blackmail!"

"It's true!" he shouted, gripping her by the arms. "Thunder take your nicety, the facts are known. It is true. He possessed a letter and he meant to make use of it as insurance if he were forced out of England by debt. You don't think he meant to live in glorious poverty in Paris, do you?"

She averted her face, refusing to believe anything so loathsome. "Papa had shocking faults, but he would not—"

"Yes, and yes, and yes!" shouted Gaylord. "He had the letter when he was in Calais. You had charge of his possessions. You must know where to find it. If I can turn it over to Duffy, we shall be freed of that sum he's attempting to squeeze out of me." Gaylord shook her arm. "Oh, Julia, will you never understand? If Papa had been the sort to live quietly and soberly he would never have countenanced such a thing. But he was run to his wit's end by losing hundreds and hundreds of pounds at a sitting with people like Fox, and Garde, and the regent. You can have no idea until you see a year's income lost on a turn of the cards. Papa was desperate enough even to try highway robbery if the notion had come into his head." Gaylord laughed. "I might myself, should it come to it." Then the anger returned to his face. "There, you are thoroughly shocked. Do I care? Not as long as you tell me where the paper is."

She glared at him, hating him. It must be true. Sir Geoffrey would have even thought of it as something of a lark. No wonder he had been so cheerful over the prospect of his exile in France. But she would never respect Gaylord again for destroying the last, untarnished piece of her father's memory. He and Sir Geoffrey and Mr. Duffy were monsters, all of them!

"I brought back Papa's strongbox," she said in a flat voice, her anger rigidly suppressed within it. "Release me, and I shall go and look there."

Gaylord obeyed with a bark of a laugh. "Be quick about it. Duffy is going to set the watch upon us shortly."

Without looking at him she turned and left the room. Little more could happen, she thought, walking quickly yet without haste to the library. There surely could be only so many disasters ordained for one's life. She tried to think about what she was doing, about how she was going to help turn a dirty, despicable letter over into Mr. Duffy's possession. It ought to be burned, and if

Gaylord were a man instead of a coward he would do so. Her father had intended blackmail in his desperation, but never committed it, while Mr. Duffy certainly would. No unexpected death would prevent him. Julia sighed as she unlocked the box and threw back the lid. How she wished Sophie were here to tell Gaylord what a fool he was. He had always heeded her more than he had Julia.

Sir Geoffrey's papers were few, and it did not take more than a moment to glance through them. Hidden within the folds of a stiff pamphlet on the evils of improper soil cultivation was a slip of a note which fluttered to the floor at her feet. She bent to pick it up and knew before her fingers touched it that she had found what she was looking for. Curiosity overcame aversion, and she read it, swiftly and with horror. Mr. Duffy had been wrong; it was not written by a reckless gentleman but by a lady of extremely notable rank, agreeing to an indiscreet meeting with Lord Garde.

The blood drained out of Julia, all in one rush, and she stood immovable, her lips parted. Then, with shaking hands, she turned over the letter and on the back was scrawled in her father's careless hand: *Received in part first payment from G.* And the date had been two days before their departure to Calais.

She ripped the letter in half before she realized what she was doing. And after that it seemed quite natural to go on ripping and ripping the shreds of paper until the tiny bits showered down around her feet, irrevocable and quite destroyed.

"What have you done?" Gaylord came rushing in just as the last bit fluttered to the floor. He threw himself down on his knees and began trying to scoop the pieces up. "You idiot! You fool!" He was white to the lips and sobbing. "I might have known you weren't to be trusted. Oh, damn! It's the end of everything!"

Julia glanced down at him, too swathed in her shock to be moved by his anguish. "The end came a very long time ago," she said and went out.

But there was nowhere in the house for her to go. Nothing seemed familiar; the furniture in the rooms seemed to belong to strangers. She wondered once if she had swooned and was dreaming she wandered about, but, no, she had fainted when she had been told the news about Du Vallon, and then she had not dreamed.

His name prodded her mind into life, and she suddenly could remember a carriage ride with him, yes, on the first day of her betrothal, when she had spoken of her father's death and of how sudden and odd it had been that a lowborn stranger, an Englishman in France, should kill him on the spot and disappear afterward. Surely any rational man would have made a denial first and attempted to brazen his way out of the accusation. Mad, the French had said and shrugged, for they could not solve the puzzle and wished to take an obvious explanation. Now she wondered. And the manner in which her father had spoken Garde's name seemed all at once sinister.

With that single doubt she was suddenly sure, although she had no proof except the conviction of her womanly instincts. She stared at the jewel Garde had set upon her finger, and then she stopped thinking altogether. Swiftly, but again without haste, she gave orders for her bonnet and the barouche. These were brought, and she set out for Garde's residence without one care for how her visit to his door would appear. At the moment the opinion of the world did not exist, for the world did not exist. There was only a cold core within her that ached until she was sure it must soon kill her.

Arriving at Garde's town house, she permitted the coachman to knock for her, and when the butler answered the door, she descended from the barouche with her chin high. "Thank you," she said coldly. "I wish to see his lordship."

The man hesitated, his eyes flicking past her to the face of her disapproving coachman. "I—I am not certain his lordship can receive you, miss."

"Of course he can. I am his betrothed." And with a flash of her violet eyes, Julia swept past him into the dim interior of the hall. The butler hastened to install her in a handsome salon, where she would not surrender her gloves or bonnet but stood eyeing him with freezing hauteur until he bowed himself away.

With a shiver of impatience she stood pulling her gloves through her hands. The opulence of the room did not sway her; she eyed it with dispassion. Above all, she did not permit herself to think, for thoughts would bring uncertainty and emotion. She must remain cold and keep the strength sustaining her.

In a few minutes she heard a bold step ringing upon the marbled floor outside, then the tall doors flew open and Garde strode in with no very pleasant expression upon his face. "Good God, whatever brought you here?" he demanded before she was more than half-turned to meet him. "An apology, I daresay. You had better have one. No woman has ever made a fool of me, my dearest, nor shall you! I am not one to be dangled from your pretty fingers while you moon over that foreign cur. I should have put a ball in his heart, damn him!"

"You have put one in his lung. I think that sufficient damage," she snapped without attempting a pointless denial. "I did not come to apologize or to listen to your chastisement. If you are vexed by my behavior, I can only say I despise yours."

He laughed loudly with a sneer on his heavy lips. "Why, the little Frenchman has used his bloodletting to gain your sympathies."

"I believe you would be well advised to listen to me," she said, wishing with a tremor her calm almost could not conceal that it were only as simple as he thought it. If only she could loathe him merely because he sought to slaughter Du Vallon, but, no, there was her father as well. She must discover the entire truth. She must know the entire depths of Garde's villainy.

Carefully, she removed his ring from her finger. He reddened and started forward, but her level look stopped him in mid-step. For a moment, they stared at each other, and again, much to her horror, she felt herself weakening before the pull of his manly attraction. The man was a devil! Shaken, she laid the jewel upon a candlestand and stepped back from it with her chin high and her eyes flashing.

"Let us speak of my father, Lord Garde," she said.

The arrogance in his face checked, and a look of calculation came into his eyes. He bent his auburn head. "I have told you before I do not care that you concealed his death."

"No doubt," she snapped, color flying in each cheek. "I know my father possessed a letter he meant to use against you. Did you hire the man who killed him?"

The awful words seemed to echo round the chamber. She could hardly believe she had said them. But what was Garde thinking? Why did he not rush to deny the accusation?

Slowly he lifted his head to look at her, and she was shocked to see him smile. "So you have guessed. Well, well! What a clever little morsel you are."

"Why?" she cried, her calm shattering around her. "Why? How could you?"

"My dear, no man ever commands my obedience in any matter," said Garde with a shrug of his muscular shoulders.

She was appalled. Was a shrug all the murder of her father meant to him? He was an animal! One trembling hand stole up to her lips. "And—and despite what you have done you would marry me?"

He raised his brows. "Yes. Just think of the irony of the situation! It struck me so when we first began our little flirtation. And then it seemed amusing, even exciting to possess my enemy's child. You have been eager enough."

She nearly choked. "But I did not know! You beast! Do you think I should defile myself? Never! When you sought to kill Du Vallon with that awful duel, I knew then I should always hate you for your bloodthirstiness. But to expect me to find titillation in the fact that my would-be husband is also the murderer of my father—"

"You can never prove I gave the order," broke in Garde smoothly. His murky eyes gleamed at her. "Sir Geoffrey Swanton was a fool. He would no doubt have gone to the lady had her uncles not been so powerful, but for him to think I could not crush him with equal swiftness was a stupid mistake. But the deed is past, and no proof lies behind me or my man." Garde's eyes ran over her in a way that made her shudder with repulsion. "Even when you stand there in that silly pose of horror you are lovely." Laughing deep in his throat, he moved toward her. "Put it behind you, my dear. When we are wed you shall have to."

Her head jerked up. "You are mad, sir! We shall never be wed. That, I may promise you!"

"Oh?" His eyes narrowed. "And do you mean to go running to the Frenchman you are so fond of?"

"Yes." She faced him with all the dignity she could muster. "He is worth a thousand of you."

"Is he?" With rough swiftness, Garde seized her arm and jerked her to him. His heavy features had grown coarse with anger. "We shall see, my dear, if you are still mine." And he crushed her protesting lips in a punishing kiss which sent white-hot fury pulsing through her every fiber.

In that moment of violation she knew at last that she was free of his evil fascination. Never again could he exercise his spell over her, for she had never in her life known such disgust and loathing. She still had one hand free. With the strength of her hatred she used it to box his ear. He swore in startlement, recoiling enough to allow her to wrench free of his grasp. At once she darted behind a chair, then backed until she was at the fireplace with the mantel pressed hard against her shoulders.

Panting, she glared at him, wild with outrage. Somehow she would see him hanged for his infamy! He had robbed her of her parent and the man she truly loved, and he would not escape his just deserts if she had any say in the matter!

"How dare you treat me as nothing but a possession you are afraid a better man might acquire!" she demanded, clenching her fists in the desire to strike him. "How dare you!"

Garde threw back his auburn head with laughter. Some predatory note in it sent a shiver through her, and involuntarily she tensed, ready for she knew not what. Fists on hips, his large teeth bared in a grin, Garde said, "Well, well, and I was used to thinking you a meek little chit, all milk and water, with just a tantalizing hint of spirit until your bluff was called."

"No one of spirit could endure you, sir!" she retorted, stung.

Again he smiled, and the way in which his eyes regarded her seemed to soil her. "If I am not to wed you, for which you may be assured I feel no overwhelming regret, I will at least have you." He laughed as her eyes widened. "Remember, my dear, that you came here, unescorted and uninvited. What else is a man to think?"

He came toward her, quite fast, and there was no time to be wasted with horror or fear. She intended to sidle down the wall, but at once she bumped into the poker stand and lost any possible chance of dodging him. For an instant panic gripped her, then courage flared into her heart, enabling her to seize the poker with both hands and brandish it warningly.

He checked, then laughed with a mockery that made her boil. "My dear, you alarm me."

Any bit of hesitation which might have hindered her was at once consumed by the heat of her fury. Drawing her lip between her teeth, she refused to let him take the advantage again, but moved first this time while he was still laughing, straight at him with fear sour enough in her throat to urge her on with a sort of fierce desperation. She swung the poker across his chest with all the strength years of handling spirited horses had given her delicate figure.

There was a dreadful dull thud as her weapon made contact with flesh and bone, and Garde fell back with a hoarse, bitten-off cry of pain.

Astonished by her success, she threw down the poker and eyed him sprawled, gasping and clutching his ribs, upon the priceless Aubusson carpet. Her violet eyes narrowed. How she should have liked to be a man just now, with a sword in her hand to run him through! He was not a gentleman, but a debased animal, and all of her principles against violence could not mean a fig at a time like this.

"You jade!" he growled, struggling to rise.

Her nostrils curled in fastidious distaste. "I shall see that you pay, sir." And with chin high, she walked out.

She rode all the way home to Clarges Street with tears streaming hot against her cheeks. There was no other reaction left to her. Twisting her reticule about in her hands, she strove and strove to think of some means of publishing Garde's villainy. But no solution came to her. How could she make the accusation when it meant she must also confess Sir Geoffrey had added blackmail to his roguish deeds?

But she could not let Garde go unpunished! Du Vallon would have known what she should do, but she had forfeited her right to his advice when she sent him out to face Garde's pistol. Beginning to weep again, Julia gave up. She simply did not know what else to do.

Reaching Swanton House, she was brought up short upon the threshold by the sight of boxes and furniture piled in the hall and cried out to see Rutledge emerging from the nether regions with a valise in one hand and a worn but impeccably brushed beaver upon his head.

"Rutledge!" she said, rushing up to block his way. "What on earth is Gaylord doing? Surely you aren't dismissed?"

The butler inclined his head with a look that spoke volumes. "Miss Julia, I believe you will recall a person by the name of Duffy?"

She fell back a step, suddenly realizing how she must look with tear stains on her face. By no means would she surrender her possessions to that odious bloodsucker! And she would weep no more lest he think he could take advantage of her weakness. "Where is he?" she demanded, a glint of steel appearing in her eyes. They could not do this to her; they could not take everything away. "And where is Gaylord? Surely he could exhibit the courage to face down the creature!"

"Mr. Duffy"—and Rutledge managed to place extreme distaste into those syllables—"is perhaps upstairs, judging by the direction of his bellow. Sir Gaylord, er, fled the house over a half an hour ago to escape the watch. Dover is, I believe, his destination."

Julia gasped, feeling her last support gone. "Then he is fleeing the country." Panic seized her. "How could he desert us? There must be someone to keep Mr. Duffy from making off with our things. Rutledge—"

But Rutledge, after visible hesitation, shook his head. "I'm sorry, Miss Julia, but I cannot help you. We servants have been dismissed and shall find the watch upon us if we are not all out within the hour." He colored a bit and bowed his head as if to escape her imploring gaze. "Indeed, I do not like it, but Lord Lewing assured me it would be best for you and Lady Elizabeth if we gave no trouble."

"Lewing!" Relief pierced her like a ray of sun through the darkness. She seized Rutledge's arm and gave it a shake. "He will tell us what to do. When did he—no, never mind. Rutledge, gather the other servants and take them out to wait in the park. The watch can do nothing to you there. Wait until I send for you." She blinked back tears. "Dear old Rutledge, I shan't let Mr. Duffy turn you out. He shan't turn any of us out."

Turning away, she pushed past a tall plant stand which was placed firmly in the doorway of the drawing room and entered to find Lewing pacing about with his hands behind his back. Sophie sat upon a corner sofa, her black silk dress framing her beautifully. There was a tranquility about them that surprised Julia, but before she could guess at it both had looked up. Lewing took a step forward, then glanced at his wife and did not speak.

Julia's eyes went to her half-sister. Breathless, she tried to summon the resistance to hold down her anger with Sophie, only to find she no longer had any anger. Nor did she hate Sophie,. The memory of that nightmare in the park was so long ago and so clouded by the tragedies which had struck since then it no longer seemed very important.

Slowly, with much grace, Sophie rose to her feet and extended one hand. "Julia," she said, and with a choke of tears Julia ran to her arms.

"Sophie. Oh, Sophie!" she said as soon as she could speak. Lewing gave her a handkerchief and she dabbed at her eyes with a poor attempt at a smile. "Forgive me. If I cry again today I shall turn as shriveled as a prune. But—" she gulped and her lips began to quiver. "My God, it's so horrible! He killed Papa and I cannot prove it!"

"Who? What's that?" demanded Lewing. "Sophie, see if you can't get some sense out of her."

But Julia was striving for self-control already. She glanced up and this time could smile. How well they both looked. Lewing had put on weight, and Sophie, why, she had softened somehow and become rosy! "How glad I am you have come."

"But of course we came," said Sophie, giving her hand a squeeze. "As soon as we heard about Papa and the scandal you'd caused. And, Julia," she paused and looked uncomfortable, "I felt I must try to dissuade you from your marriage."

"But—"

"No, don't get angry. Please, I am not meddling. Once John took me away I realized what a fool I'd been and I could not bear for you to make a similar mistake. Garde is not the man who can make you happy."

Julia bit her lip. "He has ruined my life."

"Julia!" Sophie's hand tightened upon hers.

Shaking her head, Julia continued, "He killed Papa. Not himself, but he hired someone." With a deep breath, she told all that she knew, so very grateful someone had come at last to help she could barely keep herself coherent. "There must be a way to bring him to justice," she finished, looking from one shocked face to another. "Sophie, John, I know it is dreadful. Papa was so wicked, and yet, and yet, was he worse than a murderer? I cannot think so!"

Lewing cleared his throat. "I will see about what can

be done. Wait here for me. The movers shan't disturb you."

As soon as he was gone, Julia settled back in her chair with a sigh. Almost shyly she glanced at Sophie. "Where is Aunt Beth?"

Sophie smiled ever so faintly. "Upstairs with an attack of nerves. Julia," she hesitated and began to pleat a fold of her gown. "Are you certain you have forgiven me? I know you are worn to a shadow, but when the worst of this is passed and you are feeling better, are you going to remember all the shocking things we did and said to one another?"

Julia looked at her for a long while, unable to escape the calm which hung about Sophie. It helped her to force her mind past the terrors it had so recently suffered and past the anxieties still besetting it, so that she could think of herself and the state of her own spirit. She almost wept again. It was so wonderful that Sophie should be here now at this very moment, this very day when so many terrible things had occurred. But with an effort she held back her tears and forced herself to concentrate on her answer.

"I thought I could never forgive you, Sophie. I did try when John came that day with your apology. But the forgiveness wasn't there. And now that the hurt has faded, I don't think it shall return. You are different; I can see that you are. And I have changed. Besides, for us to hate each other because of that horrible man—"

"Garde is a despicable creature," said Sophie with a spark in her green eyes. "But, Julia, you were not speaking the real truth about him when you told us of—of poor Papa."

Julia frowned as a sense of discomfort formed within her. "What do you mean?"

"Garde ruined your life. That is what you said. But then you told us about Papa."

"Yes!"

"Julia, be truthful. With yourself if not with me." Sophie leaned toward her. "I do not deny the horror of our father's fate. That Garde could order such a thing done and then set about trying to seduce me and to woo you can only show how base is his mind. But something worse than that has happened to you. I can see it in your eyes. I can hear it in your voice. Oh, Julia, what has Garde really done to you?"

Julia flinched, seeing once more the still form of Du Vallon in that stuffy sickroom. Had it only been a week since those clear gray eyes had smiled at her? Or had it been even that long? Dear God! She gasped and shook her head, unable to answer.

Sophie took her hand. "Can it be you really were in love with Dick? I always thought it was a schoolgirl fancy you'd worked yourself into. Every one of your reproaches seemed so false, so hypocritical. But, if he really is the man for you, and you cannot bear to think of what he has done to Papa—"

"No!" cried Julia, unable to bear comforting. "I hate him. I've never loved him, not since that day in the park when Lord du Vallon rescued me." Clenching her fists, she pushed herself to her feet and began to walk about the room, averting her gaze from the green tags marked "Duffy" which were affixed to the contents of the curio cabinet. "Oh, Sophie, if you have been a fool, what have I been? I could have been so happy, but I felt bound to Garde, especially after he paid my debts. I tried to shut Du Vallon out of my heart, but I couldn't. And then when he did at last offer for me I was sold to Garde and could not—I did not have the courage to do what was right. And now they have dueled, and the marquis is dying, and all I have left is the knowledge that Garde is the murderer of two men I—"

"Julia, stop!" Jumping up, Sophie gripped her hard by the arms. "You mustn't say any more or you'll weep again. I never realized. I had convinced myself I shouldn't meddle after we left town and I began to recover my good sense. But, oh, my poor dear, if only we could have confided sooner in each other!"

Now it seemed as though Sophie might cry. Clutching to the last dregs of her self-control, Julia eyed her in startlement, not failing to take note again of the glow shining behind this temporary distress, of the radiance which only seemed enhanced by the black dress. "Sophie," she said, her violet eyes widening. "You've changed so much."

"Have I?" Sophie smiled a bit self-consciously and drew her back to the chairs. "I am going to have another child."

"Sophie!"

"Yes, I am so happy, though I have not yet found the right moment to tell John. He would not have let me make this journey if he knew, which is silly, and after all, I see now I was right to come." For a moment Sophie's green eyes shone, then she dropped them. "The baby means even more because now John and I have a second chance. I was such a fool, Julia. You know how miserable I was while John was away. I grew petty and vain because I felt neglected. To show him a lesson, I began to flirt. And Garde was ever so quick to urge me on in my naughtiness." Her voice faltered. "He fascinated me so I could not help but become infatuated with him. But all the while I was still miserable because I knew even to pretend I liked Garde was to do John a terrible wrong. And then you came back from France so changed! Suddenly you weren't the dear, flighty little creature you'd always been. You were so determined, so hard! You flung at me all the reproaches my conscience brought up again and again. I was nearly mad with shame. But by then Garde had me in his spell. He is such an evil creature, so handsome, so alluring. He seemed to tempt me with all the things I'd ever been curious about, gambling, and masked balls, and wild kissing in gardens at night. If John had not come home when he did, I—I should have become wicked and ruined myself." She shivered, her voice as white as her face. "In the country it came to be as though I had been ill and lost to myself and was only at long last climbing out of my delirium. I do not deserve anyone as good as John. He has been so hurt, and yet he has forgiven me. And even begged my forgiveness! I could not decide what to do about you. I knew you hated me, and had every right to, but I also knew, having been saved from it, that Garde was too horrid for anyone. Then we received word of—of Papa, and of the advancement of your wedding. I had to come. Please don't think wrongly of me. Oh, Julia, I should so love to have you with me in the country, you and dear Auntie! We have never been close, you and I, but I should like for us to know one another better. A rest would do you good. You look so ill and tired."

Julia put out her hand, warmth rushing through her. Yes, she and Sophie could become close now. They were no longer two half-sisters, separated by different mothers and always suspicious of one another. They had shared a common hell, and now they could know a true bond.

"Thank you, Sophie," said Julia. "I am glad you spoke so freely. In these past days I have had time to sort out my thoughts and feelings. I, too, was trapped by Garde's attraction, so trapped and so inexperienced I did not realize what was wrong or that the exhilaration in his presence was so much less clean than the contentment, the deep peace and joy of spirit I knew when I was with Du Vallon. If I had had more time I would have sorted it out. But I wasn't given time." She sighed and gestured in despair. "I should love to go away. Even—even if Du Vallon should live, he could never forgive me."

Sophie shook her head. "I think he would."

"No. Some hurts are too great. I just know that having once been offered such happiness and thrown it away, I may not expect it again." She put one hand to her throat. "If only—"

A crash and heavy thud from the floor above their heads made her break off with an exclamation. "That insufferable man!" She jumped up and would have gone to do battle had Sophie not laid a hand on her arm.

"Julia, no! Please, this is all very distressing for you, I do realize. It is my home too. But protests shall only make it worse." Another thud caused them both to wince. "John examined Mr. Duffy's credentials, and he is within his rights to confiscate the house and everything inside it. It's entailed, I know, and Swantoncourt should have gone instead, but since Gaylord has sold the property—" She broke off with a little grimace.

Julia nodded. So everything was to be wrested from her. Wretched, she sank back into her chair and allowed her forehead to rest on her hand. "I suppose you are right," she said with something near to a catch in her voice. "Only, being quite worn down from—from helping tend Lord du Vallon, I cannot just . . ." Her lips trembling, she glanced at Sophie and gave her an impetuous hug. "Oh, my dear, if you had not come today, I should have been left in the street! There is my Cousin Rupert, but since he and his wife have no house of their own I could not have liked to—oh, I do not even know what I am saying. This day has been so wretched." Again she got to her feet. "No, really I must go and see what I can prevent Mr. Duffy from taking. He cannot want it all."

Leaving Sophie behind, she found a vantage point at the foot of the stairs to watch the steady stream of the furnishings flowing out of the house and into the wagons ranged about the front steps. Once again she knew the odd sensation of not really standing there, of not belonging to the house or of it belonging to her. It was as though she were a helpless stranger who wandered in to observe the proceedings.

At last Duffy passed her, red-faced and puffing from his exertions. He paused to eye her warily. "You needn't raise a fuss, missy," he said. "I've got my claim tight on this case."

Pride lifted her chin so that he could not glimpse the mist in her eyes. "I hope I may keep my clothing?" she asked with the loathing she could not suppress.

To her chagrin, he did not at once agree, but instead pursed his lips in reluctant thought. "There's a fair price to be fetched for a silk gown brought out secondhand," he said at last, but something in her expression made him blink and wave a discomfited hand. "Oh, aye, then. Keep your furbelows, missy." And pulling a handful of green tags from his pocket, he bustled off to make an inventory of the kitchen.

"Julia?" Lewing came up to her with so little warning she was obliged to dab hastily at her eyes before she could look at him. "Here, my dear child, you mustn't repine overmuch about this. It was bound to happen someday. Sophie and I shall be staying in town for a short time; she says she must shop for mourning clothes. You and Lady Elizabeth shall of course come under my roof. And when we leave for the country—"

"Thank you, John, that is very kind." Gratefully Julie pressed his hand, then gave him an anxious look "You look angry. Was nothing achieved? I did not understand where you went."

"Garde refused to see me." Lewing looked grim. "The butler gave me some nonsensical story of a fall down the stairs. I daresay he sensed what was in my mind."

Julia's eyes widened. "And what was there?"

He glanced at her, and she gasped. "John, no! You would not have stood a chance against him. Oh, I am glad I struck him down with the poker. He would have killed you."

"No." Lewing shook his head, a rueful grimace upon his lips. "You forget I am a soldier. I can shoot as well as any man, though I am not one to boast of it. Blast! I have never known such frustration!" He struck the newel post with a fist. "The man is a scoundrel! I ought to have shot him down weeks ago. But I didn't want scandal—for Sophie's sake. I love her so I could not permit it. Now—"

Julia watched his averted face a moment, then said, "But is there no other recourse? Is there no magistrate who—"

He sighed. "Your word alone against a peer's? It's a pity, but no one would countenance it. And to smirch your father's name further—" He broke off with a shrug. "I am sorry. To accuse Garde would bring us more pain than result. I hope you have forgiven Sophie this time. She is sincere, you know. Garde dropped her so abruptly she was very hurt, for she nearly threw away everything for his sake, but at least it helped her to see clearly what he is."

Julia could barely hear him for her disappointment. So nothing could be done! It was maddening! But she forced herself to smile and answer his question. "Yes, we are reconciled."

"Good. Go and fetch your things, and tell Lady Elizabeth she isn't to be left destitute in the gutter. We need not linger here." As he spoke he eyed one of the movers with distaste.

Julia hesitated. "One thing, if I may ask it. While we are here in town I should prefer to stay with my Cousin Rupert and his wife. He—I mean, I am not bound now to Garde. There can be no talk against me if—I must stay till the—" Her trembling lips could not finish.

Sophie had come out of the drawing room in time to hear. "She is speaking of Lord du Vallon, John. Perhaps it is best if she could be at his side until—"

"Yes, of course," said Lewing gently. "Go to your Frenchman. I would not wish to deny you that request."

"Thank you," said Julia through a blur of tears. She had thought so wrongly of Sophie and Lewing; why had she been too proud to go to them at the first? She gestured. "Thank you both for being so kind. I shall be ready in a thrice." And she caught up her demitrain to go hurrying up the stairs.

But while she dragged out her trunk and set Nan—who had been hiding in the attic lest she, too, be turned out—to packing her gowns, Julia was forced to press her hand against her lips to hold back a sob of despair. How unfair it was that Du Vallon should lie dying while Garde, who reeked of villainy, should continue to ride upon the crest of popularity and favor, kept safe by sheer audacity. It was not fair. It was not right. But if she could not see Garde punished, she must at least not let Du Vallon die. She must not!

The next day saw her installed into a small bedchamber near Lady Thérèse's with a small bandbox containing her necessities, and a basket of fruit and restorative pork jelly for the patient. She was terrified lest he should have slipped away during her absence, but the thin nostrils still fluttered lightly, and one lean hand was clenched upon the bedclothes. Fiercely possessive, she sat with him through the day, struggling to quiet him when his delirious tossings threatened to reopen the wound, gripping his hot hand when he moaned in pain, wishing she could make sense of his ravings in French. She stayed beside him all day until Rupert forced her to come downstairs for a distracted dinner of turbot and sauce, with a side dish of thinly sliced cucumbers, and two courses. But the next morning she was back beside Du Vallon, a heartened little figure in a gray cambric gown, her tumbled curls and anxious face making her look more childlike than ever. Surely if he had lived this long his chances must be improving. But his progress was agonizingly slow.

Sometimes she and Lady Thérèse, who looked frail and wan, her mischievous dimples rarely in evidence these days, took turns sitting with him. At other times they sat together while one of them read aloud from the Scott novels. Rupert, in seeming frustration with his uselessness in the sickroom, absented himself from the house with increasing frequency, and when he was about looked so deep in thought he might as well have been miles away in body. He knew of Garde's iniquity, for of course he had demanded an explanation concerning the end of Julia's betrothal. He had even questioned her thoroughly on all the points of the letter, and her father's activities in Calais, and Garde's bold confession. But after that one interview he had not mentioned Garde again, and for her own part Julia was glad to put the earl out of her mind. If he was beyond punishment she wanted no torment of thinking up futile plans of revenge. Her every waking moment was centered round the survival of Du Vallon. For now, his life was all that could matter.

She was there the morning when his ravings sent Thérèse flying from the room with scarlet cheeks. She was there when the doctor sounded his chest and frowned over those short, laborious breaths which rattled so dreadfully in his throat. And she was there on that glorious Sunday afternoon when his fever broke. She experienced the breathless joy of watching his gray eyes open in full consciousness of his surroundings, and her very smile was a prayer of gratitude to God for giving his life back again. Eagerly she stretched out her hand, not knowing whether to stay and savor this moment or to run for Thérèse. Her voice was gone; she could only watch him in wonder.

Then at last he saw her, and there was no doubt that he recognized her, for he paled and deliberately turned his face away.

Her agony was unspeakable. It was as though the world had ended all over again. Throughout these exhausting days she had been sustained by the hope and the conviction that, if he lived, she would have the chance to make up her mistakes. But this act of rejection could not be mistaken. Her hopes for his forgiveness were dust. He never wanted to see her again.

It was unbearable to think of his suffering more pain because of her unwanted presence, and her lacerated heart shrank from further torture for either of them. Crushed and shaken, she started up from her chair with trembling lips and tears running unheeded down her cheeks, thankful Lady Thérèse had been called from the room to confer with the cook. She must go at once. She could not—she dared not—stay; it was time she cast down the final threads of her old life and returned to the Lewings where she might set about making a new start for herself.

Stumbling to the door, and trying not to think about how awful it was going to be to know he lived and breathed and walked about somewhere apart from her, somewhere where she could never go to see him again, she let herself out in swift silence, and never looked back to see the hand he tried to stretch out to her, nor delayed long enough to hear his weak attempt to speak her name.

Chapter Eighteen

The season was over, all London was talking of the effrontery of President Monroe in calling his Congress for war, and the *ton* was making its departure to the fashionable watering place of Brighton, to check on the progress in the building of the prince regent's Pavilion. Everyone had ceased discussing the succession of scandals revolving around Julia Swanton. She had not mourned her father, but she was doing so now, and very properly. Swanton House had fallen into the clutches of a moneylender, but had been redecorated and sold to an elderly gentleman with a small household. The Earl of Garde, in spite of wealth and looks, had been jilted, but then that left him open game again for mamas with unmarried daughters. Besides, it seemed the little Swanton had not been such a fool after all. Beau Brummell had made quite a pet of her; even though she no longer appeared at functions she did sometimes receive visitors in her sister's morning room and the Beau was usually to be seen there. And, too, Emily Cowper had told Julia she was a naughty chit but not so naughty as Sally Jersey had been rude, and accordingly promised to send her new vouchers to Almack's in the fall for the little season. But most intriguingly of all, the regent was seen to cut Lord Garde dead at Gentleman Jackson's.

Julia paid little heed to any of it. She hardly went out now at all, even for the merest errand, in fear she should encounter Lord du Vallon. She knew in such an event she would never keep her composure. His health had improved to the point that he could go out upon occasion for a careful ride in a carriage. And his popularity had risen as though there had never been a hint of dishonor linked to his name. The mere fact that he had met Garde with pistols and lived was enough to exalt him in some circles. All this Julia heard from the morning callers Brummell insisted she receive. The hour was trying for her. She constantly felt she would burst into tears at any moment, and could not wait to escape to the privacy of her chamber.

In the Lewing household it had been decided that Lady Elizabeth would become Sophie's companion, and Julia a governess-playmate for young Edward, who should be increasingly neglected in the months ahead as his mama drew nearer to her confinement. Once, such an arrangement would have horrified Julia. Now she looked forward to it with relief, eager to depart for the country. She, who had always thrived on the bustle and whirl of fashionable life, now longed for peace and privacy. She had become a stranger to herself; her thoughts and emotions were all new, all different from the old ones so tightly locked away.

She learned that nothing in life could be more horrible than seeing the one she loved turn away from her. But she also learned that grief would not kill her, that no matter how much she ached inside she still lived and life still had to be dealt with. She faced the fact that the man who had ordered her father's death would never go punished. And still life went on and relentlessly on. In a way she was glad it did so, but she took no more joy from living. Her vivacity and sparkle had left her; she did not even want them back. She only wanted to escape the dirt and heat of the London streets and find a sanctuary in the country, where she could hold her shattered dreams and memories until she learned how to forget.

On the day of their departure, Rupert joined her and Lewing for breakfast. He was so late she began to think he would not come, and since Sophie and Lady Elizabeth never descended for breakfast and Lewing was engrossed in his newspaper, she was finding the meal dull. But at last Rupert strode in and winked at her before seizing a chair and sitting down. As different from Du Vallon as he was, even his accent pained her so much she could do little but busy herself buttering croissants she had no desire for.

"Good God, De Clembeau, have you heard the news?" asked Lewing with scarcely a greeting for their guest. "It is all over the *Gazette*. Garde's yacht has been caught smuggling ammunition to France. I cannot believe it. Have you ever heard the scoundrel say a good word for the French? And, yet, I spoke to Colonel Miller a half hour past and he says it is all true and more. That Garde himself has been in charge of the project from the first. The yacht's crew has all confessed."

"*Peste,*" said Rupert, accepting a plateful of eggs from Julia, whose hand was shaking so much she nearly tipped it upside down.

She stared at Lewing, who was wide-eyed but hardly looking displeased. "If only it were true!" she cried. "But, John, you are right when you say he hates the French. Why, he turns livid whenever they are mentioned. And his own brothers were soldiers."

"A convenient hatred, it would appear," murmured Rupert with a flash of teeth in his dark face.

Frowning, Julia took a second look at him and gasped. "Rupert! Why, you, but surely—"

He raised his heavy brows. "Must you resist to believe? I think it is an accusation of great cleverness. It took much work."

"Then you did set the rumor about," said Julia, beginning to smile. "If only it were true. But it isn't. It can't be." A doubt shook her. "Can it?"

"*Non.*" Rupert shrugged and accepted more eggs. "Garde is English completely. But it does him no good. I"—he thumped his chest—"have seen to it."

"But if he isn't guilty—" began Lewing.

"Ah, milord!" said Rupert, his eyes twinkling. "This *coquin* can prove no innocence. Me, I am an intriguer of the greatest skill. Did I not rescue my wife from the house of Napoleon? I think already Garde has left the country."

Lewing burst out laughing. "But this is marvelous! Totally unscrupulous of course, but marvelous all the same. Did you bribe the crew of his vessel to testify against him?"

"*Naturellement.*" Jauntily Rupert cocked his head at Julia. "Well, *petite*? The law of the English would not let me kill him, but he will never return to England, I think. He will not dare."

"Thank you, Rupert," whispered Julia, her eyes shining as she reached across the table to press his hand. "You know what it means to me—indeed, to all of us. He is such a wicked man."

"Excuse me, but I must run upstairs and give the news to my wife. She'll be delighted, I know. The matter has been causing her worry." Lewing tossed down his napkin and rushed out.

Rupert grinned after him, then let his expression soften. "*Petite,* will you not come to say farwell to Thérèse? She has missed you."

Julia dropped her fork and looked at him in dismay. "No, Rupert, I cannot return to Du Vallon's house. Don't ask it of me." Somehow, she was on her feet, choking.

Rupert rose too, and flung out a hand to steady her. "I am sorry. But you said you loved him. You tended him with such devotion. And since you left us he has—"

"I can't talk about it," she said, gasping to hold back tears. "He does not forgive me for what I did to him. What else can I do but stay away?" She had to go. She had to get out of the room before she gave way completely. Could Rupert not see how vulnerable she still was?

"But—"

"No, Rupert!" Agonized, she stopped in the doorway to look back. "Please tell Thérèse good-bye for me. I—I shall miss her too."

It took her two hours to regain her composure. By then Lewing and Sophie had departed in their private equipage, leaving Julia and Lady Elizabeth to follow in a job chaise-and-four hired for the purpose of conveying them and their belongings. At first Julia had thought she would never recover herself in time, but here she stood in the hall beside her aunt while their trunks and boxes were loaded. Her face was washed and composed, her hair neat, and her carriage dress and light pelisse a shade of violet which gave an illusion of color to her pale features. But inside she was wretched. Suddenly the journey seemed more a banishment than an escape. How she wished Rupert had spoken only of his clever disposal of Garde! Rupert was a dear creature; she knew he meant well, but surely he ought to have more sense than to meddle in a matter he knew nothing about. How she wished he had never mentioned Du Vallon at all? How she wished Du Vallon would come just now and stop her from going. In the novels her aunt was so fond of, the heroine was always granted a second chance, but Julia had learned, much too painfully, that life was exceedingly different from literature.

"Excuse me, Miss Julia," said Rutledge, who had

been acquired into the Lewing household. With a bow, he handed her a letter.

For a moment, as she saw the imposing Vallon crest upon the envelope, hope stabbed through her. She began to tremble. Could it be Rupert had worked another miracle? Could he have softened the marquis's heart? Was she forgiven?

Holding her breath, she broke the seal, only to find Lady Thérèse's signature at the end of a little note of farewell. The hope died. Julia did not even read the entire letter, but crumpled it in her hand. Nothing had come, and now she was going away and nothing would ever come.

"What is it, dearest?" asked Lady Elizabeth in the midst of involved instructions concerning where inside the carriage her birdcage and her writing desk and her jewel case were to be placed.

"Just a good-bye from an acquaintance, Aunt," said Julia and turned away swiftly lest anyone notice how she was shaking. Furious at herself for being such a hopeful fool, she followed her aunt into the chaise with a resolute expression. She could forget him! She must! She should resign herself to the fact that she had lost him more so than if he had died, and that she would be spending the rest of her days as a spinster aunt trying to keep up with grubby, energetic children who were not her own.

Depressed, she turned her gaze upon the backs of the postilions in their scarlet livery and kept it there until they were well past the outskirts of London and making a good pace along the northern turnpike road.

"Of course, however reluctant one is to admit it," said Lady Elizabeth with the tiniest of sighs, "one must face the fact that it shall be much more comfortable when we are able to cast off our mourning at last. I think Emily Cowper is the dearest creature. Of course this fall we shan't be able to do much, but I think we can go to Almack's if you do not dance. And I shall give that Jersey woman the snub of her life." Then her slight burst of temper faded and with a smile she leaned forward to pat Julia's hand. "But there! We are leaving this horrid time behind us. I am going to spend the summer teaching Sophie how to grow flowers. She has never learned the proper way of instructing the gardeners, not liking the country before, but she says dear John loves to have them about the house—flowers, I mean, not the gardeners—and so she must make an effort. I think Sophie is changing daily for the better, don't you? And you are going to spend your days playing with dear little Ned. Only think of how delightful. It is certainly to be preferred over marrying that dreadful Lord Garde. Especially after he was so inconsiderate as to shoot Lord du Vallon."

Julia made an effort to rouse herself to the conversation before it wandered further toward what she could not bear. "Yes, indeed. Ned is a darling child. Is the pace too fast for you?"

"Oh, no!" Lady Elizabeth shook her head until her chins quivered. "Pray, do not ask them to change pace. One cannot be happy at being obliged to drive past the lane to Swantoncourt, but the road is so smooth and I am in such transports at being out of Gaylord's company—although I suppose it is a dreadful thing for one to say, especially when one is an *aunt*—but I really cannot imagine becoming carriage-sick on such a splendid day."

Shifting the birdcage, which was crammed a bit tightly between herself and Nan, Julia was about to reply when, with a frightful amount of raised dust and whip-cracking, a gentleman's conveyance passed them with scant inches to spare. Annoyed by this daring whipster, she leaned out the window, despite the danger to her hat, and glared after him.

"He shall land us in the ditch!" she cried, quite outraged by the phaeton's refusal to pull on ahead and be gone. "The road is far too narrow for a race. What makes these cow-handed cawkers think they can—"

"Julia, dearest, your language," reproved Lady Elizabeth faintly as they swayed and jolted.

Julia drew in her head, flushed with vexation. "I am sorry, Aunt, but *really*! The gall of these out-and-outers is not to be—"

She was never permitted to finish her sentence, for just then a pistol shot rang out and they jerked to a violent lurching halt.

"Highwaymen!" shrieked Lady Elizabeth, turning an alarming shade. "Someone—my reticule, my vinaigrette! Oh, dear! Quick! Quick!"

Flung to the floor, Julia fought her way clear of an appalling shambles of the birdcage, which had crashed on top of her to the squawking alarm of its occupant, and the scattered contents of Lady Elizabeth's writing desk. Panting as much from anger as from the effort to regain the breath knocked from her, she emerged with her hat crushed askew over one blazing eye and battle flags of scarlet flying in each cheek.

Unable to make herself heard over the squawks of that odious bird and her aunt's and Nan's concerted hysterics, she was herself shrieking, "But highwaymen do not ride in perch phaetons!" when the door was flung open by a frankly terrified postilion and a cool, commanding voice said, "Ah, but they do, mademoiselle. *Voyons*, I am here to abduct you. Please to get out."

With a lurch of her heart, she remained frozen for a moment, unable to turn toward the speaker. No, it was impossible; something so precious as a reconciliation would not happen in this farcical manner.

Lady Elizabeth's shrieks ceased abruptly. "Why, it's only that nice Lord du Vallon," she said in a voice of wonder.

Slowly, quite pale, Julia shoved her hat out of her eyes and turned to find a thin but otherwise perfectly hale Du Vallon regarding her from the box of his equipage. She stared, unable to utter a word, her limbs like water at the very sight of him. How she had longed to be with him again—only, why was he staring at her in such a stern way as though he would prefer to beat her?

With instinctive defiance she guessed he was here not to forgive her but to insult her. She threw up her chin, her violet eyes blazing the bluest fire. If he had grown to hate her, so be it. She had just as much pride and she would die before she let him see how her very heart was pounding in desire for his smile, his kiss.

"I shall not get out," she said with a snap. "If you had wanted to converse with me you should have called in a proper manner instead of staging this rude show."

His expression became grim, and only then, with a sharp intake of breath, did she notice the pistol he was holding upon their acutely motionless coachman. "I believe I did not request mademoiselle's desires. Get out."

"I shall not!" she retorted, fists clenched. "Of all the rude—"

"Ladies of spirit must not be treated with gentleness. It renders them spoiled. I have learned never to repeat that mistake." Calmly he lifted the barrel of his pistol a fraction. "Mademoiselle will obey or monsieur the coachman will be shot."

"Miss!" The man croaked out that one hoarse word of appeal while the postilion at the door turned a shade paler and looked ready to bolt into the bushes at the first opportunity.

Julia gestured with exasperation. "Oh, come, there is nothing to fear in the least, my good man. Lord du Vallon is not about to carry out his bluff—"

The shot thundered deafeningly in her ears, and with a cry of horror she scrambled out of the chaise and looked up to see the coachman—not dead as she had for a hideous moment imagined—but simply staring in petrified terror at the gash made in the seat only an inch from his person.

Julia stamped her foot. "For heaven's sake!" she exclaimed in annoyance heightened by the fright she'd just suffered. "You could have killed him!"

For answer Du Vallon merely shrugged and produced another pistol—he seemed to be bristling with them—which he deliberately cocked and aimed. "This time I will, *je t'assure*!"

"Very well!" In considerable dudgeon she gave in and climbed up beside him. "I think you have gone stark, staring mad, but you may abduct me if you choose. Nan! Come at once."

"No!" he said sharply and the hooded, smoldering expression in his piercing gray eyes abruptly put a fatal damper on her anger and set her heart pounding rather too fast. "Not the maid."

Now she was frightened indeed when she remembered his rebuff that horrid day—the last day she'd seen him until now. And what was he doing, dragging her off by force without even a servant to ensure the final tattered shreds of her reputation were upheld? Frenchmen were impassioned, impulsive creatures; could he be plotting to murder he? He *had* come very close to finishing off the coachman. But, no, no, what an infantile thought! He could have no reason to commit violence against her. Surely he only meant to take his revenge against her, for having embroiled him into her troubles, by frightening her out of her wits. Her fists clenched as she tried to pay no heed to the violent alarm spreading through her every fiber. She would make sure he did *not* succeed!

"Julia, dearest!" cried her aunt, but he was already whipping up his horses. They headed away at a rattling fast clip.

"You," said Julia bitterly, wondering why she had

ever, *ever* been such a goose as to break her heart over him, "are nothing but a vile, conceited savage, sir! If my father were alive he would have you horsewhipped. Abduct me indeed! I have never seen such folly, nor, for that matter, anyone as impossibly, horridly *rude.* Are you foxed?"

"*Pas du tout*," he snapped, keeping his gaze on his driving so that only his taut, stern profile was visible to her.

She drew in a deep, unsteady breath, trying, for the sake of her melting courage, to concentrate less on how marvelously fit and handsome he looked and more on maintaining her irritation. "Then I believe that pistol ball touched your brain instead of your lung. Does your sister know you have escaped the house in this addle-pated way? I daresay you are confident I shall drive us to help if and when you collapse."

"I have been recovered for a week, mademoiselle," he replied, still keeping his horses at that breakneck pace.

Completely out of temper, she pounded her fists in her lap. "Then, pray explain yourself!"

"I shall." Dexterously looping his rein, he swung them onto a narrow, rutted farm lane which wound up a sloping rise, and pulled his sweating horses to a halt at the top within a shady copse of copper beeches. He turned to her. "But first I must remove this atrocity from my way." And he plucked off her ruined hat and sent it sailing into the ditch.

She tried unsuccessfully to prevent him. "How dare you go flinging my property about?" she demanded and swung up a hand to slap him for his impudence.

But he caught it and forced it down with easy strength, and his touch sent a tingle through her flesh, which only overset her composure completely. "As I told mademoiselle before, I have learned tactics *très fortes* are the necessity to tame her."

With a hammering of her heart, which threatened to suffocate her and sent an enchanting blush into her cheeks, she realized what he was about and drew back in panic. "But you quite detest me!"

"Oh, and, yes?" With a lift of his brows, he pulled her near. "You must be the complete *stupide* to believe such a thing." And before she could speak again, he bent his lips to hers in a passionate embrace which drew out all the pain in her soul and sent it soaring into ecstasy.

It was some time before she was released, gasping for breath and floating high upon a cloud of happiness. She sighed, resting her head upon his shoulder. It seemed infinitely ridiculous now to wonder further whether he had gone mad. If he had, then it was quite a glorious state to be in.

"*Chérie.*" With a gentle forefinger he tilted her face up to his. "We will have no more nonsense, *d'accord*? You ran away from me before I could believe you were really there and not just more of my delirious fancies. And then, *mon Dieu*! You would not come again."

She frowned. "I was so miserable. It was all my fault for having goaded you into such imprudence, and while you were so ill I thought I should die too."

He shushed her by laying a finger upon her lips. "*Ma petite imbécile*, I have been hurrying so much to get well before you could slip away forever. And you see? I barely caught you." He smiled in a way that made her breathless again. "Thérèse told me how good you have become; even that you broke with Garde. *Bon!* I do not have to call him out again."

"Fudge!" she said. "You wouldn't dare be so silly as to go through all that again." But the firm expression in his eyes gave her her answer, and she fell silent in confusion. How could he care for her so much? If she knew much more happiness she would burst.

"*Maintenant,*" he said, breaking into her thoughts. "I will allow you one question before I kiss you again."

She gazed up into his loving, tender eyes, still finding it hard to believe all this could be happening to her after such misery. "Yes, my lord," she said meekly and gloried in the way the corners of his eyes crinkled. "Where on earth are you taking me? Aunt is going to be frantic."

He shushed her again. "We are not concerned with Milady Beth, little one. I am taking you to our new home—a place of shabbiness incredible, but already I have workmen adding a new wing. You see, long ago when the trouble in France began, my *maman* sewed the jewels of the family into my shirt. It was most uncomfortable, but I still have enough wealth to support you and many *enfants*. And this house I have found, it will be a château worthy of my most cherished lady."

She smiled eagerly, already enchanted with the idea of her own establishment. "Where is it? What shall you call it?"

He laughed. "Why, *chérie*! Do you not recognize where you are?"

For the first time she took note of her surroundings and gasped as she looked down the hill onto the meadow where her old tree was drooping gracefully over the brook. "Swantoncourt!" She glanced at him in astonished delight. "Truly, have you bought it?"

"Yes, truly." Then he grew serious a moment, his clear eyes searching her face so intently she blushed. "You are pleased? You are *contente*? Do not let me make you do what you do not want."

His mood had changed so rapidly she tensed, but she realized at once there was no longer anything to be frightened of. This elegant, insufferable creature was the man she must spend the rest of her life with, or have no one at all. Lips parting as the rosy warmth of shy confusion rushed over her, she met his gaze with her own, equally searching and intent. He knew his mind, as she did hers; there could never again be any cause for the petty disputes which had held them so far apart in the past. She loved him with everything she possessed within her—but if she sat in silence much longer he would begin to doubt her again and suffer.

Quickly she placed her hand within his and smiled. "My dearest Lucien, I know exactly what I want, and you have provided it all!" Shy again, she whispered, "Always?"

His lips curved into a smile. "*Oui,* always." And then he had to kiss her again.

THE PASSIONATE SAVAGE

Constance Gluyas

Lucien Marsh was a loner, a man who wouldn't settle down in any one place with any one woman – however beautiful she might be. And he had two women who loved him with all their hearts and would shatter their lives to lie in his arms –

FLAMING DAWN the fiery Indian princess who broke her people's trust by giving herself to the white hunter and following him into a white man's world.

LADY SAMANTHA PIERCE the sophisticated society lady who broke her marriage vows to possess Lucien, restlessly seeking to capture her true love and desire.

THE PASSIONATE SAVAGE is the unforgettable romance of two magnificent women raging from the untamed American wilderness to the aristocratic world of Victorian London.

HISTORICAL ROMANCE 0 7221 3901 2 £2.25

Barbara Riefe

SO WICKED THE HEART

Snatched from safety and her husband's harbouring arms by the lawless corsairs of Algiers, fiery but tender Lorna Singleton is forced to obey a pirate captain's bold lusts. But Ahmed's animal passion does not lack barbaric splendour. As a Christian slave in brutal Muslim hands, Lorna must find a protector to save her from the torment and degradation that awaits her in the casbah . . . even if the price of salvation is her virtue.

SO WICKED THE HEART is a gale-force story of surging passion and turbulent love, an unabashed tale of a woman's struggle to defend the storm-wracked fortress of her heart against an onslaught of unparalleled savagery and betrayal.

HISTORICAL ROMANCE 0 7221 7363 6 £1.95

Blood Red Wine

Laurence Delaney

Alicia Orsini was beautiful, even as an unripe peasant girl. Which brought her to the notice of the old *Padrone*, feudal master of that backward part of Italy. He used her – and paid. Alicia's brother, Rafael, was forced into a grotesque act of brutality to save his family honour.

To escape retribution, Rafael fled to California, where he built up a prosperous wine-producing dynasty, a shining example of immigrant success. But the simmering feud pursued the Orsinis even there – over decades, turning Rafael's dream into a nightmare of savage vendetta that only one supreme stroke of destruction could bring to its dramatic end . . .

Moving from poverty-stricken, turbulent Italy of the 1920s to ruthless big-business in contemporary America, BLOOD RED WINE is an authentic, hugely compelling story that seizes and grips to its last, power-packed page.

HISTORICAL ROMANCE 0 7221 2994 7 £2.25